Praise for *New York Times*
and *USA Today* bestselling author
**AMELIA GREY**
and her acclaimed novels

"Grey's unconventional meet-cute, compelling series backbone, and authentic characters move an interesting plot forward. . . . An engaging series start."
—*Kirkus Reviews*

"Grey's prose is strong and her characters are fun."
—*Publishers Weekly*

"Grey launches her First Comes Love series with a perfectly matched pair of protagonists, a vividly etched supporting cast, and plenty of potent sexual chemistry and breathtaking sensuality." —*Booklist*

"Each new Amelia Grey tale is a diamond. . . . A master storyteller." —*Affaire de Coeur*

"Devilishly charming . . . A touching tale of love."
—*Library Journal*

"Sensual . . . witty and clever . . . Another great story of forbidden love." —*Fresh Fiction*

"Grey neatly matched up a sharp-witted heroine with an irresistible sexy hero and lets the romantic sparks fly."
—*Booklist*

Also by Amelia Grey

# How to Train Your Earl

## Amelia Grey

St. Martin's Paperbacks

This is a work of fiction. All of the characters, organizations, and events portrayed in this novel are either products of the author's imagination or are used fictitiously.

First published in the United States by St. Martin's Paperbacks, an imprint of St. Martin's Publishing Group

HOW TO TRAIN YOUR EARL

For information, address St. Martin's Publishing Group, 120 Broadway, New York, NY 10271.

www.stmartins.com

ISBN: 978-1-250-21880-3

Our books may be purchased in bulk for promotional, educational, or business use. Please contact your local bookseller or the Macmillan Corporate and Premium Sales Department at 1-800-221-7945, ext. 5442, or by email at MacmillanSpecialMarkets@macmillan.com.

Printed in the United States of America

St. Martin's Paperbacks edition 2021

10  9  8  7  6  5  4  3  2  1

# Chapter 1

Brina Feld should have known a lady wasn't safe from rakes, rogues, and scoundrels at a masked ball in Paris. It was a scoundrel who currently had her in his sights as she raced down one of the dimly lit corridors in the chateau with hopes of getting away from him.

A proper gentleman never forgot who he was, no matter if his face was hidden. Even in Paris. Which only confirmed that the one chasing her was no gentleman at all, and she should have never agreed to attend this grand masquerade.

Intent on finding a hiding place until it was time to meet her aunt, Brina started searching for a room. From somewhere behind her, she heard the drunken man call out to her once more, his wine-soaked voice echoing against the marble walls.

Fearful of being cornered again by him, she quickly opened the first door she came to and slammed herself inside. Feeling beneath the knob, she found the key and engaged the lock. Smugly, she turned toward the opulent room, only to stop cold.

There in the center of the classical French sitting room with its bee and acorn motifs embroidered on the draperies and cushions, a man sat in a throne-like chair in front of the fireplace. He seemed to be as startled as she. Neither of them spoke. He was clothed in a white shirt and black trousers. No coat, waistcoat, or even shoes were in sight.

With an uptick in her already racing heart, she glanced about. It appeared that aside from the exquisite figures in the sweeping murals on the walls, they were alone. Concern jolted through her. Had she escaped one menace only to find another?

But concern turned to surprise when he snapped in perfect English, "Don't just stand there, come untie me."

*Untie him?*

Brina peered more intently. Even though he was sitting, she could tell he was tall and wide through the chest and shoulders, yet his waist gave no hint of overindulgent suppers. Unlike some of the flamboyantly painted masks she'd seen throughout the evening, he wore a simple black satin cover over his eyes and bridge of his nose. More importantly, he really was tied to the chair. His wrists were secured to the arms of the chair with a long scarf.

Although she was somewhat unnerved by the power she sensed within him, she took a tentative step toward him.

"My heavens, you're bound. Why?"

"This isn't the time for questions," he stated, his commanding voice clipped as his hands turned into white-knuckled fists. "Hurry."

He struggled and strained against what held him, like a panther pulling against bindings.

In the glow of lamp and firelight she saw his muscles bulge against the fine linen of his shirt. Her heart beat a little faster. Her trepidation waned as curiosity grew.

She had always been far too enquiring and told repeatedly when younger that curiosity was not an admirable trait in a lady. Usually, she could tamp that down, but she'd never seen a man in such a state.

"Are you a thief and wanting to get away?" she asked, ignoring his command.

"A thief?" He sounded more than a little outraged and stomped his feet in frustration.

"There's the matter of your hands being bound, and you are wearing a mask."

"You're wearing one too," he answered tightly. "Everyone at the party has one."

Her fingers came to the silken demi mask her aunt had given her. That was true. The only reason she'd agreed to wear the outrageously bright pink gown and come to the masquerade ball was because identities were hidden. Which was why she wouldn't ask his name and certainly didn't want him to know hers.

"True, but not everyone is trussed up like a goose bound for the Christmas dinner table." She then considered him for a moment. "If you are not a thief or common footpad, then certainly someone caught you trying to do something you shouldn't have been doing and now has gone for the magistrate."

He glared at her. "I assure you I am no thief or criminal of any kind. Now come untie me. I don't have time for this," he said, urgency lacing every word.

Of course, the sensible thing for her to do was leave the room. She was clever enough to know it would stir an unrecoverable scandal if she were caught with a half-dressed man, even in forward-thinking Paris. But then, from behind her, the doorknob and key beneath it rattled, jarring her.

Tension coiled tightly inside her. The oaf was still looking for her.

She glanced about and saw no other escape. Clearly, fleeing back to a man who was accosting her wasn't an option. Instead, she moved closer to the stranger, deciding she was better off with this man who easily commanded a room, even tied up, than the brandy-faced scoundrel on the other side of the door.

Moments later she heard him softly call her name again, farther down the corridor and away from the door. Satisfied that threat was behind her, she stepped around a settee and noticed a black coat, red waistcoat, and white neckcloth strewn across the floor. There they were!

Her gaze swept to the man's face. His wide inflexible mouth was set in a grimace. There was a hardness to his jawline and chin. Even with the mask, she could see his eyes were a dark, deep shade of blue. Thick hair, almost as black and shiny as his disguise, fell across his forehead, down past his ears, and brushed the back of his neck.

She was unbelievably aware of him, how strongly masculine he looked and attractive he was. If one were inclined to fall for the massively arrogant type who could probably make a lady blush to the highest degree. Which, of course, she wasn't.

Though she had to admit this man stood out and piqued her interest with his unusual situation.

"Hurry," her stranger barked again.

*Her stranger?*

What was she thinking? Brina shook the thought away as ridiculous.

"Maybe you're not a thief, but a swindler or someone

equally dishonorable. You certainly didn't tie yourself to that chair, sir."

He made a growling noise that left her no doubt he was nail-spitting mad at being in such a desperate position.

"You obviously did something, and you must be dangerous. You look strong and . . ." She felt a fluttering in her chest at the thought of just how strong he did look with his shirt parted at his throat and his trousers molding to his hips and legs in a most fitting manner. "Anyway, as if it would take several men to get the best of you."

"Yes, but unfortunately only one devious woman," he muttered past clenched teeth.

"A woman?" Brina's cheeks warmed and her heart started pounding again. She could barely get her breath. Still, she stepped closer and nudged the exceedingly well-tailored waistcoat with the toe of her dainty slipper. "Well, she must have had good reason."

"That is a matter of opinion," he grumbled and renewed his struggle against the fastenings that held his wrists. "I told you I don't have time for this."

She considered him, tapping her finger to her lips, as if he'd said nothing at all. "Are you going after the woman who tied you?"

He sucked in an exasperated gulp of breath. "Certainly not. If you must know before you will give me assistance, I am going after my foolish cousin. He is about to ruin his life, and I must stop him. Now, can we get on with this?"

Brina studied him more carefully, searching what she could see of his countenance in hopes of determining the truthfulness of his words. She had to admit, she was fascinated by his predicament. After drawing in a deep breath, she released it slowly. He wanted very badly to be freed, and it was within her power to do that for him.

Oddly, she didn't feel threatened, and it wasn't because he was tied. Despite his gruffness, she felt drawn to him in a way she didn't understand. And frankly, that he'd captured her full attention at all was unusual. She'd been a widow almost five years and, in that time, hadn't given any gentleman a second glance. In truth, she'd simply never expected to be attracted to a man again. And by no means, one who was bound to a chair, brash as the day was long, and barking orders at her like a general directing his soldiers.

But there was something that pulled her in to his situation and made her want to be a part of it, if only for a short time, and even though he looked much like the drawings she'd seen of plundering pirates. She couldn't conceive of the possibility that she'd ever have the opportunity to be so close to a rake again. Certainly not to aid one.

How could she walk away without giving this further thought? Too, if she freed him, she could lock herself inside until it was time to meet her aunt.

"Before I decide whether to help you, tell me what dreadful thing your cousin is going to do?"

"He's running off to get married," he said with a hasty scoff and a stomp of his bare foot. "Would you please untie me now so I can save him?"

Curiosity struck again. "What do you have against marriage, sir?"

He blew out a deep sigh of impatience before flatly stating, "In general, nothing. When it comes to my impressionable and impulsive cousin, everything. His father should never have allowed him to come to Paris unattended. Or worse, expected me to look after him once he arrived."

It was Brina's turn to scoff at the man, and she quickly did so. "I happen to believe in love, sir."

A breath hissed through his teeth. "Love has nothing to do with this. It's his name, prestige, and money the woman is after. Specifically, his family's money and name."

Brina noticed the discarded clothing again and something occurred to her. A gasp caught in her throat. He must, indeed, be a rake and of the highest order. And he expected her to help him.

"You said you were tied up by a woman. Were you seducing your cousin's fiancée?" she exclaimed in an unladylike volume.

"What?" he asked on another sizzling breath of exasperation. "I wasn't seducing anyone. Hell's teeth. The woman in question was seducing me. And no, it was not his fiancée. Her older, wiser sister. The minx was stalling me so I wouldn't find out about the elopement until it was too late to stop the young buck. There may still be time if you will do the right thing and untie me so I can go after them. I have been a guest in the chateau many times and know of a hidden passage that will lead me out to the grounds quickly."

Hidden passages that led outside?

That aroused her interest even more. Brina wavered. By his own admission of how he became tied, she knew he wasn't a respectable man. There wasn't a reason in the world she should feel any sense of responsibility to help him, but she believed the story about his cousin. And that was what made the difference. More than most, she could understand someone wanting to protect their loved ones and keep them from making a mistake that would alter their life forever. Brina had almost made one that certainly would have changed hers.

Her gaze drifted down to the open neck of his shirt. The cadence of her breathing changed again. What she didn't want to think further about was the manner in which he became tied or how he looked in his state of half-dress. He was stirring desires in her that she couldn't possibly entertain. Such a thing wasn't for ladies to dwell on.

Not even a widow.

However, she felt a little amusement knowing it was a woman who'd gotten the best of him—no matter the reasons or means.

Nerve-racking silence stretched between them while she contemplated what to do.

"Enough of this!" he demanded fiercely. "What must I promise you in order to be released from this chair?"

A shiver stole over her, daring and courage surging together inside her. For a moment she had the unimaginable thought of kneeling before him and kissing the base of his throat. Brina had never done a reckless thing in her life, and she had the feeling he knew that. Knew of her sudden and unexpected desire to have his strong-looking arms wrapped around her, his hard body pressed against hers.

Another wild, forbidden idea suddenly entered her mind. It thrilled her down to her toes. Something that shouldn't have occurred to her. What if she told him she would untie him if he would agree to take her with him on his journey through the hidden passages to find his cousin?

But as quickly as the exciting thought surfaced, she shook it away. She couldn't entertain anything so drastic and unlike her. It would be madness. But the fleeting contemplation had sent an exhilarating rush of anticipation shooting through her that wouldn't soon pass.

"All right," she answered on a breathy sigh, knowing she was going out on a very shaky limb but willing to do it. "No promises are necessary. I'm going to have faith you are telling the truth and that I am doing the right thing in freeing you."

She hurried behind him and knelt at the back of the chair, feeling the tension in his muscles and sensing his excitement to finally be liberated as she worked the tight knots in the long, narrow scarf.

Her trusting him might be the biggest mistake of his cousin's life and quite possibly hers too, should anyone in London ever find out she was in the room with this man. Or, heaven forbid, that she had willingly freed a man who had broken the law.

He brushed off the last of the bindings and rose, standing six-feet tall or more. He was as formidable as she had suspected, with ruggedly masculine good looks. His wide shoulders narrowed to a hard-muscled waist. Just the kind of man she normally ignored. Now, she watched him move quickly and jerk back into his garments and shoes. But when she thought he would hurry away without a backward glance, he stopped, turned, and stared at her.

Brina felt a shivering awareness pass between them. It was a sensation she hadn't felt in years, and it left her feeling as if something startling, luscious, and magical had happened. Desire wasn't an appropriate emotion for this situation or for her.

Ever.

Without warning, he took the steps that separated them and caught her up into his powerful embrace. She felt the firmness of his hard chest and warmth of his taut, solid body. His hands pressed into the middle of her back, bringing her closer to him. She knew he was going to kiss her.

Sudden fear and anticipation made her heart seem as if it were trembling rather than beating. She couldn't move but watched the sensuous curve of his lips as they descended toward hers. His hold was tight, possessive, and thrilling as he bent his head to hers.

He gave her a hard, quick kiss that felt as if he were settling his claim on her. That shook her to the core. She heard a catch in his breath and knew the potency of the brief contact had surprised him too.

"Thank you," he whispered huskily, looking deeply into her eyes as if to remember something he saw in their depths.

For a second or two his arms tightened even more, and she was certain he was going to kiss her again. Instead, he let go and rushed from the room.

A flush heated her cheeks, a fluttering filled her chest, and her stomach quivered like a delicate leaf in strong wind. His scandalous behavior was shocking and exhilarating at the same time.

Brina had just been kissed by a masked rake. And she'd never felt anything so wonderful in her life.

# Chapter 2

The road to perdition was easy compared to the road to redemption. Zane Howard Veldon Dormer Browning, eighth Earl of Blacknight, should know. He'd traveled on both in his near thirty years of life. His name alone had been enough to make him want to find his own way and not be subject to long-held traditions and stiff manners he cared naught about following. Why work so hard to become the standard bearer for gentlemen when just being a man came so naturally?

And was infinitely more enjoyable.

The first thing Zane had done when he arrived in London late yesterday was to pay his respects to the Dowager Countess and offer sympathies. Her sorrow and grief were still evident and enormous. Out of regard for her suffering, he hadn't stayed long.

The second thing he'd done was find a distraction. That had come in the form of spending all night at the Brass Bull Gaming House. The sun had come up hours ago, yet he and three other men still assembled around a table in the private card room. Raucous laughter and lively scores played on the pianoforte from the night had settled down. He could now hear sounds of horses, carriage wheels, and occasional chatter from people passing by filtering in from the open windows below. The streets outside were busy with Londoners going about their usual daily lives—as was Zane.

But he couldn't forget that things had changed for him now. For the better or worse was yet to be known.

Two months ago, one of Zane's uncles, who was the Earl of Blacknight at the time, his only son, and a cousin who had been in line for the title, were killed when the bridge over Blacknight Canyon gave way and their coach tumbled to the bottom of the dry ravine. In the blink of an eye, the succession of two heirs to the earldom were gone, and Zane had become Earl of Blacknight.

After the horrific news finally reached him in Vienna, he and his errant cousin Robert had left immediately for London. Their journey had been long, beset by an enormous amount of late winter snow and followed by torrential rains that flooded roads, streams, and villages.

Movement from one of the players brought his attention back to the cards in his hands. He blinked his dry eyes several times to clear his vision. It had been a while since he'd spent all night playing cards and appreciating a bottle of fine brandy and female companionship. For his overindulgence, he now had a pounding throb at his temples.

He'd already decided he was on his last shot of the morning when he sensed someone standing not too far behind him, watching his back. None of the players at the table had given whomever it was a bother of a glance, letting Zane know the person wasn't a stranger to the small private club. He had a fairly good idea who it was—dear old Uncle Syl. Someone must have told the old bachelor Zane had made it to London.

Sylvester Browning, his father's next to the youngest brother, had taken it upon himself not only to be Zane's conscience but an unsolicited advisor after his mother passed. Uncle Syl had taken up Zane's mother's mantra and urged him to mend his roguish ways and settle down to the quiet, respectable life of a gentleman and start a family. As if there weren't enough well-thought-of Brownings populating England already.

It wasn't that Sylvester was an unlikable fellow. He wasn't, and there had never been any harsh words between them. Zane got along reasonably well with him, except when his uncle's hovering was irritating—like a bee that wouldn't be swished away. The two of them had often matched words, but they were always civil. His straight-as-an-arrow uncle wouldn't know any other way to be.

When the last card hit the table, Zane scooped up his considerable winnings from the night, pushed back his chair, and rose while bidding his fellow gamesters a good day. He dropped the coins into his small leather pouch and cinched the opening tightly. Only then did he turn to confirm his suspicions. Not only did Sylvester wait there for him, his father's youngest brother, Hector was there too. Zane muttered a curse to himself. Both were staring stone-faced at him, their collars and neckcloths pulled tight as their expressions.

Uncle Hector was something of an oddity in his father's family. Unlike the rest of the tall, powerfully fit-looking Browning men who sported thick black hair and clean-shaven faces, Hector was of average height, portly, with thinning gray hair and a bushy beard. He used a cane to help him walk and to nervously tap the floor when he was flummoxed. Sylvester, on the other hand, had all the Brownings' handsome physical traits but wore the same stern expression whether he was happy, ill-tempered, or hungry as a goat.

It had been a long time since more than one of Zane's family had deemed it necessary to seek him out at the same time. He was fairly certain the last occasion was when he was set to duel a stranger who'd had the poor judgment to call him a card cheat. That early frosty morning Uncle Syl had tried desperately to intervene and convince the young blade of Zane's expert aim and beg him to offer a public apology for the slander. There was no reasoning to be had between the two swill-headed rounders, but out of deference for his uncle's well-intentioned pleas, Zane had only grazed the man's shoulder with a clean shot.

"Uncles," Zane said with a nod, swallowing his dis-satisfaction as he swung his coat off the back of the chair and dropped his coin purse into one of the side pockets.

They bowed and said, "My lord."

Zane gave a near silent chuckle of derision and shrugged uncomfortably into his coat. Being addressed as a title was going to take a bit of getting used to. Especially when it was coming from family.

Shaking off the drum of buzzing in his head, he cleared his thoughts and made eye contact with first Hector and then Sylvester. "I've already spoken to the dowager. My condolences to each of you and the entire family."

"Enough time has passed now and most everyone is getting back to normal," Uncle Syl remarked. "We've been worried about you and Robert."

It was no wonder. Until Zane had an heir, Robert was next in line for the title.

"We made the journey as fast as we could after hear-ing the news."

"Robert told me when he managed to get home last night," Hector added. "I appreciate that you returned with my son. Last I'd heard, he'd joined you in Paris to attend the winter balls."

Hector's son was doing a bit more than that. Robert almost married a most unsuitable woman, if Zane hadn't stopped him—with the aid of an intriguing young lady he hadn't yet forgotten. And oddly, he hadn't wanted to. It was pleasing to remember the warmth of her in his arms and the taste of her on his lips. He hadn't been able to forget the strength she'd showed in questioning and studying him before making up her mind to help him. She was sagacious and beautiful. Usually when she crossed his mind, he wondered if she were still in Paris or if she'd returned to England.

"He'd never been to Vienna," Zane answered, seeing no reason to elaborate on what had happened with the French woman. "That's where your letters caught up with us. We left straightaway."

"Now that you're here, there's no time to waste. We thought it best if we joined you for your first meeting with your solicitor as Earl Blacknight," Uncle Sylvester informed him, and then quickly added, "That is, if you don't mind?"

Zane would have rather waited until later in the day or even perhaps a few days before settling into his new role, but the unsmiling expressions on his uncles' faces kept him from saying that.

"Not at all. I have much to get caught up on. I might as well get started." He motioned for them to precede him out the door and down the stairs.

"After your meeting with him," Uncle Syl said, and started down the steps first, "you'll need to do something to calm the family."

"Everyone has been in a state of shock," Hector added

before following his brother out the door, but at a much slower pace. Because of his hip injury years ago, Hector was always slow descending the stairs. "There's been no small amount of hand wringing."

That was understandable. Losing three family members was a terrible blow that Zane wasn't even sure time could heal. But, he had no idea what to say to them to ease their minds, and he doubted they wanted to hear from the family rogue anyway.

Few, if any, in Zane's family would be happy that he was now the earl. Since his mother passed a few years ago, he was more apt to have a long stay in Paris or Vienna than to gallivant around the English countryside in summer or attend the London Season. However, he always made it home for Christmastide.

Much to the chagrin of his family.

Now, for the first time in several years, he was in London during the full bloom of spring.

Zane had no memory of his father, and his fondest remembrance of his mother was how much she revered Christmas Day. She made sure everyone in her household shared her devotion as well. Church in the morning, family and neighbors around the table for a feast in the afternoon, and games of chess or cards by the fire in the evening. Some argued his paltry involvement once a year with their large and extended family should count for nothing, but Zane paid their grumblings no mind. Christmas Day with family was a code of gentlemanly honor and conduct he wouldn't forego.

Besides, returning home for the holiday gave his well-married sister, numerous aunts, uncles, and more cousins from both sides of the family than the King had horses, a reason to whisper and roll their eyes when he came walking into the manor as if he'd only left the day before. It also gave members of the ton an opportunity to trot their eligible daughters out for him to make their acquaintance. Which he always did. No man should ever pass on a chance to meet a young lady. It mattered not to the elite of Society that he was the black sheep of the family. He was from the house and lineage of Blacknight and all the privilege and prosperity that went with it.

Sylvester stopped at the first landing and waited for his younger brother.

"We'd like to suggest a dinner at your house tomorrow evening," Uncle Syl called up to Zane. "We talked to your butler this morning, and he assured us the staff is quite capable and there will be no problem getting everything prepared."

Zane grimaced. "I don't have a butler."

"Of course you do," Hector said irritably. "You have a complete household staff waiting for you at your new home; the Earl of Blacknight's house is now yours. You need to move in immediately. It's the proper thing to do. The dowager is moving out today."

"Wait a hellfire minute," Zane said, his jaw hardening with conviction. He knew being the earl was going to involve situations he wasn't prepared to deal with. "I don't want her to move out of the house. Especially not at this time. She has lost her husband, son, and nephew. It's too soon to disrupt her life."

"Nonsense. She knows propriety, expects this, and understands," Uncle Syl said calmly. "She's been planning for it. It's your house now. She's ready to leave and has only been waiting for you to return. I've made arrangements to have your personal items moved from your town house today."

"What?" Zane asked, biting back another oath as he started down the narrow stairs, mumbling to himself, "I'm quite capable of handling my own belongings and all of my affairs."

Uncle Hector stopped and tapped his cane on the stair. "You're an earl now. You don't need to be distracted by insignificant tasks when you have more important things to do, and there are plenty of people to handle such things for you."

"And it's good you've made it here as the Season is beginning as well," Sylvester added, completely ignoring any reference to Zane's comment. "You can use my tailor. He has excellent style and will have you dressed up with all you need for the parties and balls in no time."

Zane had no desire to be trussed up like a preening dandy. "I'm quite set with all the clothing I need."

"Good. We've been thinking on all this while we waited for you to return. The best thing you can do to settle everyone's frayed nerves is to show that you're ready to settle down and take your new responsibilities seriously. We hope you will avail yourself to every moment of the Season and choose a bride. There are three young belles making their debut who should be of special interest to you. One of us will make sure you're introduced to them at the first ball you attend."

Zane grunted. What did he need a bride for? He had no problems when it came to women willing to share his bed. For that reason, he stayed away from respectable young ladies of the ton. He learned early in adulthood that they were raised to assume a kiss meant a wedding would follow. It had always suited him to find his pleasure elsewhere. Doing that kept everyone safe.

He knew nothing about being a proper earl and even less about being a husband. It was best he deal with one before considering the other.

"Scouring the parties in search of a bride is not on the list of things I need to attend," he stated flatly.

"You'll learn to manage both," Uncle Syl said and trotted on down to the bottom of the stairs. "Men always do. Choose wisely and she will be a blessing not a curse."

That sounded odd coming from a man who'd never married.

"It's your duty now," Uncle Hector explained. "It will prove to everyone you intend to not only be a responsible earl, but a good caretaker of the family by producing a legitimate heir."

"I'm quite sure I have no heirs of any kind."

"All the better," Hector agreed. "After the shock we've all had, you must protect and preserve the title. The best way to do that is to marry a proper young miss who can give you as many sons as your grandfather had."

The buzzing in Zane's head and roar in his ears returned with a vengeance. He rubbed the bridge of his nose with his thumb and forefinger, determined not to let his well-meaning uncles frustrate him. He couldn't comprehend the responsibility of one son, much less five. What normal man could?

"Blast it, Uncle, I think I should get used to the idea of being an earl before I take on such an ominous role of being a husband or a father of five."

"There is no time for you to dawdle about this," Sylvester added in a decisive tone, obviously wanting to have his say in the matter as well. "The Season is upon us. Why not take advantage of it and go ahead and choose a bride?"

"I think my time will be best spent at Blacknight. I can skip the Season and go straight there and learn what I need to know about the earldom since I'm not familiar with it."

Hector stopped again. His eyes narrowed, his shoulders rolled forward a little, and his chin bobbed before he started speaking. "You spent the first ten years of your life living at the estate. How can you say you aren't familiar with it? Besides, you don't have to be. That's what you have solicitors, accountants, managers, and a host of other people for. You're an earl now, and you have more than yourself to think about. You'll best serve the family being right here in London for the greater portion of the year. This is where most of the business is conducted that concerns the title and its holdings."

"What Hector is also trying to tell you is that the Blacknight property and holdings are considerable. You now control the purse. The magnitude of the estate isn't something you can learn overnight. Your cousins are afraid to spend a penny—we all are, not knowing when the next allowance will come or *if* it will. Your aunt Beatrice is so distraught, she's having fainting spells. Your aunt Lorraine has developed a rash of red welts all over her face, and you didn't even bother to let your sister know you arrived back in Town yesterday."

Zane grimaced. He wasn't in the habit of letting family know his whereabouts. "How do you know that?"

"I went to see her this morning, looking for you. She was glad to hear you'd made it back safely, by the way, but Patricia now assumes you're upset with her."

"I'm not upset with anyone." It was always the same in his family. No peace, no privacy, and no quarter ever given to him, no matter the situation.

"Everyone's worried you'll be making changes," Sylvester said flatly.

"Changes?" Zane questioned, still trying to make sense of the fact he wasn't going to his peaceful home for a few hours of much-needed sleep.

"You have all the family in a dither about what kind of earl you'll be. How generous you will be to everyone. Naturally, the whole family—nieces, nephews, cousins—are anxiously waiting to see what you're going to do about their allowances, their houses, carriages, and what all. And there's your mother's family to consider as well. They'll be wanting to hear from you as to what you plan for their futures. Our older brother was generous to your mother's family too."

Somewhere in his past Zane had heard this. And the previous earl, his father's oldest brother, had always been more than generous to him. Which was surprising since Zane had tarnished the family name on more than one occasion with his wild ways.

"I see no reason to make changes to any of that," he said, finally deciding to sail past Hector and join Sylvester at the bottom.

"That should please everyone greatly for now, but it's up to you to tell them. You can't neglect your duty. But more importantly, you need to show them you've changed now that you have the title."

"Damnation, Uncle Hector," Zane said irritably, his head pounding as if a hammer were slamming against both sides of it. "You are acting as if I have to do everything in one day."

"It would be a good start to the recovery of your reputation if you did. Spending the whole of your first night back in London at a gaming hell will not reassure the family you have their best interests at heart, or the peerage you will work with them when you need to."

Zane had little doubt about that, but still argued, "That's what bachelors do."

"Not for you. Not anymore. Hence the need for a wife to help rein in your raffish ways, settle you down, and facilitate you being respectable and reliable to all who now look to you for protection, sustenance, and guidance."

"I didn't neglect the dowager. After seeing her, was I to pay a visit to everyone in the family?"

"That would have been a splendid thing for you to have done."

The corners of Uncle Syl's mouth tightened, and Hector's chin bobbed as he worked his mouth. Staring at his uncles' current agitation, Zane could only imagine the shock swirling through his tight-as-a-bow-string family that he was now the earl and in charge of everyone's allowances, their homes, and their way of life.

"The devil take it," he whispered, his head continuing to throb. He hadn't asked for this responsibility. "Make sure everyone knows I'll be hosting dinner tomorrow evening, and I'll listen to everyone's concerns."

"Of course," Uncle Syl said calmly, making it clear that was exactly what he wanted Zane to say. "I'll take care of that for you."

"You'll also need to start making amends for all the times you insulted half the members of Parliament," Hector added, tapping his cane once again.

Zane had to draw the line somewhere. "If I offended them, it was because they deserved it, and half of them weren't members at the time."

"No, but their fathers were, and you knew they would be one day. It's never too late to start making friends instead of enemies. It will serve you well."

"I have friends."

"And they are all rakehells like you." Sylvester sniffed and pulled on the tail of his coat and lace at his cuffs. "The less you see of them, the better. They have no reason to change. You do."

Uncle Hector made it to the bottom and Zane grabbed his cloak off the peg near the front door. His uncles were reminding him why he spent so much time away from London. The more family you had, the more worries you had. Without deliberation, he towered over Hector, who held open the door for him.

"I will accept my duties as the earl, Uncle, but don't expect me to fall in line about everything you suggest or to be as pompous as most earls are. I don't have the stomach for it."

"Of course you do," Hector said without so much as a blink of his eyes. "You just don't know it yet."

"Speaking of your stomach," Sylvester added quickly, "White's is on the way to your solicitor's office. You could probably do with a generous plate of food and tankard of hot ale after being up all night."

"I'm all right," Zane muttered as he fastened his cloak at the neck and passed under the doorway.

The brisk morning air felt good hitting his face. He breathed it deeply into his lungs, hoping it would help further clear his head of the brandy and lack of sleep. The problem with what his uncles were saying was that Zane didn't want his life to change. Being the black sheep was easy. It was what he was used to. He was good at it. Changing into the earl was going to be hard, and the damned truth of it was he didn't know if he could do it.

Stopping to settle his hat on his head, he glanced across to the opposite side of the street and was caught off balance by the glimpse of a tall, slender young lady walking down the pavement. His gut tightened. He quickly blinked several times.

It was her. The lady from the masked ball. He was certain of it. The tilt of her head, gracious lift of her chin, and sway of her shoulders as she walked were unmistakable, even though she was now dressed in sensible clothing. He might have been ocean deep into his cups, bound, and with his mind only on stopping Robert's foolish stunt, but he hadn't failed to take detailed notice of the one who freed him that night in Paris.

And he hadn't failed to remember her often.

Zane's gaze followed the lady as she passed his line

of vision, not paying him nor anyone else she swept by the slightest bit of attention. Her short cape was fashionable enough but a drab shade of mulled wine. A black bonnet covered most of her hair, but he saw the telltale sign of a silvery blond chignon at her nape.

At the ball, some of his rescuer's face had been covered by her demi mask, but there were things about her he'd never forget. The faint rustle of her soft skirts when she'd knelt beside him to untie the scarf. The sweet spring flower scent that wafted from her skin. Eyes so blue, he could have looked into their depths for the rest of the evening. Everything about her was still vivid to him, right down to her soft ivory complexion.

He was a man after all, no matter his pressing situation that night. He was more likely to forget his name than her brief appearance in his life.

Watching her now, he could feel the lingering pressure and taste of her soft lips beneath his. Had he imagined it or had she actually given in to the kiss for a second or two?

Because of her, Zane had caught up with Robert and hightailed it to Vienna with the impulsive blade. Zane wouldn't have minded staying in Paris and finding out who she was from the hostess, but he had to get Robert out of Paris for a while. He couldn't trust the randy buck not to try again to marry the French woman.

"Do you know who she is?" Zane nodded in the lady's direction as his uncles flanked him.

"Don't go setting your top hat for her," Uncle Syl immediately warned. "It will do you no good. She's one lady you won't be adding to your queue, and no one would appreciate you trying."

Tension expanded in the back of Zane's neck. "Who is she married to?"

"No one," Hector answered. "She's a widow. Mrs. Brina Feld. Her husband was killed when the *Salty Dove* sank. A shame for someone to be widowed that young."

Bits of newsprint and gossip flashed through Zane's mind. "I've never met her, but I remember the tragedy. Many drowned. It happened four or five years ago."

"At least."

"Is she someone's mistress?"

"Only her own, as far as anyone knows," Uncle Hector added. "See those girls walking behind her?"

Zane nodded but hadn't noticed the dutiful children trailing behind her like sheep following their shepherd until Hector mentioned them. There were four of them. All were dressed alike and walking as purposefully as Mrs. Feld.

"She and two other ladies started a boarding school for those girls and others like them. It's a charitable endeavor and only for the daughters and sisters of men who had worked on the *Salty Dove*."

So, she was available and obviously had a very charitable heart. Not only for men who found themselves in a literal bind and in need of help but children too.

He remembered she'd been curious but cautious when she'd come upon him in the chateau. She'd been strong in holding him to account for his predicament before she fearlessly untied him. Once she'd settled in her mind that he was trustworthy and not a footpad wanting to make off with the family silver, she'd acted in good faith and released him. That act of courage and kindness wasn't the sort of thing a man would forget.

"I'm remembering some of that story," Zane offered, as more memories of the catastrophe and the aftermath came rushing into his mind.

"The other two ladies have since married. But don't

let that give you any ideas about Mrs. Feld. She might be only twenty-four, but she's worn her widow's weeds every day since she heard the news about her husband. No one believes she's going to shed them and marry."

But.

Mrs. Feld had been at that masked ball wearing a provocative gown. Not widow's weeds. She'd worn a costume made from a tempting shade of bright pink satin. It shimmered and glistened in the firelight whenever she moved. The low neckline emphasized a fair amount of her small but delectable bosom. A large pink sapphire had rested seductively in the hollow of her throat. Smaller stones dangled from her earlobes. Her lips were full, beautifully shaped, and rosy as a late summer bloom. In her gloriously blond hair, she'd worn a coronet of leaves alternately painted gold and pink.

Today, she looked every bit the widow his uncles described. Prim and proper as a lady could get. What was the personification of a perfect widow doing in Paris at a masquerade in the dead of winter, dressed to catch the attention of every man who saw her?

Zane didn't know. But he wanted to.

Hector harrumphed and disturbed Zane's musing as Mrs. Feld rounded a corner and walked out of sight.

"She's shown no interest in any man's attentions. Probably because it's hard for any man to compete with a hero."

Damned hard, Zane thought, but it didn't keep another surge of interest from slamming all the way through him. "Was it her husband who saved the lives that day?"

"Indeed," Sylvester answered with conviction. "Not more than a handful of people survived the wreck of the *Salty Dove,* but they all told of the bravery of Mr. Stewart Feld helping passengers find pieces of wreckage they could cling to, while in the end he couldn't save himself.

Word is she's never allowed a man past her front door since. It's doubtful that will change, considering the amount of time that's passed."

Zane nodded slowly, as if in agreement, but thought if that claim were true, it sounded like a challenge to him.

"If one has made it," Uncle Hector continued, "he's kept it a secret, and that's not easy to do in this Town."

It was true, London Society laid claim to few confidences. "No doubt many have tried," Zane offered.

"And failed," Sylvester declared as if that should end any hope Zane might harbor of pursuing the widow Feld. "That's why she's garnered so much genuine affection in most circles. I suggest you set your sights a little lower if you want to be happy with the outcome of your search for a bride. Mrs. Feld is adored by many in all walks of life. Not only is she beautiful and prim to a fault, she's the epitome of all a widowed lady should be. Devoted to the memory of her husband and kind to those in need, whether they be Society or not. She's not likely to look twice at a man who is more apt to have a card game end in a back-alley duel at sunup than to have a Sunday afternoon ride in Hyde Park with a lovely lady."

His uncle certainly wasn't trying to spare his feelings. That was fine with Zane. Both were probably right about their assertion of him and Mrs. Feld, but he would just as soon find that out for himself.

But what was the best way to go about that?

Zane looked down the street again and saw the roofline of White's. He was a member of the famous gentleman's club but seldom went there. The place was deeply steeped in traditions Zane would rather avoid, so he usually stayed away. And there was the fact that he'd been thrown out more than a few times. They didn't appreciate or tolerate raucous hellraising from young men out to have a good time with their drink, games, and general fooling around.

The prestigious club was known as much for its wager book as for the exclusivity and civility of its members. Men of otherwise good character would wager on the oddest of things. From whether a man's wife would bear him a son or daughter, to what time of day a certain man would die. There was no bet too humorous or too grisly to lay down.

And that book is what gave Zane an extraordinary idea.

At first thought, it seemed an impossible, outlandish, and mostly irresponsible idea.

But it immediately sparked his interest, and he couldn't deny he wanted to accept the challenge of it. There was a thing or two he needed to consider. First and foremost is that he would be competing with the memory of Mrs. Feld's husband. That alone gave him reason to have second thoughts. There were some things that should be too sacred to disturb.

By all accounts, the man was a true hero.

The only thing Zane had ever done worthwhile was save the life of every man he'd ever dueled. He could have easily shot to kill, but he never had. He'd never actually challenged anyone to a duel. And there were those who thought even that wasn't noteworthy and a fact that was often lost in the telling because Zane accepted every challenge thrown at him. And he couldn't agree with them more. There was little heroism in duels, even if he did aim to miss.

He'd been uncommonly drawn to her when she'd swept into the room at the French chateau and looked at him the first time. He knew immediately she was an English beauty, elegant and refined and not one of the

many ladies there looking for the unrestrained sexual behavior that usually went on at such a ball.

His uncles certainly thought highly of her too. Who
wouldn't? A beautiful young lady who'd maintained un-
blemished widowhood for five years was deserving of
respect and extremely enticing at the same time. He was
up to a new challenge. What better way to get his uncles
and neurotic family off his back than to solicit help from
the one lady who had no plans to marry?

But, if he wanted to get past Mrs. Feld's front door, he
would first have to get her attention. He looked toward
the roofline of White's again and thought of that book.

Zane didn't know anything about being a proper earl,
and the hell of it was he really didn't want to learn. But
if there was one thing he knew, it was how to get a lady's
attention.

# Chapter 3

Brina Feld entered the front door of her house and caught the mouth-watering scent of fresh-baked bread, cooked fruit, and cinnamon filling the air. A pleasant change from the common smells of oil polish, beeswax, and burnt wood that so often lingered in the rooms. She could hardly wait to cut into one of Mrs. Lawton's fruit tarts, spread it with butter, and eat as many of them as she wanted.

Nothing invigorated Brina more than a brisk walk to Town when the sun was shining brightly, and the air was as chilling as dipping her bare toes into a deep winter stream. And having some of the girls from the school join her made it an especially pleasing day. Much to the girls' delight, they had spent the morning in Town looking through the collections of merchandise at several shops. None of the girls had ever had a reason to venture inside a business establishment, and it was a good learning experience for them.

Their first stop had been at the largest linen draper in London. It sold a wide variety of different fabrics. Fanny hadn't wanted to leave it. Next on the list was the haberdashery, which was Mathilda's favorite shop. The number of buttons, ribbons, and lace the store carried was astounding to them all. The last place they went into was the milliner. None of the four girls were impressed with the shop. They all wanted to sew beautiful gowns and dresses trimmed with bows, flowers, and beads. Not make hats.

It made Brina happy to see awe and wonder in their faces as they looked around the shops. She wasn't sure everyone would be pleased with her decision to parade the girls downtown and then take them into some of the stores, but she didn't care. It was an enlightening and well-deserved outing for the older ones, who had two years of schooling behind them.

Now Brina was eager for Adeline and Julia to arrive so she could tell them about some of her plans for the future. She wanted to give the girls painting lessons. Perhaps it was a bit frivolous for girls learning the seamstress trade to engage in a Society lady's pastime.

But, so be it.

Brina wanted to do all she could to see the girls had some refinement and enjoyment along with their arduous studies and the task of learning how to sew. They were all doing so well with a needle now. She'd argue that painting could prove useful in teaching them where to place bows, ribbons, and add an embroidery of flowers on a dress.

Too, she had to invite Harper to dinner soon. She'd promised her father she'd stay in touch with her cousin. And she wanted to. She'd had a lingering concern about him. The last time she'd seen Harper, he had a cut lip and the faint shade of bruising around his mouth. It hadn't seemed proper to ask him about it. Perhaps her father had seen that too and wanted Brina to make sure he was now doing fine.

Harper was a happy and mild-mannered person, but she supposed it was inevitable for a young man to get into scuffles from time to time and take one on the chin. Even well brought-up men like her cousin were sure to have disagreements that ended badly. It was part of the male nature. And it was Brina's nature to want to care for people and help them if she could.

After shedding her woolen cape, she draped it across a chair in the entry and started untying the bow under her chin. It felt wonderful to be in a home of her own. She loved her parents, but they were overwhelming at times. They doted on her, smothered her with affection, and sheltered her with protection. For a time she had needed that, but she was glad to have finally left their home to make her own way in life. The two months she'd been living in the house in front of the school had been the most contented she could remember in years.

Now that her parents were off on their journey to Northumberland to visit her mother's sister, Brina felt as if she were truly on her own, and it was a freeing feeling. The glorious spring weather had brought her many wonderful ideas. The list of things she wanted to accomplish for the girls' school and the charitable work she did for the Sisters of Pilwillow Crossings were many, and it was growing longer every day. She was going to rejoin the reading society, return to her painting, and embrace the joy of living life again after years—

"Let me help you with those things, Mrs. Feld," her housekeeper said, hurrying up the corridor toward the entrance.

"Thank you, Mrs. Lawton, but no need. I can manage

this. It smells as if your special tarts are ready to come out of the oven."

"And I have water heating for tea, but there's something I have to tell you first." She moved closer to Brina and whispered, "There's a gentleman in the drawing room waiting to see you."

A gentleman waiting for her? Brina laid her bonnet on top of her cape and started pulling on the fingers of her gloves. Because Mrs. Lawton whispered, Brina felt she must too. "You know I don't receive gentlemen callers."

"I do," the housekeeper said, softly but emphatically. "I told him you weren't here, thinking that would be the end of it and he'd go away, but instead, he said he'd wait for you. He then took it upon himself to walk right past me and into the house. I didn't know what to do but show him to the drawing room."

"That doesn't sound like something a gentleman would do."

"Oh, he's not *just* a gentleman, Mrs. Feld," she continued in her whispered, but excited voice, her wide-eyed gaze sweeping over to the masculine cloak and hat that lay on a chair on the opposite side of the vestibule. "He said he was an earl and needed to speak to you, so he'd wait."

An earl to see her? How odd. And which one? There must be close to half a dozen presently in London. Parliament was in session, and the Season's first ball was already behind them. But why would any of them want to see her? Unless . . . she studied a moment on the thought his visit might have something to do with the school in the building behind the house. She and her two friends had thought there might be protests from some people in the ton or the neighborhood when they started the small private boarding school, but that had been over two years ago.

"Did he say what he wanted?" Brina asked.

Mrs. Lawton shook her head and picked up Brina's cape and bonnet. "But of course I asked him," she admitted without guile. "Not to be rude, but wondering if I might assist him for you. He said it was a private matter he'd take up with you. Who am I to question an earl further?"

Titled or not, Brina wondered how she should confront a man who would all but barge into a lady's house. She didn't have more than a second or two before she heard the strong sure sound of masculine boots hitting the hardwood floor.

"It's all right, Mrs. Lawton." She handed the housekeeper her gloves. "I'll take care of this. You go finish preparing for Julia and Adeline."

The housekeeper quietly left, and from behind her, Brina heard a man say, "I thought I heard someone talking."

That same spark of awareness that she'd only felt one other time slithered through Brina. She went perfectly still.

*Her* masked stranger.

Here in *her* house?

Was it possible? A touch of awe and fear raced through her.

She had never seen the man's face, not all of it anyway, but she recognized his voice. She'd never forget his tone barking orders at her to free him and then saying *thank you* in the most sensual manner she could ever imagine. With a kiss that still took her breath when she thought about it.

The footsteps stopped close behind her. A dizzying wave of near panic swelled her chest. Her stomach quivered. As it had been in Paris, there was no escape for her. What was she to do? It was one thing to daydream about him, as she had, but quite another to come face-to-face with him again. Something she never thought would happen.

On the glimmer of hope she might be wrong, she turned. Their eyes met and held. It was him.

*Merciful heavens.* He was more handsome and powerful-looking than she'd remembered. Thick, black hair was combed away from his broad, masculine brow and fell to the top of his collar at the nape. His cheekbones were high and well-defined. His narrow, high-bridged nose added to the rugged look of his lightly square chin and jaw. The fit of his fawn-colored coat across his shoulders was exceptional and emphasized his broad, muscular chest. She was intensely aware of the strength and command that emanated from his body. Her pulse raced and her muscles coiled tightly at seeing him again.

In that moment, somehow she knew they'd been destined to meet again.

He nodded once. "Mrs. Feld, I am Blacknight."

Her breath caught and swirled in her chest as she stood spellbound by who he was. The way his gaze swept down her face and slowly back to her eyes sent her senses reeling. It was almost too much to take in. Unbelievably so. She had rescued the man who was known far and wide as the black sheep of the Blacknight family.

She'd heard rumors of his wild escapades for years. His father had died when he was a babe and his mother and school masters had never been able to tame him into a respectable gentleman. Just weeks ago, he had become an earl and head of the family that had all but disowned him for his ruinous behavior.

Brina managed a belated curtsey as many thoughts

became an incoherent jumble in her mind. Had he known who she was that night in Paris or found out later? That was over three months ago. What was he doing at her house now?

"I have heard of you," she said cautiously, not wanting to let on that she recognized him until she knew for sure whether he remembered her. There could be many reasons for his visit, and she didn't want to presume anything.

"I don't believe we've been formally introduced."

"No," she whispered softly. "We haven't."

He tilted his head in question before a hint of a smile played at the corners of his mouth. "But, you do remember me?"

*Oh, yes.*

She wasn't likely to forget a man who was dressed only in his shirt and trousers and tied to a chair. Or his shocking embrace and unforgettable kiss once she'd freed him. And truth be told, she'd caught herself wondering from time to time if she ever crossed his mind the way he had hers since he fled the room.

It was best to start with the most reasonable question. "How do you know my name?"

"By chance," he offered in a relaxing tone, while his gaze held tightly to hers. "I recognized you walking down the street with the girls this morning. I asked my uncle about you. I could never forget you, Mrs. Feld. Or what you did for me."

The kiss he gave her came searing across her senses again as it had so many times. And then another horror struck her. What must he be thinking about her now? She was known throughout the ton as the widow who'd never given up her widow's weeds. Yet, he'd seen her clothed in a voluminous pink satin gown. How had she lowered her defenses and allowed Aunt Josette to talk her into wearing the lavish costume? Clearly the mask had not hidden her identity as her aunt had insisted.

"Should we talk about that evening in Paris?" he asked when she remained quiet.

"Why would we?" she answered quickly, gathering some measure of control. Lifting her chin and shoulders, she hoped she didn't look as stricken as she suddenly felt.

"Perhaps because we both know why I was there, but I have no idea why you were at the ball."

Brina didn't want him to know her reasons. Motives that appeared logical at the time, now seemed foolish. But, what was he thinking? That she led two different lives?

"I don't believe an answer to that is necessary." She silently inhaled deeply to steady herself and took a step back from him. "We were at a masquerade. I trust the purpose of such evenings is things that happen there are not talked about later."

His eyes narrowed but continued to hold steady on hers. For a moment, she thought he might question her further, but thankfully, he merely nodded acceptance of her statement.

"If you're here because you fear I might tell someone about what I did for—what happened at the ball, you can rest assured I haven't spoken a word to anyone about that night."

He chuckled softly, and she found even that quite inviting. Every little thing about him made her take notice. How could that be? She didn't want to be attracted to him or any man. She had helped him when he needed it and that should be the end of their association.

"I'm not worried about that, Mrs. Feld. You could tell the whole of London how you found me, and no one would be shocked or think it out of the ordinary that you stumbled upon me in such a compromised state."

What he said was probably true. She had heard talk and knew how some in his family viewed him. However, they would be surprised to learn she was there and dressed as she was.

As if reading her mind, he added, "On my honor and the Blacknight family, I will never disclose to anyone when, how, or where we met the first time."

She believed him and gave a silent thank-you.

"I hope you were able to accomplish your mission on your nephew's behalf."

"Robert's my cousin. And I arrived just in time. I hauled him over to Vienna, and within the week, he'd found someone new to bestow his affections on."

"Yes, of course. I recognize the name Robert Browning. I've met him at parties. He's usually with my cousin, Harper Tabor, who I've always thought of as more a brother than cousin. Neither of us had siblings. I suppose it's good your cousin's heart wasn't broken for too long."

"I was sure that would be the case."

Brina cleared her throat softly before saying, "Well, thank you for stopping by to let me know he is doing well and that you know who I am. It will make it easier between us now should we meet again."

The earl made no motion to move but remained in his relaxed stance, though his expression was of a more serious nature. "I do have another reason for coming over that has nothing to do with our previous meeting. Something more important."

His words intrigued her, causing her chest to flutter again. For a fleeting moment she wondered if he might have another daring rescue to attend. Whether or not he intended it, everything about him was seductive. A fact that made it difficult to shy away from him as was her usual course with all gentlemen.

Her gaze settled fully on his. "What could that be?"

"It's something I felt obligated to tell you so it wouldn't come as a shock when you hear it from others."

Tensing, her mind flew back to the extraordinary evening in Paris. "Do others already know about Paris? Will there be gossip about us?"

The seriousness left his eyes. An engaging smile prefaced his statement. "You worry too much, Mrs. Feld. I'm sure no one in London knows about that evening unless, of course, you told someone."

"Me? No. Certainly not," she said, a bit indignant that he should even think she might tell on herself.

Brina hadn't even mentioned the incident to her best friends, Adeline and Julia. Though, she had been tempted more than once to ravish them with details about her unexpected adventure and the kiss that had stolen her breath and her thoughts ever since. Now that she knew who he was, she would be even more tempted to tell them of her discovery in that chateau.

But there was no need to let him know that.

"Then our secret is safe."

For now, she thought.

"I placed a wager in the betting book at White's a short time ago, and after doing so, I realized it was only fair that I be the one to come over and tell you about it."

Brina looked at him with almost as much inquisitiveness as she had the first time seeing him and smiled. "Why would your wagers be of interest to me, my lord?"

"Because this one concerns you."

There was something challenging in his eyes. A curl of suspicion and nip of intrigue teased her chest as she watched his eyes rake down her face with way too much interest.

"I don't understand," she offered with an unintended bit of inquisitiveness edging her voice. "Whatever are you talking about?"

"It appears that I am in great need of something specific to show my family I can be responsible and not see the earldom of Blacknight come to ruin. My family is in a near state of panic because I have become the earl. The misfortune that happened wasn't something any of us could have foreseen. Me least of all. Be that as it may, it comes with certain expectations."

No doubt. They must be shaking in their collective boots. His reputation as a gambler was well known. He certainly knew how to pique her curiosity. "Again, my lord, I'm finding that none of what you have to say has anything to do with me."

An attractive smile edged the corners of his decidedly masculine lips. "My uncles are convinced that a suitable bride would go a long way toward helping change me into the respectable head of the family I need to be and settling down all the strained nerves of the Blacknight lineage. I knew if anyone could do that for me, it would be you."

"Me?" Her voice remained calm, though she was certain she wasn't. "You can't be serious."

"Wholly serious. I wagered that you would accept my proposal of marriage and we'd announce our engagement by midnight at the last ball of the Season."

A light-headedness flashed through her. Brina had no idea if she could believe he had actually done such a thing. "What nonsense you speak of." She smiled, and then laughed a little, even though all traces of humor had left his face. He was sober, his eyes were steady and clear. Still, she added, "That's preposterous, my lord."

"Presumptuous, I'll admit to. Why would you think it preposterous I'd want to marry you?" he asked with soft intensity to his tone and his expression.

With wary amusement and a determination to remain

unruffled by his admissions, she offered sensibly, "Let's start with the fact that you don't know me."

"I know all I need to about you," he said without reservation. "You helped a stranger when he was in desperate circumstances and expected nothing in return. That speaks well of you, Mrs. Feld. So do my uncles. You are loyal, principled, and you're even more beautiful without your mask."

She felt uneasy about his praise and tactfully refrained from making a comment about it. "But what of you? Making a wager at a gentleman's club is not the proper way to propose to a lady and let her know you want to marry her."

"Which goes to my point," he offered. "I need you by my side to help me become respectable. I need to know how to say and do all the proper things expected of an earl. You could do me the honor of accepting my proposal of marriage right now. If you will, the bet would then have no relevance, and I'd be well on my way to reassuring my family that I'm capable of doing something to please them and that all was not lost when I became the earl."

This wasn't a foolhardy trick he was playing on her. He was serious. Because of that, she had to be serious too. "I have no intentions of marrying anyone," she said willfully. "Now, nor ever. When your uncle told you my name, he should have also told you that. It's not a secret."

He nodded slowly. "Though it's been a few years, I remembered your story. I know how you became a widow, about the school behind this house, and the friends who helped you start it."

"Yes. Perhaps what you don't know is that I am quite content in my unwed state. I don't know why you would do something so wild and reckless as to make a wager such as this. It's most extraordinary. Why not be prudent and simply pick from any number of young ladies who entered the marriage mart last week and would be more than willing to marry you?"

"I'm not a sensible person, Mrs. Feld." He paused and took a step closer to her. "But I never make a bet I don't intend to win."

Not sensible? How many people would admit to such a thing? But it must be true. Look what he'd done. Brina stared all the more keenly at him, refusing to give in and indulge the gentle way her abdomen rolled and tightened in response to his nearness.

"You have all the qualities of a good person that I don't have," he continued in the same calm tone. "We are a perfect match."

Anger began mixing with disbelief and shock. Her courage strengthened. "What?" Brina bristled and stood her ground. "How can you say such a false statement so innocently? We are not a perfect anything."

"I believe we are."

"No," she argued forcibly, as her arms stiffened at her sides. "We're complete opposites."

"Which will make for a very stimulating life between us. I am the blackguard of the ton, and you are an impeccable, saintly widow who's loved by all."

"Saintly," she whispered as if the word were vile.

It pierced her like a dull dagger. She felt the familiar weight of heaviness in her chest whenever she was reminded of her past. It pained her that anyone thought her such a good person. She wasn't. Grief, she'd found, could lessen, but guilt was a much heavier burden to lighten. It was a weight that never truly went away. She looked up at the earl, knowing he had no idea the haunting memories his words sent rushing back to her. Memories she decided long ago would never leave her.

"Some may think that," she said softly. "But let me

assure you, I am not flawless. Others may not know it, but I do."

His brows drew together in concern. "My words troubled you. I didn't mean for them to."

His perceptiveness unnerved her, and she lowered her head so he couldn't see more of her pain. She was beginning a new, stronger, and better life that was free of her past, her hurts, and her faults. She wasn't going to let this rogue and his shenanigans done for his own purposes upset her plans to move forward.

"You trouble me. I need you to leave, my lord," she said, shaking off the bewildering feeling of his sudden appearance and his revelation of what he wanted. "You have no right to come into my life and disrupt it in such a fashion. I want nothing to do with any of your nonsense or wagers. Nothing to do with you. I have my friends, the girls at the school, the women at the abbey, and other responsibilities that need my attention."

"I need your help too, Mrs. Feld."

"What? No. Furthermore, I don't need you."

He remained calm but seemed to study on her words for a moment before he shrugged so effortlessly she almost missed it. "Whether or not you will agree to marry me at the end of the Season doesn't need to be settled now. The fact that you will allow me to court you so you can help me with all the proper things an earl should do will help appease my family's disposition."

"Oh, so that is it," she whispered, suddenly more irritated than troubled and not afraid to let it show. Her head tilted up. "What a beast you are! Once again, you expect me to come to your aid and free you from a problem you've gotten yourself into. Well, I can't help you with this one."

His steady gaze didn't waver. "You are the only one who can."

"Don't be ridiculous," she said, folding her arms across her chest defiantly. "If you want to become a better person and act like an earl, hire someone to teach you. You don't need to court or marry anyone to learn how to put aside your bad behavior and say and do the right things by people, or to be a proper gentleman. You are the reason you misbehave, and no one can fix it but *you*."

"I am not doing this simply because you will be a mere convenience for me." He shifted his stance and lowered his voice. "There's more to why I chose you and you know it."

A shiver of something she didn't quite understand and didn't know if she wanted to chilled her. "What do you mean?" she whispered cautiously, unsure what he might say.

"There is the matter of attraction between us."

A warmth of fluttery sensations swirled in her lower stomach once again. His words were softly spoken, almost beguiling her with their honesty. Despite her anger at what he'd done, anticipation tightened her breasts. He moved even closer to her, invading a space she never allowed gentlemen to enter. With the tips of his fingers, he gently lifted her chin. His touch seared her with the desire to fall into his arms when what she should do was jerk away from him. It was impossible to keep her insides from trembling with expectancy as she looked into his deep blue eyes.

"It needs no explanation. You feel it as surely as I do," he said huskily.

Yes, she did but she didn't know why. He was considered a rake by everyone.

"You know what it is," he continued in that seductive tone that washed over her like healing warm water. "That unidentifiable feeling of interest that stirs, swells, and draws us to another person. It feeds us, fills us, and eventually overtakes our thoughts, our senses, and our lives. It makes us want to know everything about the person."

"I don't know what you are talking about," she insisted, dismayed that she knew exactly what he was describing. "There is no such thing," she fibbed to the rogue with only minimal regret. If a man was so uncouth to say such things to a lady, she shouldn't be expected to answer truthfully.

"Deny it if you must, but it's there."

Brina moved her face from his touch but put no distance between them. "Even if I were to consider your outrageous proposal, which I'm not, what would be the benefit to me other than to have my name tarnished as much as yours?"

"If we were to marry, a home. Children."

Yes, most ladies wanted that even above love from their husbands. She smiled and tilted her chin up again, confident in her answer. "I have a home, my lord. You are standing in it. I have children. Ten of them I can see every day in the school behind this house."

"Then I agree there's not much I can offer you." The inflection in his tone was conciliatory but not defeated. "No doubt a gentleman would take you at your word and not impose on your sensibilities further. However, we know I'm far from a gentleman. And because of the brief time we spent together earlier in the year, I know that you are cautious, but also curious. Intelligent, but eager to learn new things. And I believe you are more free-spirited than you want anyone to know. If nothing else, I can promise it would be an adventure filled with passion if you were married to me."

With each word he spoke, her breaths grew shorter and deeper. She believed that too, but couldn't hint to him it was true. She couldn't let this rogue upset her well-planned life. It had taken her too long to settle the past and put it behind her.

She looked him boldly in the eyes and stated, "I am not looking for adventure or passion."

The blue of his eyes seemed to darken. He gave her a quiet look of disbelief. "Our kiss was brief but passionate. You would have loved it if I had taken you with me that night in Paris. I started to offer."

Had he?

"I was tempted to grab your hand and sweep you along with me. But I had to move fast. Unfortunately, your skirts would have slowed me down as I raced through the streets. I held you so tightly, you must have felt my hesitation after our kiss."

Yes. How had he known she'd thought about insisting she go if she freed him?

But unlike him, Brina knew when she made a mistake. Attending the masquerade was one. She wasn't about to make another. Her life was settled now. She had found happiness at last. She wouldn't be drawn into this man's unacceptable lifestyle and certainly for no other reason than he needed her to make him a better person for his family.

"I am not interested in your wagers or your adventurous games, my lord," she said firmly and walked over and opened the door for him. "My advice is that you leave now and go take back your wager."

"No gambler ever withdraws his bet, Mrs. Feld."

"Perhaps not a gambler then, but a gentleman realizes when he's overstepped propriety and rectifies it. And if that were not enough to tempt you to do the right thing, you're an earl now. Surely that should give you the clout you need to call back your ill-conceived wager."

He slowly shook his head and moved to stand before

her once again. Closer than would be considered proper, but not in a threatening manner. A solicitous way. His lids lowered halfway over his eyes as his face came very close to hers. "I want you, Mrs. Feld. I'd much rather win your hand after a hard-fought battle than as an easy coup. I am a gambling man. The bet holds and I plan to win."

A chill rippled down her spine. Her composure seemed shaken as she digested his words. The way he looked at her, for a moment she thought he might catch her up in his arms and kiss her as he had in Paris. All the things she'd felt when his lips touched hers washed over her again. The moment had been divine. His arms had been strong. They wrapped completely around her and caught her up so close to his hard, warm chest. She thought she'd never feel those things again, but now he was so close to her that she only had to—

"Are we interrupting anything?"

At the sound of her friend's voice, Brina stepped away from the earl and looked toward the open doorway. Julia and Adeline stood there looking quite perplexed, glancing from Brina to Blacknight. They had never seen her alone with a man. Especially one standing so inappropriately close to her.

"No, not at all," Brina said, hoping she didn't sound as nervous and as breathless as she was. "Nothing. We weren't doing anything—but talking. I'm glad you're here. So glad. The earl was just saying goodbye." She took in a deep breath and steadied herself. Being caught with the Town rake practically had her stumbling over her words. She picked up the earl's coat and hat from the chair.

Blacknight bowed and said, "Lady Lyon. Mrs. Stockton."

Julia and Adeline curtseyed and returned the greeting.

"It's a pleasure to see you both again," the earl continued, "but as Mrs. Feld said, I was just leaving."

He took the things Brina held out for him and leaned in close to her ear. "It's been a long time since I've had to pursue a lady, Mrs. Feld. I'm looking forward to it, but don't be mistaken. I intend to go after you rigorously and win your hand. I'll see you at the grand ball Saturday evening."

# Chapter 4

Oh, he is an infuriating person!" Brina exclaimed as she shut the door and spun toward her friends. "He was the first time I met him, and still is. It would serve him right if I called his bluff and—" Brina caught herself and stopped mid-sentence.

She didn't miss the *look* that passed between Adeline and Julia, so she quickly fell silent.

"What bluff would that be?" Adeline asked, regarding her with more than casual interest while untying her bonnet and lifting if off her golden-brown hair. "And why specifically is Lord Blacknight infuriating?"

"Yes," Julia agreed, removing her gloves, but not taking her gaze off Brina's either. "As one of your dearest friends, there's much I'd like to know right now. Starting with when did you meet him the first time? Why was he here now?"

"I've heard about Zane Browning's exploits—I mean

the earl's," Adeline corrected herself. "Most of them from family members grumbling about something he has or hasn't done to upset them all. And, it's odd, but I don't remember ever meeting him. Since he acted as if we had met, I went along."

"I do recall being introduced to him some time ago," Julia offered. "He's such a dashing scoundrel and so aloof concerning the ton and everyone else from what I've heard. Who could forget him?"

Who indeed! Brina thought.

Adeline unfastened her cape. "You need to toss all your flowers onto the table and let us know exactly what's going on between you two."

While they were talking, Brina's gaze kept sweeping from one friend to the other. She needed to buy herself some time to digest her discussion with Blacknight before she tried to explain it to anyone, including herself.

"Wait," Brina said. "First things first. Where are your sons? You know I want you to always bring Chatwyn and Paston with you?"

"Sorry, but I couldn't bring Chatwyn to Adeline's this time," Julia said, brushing a strand of her chestnut-colored hair behind her ear. "It's Lyon's card club day and Garrett was coming over to play with them. A five-year-old wouldn't mix well with men intent on their pastime. I promise to bring him soon."

It was always a disappointment not to see their boys, but Brina only said, "All right. Next time. I asked you both over to discuss something I want to do for the girls. Come into the drawing room. Mrs. Lawton will bring in tea."

"We can resolve this issue quickly," Julia said. "Whatever you want to do for the girls, we're fine with it. So, that's settled. We're not going anywhere until we know what's going on with you and the most talked about man in London right now."

Brina rolled her shoulders absently. "I really don't want to talk about Lord Blacknight. He doesn't deserve a moment of our time. We have more important things to discuss."

"No, Brina. There is nothing more important than the black sheep of the Blacknight family being at your house with his nose not much more than an inch from yours."

"Right," Adeline added firmly. "Tell us now."

"He wasn't that close." Was he? Brina let out a deep breath of resignation, and as calmly as possible considering her emotional state, she said, "He wants me to marry him."

Julia went still.

Adeline gasped.

Their wide, non-blinking eyes and parted lips told Brina that perhaps she should have broken the news a little more gently. They were her dearest friends after all. They had met when struggling to make new lives for themselves. The three of them had been through much together. Society had made them acquaintances. Tragedy made them widows. Friendship made them strong. Even though Adeline and Julia now had adoring husbands and sons, the three had remained as close as sisters.

Brina supposed she needed to be the one to tell them what Lord Blacknight had done, though it still hardly seemed real. They would hear about the wager from their husbands soon enough anyway, and probably everyone else in Town. Even now the news could be spreading through Lyon's card club at Adeline's house next door.

"I know. You can't believe it either, can you?" Brina offered what she hoped to be a little laugh to make light of her announcement, but it was more an exasperated sigh.

"When did he ask you?" Adeline questioned in disbelief. "Just now?"

"Yes. Naturally, being the rake that he is, he couldn't ask for my hand in the proper way a gentleman would. He had to do it in the most incorrigible way possible."

"What do you mean?" Julia asked, still looking aghast.

"He placed a wager in the betting book at White's that I would agree to marry him by the last ball of the Season."

"That scoundrel!" Adeline whispered.

Julia gave her a surprised grin. "My heavens! What a stupendous way to get your attention."

"It was. But, of course, I won't marry him," Brina reassured them, feeling as confident as she sounded.

"I should hope not," Adeline agreed.

"What has been going on between you two that we don't know about?" Julia asked, cutting her eyes around to Adeline as if soliciting her help to get to the bottom of this.

"Nothing," Brina insisted honestly. "I hardly know him. We'd only met once before. I didn't know who he was at the time, and he didn't know me."

Julia pursed her lips before saying, "Yet, he came over today and asked you to marry him?"

"Yes. After all his wayward years, and because the title fell to him, he's looking for a sense of respectability. He thinks I can help him and that courting and marrying me will alleviate his family's misgivings about him and the kind of earl he will be."

"Wait, wait," Julia said, holding up both her hands. "I think it's time we go into the drawing room. I'd like to hear the beginning of this story."

Brina had been caught and supposed there was now

nothing to do but tell them everything. And really, she wanted to. Earl Blacknight wasn't like any man she'd ever met. She'd been with him twice now, and he didn't do anything the gentlemanly way. He'd made it clear he was going to pursue her. She needed a plan, and all the guidance her friends could give her if she was going to handle this rake.

After they were all comfortably seated with Julia and Adeline on one settee and Brina on the other, she realized her heart was still racing from Blacknight's visit. Just thinking about all the earl had said, how he'd looked at her with such intensity had her quaking inside with trepidation and, of all things, anticipation at the thought of seeing him again. And that enveloped her with delicious shivers of desire.

"Well?" Julia stated, her dark blue-violet gaze holding fast on Brina's.

Brina shook off the unexpected feelings about Blacknight and said, "It all started in Paris."

"Paris!" Adeline exclaimed. "You've known him that long?"

"And you never breathed a word to either of us about seeing him there when you returned," Julia admonished.

"I couldn't," Brina persisted. "I didn't know who he was until today. He was wearing a mask."

Adeline and Julia gave each other that *look* again.

"A mask?" Julia asked succinctly and folded her arms across her chest as pointedly. "You definitely need to start at the beginning."

"And don't leave out one tiny thing," Adeline ordered. "We need to know it all."

"Shortly after arriving in Paris, I confessed to Aunt Josette I had considered joining the Sisters of Pilwillow Crossings and the reasons I eventually decided against it. She was understanding and glad I chose to get away from London for a while. A week or so later, she suggested since I had considered a life of servitude and found it wasn't for me, it would be good to shed my widow's clothing and go out for an evening of light-hearted, free-living entertainment. She said the best way to decide what kind of life I truly wanted was to experience them all. You know Aunt Josette has always been quite liberated in her thinking and actions. And I'd—well, you know what I'd been through."

Adeline's golden-brown eyes widened again and her brow rose high. "What did you do?"

Julia moved to the edge of the settee and leaned forward.

Brina continued, "After much thought, I agreed to join Aunt Josette at a private masquerade ball. It seemed the perfect foil for me because no one would see all my face. I admit, regretfully so now, that I lulled myself into believing there might be some restorative value in participating at least once in the vastly different lifestyle of Paris's Society, so I dressed in the most glorious shade of pink I've ever seen. I'd never worn anything like that gown. It was gathered tight at the waist. The skirt was full and billowed so beautifully. It stood out to here." She held her arms out to show how wide the skirt was. "I wore a crown of painted leaves. And—"

Brina hesitated. What she was admitting had to be a shock to Adeline and Julia. To anyone who believed she'd never discarded dark clothing since her husband's death.

"And what?" Adeline asked breathlessly, motioning with her hands for Brina to hurry along.

"She spent the night in the earl's arms!" Julia whispered.

"No," Brina answered earnestly. "I didn't. I swear, I didn't. He's a rake of the highest order. How can you think that?"

"But you didn't know that at the time and you wanted to," Julia added as if encouraging her to answer truthfully.

Had she?

"No. No. That never entered my mind." Not that night anyway. The truth was that it might have crossed her mind a time or two since then. Well, maybe more than a time or two, but she'd stopped those thoughts as quickly as possible. Sometimes. But she didn't need to tell her friends every little detail of what happened and how she felt about it then or since.

She needed to keep a few secrets to herself.

After a few more moments of hesitancy, Brina continued, "There wasn't time to think about anything like that. When I came upon him in the room, I thought he was a thief. He was only half-dressed and tied to a chair with a lady's silk scarf."

Julia and Adeline rose to their feet and stared down at Brina. Neither of them uttered a word. She'd silenced them.

"Sit back down," Brina said, trying to will away her frustration and anger about the chaos the earl had brought into her life because of his wager. "I'll tell you everything that happened."

And in a rush of excited words, she did.

Almost everything.

She started her tale when she entered the chateau and was immediately accosted by a drunken man. During her story, she was interrupted numerous times with ohs and ahs and with questions and comments along the way. Mrs. Lawton brought in tea and piping hot apricot tarts. Brina admitted to the unexpected shock of the brief kiss—but didn't tell them about the lingering, disturbing, and wondrous feelings that still plagued her. No need for that. She finished her story at the point where Julia and Adeline had appeared in her doorway.

"Now I know why he's called the scoundrel of the ton!" Adeline exclaimed. "It's beyond the pale for him to think you'd marry a man with his reputation. And what arrogance. It's astounding. To think you'd do it only to help him seem more respectable so he can find favor with his family now that he's the earl."

"I know. He must do something more than marry me to convince them he's changed. It would serve him right if I came up with a wager of my own," Brina grumbled. "How do you think he would like it if I asked all the ladies I know to place a bet that I won't agree to marry him by the last ball of the Season? I wonder if he'd react favorably to that."

"He wouldn't like it at all," Adeline agreed.

Julia placed her teacup onto the small table that stood between the two settees, leaned back, and said, "I think you might be on to something, Brina."

"What do you mean?" she asked, a little concerned by Julia's confident expression.

"Maybe you *should* consider his proposal."

"Absolutely not!" Adeline injected.

"Ha! I agree. I never would."

"Let me explain," Julia argued, holding up her hand as if asking for calm. "There seemed to be something between the two of you when you looked at each other a few minutes ago."

Adeline whipped her gaze over to Brina for confirmation. "Was there?"

"Well—" Brina hedged.

"Really? He's the devil of depravity and debauchery, which is why he's spent so much time in Paris. That you found him tied to a chair—and by a woman, no less—shows he is living up to everything we've heard about him. He cares for no one but himself, stays separated from his family for most of the year, and when he is in

Town, he never visits to even ask about their welfare. I don't know what Julia is thinking, but you can't possibly consider this travesty he's pressed upon you for one second."

Brina knew all of what Adeline said wasn't true, even though it was accepted as fact. And she was upset with him about it. But he obviously cared for some of his family. He'd saved his cousin from a marriage that would have probably been an unfortunate one. For both, considering how quickly the young man went on to find another woman's affections.

But . . .

"Of course, I can't and won't consider such an idea," Brina stated again. "He's a scoundrel for doing this. You both know that." She turned to Julia and saw her friend wasn't convinced. "All right, there was, or perhaps I should say there is a spark of something when I look at him. It's true. I might avoid telling you all the truth, but I won't lie to you about anything. I suppose my feelings have something to do with the fact he seems dangerous to me, and yet safe at the same time. I can't explain it. It's just there, but I certainly don't intend to act upon those feelings. As his reputation bears out, he seems to have skipped all civility in something as sacred as a marriage proposal and placed a wager on it."

"I understand all you say and agree," Julia replied calmly. "Both of you indulge me and let me finish. Before you went to France, Brina, I remember asking you why you thought you would be happy joining the Sisters of Pilwillow Crossings and you said, 'Because I'm not happy where I am.' Tell me, are you happy where you are now?"

Brina had lived the past five years thinking she'd never be happy again because of Stewart's death and the subsequent things that came close to driving her to madness. Now, living in the house in front of the girls' school and helping the Sisters at Pilwillow Crossings, she'd found a certain amount of contentment.

Until today. Now, along with the feelings of resentment toward the earl, she felt an anxious excitement coiling inside her too. As if that passageway to adventure the earl talked about was before her, and all she had to do was step into it.

"I believe I was until Blacknight showed up and announced his preposterous wager."

"Well, he obviously didn't want you to agree to marry him today."

"Didn't he?" Brina asked.

"No. He wouldn't have made the wager if he had. He would have simply come over and asked for your hand like any gentleman would have. He's a different kind of man. Strong, self-confident men want to pursue the lady they are after. What would be the pleasure for either of you if he asked you to marry him and you said yes or no immediately? There wouldn't be any value in that. Declining gave him exactly what he wanted. A reason for you to run and for him to pursue you."

"You may be right," Brina said, thinking back on the earl's shenanigans in a whole new light. "He said something similar."

Julia pursed her lips in thought again. "Your first inclination was the right one, Brina. You should find a way to turn the tables on him and agree to marry him but with conditions he can't possibly accept."

"What?" Adeline exclaimed, looking at Julia as if she'd lost her mind.

"No," Brina persisted. "I don't want to marry him."

"I know. I'm not suggesting that. Only that you get even with the rake. He's made a very public wager involving you, but you have no say in it. Only the men at

White's can put up a bet. You should stand up to him and make your own wager."

"I can't believe it, but think I'm agreeing to this too," Adeline added, placing her cup on the tray beside Julia's. "He needs to be taught a lesson he won't soon forget."

The idea of doing something to upset the earl's life as he had upended hers was intriguing. It would serve him right if she could get the upper hand in the situation he'd created and beat him at his own game by forcing him to accept a wager from her. One he couldn't possibly win.

"I don't know," Brina answered soberly, shaking her head. "The possibility sounds good, but I'm not sure I can do it."

"Sure you can," Julia encouraged. "As an example, everyone has heard Blacknight's instincts are superb when it comes to gambling, and he's certainly fought more than one duel over a card game. I've heard few can match his gaming skills. Maybe you could say if he can manage not to gamble during the rest of the Season, you will marry him. Of course, he can't quit. He's a master at it. Men seek him out to play against him. So, he will lose the bet and your hand in marriage."

"So—what would you win if he lost?" Adeline asked Brina. "A bet has to work both ways. He loses you, but what do you win?"

"I don't know," Brina said. "What?"

Julia shook her head. "That is up to you. What do you want, Brina? What is something the earl could give that would make you happy if he lost? Only you can decide what that is."

Brina studied on Julia's words. Didn't she have what she wanted? A home of her own and a life that was filled with people who needed her to help them. A way to atone for what she'd done. What she didn't need was a man.

"If you are going to consider what Julia is suggesting," Adeline said. "One thing you must remember is this is a very serious matter the earl has brought to your door. If you offer him a wager, and he accepts, you have to ponder the consequences of what will happen if you lose."

*Marriage.*

That possibility was too hurtful to even think about. Brina threw her napkin on top of the tea tray, rattling the empty cups. She rose and walked over to the window and looked out at the spring day. It had been perfect until the earl had arrived at her door. She had come through the dark times in her life and had definite plans. Now she was not only unsettled, she was angry with Blacknight for inserting himself into her life, making her think about the possibility of doing something to get even with him, and worse, making her feel the wonderful, sensuous sensation of desire once again.

Love and marriage were two things she never wanted in her life again under any circumstances.

She didn't want to ever have the possibility of going through the kind of heartbreaking loss, hot, bitter anger, and soul-destroying despair that had crippled her for years. The only thing she really wanted was something the earl couldn't give her.

Redemption for what she'd done had to come from someone much higher up than the Earl of Blacknight.

# Chapter 5

Zane walked through the wide double doors and into the spacious entryway of the Grand Hall, where the premier parties and dances of the Season were always held. Its marbled floors led to the famous ballroom as well as secret little alcoves and candlelit corridors that were perfect for romantic rendezvous between young ladies and courtly beaus or star-crossed lovers.

After shedding his black velvet evening cloak, he came face-to-face with his older sister, Patricia. She'd undoubtedly been waiting for him to arrive.

Smiling in her usual impatient way, she curtsied and said, "My lord, I'm glad to see you actually came tonight. I wondered if you would."

"Good evening, Pat. You're looking lovely this evening in your sky-blue gown." And she was. She was eight years older than Zane but not one year of it showed in her face or appearance. Patricia had inherited the regal good looks of most of the Browning family. Tall, slender, and with hair and eyes dark enough to give a mysterious appeal but light enough to remain approachable. "I told everyone at the family dinner I'd be here."

She reached up to accept the kiss he gave to her cheek. "Yes, I know, but I wasn't sure I could believe you. No one else was either. Must I count the times the family expected you to join us for an event and you never arrived?"

"Probably not," he answered.

"It's downright unchivalrous of you to actually attend and prove us all wrong for the first time in years."

"But necessary, I think you'll agree." He handed his cloak and hat off to the attendant, but unfortunately not his gloves. For such a formal evening as this, they must be worn. Otherwise he might accidently touch a young lady's bare arm. Zane considered it more useless Society rules.

"After what you did to the gracious Mrs. Feld this week, I certainly do. The wager you placed was shocking to everyone in the ton. If you thought it would make anyone think you had settled down and were ready to seriously take on your responsibilities, you are mistaken."

"You can't say I didn't try," Zane offered with a wry smile.

Patricia rolled her eyes as if rejecting that claim, but said, "It was quite clever of you. Of course, it didn't fool any of us for a moment. We know you have a better chance of winning a foot race with a horse than taking Mrs. Feld's hand to the altar in marriage."

Zane chuckled as music and chatter from the large ballroom drifted toward him when they started walking.

"I'm flattered by the abundance of confidence you have in me."

"I'm only being realistic," Patricia offered without conceit, reaching up to push a pearl-tipped comb farther into her dark tresses. "You should be too. Men have been trying to put a dent in Mrs. Feld's armor for years now. You're not likely to be the first, even with your generous good looks, title, and ingenious exploit to gain her attention." She gave him a quick appreciative smile. "I'm not surprised you have the courage to try. You always have been a devil when it comes to behaving badly."

"You know I can't resist a challenge," he said.

"Nor a wager, it seems. No reason you should, but climbing a steep hill is a challenge. What you are trying to accomplish is folly."

"Folly can be quite enjoyable," he reminded her.

"For a time, anyway," Patricia answered in a somber tone and nodded to a couple who walked past them before giving her attention back to Zane. "If only Cranston were up to a little folly, I should welcome it."

"You mentioned last night he was ill. How is he today?"

"Miserable. The cough lingers and he's a dear about it. Kind enough not to want it to bother anyone."

"I'll drop by and say hello to him."

"That should cheer him. He's rather pleased I'm now the sister of an earl."

Zane smiled indulgently.

"I don't know if you've heard, but some of the matrons in Society are upset with you for placing the wager, though none of them would dare say a word to you about it. Now that you're an earl, they'll all want to remain in good standing with you, no matter what they say behind your back."

"I'll consider that useful information I don't need," he answered dryly. He hadn't expected anyone to approve of what he'd done. And he wasn't sorry for it. He had no doubt Mrs. Feld would make it a lively chase.

"I don't know Mrs. Feld well enough to say much

about her, but apparently there are those who do consider her saintly because of the work she does for the Sisters of Pilwillow Crossings."

"The abbey?"

"Yes. Not many have the courage to go and offer assistance for the charitable work they do. Including me."

An unusual twinge of guilt tightened his chest. "Does she support it as she does the girl's school?"

"One would assume. Quite frankly, not many really want to know. They'd rather pretend she doesn't go there at all. As I said, I don't know her well, but I'm never above prying if—"

"No," Zane cut in and said firmly. He would find out anything he wanted to know about Mrs. Feld without his sister's help.

Patricia moved her shoulders a little and smiled knowingly. "As you wish, my lord. I had some flowers delivered to her, by the way. I thought I should do something nice to let her know not everyone in the family has your propensities to be uncivil."

"Thank you." What else could he say? He was glad Patricia had.

Zane wasn't surprised the older ladies of the ton found his wager abominable. Men, on the other hand, were entirely different creatures. They might say he'd done an abhorrent thing but most, if not all, the members of White's he'd talked to had already put down their money. The great majority collected was against him winning her hand. That was unexpected. But he hadn't heard of anyone, including his uncles, thinking it beyond the pale to have put up the bet, except of course, Mrs. Feld.

Remembrance of her teased his senses and aroused an eagerness to see her.

"I meant no harm of any kind to Mrs. Feld," Zane offered. "Unusual wagers at White's is commonplace. I hope no one is thinking she was a willing participant in what was my doing."

"Gracious no." Patricia gave a polite nod of greeting to someone behind Zane. "The ladies are all jealous as thieving mice because you didn't go after them or one of their daughters. Who can blame them? At least with one of them, you would have had a chance to win their hand. I'm sure some of them will try to lure you in anyway. Now tell me, have you given any thought to the request I made of you Tuesday evening?"

So, they were finally getting around to the reason she was waiting in the atrium for him to arrive. He thought back to the dinner his uncles had arranged. What was it his sister had wanted?

"If you'll remember," he said, stalling for enough time to recall her particular wish, "there were two dozen family members there and many appeals were made to me by everyone."

"Yes, but I'm your sister. Surely that gives me some measure of special consideration in the long list of favors you were asked to grant."

"I don't mind financing your travel, Pat," he offered as what she'd asked for finally popped into mind. "Go, if you want, but why the devil do you want to go to the Americas?"

"The experience, of course. Besides, a visit there is all the rage right now. I don't want to be the last person in the ton to see what it's like. I've heard summers in Boston are quite nice and some have even bought homes—the Chesters, the Graveses, and the Mickletons. I'd like to assess the place for myself. So, thank you. But, of course, once I see their fashions, I might need to have some dresses and gowns made while there. You understand, don't you?"

She was thinking about clothing, of which she had

plenty, while he was still trying to go through the immense number of account books concerning the holdings for the entailed property in order to understand exactly what he was supposed to be in control of. Zane was finding out quickly that he was used to a much more leisurely day than that of an earl with many properties and businesses. His uncles arrived early and stayed late. The solicitor and two accountants spent most of the day with him as well.

And that was only the half of it. In addition to his family's requests, he'd been bombarded with various gentlemen who wanted to know where he stood on the politics of London, England, and the rest of the world including America. He'd never had a reason to take sides in Parliament. Apparently, that would now be required of him, but not immediately. He assured them he was a fair man and would treat everyone equally and with respect, no matter if he was a farmer, silversmith, blacksmith, or earl.

Zane lost count of the men who wanted him to consider their daughters, dowries, and wedding offers that would profit him much more than the gentle Mrs. Feld's properties.

He wasn't interested in any of them. He'd much rather be left alone to pursue her at a leisurely pace and as he so desired. His uncles would have none of that. They would have rather he married her yesterday.

"As promised, Pat, I will look into everyone's allowances and see what I can do to increase them all, but right now, there are more important matters concerning the estates I must take care of."

"I understand." She held up a hand, seeming content that she'd received from him most of what she wanted. "A consideration is all I ask."

They stopped in front of the two sets of double doors

that had been swung wide to allow entrance into the ballroom. It had been a couple of years, or maybe more, since Zane had attended such a grand affair of the Season given by the elite members of the ton. Young ladies who had come of age in the past year were officially available for all eligible men to consider for marriage. And, it was the beginning of the husband hunt for the young ladies as well. For Society, the entire Season was more about that intricate dance of manners and settlements than the thrill of romance.

The Grand Hall was teeming with ladies dressed in colorful silk gowns, beautifully adorned with beads, bows, and lace. Their elaborate headpieces rivaled the latest fashions in Paris. Gentlemen wore their usual starched white shirts, neckcloths, waistcoats, and black evening coats with long tails.

The ballroom wasn't without its share of glamour either. It was decorated to the hilt with vases and urns overflowing with colorful flowers. Lengths of shimmering silk streamed from the towering ceilings and cascading ribbons of satin fluttered around the fluted columns, chandeliers, and every gleaming sconce on the walls. Zane had never seen so many brightly burning candles. Servants roamed about holding trays filled with glasses of champagne for everyone to indulge in. On the far end of the ballroom, a well-tuned orchestra played one melodious score after another and would continue into the wee hours of the morning.

Zane had forgotten how lavish the parties were. And the hell of it was that his family thought *he* lived a self-indulgent life.

He quickly scanned the ballroom for Mrs. Feld, but he didn't see her among the gathering. His stomach tightened at the thought she might not be in attendance. The gossip about his wager was all over Town. Maybe she wasn't as strong as he'd thought. He scanned the room again with more care the second time. A leap in his breath caught solid in his chest. His pulse ticked up at the sight of her silvery-blond hair. She was standing with another lady next to a line of chairs that had been set up along the side wall near the dance floor for the widows, wallflowers, and spinsters.

Stifling feelings of wanting to rush over to her, he relaxed and smiled. He didn't know how badly he'd wanted to see her until he was afraid he wouldn't.

Time for the evening to begin.

Turning back to Patricia, he said, "I heard the call for dancers to line up." Taking hold of his sister's hand, he placed it in the crook of his arm. "Do you think Cranston will mind if I have my first dance of the evening with you?"

"Not at all," she said sweetly, seemingly surprised and delighted that he'd asked her. "He would love it and so would I. And don't forget your cousin Thelma is here tonight. Be sure to ask her for a dance too. She came out last year but didn't make a match, the poor dear. Perhaps you can help her find a suitable husband."

He cleared his throat. "I'll be happy to dance with her, but I'll leave the matchmaking to other members of the family."

"Nonsense. It's your place to do it now. The family expects it."

Zane grimaced. The list of all the family required of him grew longer each day.

More than an hour later, Zane moved away from the crowd and leaned a shoulder against one of the columns in the ballroom. The only thing on his mind was having a dance with Mrs. Feld. As London's newest peer, he hadn't been idle since entering the ballroom. He'd indulged his uncles Syl and Hector by dancing with two of the young ladies making their debuts and had conversations with half a dozen others. They were all beautiful, intelligent, and inviting in different ways, but none of them controlled his interest in the way he desired a chat and dance with Mrs. Feld. It was impossible to consider anyone but her. She was the one he'd been waiting for. Seemingly patient, but not really, he felt twisted in a knot that only she could untie. And he was ready for that release. He wanted to know if she'd found it in her heart to forgive him, if only a little, for placing the wager.

He might have been busy with others in the room as the evening progressed, but so was she. He hadn't failed to notice where she was at all times. And who she was with. She'd glanced his way a few times too. When two people were interested in each other, there was no easy way to hide it. Though she continued to try.

Her attire was modest compared to most of the ladies', but her elegance was unsurpassed. Her gown was such a deep shade of blue, he'd first thought she wore black. When he detected the variance, he realized the subdued color enhanced the beauty of her hair and ivory complexion. There was a swath of cream-colored lace at the cuffs of her long sleeves but no garnish in her hair or hanging from her ears. A short, single strand of pearls adorned the neckline of her gown.

When she wasn't talking to someone or dancing, as had happened three times since he'd been there, she seated herself alongside the wall with other ladies who watched the dancers and chatted happily among themselves. He kept thinking she didn't belong there, among the women who, for whatever reason, had given up thought, hope, or desire of marrying.

It was up to him to let her know her destiny wasn't there. No time like the present to do that.

He straightened and set off in her direction. As he

drew closer, he felt as if every pair of eyes in the room were focused on him. It was as if they all had been waiting for him to seek her out, so they could witness her response. It was his idea to go public with this pursuit. The chatter around him lowered as he passed. He didn't mind. There was no reason for him to complain about the open display. It was of his own making.

Zane kept his gaze firmly on Mrs. Feld as he headed to the far wall where she was sitting. He didn't allow anyone's movements or talking to distract him until he stood in front of her.

When she looked up at him, his stomach tightened, and his senses stirred restlessly. Damnation, he had no doubts he'd made the right choice in choosing her. His gaze did a slow, detailed sweep of her beautiful face before centering on her bright blue eyes. For a moment, he thought he saw surprise in their depths. Surely, she knew he would approach her before the evening was over.

He bowed. "Mrs. Feld. It's good to see you again."

She glanced about cautiously, rose, and curtsied. "My lord."

He reached for her gloved hand and the second his fingers closed around hers, he felt a deep, rousing hunger shudder through him. He knew then she heated his blood like no other woman ever had. In the candlelight her eyes were captivating. He gave her the accepted, formal kiss on the back of her palm and then moved between her and the row of ladies behind her to give them a degree of privacy.

"Would you join me for this next dance?" he asked.

She inhaled deeply before saying, "And further more gossip about us? No, my lord, I believe you've done quite enough without any help from me, and I don't think it would be in my best interest to accept."

Her response wasn't completely unexpected, so he

took no offense. He relented with a smile. "All right. I suppose I deserved that rebuff after the wager."

"Yes, and much more. After what I've been through the past three days, were I capable of calling you out, I probably would have."

Her saucy response made him chuckle softly. He gave her a nod of appreciation. "I believe you, and I'm a lucky man you can't. You would be a formidable opponent. I have a feeling you'll find a way of getting even with me."

"I've considered it and wish I could," she said adamantly. "However, it's your good fortune I wouldn't dare stoop so low."

She was still angry with him, and with just cause. Yet even in her ire, there was a softness and gentleness about her that drew him.

"I'm glad to see my ill behavior hasn't kept you from enjoying yourself this evening."

"No, it hasn't," she said, confidently lifting her chin. "You seem surprised that is the case."

"I'm delighted. You're a strong lady. I had no doubt you would carry on as normal."

"Normal?" she asked with a breath of extreme exasperation. Her gaze focused tightly on his as she took a step toward him, seeming not to care that everyone was watching. "Really, my lord? You don't know the half of it, so don't tell me you are delighted about anything concerning me."

He noticed her hands made fists at her sides. "That wasn't my intention."

"What was? You have completely disrupted my orderly life in the most tumultuous way possible. Because of you I've had a steady stream of ladies calling on me to make sure I haven't taken to a sick bed over this wager you made. Some have sent baskets of flowers and others boxes of sweet confections to cheer me. I've received packages of handkerchiefs, which I can only assume they felt I needed from all the crying I must be doing over your arrogant machinations. An anonymous person sent me an essay on Ophelia—of all things. Even the vicar paid me a visit to ask about my welfare. That you have the nerve to think I'm carrying on as normal is outrageous."

She was magnificent!

Her words and tone were heartfelt. He could almost taste her anger. By the time she'd finished, a flush had heightened her face with indignation. It made her stunning. If they had been alone, he would have caught her up to his chest and kissed her, giving an outlet for all the passion pent up inside her. And there was plenty of it. But since they were far from alone, he offered the truth instead.

"I didn't stop to think of the many different ways this might affect your life."

"Indeed!" She almost gasped after saying the word.

"I'm sorry for that, but not for making the wager."

Disbelief danced in her bright eyes and made her all the more tempting. "I can't believe you can say that so seriously. What kind of gentleman would do what you did?"

"A gentleman wouldn't," he answered with ease.

"Exactly! Because of you, we're the talk of Society. Everyone has been looking at us and whispering about us all night, as they are doing right now. You are right. Manners and respect are taught, not born. You do need someone to teach you how to be a proper gentleman, but it won't be me. Now, excuse me, my lord, but we are finished."

She turned away from him and sat back down in the row of ladies, all of whom were giving him the evil eye.

Tension flashed through him at her abrupt dismissal.

His eyes narrowed, but then he looked at the beautiful curve of her lips set in a firm line, the satiny appearance of her skin and pillow-soft swell of her breasts beneath her widow's gown. Despite the prim exterior, he knew she was a deeply passionate woman and he wanted her.

No. He wouldn't give up. Not for anything in the world. He hadn't realized it until he saw her again, but she'd left him with a need that no other woman ever had.

She may not be aware of it, but she was a temptress, a curious mix of defiance and vulnerability. He understood that, accepted it, and could deal with it.

On the other hand, Zane had played enough cards to know there were times when you needed to cut your losses and save what you had for another game. Reluctantly, he would have to do that now—difficult as it was.

Mrs. Feld was more than mildly upset with him about the wager and that made her as enticing as seeing a piece of spice cake on Christmas morning. Her vigor and fervor were seductive. He was going to relish every moment he spent with her. He wanted her to see him as the man she wanted to make her life complete.

As angry as she was with him, that wasn't going to be easy to do.

# Chapter 6

Zane had lost the first battle, but the night wasn't over. He nodded once to Mrs. Feld, turned, and started walking away. The crowd that had somehow inched around them parted as he strode away. A few of them were close enough to have heard some of what she had to say. They could guess the rest.

"That didn't go well," Uncle Hector said, coming up beside him almost immediately.

"I don't need you walking with me, Uncle. I'm quite capable of handling the rejection of a lady refusing to dance with me."

"Oh, I know that. I only wanted to remind you, I tried to tell you she wasn't one you should court. There are more than a dozen ladies who would accept a proposal from you tonight. Best you put her and thoughts of winning your wager aside and get on to a young lady who's looking for a husband. I have two more in mind."

"It seems you don't know me well, Uncle," Zane offered, with no irritation at the man's lack of understanding. Mrs. Feld was the one he wanted. "I always play to win and the game's just started."

"You are usually playing against a man," Hector offered, struggling to keep up with Zane's longer stride.

"Are you suggesting ladies don't play fair, Uncle?"

"Certainly not. Though some do make that claim. I'm suggesting if it's a widow you want to marry, look more closely at Mrs. Pinewiffle. She's not as lovely as Mrs. Feld, but she's younger and I think she'll be more accommodating to your marriage proposal. She appears healthy enough to give you as many sons as you want."

"I'll keep that suggestion in mind," Zane said as Sylvester appeared at his other side.

"If you were trying to keep the gossip going about you and Mrs. Feld, congratulations," he said. "That was an excellent way to do it. Most of us couldn't hear all of what was said, but we could see well enough to know she was giving you a dressing down you won't soon forget."

And a fiery, delicious one it was, Zane thought and then chuckled. He didn't want to forget it. He wanted to relish it. All her outrage did was heat his blood more for her.

"Uncles," Zane said and stopped walking to look at them. "You're both acting as if this is the first time a lady has declined to dance with me."

"It probably is," Sylvester offered without a hint of a smile. "Perhaps if you sent her flowers instead of wagers, she'd be more affable."

A server walked by and Zane stopped him. Grabbing two glasses of champagne for his uncles and then one for himself, he said, "No more lectures or suggestions. This is a ball. Let's enjoy ourselves."

And Zane did. For at least another hour he danced, talked, and laughed among the other guests. As did

Mrs. Feld. But he soon found himself drinking yet another glass of champagne and contemplating a second request for a dance with her.

"Lord Blacknight."

Zane didn't recognize the voice, but he did the man when he turned to see the well-respected Earl of Lyonwood behind him. Lyon was the husband of one of Mrs. Feld's best friends. Zane didn't know the tall, broadshouldered man standing beside Lyon, but it was a safe bet he was the husband of Mrs. Feld's other good friend.

He didn't think Mrs. Feld had said a word about him to the men standing before him. However, she'd probably talked to their wives at length after he'd seen them at her house a few days ago. And *they* had probably talked to *their* husbands. He appreciated the men's show of force in approaching him and didn't mind. As long as all they were doing was letting him know they were around in case Mrs. Feld needed them.

A breath of a smile lifted the corner of Zane's mouth. They must have noticed him watching Mrs. Feld and assumed, rightly so, he was contemplating asking her to dance *one more time* before the evening ended.

"Lord Lyonwood," Zane said, dipping his chin in proper greeting. "It's been a while since I've seen you."

"Welcome back to London, even though the circumstances for your return weren't what you would have wanted."

"That's true," Zane said honestly, and looked at the man standing beside Lyon.

"May I present Mr. Garrett Stockton?" Lyon asked.

*May I present* was a fraction of the manners and protocol of Society life Zane would prefer to ignore. He'd much rather have someone say the more informal *have you met* and not be so damned proper. But Lord Lyonwood had always known how to be a gentleman.

Though he'd never met Stockton, Zane had heard about him and had a great deal of respect for the man, who had been known as an adventurer. He shook off the trappings of gentlemanly life for a time and traveled the seas to distant lands. Zane admired that kind of courage and free-thinking. He wouldn't mind talking to him about his adventures over a glass of brandy.

"Yes, Mr. Stockton," Zane offered with a nod. "I don't think our paths have ever crossed, but I've heard of you and the success of your company. I trust all is well."

"I've had good winds and fair seas as the old sea dogs like to say."

"No doubt. I've never sailed the distances you have, Mr. Stockton, but I might want to do that one day. I've heard you've been to the East."

"Singapore. It's a long voyage and not for anyone who wasn't sure he could spend a lot of time on the close quarters of a ship."

"Understood. I have no doubt it's a fascinating country and worth the length of the journey for those who can endure it."

"I'd be happy to talk more with you about it anytime, and it's Garrett, if you would prefer."

Zane nodded, appreciating Garrett's friendly manner. The more protocols he could dispense with, the better. Courtesy to your fellow man didn't have to be as rigid as Society made it.

"Do you expect to be in London for all of the Season?" Lyon asked.

"That's my plan," Zane answered.

"Good. As you have probably heard, I have a card club that meets at my house once a week. We're short a player this year. I wanted to invite you to join us if you have an interest."

Zane held his surprise in check. All esteemed game-sters and common gamblers alike had heard about Lord Lyonwood's distinguished card club. Most of them would pay heavily for a chance to play with any of the members. Lyon's father, the Marquis of Marksworth, was one of them and greatly respected not only in Society but all of London too. Being invited to join the earl's group would certainly make his uncles happy. They'd much rather see him playing cards in a home with titled gen-tlemen than the rowdy gaming hells near Bond Street. Zane was comfortable playing anywhere. So, hell yes, he welcomed this invitation. This news, and the fact he was pursuing Mrs. Feld, should go a long way in settling down the family a bit more.

"We usually start at half past two on Thursdays," Lyon continued calmly, showing no sign of being affronted when Zane didn't immediately answer. "We keep it friendly but lively enough to appreciate the afternoon."

"I've heard a few stories," Zane answered, wondering if Lyon had issued the invitation for the sole purpose of keeping an eye on him since he was pursuing Mrs. Feld. Zane was all right with that too. He would have done the same if their roles were reversed.

Lyon quirked his head and studied Zane. "So have I. Not all of them are true."

Zane smiled. "I didn't think they were."

"Can I count on you to join us?"

"I can manage that. Good of you to ask."

From the corner of his eye, Zane saw Mrs. Feld walk-ing toward the entrance. He didn't know if she was leav-ing, but didn't want to take the chance. He wanted to talk to her again. "Gentlemen, if you'll both excuse me. I was about to ask someone to dance."

His pursuit of the widow might have been started only to help settle his family's jitters about the kind of earl he'd be. That changed fast after meeting with her earlier in the week. There was real desire for her in his quest. He hadn't expected to get caught up with her so quickly, but she had filled his thoughts with an eager excitement he couldn't remember ever feeling before. Obtaining the attention of a lady he was interested in had never been a problem. Mrs. Feld had already proven she would not dutifully fall in line as so many others had.

The ton loved drama and gossip more than anything, and Zane was about to give it to them in spades. He'd never been known for his self-restraint, and there was no reason to curb what came naturally to him tonight.

After having set his glass on a table, he caught up beside Mrs. Feld. She didn't slow her step or look over at him, but there was no doubt she stiffened when she realized he was walking with her.

"I heard the call for a dance," he said casually.

"Did you?" she said coolly.

"Would you join me for this one?"

Brina stopped and faced him. Her big, beautiful eyes narrowed, and a tiny wrinkle formed in her forehead. "I can't believe you're asking again."

Obviously, time and the champagne he'd seen her sip hadn't smoothed her ruffled feathers. He didn't think she'd expected him to ask a second time. Most men wouldn't if turned down once in an evening, but that was another one of those accepted rules Zane had never followed.

Everything about Mrs. Feld intrigued him. When he looked at her, there was an aura about her that had nothing to do with her beauty, sophistication, or her past experiences. But it was there, and it drew him. She didn't cower from his nearness but casually looked around the room, as if hoping no one was watching her converse with him. But of course, everyone had directed their attention to the two of them, even if most pretended not to.

He remained relaxed as he took a slow, small step closer to her. "Did you really expect I wouldn't?"

"Yes." Her eyes narrowed more. "You should never ask a lady to dance twice in the same evening. Especially if she turns you down the first time."

"I'm not like most men, Mrs. Feld."

"So I have found out. The hard way."

He gave her a twitch of a smile, not minding that her temper hadn't cooled. He was finding she stirred him like no other, no matter her temperament. "Why would any man give up trying to get something he wanted after only one attempt?"

She seemed to ponder on that before saying, "I'm not saying in all things, but it's the proper thing to do in this instance."

"And because that is the way of it," she continued. "You aren't supposed to break the rules and certainly not in front of the elite of Society. Probably most everyone in the ballroom is staring at us right now. I think that must be what you really wanted."

He gave her a half smile. "Didn't it cross your mind they were looking our way because you are beautiful?"

"What?" She blinked in horror for a second. Her cheeks flushed to a tempting shade of pink and her expression softened. "No, no, of course not. I would never think anything of the kind."

"It's true," he said softly, letting his gaze sweep slowly down her face and back to her eyes. He knew he was vexing her, but he wasn't trying to. Only stating the truth. "Everyone looks at you whether or not you are standing near the entrance with me or seated with the ladies. You're beautiful, kind, and quite simply, Mrs. Feld, you fascinate them."

"Stop it." She lowered her lashes for only a second and then looked around the room again. "You don't know what you're talking about. I won't hear any more of it. Every lady here tonight is beautiful."

"I stand corrected. What I should have said is that you fascinate me. And you are the only lady in the room who does."

"Oh, you are an impossible man to talk to," she said, looking back at him again.

"I'm determined."

She clasped her hands together in front of her. "Yes. I suppose you could call it that as well."

"I'm still trying to settle in my mind that you aren't the young maiden I thought you were that night in Paris, but a strong-minded capable lady who has created a good and noble life for herself and others." He lowered his voice to a husky whisper, and said, "I want to dance with you."

"Why are you being so insistent?"

"Why are you refusing?" He kept his tone soft. "I'm not asking for your hand in marriage tonight, Mrs. Feld. Just for a dance. Everyone who is looking at us right now is thinking: *Will she say yes to him this time or turn him away again?*"

Her expression turned tense. "Tell me, my lord, would you be happy and want to dance with me if I had done to you what you did to me?"

*Hell no.*

"I would be flattered if a lady wanted to, no matter the reason."

"Oh, don't try to sell that poppycock to me," she said sternly but quietly as one hand jerked to settle on her waist in frustration. "I don't believe a word of it. Don't pretend not to know every eligible lady in this room would marry you in a heartbeat. You are every lady's dream. You are beyond handsome, a wild rake, and you are now an earl. What more could a lady want?"

He kept his gaze tightly on hers and gave his head a light shake as he smiled. "You tell me. I'm only interested in you. All I'm asking for is a dance."

"If our situations were reversed, and I had come back from Paris and pledged a wager I was going to marry you by the end of the Season, how would you have handled it?"

He took in a long deep breath. "Carefully."

"Which is exactly what I'm doing."

He gave her another twitch of a smile. "But I would have never refused a dance with you, Mrs. Feld."

"All right," she said confidently as if she'd suddenly found courage she didn't know she had. "Let's get this over with. One is about to start. We'll have to hurry."

She marched off toward the dance floor. Zane stayed right beside her. They quickly positioned themselves in line with the others already in position for the cotillion. Ladies in a straight line faced their gentlemen partners. As the first chords were struck, they bowed to each other and the intricate dance began. It involved precise steps, perfectly timed moves, gentle touching of their gloved hands, and an occasional light gripping of their fingers as she walked underneath his upheld arm.

Zane performed the intricate maneuvers with impeccable decorum considering he wanted to grasp her small waist, pull her close to his chest, pick her up, and swing her around in his arms until they were both dizzy with delight. But that was for women in a bawdy house. Polite people didn't dance that way.

He'd always appreciated a waltz and a lively quadrille, but he'd never cared for the older, more formal dances of Society.

Until now. He was absolutely mesmerized by her.

As the dance progressed, he had to admit it was erotic in a way it had never been for him. There was a focused commitment and deliberation in each step that he'd never noticed. Her fluttering skirts brushed his legs seductively. The technique in how their hands touched ever so lightly, how she faced him so boldly before quickly turning away gave a feeling of intimacy with her. They moved in time with each other and with remarkable compatibility.

With Mrs. Feld, the dance was a slow, sensual repeating method of pursue, catch, and release. How had he never noticed that before?

"Have you thought anymore about my proposal?" he asked as she passed under his arm for a slow twirl.

"Yes," she answered. "I've been steaming about it since you were at my house."

That was the spirit that drew him.

"I'm glad to hear it," he answered, their open palms touching lightly again. He was tempted to let his thumb brush against her wrist when they stepped back and bowed again but refrained. He didn't want to send her rushing from the dance floor.

They walked around in a tight circle, and when they faced each other, her eyes pierced him with a determination he hadn't seen from her before, and suddenly, she said, "You have vexed me, my lord, to the point I think I *will* allow you to court me."

A wave of anticipation swept through him like fire through dry brush. Zane nearly missed a step. Was she teasing him with her words as well as with the dance?

He remained silent and waited, sensing she would say more.

"And while doing so, I will do my best to make a proper gentleman out of you, not only for your family but the benefit for all ladies who come in contact with you."

Her gaze stayed riveted on his as she passed in front of him. "And if I succeed, I will accept your proposal by midnight at the last ball of the Season and marry you."

Their palms met again as they stepped forward. The pressure from her touch was strong, sure. She was confident in what she was saying. His stomach tightened and his fingers closed over hers as she walked in a circle under his arm. The scent of wildflowers tempted his senses along with visions of kissing her lips, cheeks, and long, slender neck.

Taking in a deep breath, he asked, "Am I to believe you?"

Her fingers slipped out of his grip. They stepped away from each other and bowed before coming together again. "I don't make promises I can't keep, my lord. The question is, do you?"

With his gaze locked on hers, he vowed, "I keep my word, Mrs. Feld."

"If that is true, I will marry you. But first, you must prove you're capable of becoming a proper gentleman."

"That should be easy enough," he murmured as they walked in a tight circle. He'd been properly trained in how to be a gentleman.

"Will it?" she asked.

That's when Zane knew all wasn't as it seemed.

"During the remaining weeks of the Season, you must give up wine, brandy, ale, and all spirits of any kind."

Zane gave a little snort as he clasped both her hands possessively and they twirled under each other's arms. "Most gentlemen have a drink or two each day," he said as her fingers slipped from his grasp again, but not before he let his thumb trace up and down her wrist a couple of times. "If you'd rather I not, I'll give it up for you."

Surely, he could manage not to take a drink for a few weeks. He'd never had a reason not to but was certain he could. Since that was all she was asking, it seemed a small price to pay for what he would get in the end.

"You must also give up cards, dice, and all forms of gambling and wagering of any kind and for any reason."

Zane's body stiffened. They continued to move through the painstaking steps of the complicated dance. Her courage was unbelievable. To even ask such a thing of an earl or any man was daring. Not only that—he'd just been invited to join the most sought-after card club in all of London. This demand wasn't something he could take lightly.

He was finding out he couldn't take her lightly either. The trouble was that he was falling for all of it.

"Again, Mrs. Feld," he said from stiff lips, unable to suppress his disagreement in his tone. "Most gentlemen play cards, whether or not they gamble. It's a way of life that's not usually questioned."

"But you do both to excess," she informed him, lifting her chin, making it clear she wouldn't give an inch on this point. "The wager you placed at White's is proof of that. But if you aren't willing to try, I'll withdraw my offer."

She was as cool as an early autumn morning. What she asked wouldn't be easy. Yet. Everything about her was compelling. He considered once again what he would be giving up and what he would be getting in return.

"All right," he finally said and could see from the tension around her eyes that she hadn't expected him to agree to the second term of her agreement. Good. It was about time he got the upper hand in this matter, or at least caught up with her.

"You don't think I can do it," he offered.

"Maybe for a night but not until midnight of the last ball."

What a lovely spitfire she was turning out to be. He'd

heard she was a nurturer. She enjoyed helping people. Taking care of them. Apparently, that didn't include him.

"And there will be no swearing or cursing."

"What?" he snapped. "Blast it, Mrs. Feld," he whispered, missing a step. The man next to him bumped his arm and gave him a foul look. Zane paid him no mind. His eyes were set only on his partner. "You go too far."

"No, you did that."

"Swearing is in a man's nature and there's no getting around it."

Her expression became more determined than ever, and she leaned in toward him. "A well-educated gentleman such as yourself can find words to say other than swears, curses, and cusses whether he's with men, ladies, or horses."

Obviously, she could be fierce when she wanted to be. Zane bit back an oath and several vile bloody cuss words he wanted to say and simply ground out, "Fine. Consider it done. Are you finished now?"

"No," she said as he lifted his arm for her to walk under.

"What more could there be? I refuse to be in church every Sunday morning. I go on Christmas Day like most respectable people and that's enough."

"No women."

*No women?*

Zane felt a twitch between his shoulder blades that ran up the back of his neck and throbbed in his temples. His fingers tightened on hers again. Where did she get the nerve to demand such compliance from him? The truth was he hadn't wanted to be with another woman since he'd seen her again, but he didn't want her telling him he couldn't be with someone if he wanted to.

She blinked rapidly and her shapely lips were set in a firm line. He was certain she'd said *no women* impulsively. It wasn't something a genteel lady of the ton would say to a man. But he also knew now she had uttered it, she'd never take it back.

"That's going—"

Mrs. Feld froze and dropped her hands to her side and fixed her gaze on his. From the corner of his eye, Zane watched as the other dancers slowly realized what was going on and the line stopped in sequence. The music slowly died away and so did the chatter of the crowd.

Intensity radiated from her stance, her expression, and her countenance. She couldn't have been more serious. And he knew why. She didn't think he could do any of it.

"No women, no cards, no wagering, and no swearing," she said unwaveringly.

"Are you trying to make me a saint?" he said a little louder than he intended.

"No. Only a gentleman. But I will end proving you can't change your rakish ways, and furthermore, that you don't want to." She scoffed. "But if you can—" Suddenly her countenance changed. She relaxed her inflexible stance and smiled confidently. "I'm yours."

The ballroom was as quiet as a sealed tomb. Realization of what was happening hit him. The kind, beautiful, and perfect widow he thought would make him respectable was really going to try to make him respectable.

He bent closer toward her ear and whispered so only she could hear, "I hope *no women* doesn't include kissing. I have to kiss a lady's hand, my sister's and cousins' cheeks."

She held her ground unflinchingly as she seemed to consider what he said. "Understood," she acknowledged in a tone as low as his. "Kissing accepted."

Over Mrs. Feld's shoulder, Zane watched Lyon and Garrett push through the gathered crowd and move into his view. Their wives nudged their way beside them. They were taking a stand and making sure he knew in no uncertain terms they were there to protect her if she needed them. Movement on the other side of the room caught his eye. Patricia and his uncles stepped forward too and looked on with keen interest. But were they on his side or Mrs. Feld's?

The gauntlet had been thrown down, but Zane wasn't sure if he'd thrown it or Mrs. Feld had. One thing was sure, this cat-and-mouse game that only the two of them were playing had been witnessed by many.

From the crowd, Zane heard whispers that did nothing to aid his thoughts on what happened between the two of them.

*"He can't do it,"* a man said.

*"No, he won't accept her terms,"* someone else added.

*"Can't say as I blame him."*

*"What respectable gentleman would be willing to give up his ale and cards in the afternoons and his brandy in the evenings?"*

*"Or women?"*

*"He'd be a fool to try,"* a different man answered.

*"I'd say she got the best of him."*

Not yet, she hadn't, Zane thought. His pursuit of Mrs. Feld had only just begun.

# Chapter 7

The only sound Brina heard was her own breathing.
She knew there had been times in life when
things got out of hand, but those times usually happened
to Julia. Her friend was noted for unintentional mishaps
and was more adept at handling unexpected surprises of
her own making. But really, Brina must put the blame
for this catastrophe exactly where it rightly belonged.
On the Earl of Blacknight's more than ample shoulders.

It was almost as if he'd goaded her into making demands by accepting the first one. Why had he done that?

She wouldn't have said a word to him if he hadn't
asked her for a dance the *second* time. Something no
proper gentleman would have ever done. And despite
her resolve to ignore him, he'd seemingly so innocently
pulled her into a discussion she didn't want to have, making it easy for her to trade words with him. Most disturbing of all was how their exchange made her feel

invigorated—alive. Their entire conversation had been astounding. They were quibbling over the possibility of marriage. A subject that should always be handled delicately and in private.

They had an entire ballroom looking on and trying to listen.

Obviously, nothing was sacred to Blacknight. He *did* need someone to teach him proper conduct. Suddenly, there was something immensely thrilling about being the one who was going to do that.

He was a powerfully built man. Handsome. Tempting. She wasn't immune to his physical presence. Much as she'd like to be. It was the intensity with which she felt the attraction that unsettled her. Sensations too rapturous to think about stirred within her when she looked at him. She was a widow. Seasoned and rational. She shouldn't be giving in to the feelings he stirred up inside her.

Seconds ticked by as they stood silently in front of each other as if they were daring the other to be the next to speak. The crowd remained quiet too and continued to watch them. She had no idea how much of their conversation some had heard.

But enough.

Where had she gotten the nerve, the fortitude to be so bold to an earl who was known for his gambling, drinking, and carousing with women? And in front of so many people? She wasn't the kind of person to need attention or affirmation.

If she'd ever wanted to back down from anything in her life, it was now. But, of course, she couldn't. She'd gone too far. Somehow the earl had drawn her into bargaining with him for something she didn't want.

Marriage.

It was insane.

But it was done. And the black-hearted rake that he was, he'd agreed to all her demands.

In truth, there was no one to blame or thank but herself for the position she was in.

With her wits finally returning, there was no time to ponder further the ins and outs of the ways this man aroused her. She needed to bring this spectacle in front of everyone to a close. Filled with resolve, she leaned in toward him and said, "We have one more thing to discuss before this is settled."

He followed her lead and inclined closer to her too. "You drive a hard bargain, Mrs. Feld."

With her courage returned, she replied, "You are asking me to give up my freedom. If there is even the slightest possibility that you might win, I want to make sure you're going to be worth it. Walk with me. I need a glass of champagne."

"I need one too," he muttered under his breath.

Brina cut her eyes around to his as her brows rose, and she set her lips in a firm line.

"But I won't be having one," he added under his breath. "I'll be happy to get a glass for you."

They started walking away from the dance floor and toward a refreshment table that had been set up on the far side of the ballroom.

There were more whispers and murmurings from the crowd. Brina tried not to pay attention, but it was difficult not to hear some of them.

*"What are they going to do now?"*

*"I think she handled him quite well."*

*"It's about time someone did. His family never could."*

*"A lovely lady like her shouldn't have to put up with such a scoundrel."*

*"I'll be at White's first thing in the morning, and I'm putting my money on Mrs. Feld."*

*"I believe I will too."*

Tension and frustration shook through her, but she kept walking.

"You were quite spectacular just now, Mrs. Feld," he said with guarded praise.

Yes, she was, but she'd be the talk of the gossip sheets tomorrow. More ladies would flood her with flowers, sweets, and kind words next week, but this man was making her feel like smiling with his high praise. Her impossible demands had been a shock to him. They were to her. There was no way he could adhere to one of them, let alone all of them. It was startling to think she had the courage to tell him *no women*.

Where had that idea even come from?

He was perturbed by it, but so far, obviously not deterred.

"What else do we need to settle?" Blacknight grumbled, as they moved farther away from the thick of the crowd. "I think I've already agreed to give up every sin known to man."

"You have some nerve being peeved with me," she countered. "After your actions."

"If I'm remembering correctly, Mrs. Feld, you were the one who did most of the talking tonight. All I wanted was a dance."

"I was referring to you involving me in your scandalous wager in the first place. Not the conditions I attached to it."

"Of which you said you had another. I can hardly wait to hear what the next one is."

Brina glanced over at him. She had really gotten to him with her unprecedented requirements. That pleased her. Much as she would like to deny it, he was immensely compelling when upset with her.

"The one I haven't stated is the most important."

"Maybe to you," he mumbled and picked up a filled glass from a server who passed by.

The orchestra returned playing, and the people continued talking in their hushed whispers as they dispersed. She had no doubt who they whispered about. But she couldn't worry about that right now. She had to finish what she'd started.

They stopped in a corner, and he handed her the champagne. "I don't know what else you could want from me."

"Humility would be nice," she answered.

"That might prove as difficult as giving up an afternoon game of cards is going to be."

"Which is why I'm certain in the end, I will win this wager. However, let's look at the facts. If you should somehow miraculously win, you would get me and the money from the gentlemen's wagers you placed at White's. I've been told it's considerable."

He nodded confidently. "After tonight, it could quite possibly reach to the stars."

She shrugged as if it hardly mattered but actually concurred. "I have the conditions set forth for you, but we need to talk about what I get if you lose."

"An earl for a husband," he answered quickly and without an ounce of boasting.

She scoffed. "What possible value could there be for me in something I don't want?"

His head tilted in question for a moment before a flicker of admiration sparked in his expression. "I agree. You should be entitled to something of your choosing if you win. What do you want from me?"

"Nothing," she whispered softly, knowing it to be true.

His eyebrows quirked upward as he considered her question. "No. It's only fair you receive something I can give you."

When he said that, she remembered the kiss he'd given her as a thank-you. Her heartbeat quickened. He'd held her so tightly, she felt treasured, kissed so briefly but so thoroughly, she couldn't erase it from her memory.

Heat flushed her cheeks.

To cover the sudden, unbidden sensations, she quickly said, "Since from the beginning you made this wager a public one, we will end it the same way. I want everyone to hear your apology when you lose."

"What else?"

Brina blinked. "Nothing else."

"You have almost half a dozen conditions for me to follow in the next four weeks. Surely you want more than an *I'm sorry* if you win. Money? Jewels? Land? There must be something."

"No. No, I don't," she said earnestly. "Money or land? What kind of person do you think I am?"

He leaned back to study her. His expression turned gentle, almost comforting, and he slowly nodded. "A good one. I know you wouldn't ask anything for yourself, but I thought you might ask something for your school or the sisters."

She appreciated he realized he'd misjudged her motives and had no trouble admitting it. The boarding school was well-funded. She could have asked him for money to aid the sisters' work at Pilwillow Crossings. They could always use more donations. But being benevolent to a charitable organization would be too easy for him. It would require nothing of him but giving money.

He needed to do something that would be difficult for him.

Only one thing would do.

"I want nothing from you other than a public apology for getting me mixed up in this terrible scheme of yours and upsetting my life without any care for what it would do to me or how it would make me feel to be a part of your questionable behavior."

It might seem unimportant or perhaps even unnecessary to him or others, but it was important to her. Instead of the peaceful life of serving others she'd expected to live when she returned from France, she now had to train a man on proper behavior befitting an earl and head of his family. And knowing how to say *I was wrong* and *I'm sorry* were two of the first things he needed to learn.

Besides, she had a feeling that to this gambling man, losing a wager—to a lady—and then having to apologize wouldn't come easy.

No matter that right now he thought it would be easy to do.

"You have my word," he said with an unusual tenderness.

His expression was gentle and his promise heartfelt and nourishing after the battle they'd had. One she felt she had won—at least for now.

"If that's all you want, I'll do the grandest of apologies," he added. "Instead of the banns to announce our forthcoming marriage, I'll take out an ad in the *Times* and all the newsprints proclaiming the errors of my ways and your victory. Would that make you happy, Mrs. Feld?"

She drew in a heavy breath. "I don't need anything so ostentatious. At midnight, the last ball of the Season, a simple apology will do."

"If I fail and you win, I will comply." He folded his arms across his chest. "If I refrain from all you have dictated, at midnight, the last ball of the Season, you will agree to accept my proposal of marriage."

Brina swallowed hard. Suddenly she didn't want to agree. Fear he might somehow win pounded in her chest.

It had been easy when they were dancing and their hands touching to play tit-for-tat with their words. But now, this was serious.

Could she go back on her word?

"Do we have a bargain, Mrs. Feld?"

She willed herself to be calm once again and remember she had proof of his rogue ways and had to believe with all confidence he could not change them for her. "Yes."

He answered with a nod. "I assume you know the stipulations you've placed on this arrangement of ours means we'll be spending a lot of time together."

Brina felt a twinge of unease. *A lot?* That was something she hadn't thought about. "Even though I'm committed to try, I'm not sure how much time I can devote to helping you in your endeavor to change your ways."

"It's not only that. You'll want to be with me as much as possible to make sure I don't swear, take a drink, or—"

She suddenly cleared her throat and he paused.

"Commit any other offense that would keep me from upholding my end of the bargain and winning your hand."

A humorous light shone in his eyes, and despite her best effort she warmed to it. It should infuriate her, but now that their connection was set, she found his easy-going manner charming and tempting her to go along. This entire affair should have her feeling wretched. She didn't want a man in her life. In any capacity.

"I have other commitments, my lord. People who depend on me for certain things. I cannot be constantly watching to make sure your behavior is acceptable, and I don't believe I need to. Different people heard portions of our exchange tonight. By tomorrow everyone will put together the bits and pieces they heard and the terms of our agreement will be known."

She stopped and drew in a deep breath, wondering if she could handle the scandal of it. "Anyway," she added. "You will have a thousand eyes watching you. If you step out of line once, someone will see or hear, and I have no doubt they will let me know if you stray."

"I have no doubt of that either, but just in case, I'll be over tomorrow afternoon and we'll ride in the park."

*Tomorrow?*

Tension caused by what she'd done coiled inside her once more. "We certainly don't have to start this charade that soon. No reason to hurry with anything."

"I want to." He stepped closer to her once again and lowered his voice. "You have much to teach me, Mrs. Feld, and I am eager to learn."

His closeness always filled her with a shiver of desire and made Brina wonder if it would really be the other way around. She had unwittingly given Lord Blacknight a reason and a way to pursue her in front of everyone.

And he had just started.

A faint gleam of humor shone in his eyes. "No time to waste. If I'm going to have to live without a game of cards, no drinking, and other things of a nature too primal for a gentleman to mention in your presence, you will have to live with seeing me. Often."

"Oh, you are a beast," she exclaimed in a frustrated tone. "Because you will be suffering, you want me to as well."

He gave her such a charming grin, her displeasure over the entire affair almost faded away. Brina had no idea exactly what she'd gotten herself into. Yet, much to her chagrin, apprehension and anticipation twisted together inside her, troubling her even more.

"All right," she said, feeling somewhat like she'd agreed to a prison sentence. "If you insist, half past two for a ride in the park will be fine."

"There's one thing I should remind you of before we seal this," he said. "I always play to win."

Her chin lifted. "And you should know, I've never put a wager on anything in my life—I wouldn't be doing it now if I had any concern about losing."

"I will take no mercy on you because you are a lady."

"I would be affronted if you tried." She took a sip of champagne, looked at him, and smiled. "Oh, my, this tastes so wonderful. Cooling after such heated talk."

He gave her a twisted grin. "You are a delight when you're being wicked, Mrs. Feld."

She took another sip and it went down hard and ended with a heavy breath. "This is madness. I can't believe I'm going to be spending time with you when I could be doing something to help someone in true need. I have important things to do during the day. Taking jolly rides around the parks with you wasn't in my schedule." She stopped. Her gaze froze onto his. "Why did you get me mixed up in this? I was just beginning to get my life—" She bit off the words and ended with an exasperated sigh.

His expression softened, and he leaned toward her in a concerned way. "You were beginning to do what?"

Warmed by his sincere tone, her earlier confidence evaporated in an instant and in its place was the crushing need to be held against his strong chest and comforted. Blacknight was offering her the opportunity to share her heartache with him. And strange as it was, for a moment she wanted nothing more than to do that.

But no. She couldn't. Ever.

She wasn't going to pour out her heart to him about how she'd struggled since her husband died. First with the denial, then shock, and later the overwhelming anger that nearly destroyed her. Oh, the anger had been so difficult to deal with. She hadn't even shared her deepest feelings with Julia and Adeline. It was too horrible for anyone to know.

Brina took a step back from the earl. "Nothing," she said cautiously, displeased she'd allowed some of her inner struggles to show to the earl. "Nothing at all. Why are you looking at me so intensely?"

"I was making sure you are all right and—"

"And what?" she insisted, keeping her gaze directly on his.

"Thinking I might need a list of words that you believe are swears, curses, and cusses. You know, just so I'm safe. Everyone has their own ideas about words that are acceptable."

"Oh, yes." She relaxed and smiled. "I suppose I did get a little carried away with that one. I meant only—"

His brow rose. He wasn't going to let this pass. "I'm listening."

"Only the supremely coarse ones."

"Good." He gave her a bit of a smile. "That, I'm certain I can manage."

"Can you?" She sighed and shook her head. "I've never been one to wish ill-fortune on anyone, my lord, but so we're clear, you *can't* be safe." Her words were calmly spoken. "I'm not happy about this bargain we have struck. But know this, I don't believe you can change, and I am committed to remaining a widow. In a way it seems unfair to you to go through with this."

His determined expression slowly relaxed and his lips formed a half smile. "Maybe I forgot to tell you, I always win."

The earl caressed her face with his gaze so intently, it was as if he were caressing her skin with his fingers.

The air around them seemed to crackle with words that weren't being said and feelings that weren't being expressed.

"Not this time," she asserted, handed him her glass, and walked away.

# Chapter 8

As soon as Brina had awakened and remembered the earl was taking her for a ride, she felt a humming of excitement deep in her chest. At the time, she'd immediately put the sensation down to the chill in her room. Later she told herself it was common nerves. When it continued, she realized it was because she was annoyed with herself for becoming overwrought at the ball and had started making all those demands on him, and that she'd actually told him she would marry him if he complied.

She didn't know what emotion had taken hold and caused her to literally put herself at such a high risk. That was certainly reason enough to give her a case of the jitters, but she shouldn't still be experiencing the troubling stirs. By the time summer arrived, she'd be twenty-five. Plenty old enough not to allow a rake like Blacknight make her feel as if she were a young belle getting her first ride in a landau with a handsome gentleman.

It wasn't the best day for a ride in St. James's Park, but Brina would manage. Skies were gray and the air was downright cold for mid-spring. A gusty strong wind had whistled around the corner of the house all morning. Two days ago she'd heard birds chirping and the sun blazed hot on her cheeks when she was in the garden. Now, spring had seemed to disappear overnight and left a winter's day in its place.

Brina prepared for her outing with the earl by donning a thick fabric chemise, a heavy forest-green carriage dress with matching velvet pelisse, and fine woolen stockings. At the last moment, she changed from a low-heeled pump to her most comfortable pair of walking boots in case they decided to stop the carriage and take a stroll.

"Should I go up to your room and fetch your black cape, Mrs. Feld?" the housekeeper asked, handing her the wide-brimmed bonnet banded with satin ribbon.

"No, I should be fine. I don't expect to be out of the house long this afternoon."

Brina knew if she were too cold, it would be a good reason to cut short her excursion with Blacknight. She wouldn't admit to actually planning it, but a shiver or two from her should make him recognize her discomfort and suggest the need to return home.

After tying a bow under her chin, she started pulling on her gloves, wanting to be ready when the earl arrived. There was no reason to prolong their time together by inviting him inside and offering tea. It would have been a proper thing to do, and necessary if she'd still been living at her parents' house. They would have insisted on saying hello to the new earl. Though Brina was quite sure they wouldn't be pleased Lord Blacknight had placed a wager at White's stating she would accept his proposal by the end of the Season. Hopefully they wouldn't know until it was all over. By now, her parents should be safely ensconced at her aunt's estate in Northumberland and far away from all the gossip.

Brina adored her mother and father. They had always been good to her, but she was glad she no longer had to depend on their unwavering support. After Stewart's death she needed them close.

And not without good reason. The shock of losing her husband and the denial that persisted far too long had provoked unhealthy emotions she was still trying to recover from.

A stirring from the past teased Brina's mind as she tightened the gloves around her fingers. She tried to brush the unwanted memories away, but they lingered like cold morning fog on a gray day.

For a time, Brina thought she might be going insane. Perhaps she even had a little. For a while.

She'd loved her husband and considered it an act of faithfulness and honor to refuse to believe he was dead. After all, they'd only been married three months when she was told the sea had taken him. There were reports he'd saved the lives of several people by helping them grab onto pieces of wreckage. He was young, strong. Surely, he'd saved himself too. He had to be somewhere. Injured perhaps and hadn't been found. Days turned into weeks. Months passed. He didn't return.

Brina finally had to accept he wasn't coming back.

He was dead, and she had stopped living. She couldn't cope with the deep, pulsing sadness of losing him.

But then, when she felt she couldn't bear the pain and anger of loss any longer, she met Julia and Adeline that sad day at a square near the docks at London's Harbor. It wasn't a place widows of Society should ever find themselves, nevertheless it was where the few personal belongings that had been recovered from the sinking of the *Salty Dove* had been displayed. The items were lined up in rows, available for family members who wanted to look through and retrieve loved ones' final possessions.

Seagulls had squawked all afternoon. The smell of putrid water hung in the air. Lonesome, distant sounds of riggings clanking against wooden masts would never fully leave her mind. Nor would the suffering families of the stewards, attendants, and other workers on the ship. They had gathered and huddled there too that day. Mostly women and children poorly dressed. They hugged, talked softly, and comforted one another.

That was the day Adeline had the idea of starting a school for the unfortunate children who were left fatherless by the downed ship. Polite Society would take care of their own, but who would take care of the workers' offspring? The three Society widows decided they would, and the inception of the Seafarer's School for Girls had been born.

And it had saved Brina's life.

"Would you like for me to ask your maid to bring you a different pair of gloves?"

"What?" Brina blinked back the past and looked down at her hands. She had put on the gloves and now taken them off. Shaking her head, she smiled at Mrs. Lawton, happy to have a reason to put the unwanted memories to bed once again. "No, no. They fit fine. I was simply distracted for a few moments."

A tap sounded on the door knocker. Brina's stomach tightened. She started pulling on her gloves again. "At last, he's here. There's nothing like getting something started so you can look forward to the finish."

Mrs. Lawton headed for the door. Brina slipped the braided ribbons of her reticule over her wrist and settled them at the top of her gloves. She then scooted from behind her housekeeper, intent on rushing outside, but at seeing the earl looking so splendid and dashing in his dark-blue coat, fawn-colored trousers, and quilted beige waistcoat, she had to stop and drink in the sight of him.

Reality came swift. It hadn't been nerves or annoyance she'd felt all morning. It was guilty excitement at the thought of spending time with him. His towering height and perfect physique sent a thrill of desire flashing through her, and she simply wanted to take pleasure in it.

From the moment she'd first seen him, she'd been attracted, and despite her valiant efforts, that hadn't changed. But right now, she had to rein in those feminine emotions and stay calm.

"My lord," she greeted him and curtsied.

He took off his hat and nodded. "Mrs. Feld."

She stepped outside. "You're right on time and I'm ready."

His eyes narrowed and he hesitated. "You might need a cape. It's windy today."

"I should be warm enough." She hummed to herself and started down the stone steps toward the street. The closer she got to the pavement, the slower she walked. No carriage was parked in front of the house. There were three horses and a groom standing with them.

A feeling of suspicion rose from within her. She stopped and turned to stare at the earl while her brain tried to focus on the situation she saw unfolding before her.

"These are horses," she said.

He regarded her closely as he came up beside her. "Well-schooled mares. I picked a gentle one for you. You do ride, don't you?"

Brina was so astounded, she wasn't sure she could speak at first. Her breath seemed to clog at the base of her throat. "Yes, I do," she managed to say. Not well, but she could manage a horse. Somewhat. "Why did you bring horses?"

"You look concerned," he said, though his tone was light, making it clear he was anything but concerned that she could not handle the task he'd brought to her. He casually folded his arms across his chest. "I said we'd go for a ride in the park."

The Earl of Blacknight had to be the most unbelievable man in all of London. And England. The whole world. And he was standing in front of her. Pursuing her. Tempting her with intriguing charm.

"This is not what it means when you ask a lady to go for a ride." Brina sucked in a deep, soundless breath of exasperation. "It means you will bring a curricle to her house, or perhaps a shiny landau with the top down. You don't bring horses. How could doing something like this have even entered your mind?"

He remained at ease and offered her only a trace of a smile. One that teased her senses and irritated her disposition at the same time. That he'd made such an assumption and she was perturbed didn't seem to bother him at all.

"It's not a problem," he said so smoothly, his words washed over her as if they were a goose feather trickling against her skin. "I'll return to the stable and get a proper carriage for you."

"No, no." Brina shook her head, walked over to the smaller horse, and rubbed down the long brown nose. She was practical. The horses were already here. Besides, she rather liked the idea. "I don't want you to do that. I haven't ridden in a long time and I'm not properly attired, but I'll manage."

"Only if you're sure," he said with conviction.

The mare nudged her hand gingerly so Brina patted her firm neck. She seemed to like that and prodded

Brina again. The animal was friendly, and Brina warmed to her immediately. Blacknight had made a wise choice.

She looked over at him and gave him an expression of approval. "I am."

How could she stay upset with a man who brought her a horse to ride? A man who continually surprised her? It was frustrating that he was so stimulating. She had a feeling he wasn't nearly as oblivious to the rules of gentlemanly behavior as he claimed and others liked to think.

The groom placed the two-step stool down by her, and the earl reached for her hand. His grip was firm and reassuring. Within the bounds of propriety, he helped position her perfectly in the side saddle with her booted feet properly settled in the stirrups.

He held onto the reins as he gazed into her eyes, "You look very capable sitting up there, but would you like for me to lead your horse?"

"Absolutely not." She tried to feel annoyed at him, but there was no way she could. She was delighted to be in the saddle again. Riding was an enjoyable pastime and the thought of doing it made her feel good and excited to get started. "I'll be fine," she answered, holding out her palm. "It may have been a few years since I've ridden, but I don't think I've forgotten how to guide a horse."

He placed the ribbons in her hands. "And you're right. You don't need a cape. I brought a blanket for us to sit on and have refreshments when we get to the park." He walked over to the groom's horse and pulled a gray wool blanket from behind a basket. He laid it over her lap and said, "Hold on to this end to keep it from falling off."

"Thank you," she said, tucking the heavy fabric around her waist and under her hips. Giving her the blanket was not only mannerly of him but thoughtful of her comfort as well.

"If at any time you feel you can't control the horse, let me know."

Brina knew he was playfully teasing her as the mare hadn't so much as snorted. She gave the earl enough of a smile to let him know she understood exactly what he was doing.

"I fear the only thing I can't control is you." Or the way she felt when he was near.

He chuckled and climbed atop his horse with the ease of a man who was well-seasoned to a saddle and knew how to handle the animal beneath him. Brina gave a gentle kick to the horse's flank with her heel, and they started down the quiet street.

After passing only a few houses she felt exhilarated. She was enjoying the ride immensely and wondering why she hadn't done it for so long. The mare had a smooth gait and ambled along at the right pace, giving her time to get used to being in the saddle after a long absence. From atop the horse she could see more of her surroundings. Her perspective of the houses and trees was different than when sitting inside a carriage or taking a stroll.

When more than a few moments of silence had passed, she offered, "You do know that even if we were going to ride horses, we should have arrived at the park in a carriage and had the groom waiting there for us?"

"If I'd done that, you would have missed some of the thrill of the afternoon."

She scoffed with confidence. "You can't fool me. What you mean is that you would have missed the amusement of seeing how startled I was at what you had done."

"That too," he admitted without qualms.

Even with the dreary cold day, he still had a twinkle in his eyes. How could she ignore that? When he wasn't being a rake, he was so charming. And that was what she had to be careful of.

"How are you doing?" he asked. "Warm enough?"

She was actually doing wonderful as she was sure he expected. A cape would have kept the chill of the wind from blowing down her neck, but she was fine with the heat of the horse beneath her legs and the warmth of the blanket he'd politely placed on her lap.

"You brought the horses on purpose, didn't you?" she asked.

He shrugged. "I thought you might be getting a little tired of doing the same thing each day and ready for something different."

A prickle of something she couldn't describe skittered over her. It was alarming how well he seemed to know her. She'd wondered how he'd known she wanted to flee down the stone corridors and tunnel beneath the Paris chateau with him. Now, how had he known she needed to do something she hadn't done in years but used to enjoy? Something as simple, peaceful, and pleasurable as riding a horse.

Brina had shied away from any closeness to men for years. Now, this one, with his bold wager and her demands, had found a way to insert himself into her very private life. For now, there was nothing to do about it but cope.

Their pact was sealed.

"You must have known I could ride or you wouldn't have chanced bringing the horses."

"Wouldn't I?"

*Well, perhaps he would.*

"If you didn't know for sure, it was very brazen of you."

He remained silent so she asked, "How did you find out?"

"Must you know all my secrets, Mrs. Feld?"

His voice was calm and as easy as their ride. She had

to be careful with him. There were so many things about him that tugged at her senses and brought them to life.

"I'm curious," she conceded and added a mischievous smile when he turned his head and looked at her.

"I asked your cousin Harper when I saw him. He was with my cousin Robert last night."

"Really? I didn't see Harper at the ball. He must have arrived after I left. But it was already late by then. Did he look all right to you?"

"Yes. Why do you ask?"

"My father asked that I stay in touch with him, invite him over while he and my mother are away visiting his parents in Northumberland. I'm afraid I haven't done that." She paused long enough to reprimand herself once again for not having yet done so. "I've had other things to attend to, and it's only been a little over a week since they left. It was odd my father asked me specifically to stay in touch with him. Almost as if he was concerned about him."

"Does he have reason to be?"

"No, I'm sure not. Not having a son, Papa has always been attentive to Harper. I'm feeling quite guilty I haven't reached out to him yet. I'll do that tomorrow for sure."

"He looked as if he were doing quite well last night. I left the ball shortly after you. I saw him and Robert at a gaming house, and they were making a good showing at the tables."

A carriage came up behind them suddenly and quickly whipped around, passing them at a fast clip. The driver, a young buck, was obviously desperate to get somewhere. Though Brina was annoyed by the man's lack of common courtesy, neither Blacknight nor the horses they were riding gave the incident notice.

"So, you went to a club after the ball," she stated in a

more pleased manner than she intended. But really, she was very happy. How could a gambler stay away from the excitement of the games? This is what she had expected him to do.

"It's my usual habit." He looked over at her and flashed a bit of a grin.

"Yes, I know, but it is good news to hear you were at your club where there is much gaming, drinking spirits, and other pursuits."

A soft chuckle rumbled from his chest. "Don't get your hopes up, Mrs. Feld. You'll not hear anyone say I had a drink or played a game. I merely walked around and talked with those who were partaking in both and enjoying themselves."

She gave him a confident lift of her chin. "I'm not worried, my lord. If not last night, nor tonight, nor even tomorrow. Some night. Soon. It will only be a matter of time until you give in to your nature and old habits and have a howling good time at the tables with a glass of the finest brandy."

"Perhaps you are the one who should be careful, Mrs. Feld." He gave another short laugh. "When you say things like that, it only makes me want to prove you wrong all the more."

She turned her head away from him as if to be dismissive of his warning, but of course, she couldn't stay silent after his comment. "I know how men like their vices. Tell me, did you have a headache this morning?"

"Yes. From not drinking."

She suppressed a grin because she knew he was looking at her. "And how did you sleep?"

"Well—once I managed to stop the shakes."

A genuine, playful laugh fell from her lips and she faced him again. "You are teasing me," she chided lightly.

"As you are me."

It felt good to listen to his humor. She could tell by the way he looked at her, he knew how much she was enjoying herself. The awareness that always seemed to be between them heated her cold cheeks and caused a ripple of what she could only describe as desire to curl and wind its way slowly through her.

"So, what did you do at the club if you weren't having a brandy and a game?"

He shrugged and looked away from her. "I watched a couple of old masters play billiards and some of the younger ones roll dice and play cards. I don't always have to participate to appreciate whatever game is being played. One way to get better at anything is to watch how others do it well. It helps to discover their weaknesses and strengths and then apply them to your own game."

"Yes. I can see where that would be beneficial." She needed to study him. At times like this, when she was happy to be with him, she had to remind herself they were in a fight. And she had to win.

They rode in silence for a few moments before her more solemn self returned, and she turned to him and offered, "Obviously, I'm a little more troubled about our hastily made arrangement than you are. You can take it lightly."

He arched his eyebrows and quickly said, "I take nothing lightly, Mrs. Feld. Least of all you."

Her shoulders lifted and her chin tilted up as she looked at him with a questioning glance. "That is a matter of opinion. It's true I have more to lose than you."

"That is also a matter of opinion," he answered calmly as his horse snickered and pulled against the bridle. "There wasn't a man in London who woke this morning without knowing what I agreed to last night. Your demands are rigid."

Brina gave him an expression of satisfaction. "As I intended."

She believed it was only a matter of time before the seemingly strong-willed earl tired of adhering to his new life without the things he wanted and gave up the fight in favor of his nature.

They came upon the one busy street to cross before entering St. James's Park. Instead of stopping the horses and waiting for traffic to clear as she expected him to do, Blacknight motioned for her to follow him. He inched his horse into the lane of traffic and said, "Tighten your reins and keep the mare directly behind mine. She'll stay calm as long as you do."

"Don't worry about me, my lord. I'm doing quite well and can handle her. You take care of yourself and your horse."

He threw her an admirable grin before giving his attention back to the matter at hand.

The carriages, wagons, and other horses stopped as he commanded by lifting his arm, and he maneuvered them across the street, safely onto the other side, where they entered the park. Only a few people were milling about. It was no wonder with the day so blustery. Some were walking and others rode in open carriages. A handful of people were seated on blankets. Small sections of St. James's were thick with small trees and undergrowth. Some of the terrain appeared wild and woodsy while other areas resembled open grasslands where trees were spaced far apart.

Lord Blacknight led them to a flat area near the beginning of a heavy growth of bushes sprouting their spring leaves. He stopped beside a large tree where they would be blocked from the worst of the wind by the wide, sturdy trunk.

Brina kicked out of the stirrups while he dismounted.

After throwing the blanket to the groom, he reached up for her. She expected him to take her hand and gently help her down. Instead, he clasped his strong hands firmly around her waist, and in one quick puff of breath and fluid motion, he lifted her out of the saddle and down onto the ground. His grip was firm, capable yet somehow caressing. A thrill of warmth shuddered through her.

His hands lingered only a couple of seconds before he released her and offered reasoning. "It's so much easier that way." A quick glance from one side of the park to the other. "And it doesn't appear as if anyone close by took notice. Your reputation should be intact."

Trying to forget about the heat of his touch and nearness, she gave him a perturbed glance and looked around the park for observers too. It appeared he was right and no one was paying them any attention.

"It's not my reputation so much as it's *not* something you should do—putting your hands around a lady's waist is highly improper. Since it's already done, I don't know what I can do about it."

His brows rose and he gave her a curiously genuine smile before saying, "I was liking our conversation so much, I had forgotten that part of our bargain is for you to help me know what I should and shouldn't do. I like the way I do it better."

"I'm sure of that. And it's what I'm relying on. Yet, in fairness to our wager and my pledge, I must let you know when you're being improper."

He leaned in close to her. The corner of his mouth twitched engagingly. "I haven't been improper yet, Mrs. Feld."

His words were low, husky, and revealing. A breathless fluttering rushed through her. Yet, she stood still. Quiet. Hardly breathing, wanting to ask him what he considered improper. For a light-headed moment she wanted to tempt him to go further with his statement and show her what he meant.

Instead, her good sense returned with a gasp of indignation and she asked, "How can you say that? You kissed me in Paris. You involved me in a shameful wager which prompted me to respond in kind."

As if to calm her, he gave a reluctant nod and in the same low voice, he answered, "I would do it all again for the chance to be with you. I regret nothing."

His honesty flushed her cold cheeks and caused ripples of desire to shoot through her. A hint of enchanting devilment sparked in his eyes and much to her obvious distress she reveled in it. It appeared they were both benefiting from this afternoon tête-à-tête.

And that could only mean trouble for her. She hoped he took a drink soon.

The horse nudged Brina's back, breaking her concentration. She stepped away from the earl. Being around him wasn't going to be easy. He made her smile, laugh, and feel things she thought she'd never experience again. It was going to be difficult to deny herself such tempting emotions.

They walked over to where the groom had spread the blanket and placed the basket. Brina settled herself on one side and the earl on the other. The gray clouds were beginning to scatter but the wind was still brisk as a winter day. It rustled the budding leaves on the trees and whipped at her bonnet. In the distance, she heard carriage wheels rumbling and shouts from children playing. Yet, even with the sounds, there was always something peaceful about being in the park.

After taking off his hat and gloves, Lord Black-night unbuttoned his overcoat and pulled the dark beige scarf from his neck. He extended it toward her. "I think it's large enough you can use it as a shawl. It will keep you warmer now that you don't have the blanket for cover."

There was a softness in his voice she couldn't refuse. His gentleness and thoughtfulness were astounding at times. "Thank you," she whispered and took it from his hands.

Brina wrapped the wool high around her nape, spread its width over her back and shoulders, tying the long ends across her breasts. The fine wool fabric held the fresh heavenly fragrance of his shaving soap. She breathed the scent in deeply. Heat from his body clung to it and soothed her chill instantly, making her want to sink and cuddle into it.

"Let's see what my cook prepared for us."

He moved the basket closer and opened it. A large napkin was the first thing he took out and lay in front of her. Next came two teacups and saucers. After taking the stopper out of a pewter bottle, he put it to his nose and smelled.

"Good. It's chocolate. I was afraid it might be tea."

"Afraid? That's an unusual comment coming from you."

"A poor choice of words to be sure." He carefully poured some of it into a cup.

"Do you not have an appreciation for tea?"

"I was only thinking of you. My cook serves tea warm but chocolate she makes piping hot. So, it should still be heated for you on this chilly afternoon."

His consideration warmed her as much as his scarf. She supposed there were times she judged him too harshly.

He handed her the cup and she sipped. "It is. I thought

you were going to tell me she usually adds a splash or two of brandy to your chocolate but not your tea."

The earl looked at her over his cup, his expression gentle but probing. She quirked her head as if to question him.

"Is that the way your husband liked it?" he asked.

# Chapter 9

The mention of Stewart startled Brina. She swallowed hard and slowly lowered her lashes, hoping Blacknight wouldn't see how affected she was by his mention of her husband. She supposed it was a reasonable inquiry, but not one she expected from him. From anyone. Still, she didn't want to overreact, but had to take a moment to collect herself.

That meant not looking at the earl. She glanced away and watched a carriage roll past them in the distance. A lone rider had his horse cantering, and a couple walked arm in arm. Life was carrying on. Just as she'd had to do.

She carefully settled the cup back on the saucer. After sucking in a deep breath of the cold, windy air, she cleared her throat, kept her eyes averted, and answered, "No, Stewart wasn't a man with many vices. He seldom drank anything other than tea. He did love horse racing, but if he ever made wagers, he kept them to himself and didn't speak of them."

"Did I disturb you by mentioning him?"

She lifted her gaze back to the earl's. He watched her intently. She was not sure what, if anything, she should say. Talking about her husband wasn't improper, though it had been a while since she'd discussed Stewart with anyone.

Blacknight stared at her long enough for her to know silence wasn't an answer. She had to shake off her mild uneasiness that he was the first one to mention Stewart in a very long time and continue.

"All right, no. I mean, yes. In a way, I suppose. Oh, who am I trying to persuade? Yes, of course it did. How could it not?"

"That wasn't my purpose," he offered gently.

"I know," she answered in a controlled voice. "It's that people seldom speak of him anymore. Not that I blame them. He's been gone so long. It's hard to— Everyone still calls me Mrs. Feld, but no one seems to remember Mr. Feld."

Blacknight nodded as if he understood when really she wasn't sure she did.

"I didn't know him," the earl admitted. "But I'll talk with you about him anytime you want."

His soft expression and somber, sincere words suddenly made her feel like crying. She was thankful the chilling wind kept her eyes dry, and that the sensation passed quickly. Reflecting on her short marriage to Stewart wasn't something she wanted to do with the very desirable man sitting across from her. The sadness of losing Stewart would never completely go away. She believed that was the way it was supposed to be for a man who had been as good as her husband.

She swallowed and then took another sip from her cup. "Thank you, but no. I wouldn't want to do that."

"All right but my offer stands."

She made no further comment about that, but said, "The chocolate is still warm and delicious. Not too sweet."

He looked in the basket again. Grateful he wasn't going to press her to say more, she watched him pull out another napkin, open it, and display little fruit-topped biscuits. They looked delicious, but she was sure she couldn't eat a bite.

"How is your cousin Robert?" she asked, wanting only to change the subject.

The earl kept his gaze concentrated on hers. "Did you forget we talked about Robert and Harper on the ride over here?"

*Oh, my.* Yes, she had. In her haste to forget about Stewart, she'd asked the first thing that came to her mind.

"But, I'm glad you mentioned him," Blacknight said, not giving her time to respond to his question. "It gives me the chance to say I do think he appeared restless last night when I saw him at the club, even though he was winning. London has a much slower and more determined pace than Paris or Vienna. The people here are sometimes unbending in their outlook on life. I'm assuming that was the reason for his impatient behavior. It may take a while for him to settle down to Society's ways again."

"And what about you?" she asked, hoping her cup remained steady in her hands. "Restless, too, in tired old, stodgy London? Are you yearning to race through underground tunnels in Paris again?"

He shrugged blithely and then chuckled as he made himself more comfortable by leaning on his elbow and stretching his long, powerful legs out on the blanket, crossing his booted feet at the ankles. It was highly irregular for a man to be so relaxed in front of a lady he wasn't married to. Should anyone they know pass by and see them, there could be talk enough to turn into a scandal. Still, Brina couldn't bring herself to remind him of the indiscretion he was exhibiting. Looking at him was simply too tempting to deny herself the joy.

"There's no time now for such idle thinking as was my pastime in France," he told her. "I'm still trying to make sense of the evils of fate."

"Ah, is that all? Well, my lord, let me assure you that can't be done. I've tried to figure it out myself."

"I'm sure you have."

Her gaze held a moment too long on his, so she cleared her throat and finished off the last sip of chocolate before placing her cup on the saucer in front of her. She hadn't meant to return their conversation to such a troubling one.

He saved her from having to reply to his softly spoken sentence by adding, "It's more than just that I never *wanted* to be an earl." He absently opened the chocolate, poured more into her cup, and handed it to her. "The thought of ever being the earl and head of my family never entered my mind. There were too many male relatives in line for the title for it to have been possible. If not for that cruel stroke of fate. I've been Zane Browning, the black sheep of the family for as long as I can remember. It's hard to stop being him."

From experience, Brina knew no one could help him settle his issues with how his life had changed and the reasons for it. She'd tried it herself for years. She could be a buttress, but not an anchor, nor an answer.

"That's why you wanted to court me, was it not? To help you adjust to the proprieties of being an earl rather than a rake."

"If only that had turned out the way I had planned."

He chuckled good-naturedly. "You have not made my way easier. You have made it even harder."

She needed to hear that. "As was my intention. Now, tell me, what did you do today?"

He looked at her as if she were asking him a trick question. "Are you thinking I might have mumbled a coarse curse or two when my uncles and solicitor arrived at the door before my morning coffee?"

"Of course not." She twitched him a smile. "But I do expect that if you do, you'll let me know so we can end our arrangement. In the meantime, if you are going to insist we spend some time together, we must have something to talk about or things will become quite boring."

"I could never get weary looking at you, Mrs. Feld."

"You say that now, but I doubt you would feel the same three weeks from now, if you by chance make it that long, and we had nothing to talk about."

"All right. My uncles, solicitors, and accountants continue their long list of instructions for all the things I'm now responsible for, decisions I have to make concerning businesses, tenants, contracts, families, allowances. Frankly, Mrs. Feld, I was happy for them to rush me out to make sure I wasn't late to your house."

"Speaking of lists. It so happens I have something for you." Picking up her reticule, she pulled it open and reached inside. She took out a small book and folded sheet of vellum. She handed the book to him. "It's a little worn because I've read it several times. It's small and will fit very nicely in your coat pocket."

He glanced down at the front of it before catching her gaze again. "It's poetry."

"Yes," she said as seriously as possible, considering the confused expression on his face filled her with glee. "Every gentleman, especially earls, should always have a little book of poetry with them. For you, specifically, whenever you feel the need to gamble, drink, or whatever—pull it out of your pocket instead. You'll find it will quiet you and help curb your urges."

Wrinkles formed on his forehead and around his eyes. "That sounds very much like a prison sentence to me, Mrs. Feld."

Good, she thought. He was making it difficult for her not to laugh. "Poetry strengthens the mind, the heart, and the soul. You can't absorb too much of it. You'll find it sustaining in your weaker moments."

"You are a clever one," he chided lightly, and pointed to the sheet of paper in her lap. "So, what's this? You give me an entire book to read, but you only have one piece of paper. That hardly seems fair."

His attitude was perfect, and she was quite happy. He needed to be a little irritated with her. It was far better for her. "That's because these are my notes, and I am going to be studying them while you read on this windy day. Imagine how delighted your uncles would be if they came riding or walking by and saw you sitting in the park, reading the much-maligned poet John Keats."

His expression was relaxed and he was so easy to look at. The allure of him suddenly made her shiver and she pulled his scarf tighter about her shoulders.

"They would indeed be shocked. No doubt about that, Mrs. Feld. They've never forgiven me for not being a better student of subjects such as poetry when I was at Oxford."

"You had things other than your studies on your mind, did you?"

"Always, but they were happy to know I did well enough to comprehend all the intricate notations and explanations of numbers in the account books they have placed in front of me. It shouldn't have surprised them.

I've always been good with numbers. They seem to stay in my mind without me trying to make them."

"I'm sure that's been helpful for you when playing cards."

"Immensely. The natural talent added with the skills I've learned has been good to me."

"It sounds as if authority and responsibility weren't the things you wanted fate to gift you."

"No, but now that it has, I will do my dam—duty and my best to be good at them." His brow wrinkled, and his head tilted a fraction. "That was only a small slip of the tongue."

She lifted her eyebrows in a knowing way. "I suppose I can say you caught yourself in time—this time."

He shifted his position and asked, "What kind of notes will you be studying?"

"Things I had planned to do in the coming weeks. I doubt you'd be interested as none of them included you appearing in my life and wanting me to help you be a better gentleman, but I will manage."

He sucked in a low chuckle. "Being with me today hasn't been all bad, has it?"

She couldn't lie. "No. It hasn't." *It has been pleasurable.* Brina gave herself an internal shake. That was dangerous thinking. She needed to avoid getting too comfortable with him. "I enjoyed the ride over here and the chocolate. Tell me, do you really want to know my plans or are you only wanting to avoid reading poetry?"

He seemed to debate that, then said, "Both."

"Fair enough." She unfolded the paper. "The top of my list is to start a weekly art class at the girls' school. Julia and Adeline have agreed. I don't know how much you know about the school, but the students are being taught how to read, write, and add their numbers as well as the seamstress trade so they can earn a living for themselves and their families one day. I think it will also be nice for them to have an appreciation of creating beauty with paints as well as fabrics. Lyon, Adeline's husband, gave the school a pianoforte and they love singing. I hear them every morning. So, this will be another way for them to express themselves that doesn't have to do with a form of labor."

"I can see this idea makes you happy."

"It does. The girls are eager to learn all that's put before them. It's refreshing to talk with them. I received so many flowers recently that I took some of the bouquets over to the school for the girls. One of them reached out and touched a rose. I could tell how much she appreciated the velvety smooth petal and delicate beauty of it, and I thought, she needs to learn how to paint a flower."

"I suppose the more good things one can be exposed to, the better life one will have," he offered as an observation.

"Yes," she agreed, heartened that even this rake thought her idea a good one. "I feel the same way. I was going to spend some time this afternoon getting things ready for art lessons, but now, I'll do that another day."

"What else is on your list?"

"I have some weekly things I do for the Sisters of Pilwillow Crossings. I help with their charitable efforts. And I want to walk around town and look at some buildings."

A gust of wind whipped around the tree and she pulled his scarf higher on her neck. The earl suddenly stood up and reached for her hand. "Let's move around. I can see you're getting cold."

Oddly, she hadn't noticed the chill. She took his hand

and rose. Even though his gloves had been off for some time, when his fingers closed around hers, she felt their warmth, but quickly slid her hand out of his grasp.

"Strolling downtown is something we can do together," he said but made no move to start walking, so they stayed in front of the tree.

"I'm afraid you would find it quite boring. I won't be doing it to admire the architecture. The girls will need a place to open a seamstress shop one day. They will have to do an apprenticeship with someone first, but I want them to eventually have their own building. It's never too early to start looking for options in different sections of Town. Not only that, I've noticed there's a small building directly behind the abbey. I want to look into the possibility of buying that for the sisters one day. So, you see," she added with confidence. "I simply won't be able to see you every day."

"What would that building be for?"

"A chapel. They don't have a real one—well, that's not to say it isn't real. Of course it is, but it's only a small room inside the abbey. I thought a larger space for their relics, prayer books, and gatherings of quiet reflection time would be nice."

He stared into her eyes for a long time, as if he were taking stock of her. His eyes and the way he looked at her were tender, as they had been when they spoke about Stewart.

"I'm not sure I'm at all comfortable with the way you are staring at me, my lord."

"I was trying to merge the soft, compassionate lady you are now with the bold and magnificent lady who had the command of everyone in the ballroom last night."

Her breaths became shallow and short. "It wasn't my intention to make our conversation so public. I meant for only you to hear me."

"I heard you, and every man there was wishing he was in my shoes and had the opportunity I have."

She was caught under the sensual spell he was casting over her and wondering how she was going to break free. "What do you mean?" she asked quietly. "That's ridiculous. No man wants to be told he can't drink, swear, gamble, or indulge in other manly pursuits. Most of all you."

He moved closer to her and lowered his head toward hers. "No, but every man saw and felt your raw, determined passion. It's in a man's nature to be drawn to that, to want to seize it for their own and possess it."

Brina felt a flush rising in her cheeks. "You talk nonsense at times, my lord. You should pay calls on other ladies and not be so fixated on me."

His gaze swept up and down her face, lingering on her lips for a few seconds before capturing her eyes again. "You are the one I want. I knew it the moment I saw you walking down the street with the girls marching behind you."

Perhaps the earl had already read the romantic poets. His intense gaze, his genuine expression of wanting her were beguiling, and she had to somehow fight them.

His eyes narrowed and he leaned toward her. "Tell me, Mrs. Feld, did you read the scandal sheets this morning?"

"Heavens, no," she answered, looking past him and over the spacious park. "I couldn't bring myself to read them. I don't want to know what they are saying about me. I heard enough whispers last night."

"They were kind to you. The one I read had only high praise for you and your ultimatums. Though it was clear the author of the gossip column had not a hope in hel— heaven that you or my family could change me and make me worthy of the title earl."

She didn't know why, but her gaze fell to the sensuous curve of his lips and she imagined them on hers again.

"Do you think you can change?" she asked.

In the blink of an eye, he caught her shoulders in his hands, pulled her up to him, closed his eyes, and pressed his lips against hers.

Brina expected the same wild, short kiss he'd given her in Paris. Instead, his lips landed softly on hers with infinite care. They were warm, pliant with merely a hint of delicate pressure. The back and forth movement was a light, feathery teasing sensation that caused her abdomen to tighten in response to the gentleness of his caress.

For a fleeting second, she thought to make a feeble attempt to resist him, but the mindless pleasure of being held so tightly and kissed again—and so thoroughly, it put a stop to the idea almost instantly. With little effort, his mouth gently coaxed her lips apart and the kiss continued with a sweetness she wouldn't have thought possible from this man who had wagered at a club for her hand. Any notion of the kiss not continuing faded as quickly as resistance had, and in its place was the very selfish thought that after so long, she deserved this tender embrace.

There was really no other choice. Brina wanted to accept and join in the pleasure he was giving. She didn't want to deny herself these few brief moments in his arms, even though at the back of her mind she knew they were standing under a tree in a park where anyone could happen by, see them, and blab to the world.

Not even that mattered. This moment with this man was worth the chance of getting caught, being disgraced.

There had always been an inexplicable, unrelenting attraction between them since the moment they'd met, and right now it was sizzling hot.

Her lips parted farther, a sigh of wanting escaped as

passion flared brightly inside her. The sheer intensity of how fast a deep longing for more filled her, almost overwhelmed her. Without forethought, her hands flattened against his hard chest and skimmed up the buttons on his waistcoat to grasp the warmth of his neck and pull him closer.

His fingers squeezed on her shoulders, digging into the soft flesh beneath her clothing. He held on to her possessively, as if she were something too precious to let go. In response, her fingers meshed into the length of his black hair, holding his head, and clinging to him as if he were her nourishment. The kiss deepened, their tongues met, played, and sought. The taste and thrill of his mouth on hers was exciting.

Brina forgot everything but his touch until slowly he raised his head and looked down into her eyes with a penetrating gaze that left her dizzy.

On a ragged breath with a raspy voice, he whispered, "I don't know if I can change, Mrs. Feld. What do you think?"

For reasons she had no desire to contemplate, she couldn't answer. After their kisses, she wasn't sure she wanted him to change. She had no doubts about not wanting to marry him, but his kisses—yes. She could quite happily endure every one.

# Chapter 10

Zane walked through the front door of the earl's home shedding his outer clothing and stopped suddenly.

What was he thinking? It was his home now. He was the earl. Not his uncle, nor his uncle's son, nor his older cousin. But him. They were all gone.

*Damnation!*

Why had all three of them been riding in the same carriage together that day anyway? Why hadn't someone inspected the damned bridge over the canyon since there'd been weeks of torrential rain? Didn't they know he was ill-prepared to take over for them?

He wasn't supposed to be the earl.

Zane rubbed his hand across the back of his neck. He needed a drink.

Huffing another silent curse of frustration, he felt something, reached into his pocket, and pulled out the book of poetry Mrs. Feld had given him. He scoffed a laugh and wondered if she would take him to task if she knew he was swearing like the devil in his thoughts.

Probably.

He laid the book on the side table but then picked it up. The corners were worn. She'd read it often. Maybe he'd give it a try. After all, he had pursued her in an ungentlemanly manner. Consciously, maybe even willfully. She hadn't deserved it, but he wasn't sorry he had done it.

In return she'd given as good as she got.

She was uncommonly headstrong for someone who had the look of a fragile night fairy with her glistening blond hair, big bright eyes, and fair, delicate-looking skin.

He hadn't planned to kiss her in the park, but it was a damned good thing he'd thought to exempt kissing. She'd been particular with the rules set forth. Her passion had been just as strong when in his arms as it had been when she laid out her demands for acceptance of his proposal. He had no doubt that she would claim victory if he so much as sniffed a brandy, and that strength challenged him to be stronger. That passion inside her was what drew him. He'd sensed it that night in the chateau, and ever since he'd wanted to taste her lips once more.

For the better part of half an hour during the afternoon, he'd watched her be composed and measured in everything she said at the park. Her beautiful lips smiling at him, her graceful hands had laid clasped in repose on her lap. She'd been the personification of everything he'd heard about her. Kissing her had awakened an aching need inside him that he still carried.

After dropping his great coat, hat, and gloves onto a chair in the entryway, he slid his scarf from around his neck and gathered the center of it into his hands to press into his face. The flowery scent of her perfume had held in the wool, teasing him with her fragrance.

He inhaled again, deeper, letting the memory of her in his arms wash slowly through him. It had an eager, rousing effect on him.

Thoughts of her sparkling eyes, the wind grabbing at strands of her hair and blowing it across her soft cheeks drifted pleasantly through his mind before suddenly he remembered how still she'd become when he mentioned her husband.

His question had surprised her.

It had surprised Zane too.

There was no reason to ask about him other than it had suddenly crossed his mind she might be thinking about him when she mentioned the chocolate. Plenty of men and women added a dash of brandy in the sweet liquid. Evidently, she hadn't been thinking of her husband. That pleased Zane, but he wondered if she always looked as if she was barely holding back tears when she spoke of him, or if it was only that Zane so unexpectedly asked about him. That couldn't have been easy for her, yet she'd handled his surprising question well.

The tragedy of becoming a widow must have changed her to some degree. He wondered what she was like before that happened. She hadn't been ready to talk about Mr. Feld with him. Without her doing that, he couldn't get an idea of how deep her wounds of loss were now that time had passed. He wanted to know, even though he was very sure of one thing—it made no difference to him. It was to her credit that five years after Mr. Feld's death, she still was moved by talking about him. That she had great respect for him was evident. That was one more thing to admire about her.

He also knew Mrs. Feld wasn't indifferent to his touch. It was who she was today that had him caught in her un-intended snare. How could he not be drawn to a lady who had stayed respectful of her husband's memory, wanted to teach girls the beautiful art of painting, and helped nuns take care of unfortunate people?

Zane closed his eyes, letting the memory of her fill him again. His mind drifted back to their kiss and the feel and taste of her cool, enticing lips beneath his. Her hands had moved with hunger up his chest before they settled in womanly comfort around his neck. Their lingering kiss in the park had proven what he'd known since Paris and she had to believe now as well. She was as attracted to him as he was to her. So, to her question he never answered, hell, no. He didn't want to stop being bad. He wanted to tumble her onto the bed and press—

Multiple footfalls and the familiar tapping of Uncle Hector's cane sounded down the corridor. Zane looked up to see his uncles Syl and Hector coming toward him at a jaunty pace.

"There you are," Uncle Sylvester called. "Finally home, I see."

"How did it go?" Hector asked in a jovial tone as he stopped in front of Zane and leaned on his cane.

"Was she cordial?" Sylvester echoed with an enthusiasm he didn't try to keep hidden either.

Zane blinked. "What are you—were you two waiting here for me to return?"

"Of course," Uncle Syl replied. "You didn't expect us to leave, did you?"

Zane's eyes narrowed and he frowned. "Yes, I did."

These two men were unbelievable. Their counsel with the family and helping him learn the affairs of his estates were appreciated. He really did need their help with those things, but sometimes they were a bit overwhelming. He didn't need them playing the role of nursemaid.

Sylvester pressed his hands down the sides of his coat and took a proud stance. "How would we find out how your afternoon went if we'd gone home?"

"You wouldn't," Zane argued.

"That's what we thought, so considered it best we stay in case there was anything we could help with."

"Tell us all about it," Uncle Hector encouraged.

"No," Zane said in a rather forceful tone. "I have no intentions of sharing anything of my afternoon with Mrs. Feld with you two or anyone else."

His uncles glanced at each other as if they were facing a grave situation they didn't know how to handle before centering their attention back to their nephew.

"I take it that means it didn't go well." Hector emphasized his words with a sudden hard rap of his cane to the floor.

It went very well, Zane thought, but felt no inclination to satisfy these two ninny grumps.

"He probably didn't watch his language as closely as he should have," Uncle Syl offered. "Ladies don't like to be spoken to in an ungentlemanly manner."

"That's difficult for most of us on occasion," Hector supplied. "But we learn to do it."

"I suppose it will take time," his brother mumbled quietly as if he didn't want Zane to hear him. "We may be expecting too much, too soon."

"Did she at least enjoy the ride in the new curricle your uncle had built last winter?"

That caught Zane's interest. "The earl has a new carriage?"

"Yes," Uncle Syl informed him. "Quite a pricey one from what I heard. I'm not sure he had it out more than a time or two before the winter weather took a turn for the worse."

"Why haven't you told me about this before now?"

Hector and Sylvester looked at each other. It appeared neither of them had thought to mention what was by all accounts considered a younger man's transportation and something Zane would want to know about.

"We've had more important matters to discuss with you than a sporting carriage," Syl argued.

Zane would make sure to take it out for a jaunt first thing tomorrow morning—before his uncles arrived.

"This afternoon with Mrs. Feld is in the past," Hector continued in a disappointed tone. "Nothing to do about that now. Best to move forward and do better. What dinner party will the two of you be attending tonight?"

"What do you mean?" Zane questioned.

"It's the Season, my lord," Uncle Syl said in an irritated tone where Hector left off. "There are several parties in Mayfair and other places about Town. Didn't you arrange to meet with Mrs. Feld at one of them—at a certain time?"

"No." Tonight hadn't crossed his mind. He'd been too busy taking pleasure in the afternoon. Their conversation, their kiss, and the way his kiss had caused her cheeks to flush as she melted against his chest.

Uncle Hector's cane made another sharp click on the floor. His gray, full eyebrows seemed to grow together tightly right before Zane's eyes. "Then how will you know where she will be and at what time, so you can be there as well? If you are going to pursue her, my lord, you must *pursue* her."

Tension started in the back of Zane's neck.

Sylvester made a motion with his hands as if to calm the more excitable Hector. "Don't get too riled about this. It's easy enough to remedy. He can send over a note to her and ask where she plans to be at half past nine and meet her there."

"It's a bit late in the day for that. She may not answer him now that he didn't ask her at the proper time."

"No, no. It's not." Uncle Syl looked at Zane. "I know about these things. I'll help you compose the note. I'm quite eloquent on occasions like this."

This was maddening. Uncle Syl had never married. How could he know what to say to a lady? The only thing Zane wanted to do was pour himself a glass of claret, relax by the warm, crackling fire in his book room, and reminisce on the afternoon with Mrs. Feld. Thinking about her was certainly much more pleasant than listening to his uncles blather or reflect on their priorities.

Making the circle of parties during the Season wasn't something Zane had ever cared to do. Which was why he'd never spent much time doing it. He didn't see the sense of playing this game with Mrs. Feld. She was a widow after all. Not an innocent maiden who always had to be guarded. If he wanted to see her, why couldn't he just go to her house and spend an evening with her?

Because of rules, manners, and Society's strict code of acceptable behavior. Blast them all.

His uncles continued to look at him, waiting for a response. "I will figure out something for later in the week."

"Later?" Hector exclaimed as his chin bobbed and the cane tapped. "You have four weeks to win her hand, and you are talking about later?"

"I will pursue Mrs. Feld in my own way, Uncles. I need no instructions or rules from either of you on that. She has already given me enough to follow. Now, have Fulton get your coats and go home. We are through for the day."

"Yes, yes, we're going," Uncle Syl said, once again giving his brother the signal to be calmer. "Before we do, I wanted to tell you that a friend of yours, Mr. Robins, dropped by to see you."

"Harry was here? Did you entertain one of my guests?"

"No, not at all. Naturally, when we heard someone at the door, we came out of the book room, thinking it might be you. At that point, we had to speak to him, but he decided not to wait when he found out we were already waiting."

That was best, Zane thought. Harry wasn't the kind of man who would find favor with his uncles. Nor them with him.

"He was kind enough to tell us what he wanted."

Zane couldn't believe what he was hearing. "Did you ask him?"

"Not exactly," Syl said, his brow rising.

"What someone wants with me and why they come to my door is none of your business," Zane said in a tone that would have let an ordinary man know he had stepped over the line. He couldn't be sure these two would understand.

"Oh, we couldn't agree more," Uncle Syl agreed with so much pride, his chest puffed. "But we are happy he relayed to us that the bets at White's are up tenfold today."

"But unfortunately, not in your favor it seems," Uncle Hector added. "Hardly anyone thinks you will win Mrs. Feld's hand. We expected that but are pleased everyone wants a stake in the outcome of your wager."

Zane shook his head. Not only did he have to deal with these two, it seemed as if he'd become both an earl and a saint almost overnight. If not for Mrs. Feld's requirements, he'd be swearing like a drunken idiot and downing all the liquor he could get his hands on.

Out of the corner of his eye, Zane saw movement down the hallway. "Fulton," he called. "My uncles are leaving. Get their coats."

"Yes, yes, of course, we're on our way," Uncle Sylvester remarked, pulling down on the lapels of his stylish tweed coat. "We have things to do. But one more thing before we go. Did you consider whether you'll grant your cousin Pelroy the right to build a home on the south end of Blacknight? He only wants a small cottage by the stream that runs through that hollow."

"No," Zane answered irritably. "You made the request this morning. As I told you and all the family a few nights ago, I'd rather know all that I'm in charge of before I start giving grants away. Everyone keeps what allowances they have, but that's all I'm willing to do for now."

"In that case, I'll tell him it's still under consideration. And what about Ivan?" Uncle Hector continued as if Zane hadn't said what he'd just said.

Zane searched his memory for someone in the family named Ivan and came up blank. "I'll let you know later."

"Yes, do. Your aunt Beatrice would appreciate it if you'd see fit to buy him a commission in the army."

Now, Zane remembered. Ivan wasn't a Browning. He was Hector's wife's sister's son. All these requests could make a strong, stable man stumble. How would he keep them all straight? He would find a way, and Zane would grant his aunt's wish. He wanted to help any man ready to take up arms and fight for England. "I'll set time aside in the coming days to go over all the requests."

"Fair enough," Sylvester answered. "There will probably be more later in the week. Now, we'll see you tomorrow morning. Bright and early as usual."

"I wouldn't have it any other way," Zane murmured tightly.

Leaving his butler to see his uncles out, Zane strode toward the book room. The tapping of Hector's cane echoed down the corridor. He didn't know if it was his uncles' unwanted presence when he'd returned or the need for a drink that gave him a headache.

Rounding the doorway, he saw the mountain of ledgers still on his desk as he'd left them. A fire burned. The room was warm, quiet. What he really wanted to do was have a drink. A quick one followed by a long one, and then pick up his coat and gloves and head out to his club for a game of cards.

But he'd promised the prim widow he wouldn't. He was going to play by her rules if it killed him.

He wanted to forget the stack of ledgers, forget about the fact that he was now the earl. That it was his responsibility to consider and answer when his family wanted something.

Damnation, he didn't want to do it.

Life had prepared him to be a gamester not an earl. Which suddenly reminded him to write a note to Lord Lyonwood regretting that he would not be joining his card club. He would have thoroughly relished the chance to sit around the table and match skills with any one of the men in that circle.

He supposed he'd have to do some things the way Mrs. Feld, Society, and his uncles expected him to. But he didn't have to like it, and it sure as hell wouldn't keep him from wishing he had his old life back.

Zane seated himself behind the desk, determined to put his nose into the account ledgers and keep his uncles and Mrs. Feld off his mind. He wanted to concentrate only on what was before him—the Blacknight earldom and all its entities.

Later, obviously much later, Zane rose from the desk to stretch. Sometime during the late afternoon he had shed his coat and Fulton had come in to light the lamps and stoke the fire. Without thinking, he walked over to the side table and started to pour himself a nip of the expensive brandy that had been poured into the decanter yesterday. But as his hand reached for it, he remembered his promise.

*No drink.*

He slowly and with great reluctance withdrew his hand. It had taken a strong will for her to have the nerve to challenge his way of life, and she did so only because she didn't think he could change. She'd said as much. She expected him to fail and have that drink. And she had good reason to believe that. He wanted a drink desperately. But difficult as it would be, he had to match that iron will of hers and show her he could keep his commitment. He turned away from the brandy.

Only a day had passed and already he knew it wasn't going to be easy living up to Mrs. Feld's standards. Long-developed habits were difficult to break.

What was he to do tonight? Spend it watching others play. He could do it; though, as he found out last night, it wasn't as enticing as it used to be when he was young and eager to learn all he could about cards and billiards. Blast it, Hector was right. He should have asked Mrs. Feld which parties she would be attending and planned to meet her.

Zane walked over to the window and looked out. Through the tops of the trees and tall yew hedge a few lights flickered from windows of his neighbors' houses. The twinkling sparkle reminded him of Mrs. Fe— Brina's eyes.

Yes, he liked thinking of her as Brina. She wasn't a Mrs. anymore. As she had so reverently pointed out, there wasn't a Mr. Feld. She wasn't married.

"Excuse me, my lord."

"Yes, Fulton?"

"Mr. Robert Browning is here and wanted to know if you were available to see him."

"Yes, tell him to join me."

Zane didn't know if he'd ever get used to the formality of being an earl. But he would try. For the family. He'd never minded Robert seeing him in a casual state when they were in Paris or Vienna, but things were different now. Zane strode over to the corner of the desk, picked up the coat he'd discarded earlier, and was stuffing his arms into the sleeves when Robert walked in.

The strapping twenty-two-year old man with a head full of dark-brown hair and laughing eyes stopped and bowed. "My lord. How gracious of you to receive me without benefit of a prior appointment."

Zane acknowledged him with a smile and they both laughed. Standing on ceremony with his cousin after all the time spent together wouldn't happen anytime soon. They'd been too at ease with each other during their travels. In the meantime, it was good to know someone in the family was all right with him still being Zane.

"It looks as if you are settling into your new role as earl quite well," Robert offered.

"I'm adjusting, and glad you stopped by." Zane leaned a hip against his desk and pointed toward a chair. "Sit down."

"Thank you, but I wasn't going to stay long. I know how busy you are. I overheard Father telling Mama that you had a lot to learn—well, yes, I will sit, but only for a minute."

"Don't get nervous, Robert. I know what your father is saying about me. Hector is not a shy man. Especially not with me."

"No, he isn't," his cousin answered as he made himself comfortable in the upholstered chair. "In case you haven't heard, I wanted to let you know that wagers similar to the one at White's concerning you and Mrs. Feld are being made in other clubs in London."

"No," Zane muttered with no small amount of interest. "I hadn't heard that."

Making a wager in the prestigious White's was one thing—a gentleman's right. He hadn't expected the wager would become commonplace and Brina's name would be bandied about other clubs and gaming houses in Town. He hadn't thought through all the ramifications of his ploy before he'd acted on it. And Brina's deed, with all her conditions for him, was bound to have had an impact on what was happening too.

Not that he blamed her for anything she'd done. He admired her for fighting back. He did take issue with how clever her tactics were.

"I've been introduced to her, but I can't say I know her. She's quite beautiful."

*She is stunning.*

"Another reason I stopped by is that I was hoping you could spare me another one hundred pounds. There's a game at the Brass Bull that Harper and I have been invited to join tonight. My pockets are too light right now to get into the first game."

Robert's words disturbed Zane. "You don't need to be involved in high stakes games at your age or because of the amount of your allowance."

"I've been assured the games won't be steep initially, but of course, it really depends on the number who join. But Mr. Remick wants to make sure we can cover bets."

"And Harper?"

"His pockets have always been plumper than mine. He's an only child and his father has been generous. I think his uncle—Mrs. Feld's father—helps him from time to time as well."

That would follow what Brina said about her father asking her to keep an eye on Harper. "Is he a good player?"

"I'd say we are even."

"Good," Zane said and looked at his affable cousin. He liked the cheeky lad, but they were home now. Robert was Hector's responsibility. "I gave you an extra hundred at the family dinner last week. You should still have more than enough to see you by until your allowance releases again."

"I know." He moved to the edge of his seat. "And I don't want you to think I'm not grateful for your generosity. I am. All it takes is a few bad hands to get behind. You know that. Either luck is with you or she isn't. It's only a matter of time before my fortune turns bright again."

Zane regarded Robert more carefully. One of the first rules of gaming that he tried to instill in his cousin was that sometimes fortune didn't return. Some people were not meant to be gamesters. A hand or two of cards after a dinner party or on a rainy afternoon at one of his clubs was all the playing some gentlemen needed to do. He was thinking his cousin might be that type person.

When Robert arrived unannounced in Paris, Zane hadn't expected or wanted to become the young man's caretaker, but out of respect for Hector, he had taken him under his protection and started schooling him in the games. It appeared his cousin wanted to keep it that way, even though he was under his father's roof again. Robert was studious at times, but more often than not, he was given to bouts of imprudent, impulsive gambling rather than taking it slow, steady, and judicious. At the time, it had suited Zane to tutor him and keep him out of trouble, which he found out included matrimony.

Zane had no other pressing priorities during his travels.

Now he had too many. He would never again have the carefree life he lived before he became the earl. And he was finding out that he no longer had the patience, time, or the inclination for such tutelage. Robert was going to have to understand and rely on Hector for fatherly advice and extra funds.

"I've tried to explain to you how important it is to get out of a game before you lose all you have," Zane stated, trying not to sound as if he were giving a lecture. "You always save enough to play for another day. That's how you learn to be good at gambling. Remember we talked about when your money runs low, you go."

"I know." Robert's expression was sincere. "I remember everything you taught me. A gamester shouldn't hesitate. He needs to know how and which card to play as soon as it hits his hands. I do try to gain skill and play your way every time, but so often, it seems what I have becomes less and less each night until it's gone."

"We went over this when we were in Vienna. You either get better at remembering the cards that have been played, how to use what you have, or you don't play as often or as deep."

"I do," he said convincingly. "If you'll let me have a hundred for tonight, I promise I'll be more careful with it. I'm sure it was the excitement of being back in London with old friends. I wasn't giving enough attention to the game."

Zane considered Robert's request. Unlike the night with all his family members asking for favors, this was something his cousin would have asked whether or not Zane was the earl. Money wasn't something Zane had ever had to worry about. In addition to the allowance from the previous earl, Zane's grandfather on his mother's side had left him an inheritance that had served him well over the years, and he'd never abused income from it.

"This is what I'm going to do. I'll loan you the money. No more handouts. A man, no matter his station in life, needs to gamble with his own money and pay his own debts. So, consider this another lesson in how the game is played. The money will have to be repaid, and there will be no more forthcoming. Do we understand each other on this?"

"Yes, of course and I agree." He nodded, rose, and looked as if he'd walk away without saying more but suddenly turned back. "It's just that sometimes it's difficult to leave the table. Especially when there is something on top of it that you want, and you think you can win it all with one more shot. It's hard to walk away."

Zane knew exactly what Robert was saying but wasn't thinking about cards. His cousin's words brought Brina to his mind. She was the treasure he was trying to win, and he had to be as clever with her as he was expecting Robert to be with cards.

The most important thing he had to remember was Brina expected him to fail.

# Chapter 11

The décor of the small town house was opulent from the floors to ceilings. Grand crystal chandeliers hung in every room. Every piece of gilt fretwork and carved moldings were exquisite in detail and style. Rich colors of velvet draperies graced the frames of all the windows. The cushions on the settees and chairs displayed the finest fabrics with classic English floral patterns and scenes.

Brina knew the home well. The hostesses for the evening had been her parents' neighbors all her life. She'd been welcomed into their home many times.

So had numerous other guests present at the soiree. The well-designed drawing room was packed with people, including a cellist and violinist who had been squeezed into a tight corner by the pianoforte. The chatter and laughter of the crowd often drowned out the beautiful music they were playing. No one seemed to notice. It was a party, and everyone was delighting in the merriment of the Season.

A buffet that looked as if it had been set for the Prince was in the dining room. Brina had only seen it as she passed in front of the open double doors. She hadn't made it inside to sample any of the delicacies splendidly arranged on the white linen–draped table. There was always someone to distract her with conversation.

Adeline and Lyon had picked her up for the party, and as soon as she entered, Julia joined them, but so did a host of other ladies all wanting to know how she was managing after her showdown with the new earl. She kept all her answers short and as vague as possible, insisting she was doing extremely well and not letting any of the machinations of the past few days hinder her from her work. The surprising thing was that most of them seemed to believe her.

One by one the ladies started drifting away, including Adeline and Julia when the handsome Mr. Inwood came up to talk to Brina. They had found other people to converse with on the other side of the room.

Currently Brina had three handsome bachelors standing in front of her, vying for attention, making it clear they now considered her eligible to pursue. It was her fault, of course. She had opened the door to such attention by agreeing Lord Blacknight could call on her. Now, apparently every man thought he should be given equal opportunity to win her hand. Like her, none of them expected the earl to adhere to all her demands. Even the younger bachelors were trying to woo her. Brina wasn't attracted to any of them.

It was a bit disconcerting to have heard tonight that in addition to Blacknight's wager at White's, many side bets were being arranged in gaming hells all over Town and private wagers among friends too. Brina consid-ered all of it madness of the highest order. It was as if a raging fire had swept through the ton and there was no water to put it out.

The earl certainly knew how to get her attention and everyone else's.

Unfortunately, she had unwittingly added kindling to the flames. She'd had no definite plans to make any demands on the earl until they started dancing. It must have been the touch of his hands, tilt of his head, or maybe it was the look in his eyes that made her end up giving in to his uncommon, yet persuasive assault to pay her court. Even he kept insisting he only wanted a dance. There wasn't anything she could do about it now but weather the storm and adjust to being pursued.

Not only by the earl but others.

It wasn't that Blacknight didn't need her to help him. He obviously did. He continued to prove he didn't always do the proper thing.

By design, she was sure.

Like bringing horses to her house, and kissing her in the park where anyone could have seen them. Though, she couldn't say she had overly objected much at the time. Oh, who was she kidding? She hadn't objected at all. She'd loved riding the horse and welcomed the kiss with a passion she hadn't thought possible anymore. And she hadn't wanted it to end. So much for her declaration of no women for him—though in truth—at the time she'd said it, she hadn't been thinking of kisses. She was thinking about visits to a mistress for what men pay vis-its to mistresses for.

She felt a sudden uptick in her breathing. It was ridicu-lous. Just thinking about Lord Blacknight had—

"What is your favorite flower, Mrs. Feld?" the tallest of the gentlemen standing with her asked.

Brina blinked for a moment as she stared at his boyish face. "Pink," she answered, trying to return her thoughts to the conversation at hand. "That is to say, any pink flower. I would choose that color over any other in the garden no matter if it were a lily, peony, or rose."

"I shall remember that. It's a color I'm fond of as well. It would look beautiful on you."

Suddenly Brina remembered the revealing pink gown she'd worn in Paris. "Thank you, Mr. Inwood, but I doubt I shall ever wear that color again," she said softly. "I believe it's more suited for ladies much younger than me." She looked over at Adeline and Julia. She could really use their help right now, but neither of them paid her any mind. "However," she continued when the bachelor seemed to expect her to say more, "I saw that flowers have been planted in window boxes on most every street. Have you noticed?"

After that question, the four of them engaged in an extended conversation about the new flowers planted in Hyde and St. James's Parks and various gardens for the upcoming May celebration. While continuing to converse, Brina kept glancing at Adeline and Julia, hoping to give them the signal to come over and give her a reason to excuse herself from the young men. She kept spearing her attention their way. All to no avail. It was as if they were both ignoring her.

She glanced toward the doorway and not the first time since arriving. Right now, she'd even welcome the earl to come and give her a reason to excuse herself.

Finally, deciding she must save herself, she conveniently moved the subject to horses. Something all gentlemen liked to discuss. Within a few seconds, they were robustly discussing a recent midnight horse race down Rotten Row and seemed happy to leave her out of the current conversation.

It was the perfect time to excuse herself, which she happily did and made a straight line to Adeline and Julia, who were standing near the entryway into the sitting room.

"What's wrong with you two?" Brina complained, walking up to her friends. "Couldn't you see I wanted you to politely untangle me from my new admirers?"

"You needed no such thing," Adeline answered with confidence. "You can more than handle all three gentlemen at the same time."

"But we did keep check on you from time to time, in case you required us," Julia added. "We were actually watching the door more and hoping Lord Blacknight would get here in time to see all the beaus crowded around you."

Brina coughed out a light laugh. "What do you mean? I'm not trying to make him jealous. I have no need for him to see me at a party. Have you forgotten? I need him to be at White's tonight playing cards and drinking brandy until dawn. Were that the case, I would know this bargain we've struck is over, and I could return to the peaceful, normal life I expected to have when I returned to London."

"Where is he?" Julia asked.

"I have no idea," Brina answered, not wanting to admit that she had looked at the door more than a time or two, wondering if she might see him. "I haven't heard from him since our ride in the park. We didn't talk about which, if any, parties we'd be attending in the coming days."

After their kiss, Brina hadn't been able to think about anything, so she'd suggested they pack up the basket, get back on the horses for a ride through the park. Which they'd done. Thankfully, he'd decided to be a gentleman and hadn't mentioned the kiss when they'd dismounted in front of her house. She had hoped he wouldn't. But there was no way he hadn't noticed how utterly eager she'd responded to his ardent embrace.

"He has no inkling you are here tonight?"

"I don't know how he could. I chose this dinner because my parents would never forgive me if I hadn't shown up at their neighbors' party." She looked at Adeline and smiled. "Thank you again for letting me come with you and Lyon. It would be tiresome if I were forced to have a constant companion. It's much easier to come with you or Julia."

"One of us will always pick you up and be with you at every party you attend."

"Thank you," Brina said gratefully.

"Which," Julia said, "leads me to ask what you and Lord Blacknight talked about yesterday afternoon?"

Brina didn't know. All she remembered was the glorious kiss that had made her breathless and warmed her all the way down to her toes. Most troubling of all was the way his touch had made her want much more than kisses and caresses from him.

Those feelings she would keep to herself and not share with her friends.

"Many things" was all Brina answered, as she glanced toward the entrance. How could it be that she was watching for the earl, hoping to see him standing there looking for her among the crowd in the room? A week ago, it would have been inconceivable that she would be watching for him or any man. Oh, why did he have to come into her life? She was settled. Happy. Now, she was—eager.

"Was he a gentleman toward you?" Adeline asked.

"Of course not," Brina said without thinking. "Far from it."

Adeline moved closer again and whispered, "What did he do?"

"Did he kiss you?" Julia asked, her eyes growing wide with curiosity.

Brina ignored her probing question and replied, "When he came to my house, he brought horses for us to ride to the park instead of a well-tooled carriage."

Adeline's jaw dropped. "You can't be serious."

Julia grinned with surprise. "You are serious."

"Of course I am," she exclaimed softly, and then glanced around to see if anyone was watching them. "I can't make this up. He did have a proper refreshment basket with him, and I gave him a book of poetry. Blacknight is different. I don't know what to make of him. He's unsettled my life, me. It's no wonder he's had such problems with his family. I'm sure it's because they've never known what to expect from him."

"But he intrigues you," Julia offered as if to finish her thought.

"Yes, he does," Brina said without any hesitancy. "Immensely so. I've admitted that and it distresses me that he does. I simply must stop thinking about him. Or talking about him. So, enough about the earl. I must keep my mind on other things. As I've told you, I want to give the girls art lessons once a week and teach them to paint."

"When did you mention this?" Adeline questioned as her gaze darted over to Julia for confirmation.

Julia's eyebrows rose and she lifted her hands as if to say *I have no idea what she's talking about.*

"Last week when you came over without your sons and Blacknight was there. Maybe I never actually got around to telling you exactly what I had in mind. The earl seemed to take up most of our conversation, but I did say I wanted to do something more with the girls, and both of you said whatever it was, you'd agree."

"I vaguely recollect that," Julia said with a hint of uncertainty in her tone. "But, Brina, it takes time to learn how to paint. Unless one has a natural talent like you, it can be a very frustrating pursuit."

"I know," Brina answered, a bit disappointed Julia wasn't as excited about the prospect as she was. "I think some of them might be gifted. It will be easy enough to tell as time goes on."

"You'll need paints, brushes, aprons, easels for them all. Not to mention that Mrs. Tallon will object strongly to this."

A server holding a tray of champagne offered them a glass, but all three declined. While shaking her head at the man, Brina noticed one of the young bachelors she'd been talking to was watching her. He smiled when she saw him. She returned the greeting and turned away.

With the server gone, Brina continued. "I've thought about all of your concerns, including the headmistress. She won't be happy about it. I'll be gentle with her but make her see things my way. I realize I can't go over and set up an easel and palette for everyone. At first, I'll use my own and my mother's since she is out of town and hasn't painted in years. Anyway, I was hoping the two of you would share your supplies. That will give us four. If I buy another, we'll have one to share between every two girls."

Brina stopped and waited for one of them to say something.

"Of course, we'll be happy to send over our painting materials," Adeline said with a determined smile. "We're in the school together and always will be. Whatever needs to be done we will do."

"Thank you. I've received so many flowers recently, I took some of them to the girls. With Mrs. Tallon and her helpers, we gave them a lesson in flowers. We let the girls gently take the petals off some of the blooms and draw the parts of the flowers on their chalkboards. Doing things like that will help them when they start making flowers to add to dresses, gowns, and capes."

"What an excellent idea," Adeline praised. "I'll see to it my easel and palette are delivered to the school tomorrow."

"I'll do the same," Julia agreed.

"No, not yet. There's no hurry." Brina held up her hands. "I must speak to Mrs. Tallon first."

"You'll be a good teacher, Brina," Adeline said softly. "You let us know what to do and when."

Brina felt compelled to add, "I know it might seem I'm overstepping my boundaries, but I do believe this will be helpful to them in how they choose and blend colors and where to place flowers, beads, and bows. You both have your sons to help keep you busy and content. I need something more to do too."

"Brina, we want you to find happi—"

"No, don't," she said softly, cutting off Julia's words. She then lifted her chin and saw the tall, handsome young bachelor was still looking at her and smiling. The gaiety everyone was feeling showed on their faces and in their noisy chatter. She had long come to terms with the fact that life had to go on after her husband died, but she had to do more with her life than dress for parties and afternoon strolls in the park. Her life had to have more meaning than attending happy social gatherings like this one, and she was determined it would.

Suddenly feeling stronger, she gave her attention back to her friends. "Don't even hint that you are feeling sorry for me, Julia."

"No, I don't," she answered earnestly. "You know that wasn't my intention."

"That's how it sounded. I need no one's sympathy because I'm not unhappy anymore. I have a full life." Brina gave her a faint, indulging smile. "I know you don't understand my need to be of assistance to others. Even the untrainable earl—who I'm determined to make into a better gentleman if it tatters my own reputation."

Julia reached over and touched Brina's hand affectionately. "I will help you give them the lessons."

Brina squeezed her fingertips and smiled. "Never. You are terrible at painting."

The three friends laughed.

"Wait," Adeline suddenly whispered. "Don't either of you glance toward the doorway right now, but I think the Earl of Blacknight just walked into the room."

Brina's pulse raced with anticipation. She turned immediately to look at the doorway.

So did Julia.

"I told you not to look," Adeline grumbled. "Now he will see the three of us staring at him."

Brina's hopes plummeted. "No, it's not him. It's his younger cousin, Robert. They do favor, but then, all the Browning men are tall, have that thick black hair, and are handsome."

"Yes," Julia agreed. "It's not the earl, but he might as well be. Every young lady in the room is gaping at him. I suppose they are thinking if they can't have Blacknight, they'll take his cousin."

"I really felt strange for a moment when you said his name," Brina offered, watching how at ease Robert seemed while saying hello to someone. "I wondered how Blacknight could know I was here with so many other parties being held."

"That's easy enough," Julia suggested with a sheepish smile. "He could have followed you. It wouldn't be the first time a gentleman behaved in such an ungentlemanly manner in order to know where a certain young lady might be on a given night."

"Or," Adeline countered, "we could have assumed it was a lucky guess. Lyon says he's considered lucky with cards."

"Garrett told me that as well," Julia injected. "He tells me the earl's skill is unmatched when playing. Maybe he's fortunate in everything else too."

Adeline nodded. "Gentlemen consider it an honor to play with him and against him. In fact, Lyon invited him to join his weekly card game but now that he can't gamb—" She stopped and her golden-brown eyes zeroed in on Brina's.

An odd feeling washed over Brina. "Lyon asked him to join his club?"

"Yes. But he won't be joining. He sent Lyon a note saying it wasn't a convenient time for him to participate."

"Adeline," Brina asked, suddenly a little suspicious of her friends' motives, wondering if they felt the need to watch over her concerning the earl. "Did you ask Lyon to invite Lord Blacknight to be a member of his club so Lyon could keep an eye on him?"

"Absolutely not," Adeline admonished. "I would never do that. First and foremost, I'd never try to interfere with Lyon's card club in any way. Second, if I were going to do anything of the kind, I would tell you. Lyon invited Lord Blacknight because his skill at cards is legendary and most gentlemen would pay for the chance to play with him."

"Oh, I should have known you wouldn't do anything like that." Brina shook her head in bafflement. "I don't know why I'm so prickly concerning him. The earl keeps me bristling with emotions I've not wanted to deal with for years. I don't even want to think about the man, but I do."

"We understand," Julia insisted softly. "It must be hard for someone as self-possessed as you are, but why don't you face the fact that he appeals to you, and delight in it rather than fighting it?"

Brina glanced over to the young and handsome Mr. Inwood. There were no butterflies in her stomach, nor tightness in her chest or throat at the sight of him. But always with the earl, she found it difficult to catch her breath.

"I never thought to look at another man with interest. It's perplexing."

"And I have no doubt you have confounded him," Adeline offered with a smile. "What gentleman wants to give up his cards or his wine?"

"Or his women?" Julia added with a satisfied smile. "I thought that was brilliant."

"Indeed! It was superb," Adeline agreed with a laugh.

"Four weeks is a long time for a man to be so saintly. I couldn't believe you were being so bold."

"I surprised myself," Brina said honestly. "But once we started talking, the words came tumbling out and the demands got more personal. I truly expected he was going to say no, but he kept saying yes."

"Once you got started, you didn't stop, and it was so satisfying for us to see you getting the upper hand," Julia told her. "You are usually too worried about being good to ever do anything so bad."

"I know," Brina said with a laugh, shaking her head again. "I kept thinking he was going to say, 'Enough of this! Forget the whole idea!' and give up on courting me. I wasn't making it easy on him, but he agreed to everything. Once I made the demands, I couldn't back down."

"And you shouldn't have."

"Right," Adeline agreed. "If a man wants to marry you, there's nothing wrong with making him work to win your hand."

*Marry him.*

"You know I don't want to marry," she said honestly. She probably should have added that she was definitely conflicted about him too. But how much did she want to share with her friends? Especially when she wasn't sure what exactly she was feeling and certainly not why she was feeling it.

"But you wouldn't mind having him as a lover," Julia stated as if it were already a settled fact between them.

Brina opened her mouth to agree, but stopped when she saw Harper enter the room. If she hadn't been so busy thinking about the earl, she would have wondered if he had come when she saw Blacknight's cousin. "Excuse me, I saw Harper come in, and I'd like to speak to him before he gets caught up with all the beautiful young ladies here."

"Are you really going to brush us off just when the conversation was getting so interesting?" Julia asked.

"I fear I am, but only for now. Not forever. We will speak of this again later in the evening."

With those parting words, Brina headed toward the entryway. Harper saw her, gave her a big smile, and started walking to meet her.

Harper Tabor was the kind of young man who walked into the room with a light step and friendly expression. Wherever he went, he always had the look about him as if he expected something wonderful to happen and he was going to be a part of it. His step was lively and sure, and his eyes were always full of warmth. He was of average height for a man, clean-shaven, and thin. Light sandy-brown hair was combed away from his face and fell above his collar in an attractive wave. He'd inherited the family trait of big blue eyes.

"Harper," Brina said with a beam of happiness she

didn't try to contain. "It's so good to see you. I'm sorry I was out when you called on me yesterday. How have you been?"

"I'm well," he answered, and gave her a cousinly kiss on each cheek. "You get lovelier every time I see you. How do you do it?"

Brina smiled at his flattering comment and couldn't help but give his lip and chin a good once over. All signs of bruising were gone. "And I think you are more charming every time I see you."

"No," he said with a twinkle in his eyes. "I'm only hoping for an invitation to dinner one night this week."

Brina laughed. "Consider yourself invited. I should have done so already, and I had plans to, but—" But she'd had the unexpected nuisance of the earl to think about and require her attention. "Why don't you come late tomorrow evening and we'll have supper together."

After a brief hesitation, he responded, "Tomorrow's probably not good, cousin, but I will make it soon. I promised your parents I'd check on you while they are out of Town, and I will."

"Did you?" she asked with a feeling of delight. "Papa asked me to keep in touch with you. I don't know how you feel, but I need no one checking on me, Harper. A pleasant visit will do."

He nodded. "Same for me and we'll do that soon."

"Why didn't you go with my parents to see your mother? It would have been the perfect opportunity. I'm sure she misses you."

"And I miss her, but I don't want to leave London right now." His gaze drifted from hers and scanned the room before he thoughtfully added, "I've left the nest, as they say. I'll go, but not until summer comes around or perhaps I'll even wait until autumn. It will do the sisters good to have some time together, don't you think? If I were there, Mum would want to divide her attention between the two of us. Besides, I didn't want to miss the Season. So many new people are in Town."

"And I see two beautiful belles huddled together looking at you right now and wishing you were speaking to them and not me."

He looked over at them, smiled, and nodded a couple of times. "They are lovely, aren't they? I know the Season is for making a match, but I'm not wanting to do that this year. Best I stay away from the ladies. But what of you? The reason I stopped by yesterday was to see how you are bearing the scandal Lord Blacknight brought to your door. You certainly don't seem as if it's gotten you down. You look splendid."

She saw sincerity in his expression and it warmed her. "I'm managing well. Thank you for asking, Harper."

His eyes engaged with hers. "You do know you can call on me if you need to."

"I do, but there hasn't been anything the earl has said or done that I can't—" Brina's words fell away as she thought for a split second the Earl of Blacknight had come up beside Harper.

"You remember my friend Robert Browning, don't you?" Harper asked.

Robert was probably as tall as Blacknight but thinner through the chest and shoulders as was the usual case with younger men. His hair was as dark as the earl's, and there was no doubt he had the same handsome features.

"Yes, of course I do. How are you, Mr. Browning?"

"Well, Mrs. Feld," he said with a smile. "You always look so lovely and especially tonight."

Brina could tell both Harper and Lord Blacknight's

cousin had been taught the art of flattery. She returned his smile and said, "That's kind of you to say."

"I was visiting Lord Blacknight recently, but I didn't stay long. He seemed busy. There were books and papers all over his desk." "Have you seen him tonight?"

"No." She smiled again, deciding not to say more than her one-word answer.

"Perhaps we'll see him somewhere later in the evening," Mr. Browning offered.

"Brina," Harper said, "Robert and I are going to have something to eat before we go. Would you like to join us?"

"Go? You just arrived."

"I know. We've said hello to most everyone. Come dine with us. It will give us time to chat and give Robert a chance to get to know you."

"Yes, do, Mrs. Feld," Mr. Browning encouraged, his smile as genuine as Harper's.

"Well, yes, I will. I'm surprised you don't intend to stay and visit with—everyone. Your hosts and all the young ladies. I didn't expect you'd rush away."

"We must tonight." He glanced at Robert. "We have a card game and don't want to be late."

"Cards?" she queried.

"Yes," Mr. Browning answered for Harper. "I was introduced to a gentleman who's starting a new club. We want to play a few hands and see if we think it's one we might be interested in joining."

"Terribly rude of us to eat and run, I know," Harper said. "We're hoping to slip out without anyone noticing."

Harper politely held out his arm to escort her into the dining room. Brina smiled and hooked her hand around his elbow.

Men and their cards. There was something about the

two of them that made her uneasy. She couldn't imagine what it could be. But something had her thinking that not all was quite right. And she wasn't so sure Harper should be spending so much time with the earl's cousin.

# Chapter 12

Brina decided to forgo bonnet and cape since the school was only a short distance away. The midday sun was shining down, and that, along with her simple long-sleeved, dark-gray dress, warmed her aplenty for no longer than she planned to be out of the house.

She walked out the back door, down the steps, and into the small portion of garden that separated her house from the three-story building that used to be a servants' quarters. There was no intricate lattice work or fancy outside moldings on it. Only a plain sign over the door that read THE SEAFARER'S SCHOOL FOR GIRLS. A few paces later, she came to the tall yew hedge that served as a boundary on both sides of the house. In the middle of the shrubbery was a vine-covered trellis that had been built so the servants could easily come and go from the main house. The archway now served as entrance to the grounds of the school.

Finding such a perfect property had been a dream

come true for Brina, Adeline, and Julia four years ago. Situated in the middle of a privately secluded cul-de-sac near the business district of St. James's made it valuable. After hearing what they wanted to do, the owner had made it affordable. Now that Brina lived on the grounds, she was convinced they couldn't have found a better place in all of London.

The school started with nine girls. All from families that had lost either a father or brother who worked on the *Salty Dove*. It had taken time for their solicitor to track down eligible girls and explain what the widows wanted to do for them. Persuading their relatives to allow them to come live at a boarding school and be taught to read and write as well as the seamstress trade hadn't been as easy as Brina thought it would be. Boarding schools for girls were rare. Free ones almost nonexistent.

Another child had been added the first year. Little Nora. At only five, she was younger than the other children. Brina, Adeline, and Julia knew they had no choice but to take her in after her mother abandoned her there shortly after the school opened.

Nora was the illegitimate child of Adeline's first husband. There had been numerous attempts to find the girl's mother, but no leads to her whereabouts had been discovered. Their hope was that one day the mother's circumstances would change and she would come back for her child. In the meantime, her daughter was being well-cared for and educated, and would one day be earning her own way in life as a skilled seamstress.

Brina knocked on the door of the school and opened it, calling, "Hello," as she entered.

The ten girls immediately pushed back their chairs from the long rectangular table and rose. So did Mrs. Tallon and her two helpers.

"Good afternoon," Brina said, walking into the large,

square room with enough windows to let in plenty of light. "I hope I'm not interrupting anything too important."

"Not at all, Mrs. Feld," the headmistress said with her usual pinched expression. "Your presence is never a disturbance for us. We welcome you anytime. Say hello, girls."

"Good afternoon, Mrs. Feld. How are you today?" they asked, all speaking together.

Brina beamed as the chorus of greetings echoed around the room. Fanny, one of the oldest students, was always easy to spot with her long, vibrant red hair. Recently, she'd learned how to somewhat tame her unruly curly locks by pulling half of them up and away from her face, tying them at the back of her head with a ribbon. Fanny wasn't tall, but she made up for height in her personality. Unlike the other girls, she was never shy around Brina, always lifting her hand to wave as she said hello. Brina acknowledged her with a slight nod.

"I'm good," she answered the girls. "Thank you for asking. I don't know if you've been outside today, but the sun has chased away the cold wind and the weather has warmed considerably again." They looked at Brina but said nothing, so she added, "I enjoyed hearing you sing this morning. Your voices were pure and enchanting. Angelic. I thought I was listening to a choir in a cathedral."

Ahhs and gasps of surprise sounded around the room. The girls looked at one another and smiled. Brina was glad her compliment pleased them.

"We've continued to work on the flowers you brought us, Mrs. Feld," Fanny said.

"That's wonderful to hear," Brina moved a little closer to the table. "I'll send over some more. One can never have too many flowers to study."

"I drew a beautiful snowdrop yesterday," the tall and thin Mathilda said in an eager voice.

"Did you? How lovely."

"I drew one too," one of the other students chimed in cheerfully. "Mine was bigger."

"But it wasn't as pretty as mine," another girl cut in quickly.

"Yes, it was," Fanny remarked tartly, taking up for her taller, crestfallen friend. "Yours didn't have any leaves on the stem."

"We were told to draw a flower, not leaves," she remarked right back to Fanny, jerking her hands to her waist and sticking out her tongue when she finished.

"I drew a garden of flowers this morning and everyone said mine was the best," Mathilda injected excitedly, seeming not to want to be outdone by any of the other students.

"That's because no one else drew flowers today," one girl added with a high-pitched giggle at the end of her sentence.

Suddenly, in the space of a few seconds, all the girls were talking at once, and Brina couldn't hear one over the other. She hadn't realized how competitive they were.

"Girls," Mrs. Tallon called above their loud, excited chatter. "You can all sit back down now and go back to your work."

Quietness quickly settled over the room once more, except for the sounds of chair legs scraping across the wooden floor.

The headmistress walked over to Brina. The skin around her eyes and forehead had tightened, though her lips formed a smile. "Was there something in particular I could help you with today, Mrs. Feld?" She spoke in a hushed tone. "If so, perhaps we can discuss it outside so as not to hinder the students any longer."

"That's not necessary. I won't be long."

Mrs. Tallon was by no means disrespectful, but Brina felt she was never happy for her to come over and visit the girls. The head mistress had once suggested it might be better if Brina sent a note over and ask Mrs. Tallon to visit her. Brina didn't want to do that. She enjoyed seeing the girls, looking at their happy faces and hearing their voices.

She supposed she could understand why Mrs. Tallon thought she was interrupting their lessons, but Brina didn't want to stop, no matter if Mrs. Tallon wished otherwise. Besides, children needed a break from their studies once in a while. And everyone loved unexpected surprises if they were good ones. She knew the girls liked for her to visit them.

"I wanted you to know that with Lady Lyonwood and Mrs. Stockton's approval, I will be giving the girls painting lessons. I'm not sure of all the details yet."

Mrs. Tallon's smile faded rather quickly. "Painting? I believe that would take up a lot of valuable time, Mrs. Feld."

Brina remained undaunted. "Not really. My plan is to stop reading to them, as I realize most are now reading quite well on their own. So, I won't be disrupting them for that or taking any more time from their usual studies and sewing preparations. The painting will be in place of the reading."

"Yes, of course, Mrs. Feld," she said tightly. "I do thank you for that consideration. As I stated when I came to work at the school, I believe in discipline, decisiveness, and dedication to the art of sewing. If you feel the art of painting will help them achieve my objectives to make them valuable to the community one day, I will yield the time to you for painting lessons."

Brina felt that went easier than she expected until she realized the headmistress wasn't finished.

Mrs. Tallon's lips widened, but there was no pleasure in her smile. "However, I do feel if we find that some of the girls are not inclined to do well with a paintbrush, as many don't, we must allow them to do something else. Just as we've discovered some are better with cutting the fabric and others with the needle, and still others with tying ribbons into a bow and making a shapely rosette."

"I understand, Mrs. Tallon, and think that's a reasonable request. I'll be happy to revisit this if that is the case."

Mrs. Tallon's eyes slowly returned to normal and her expression softened a smidgen.

Brina knew she was supposed to let Mrs. Tallon make all the decisions concerning the school but she needed to help in some way. "I'll be in touch. Don't hesitate to let me know if you need anything."

After saying goodbye to everyone, Brina stepped outside, closed the door, and leaned against it, wondering if it was natural to want to help the girls have a more fulfilled life. Was she interfering more than helping? Was it unusual for her to want them to need her for something? What would she do if she couldn't help them? Brina knew other ladies in Society successfully lived as widows and seemed perfectly happy without needing the satisfaction she received from being with the girls and the sisters.

Brina took in a deep breath, feeling as if she were an interloper in the school. Perhaps she would go visit the sisters at Pilwillow Crossings and take the bandages she rolled last night. It always seemed to cheer her to talk with them. Surely they couldn't receive too many donations to give out to the unfortunate who depended on the abbey's help.

Feeling unsettled by the very real prospects of not actually being needed by anyone, she lifted the hem of her skirt and started down the three steps. As she made it to the bottom, she heard a squeak of metal and looked over at her side gate. A sudden rush of expectancy tightened in her chest and halted her steps.

Blacknight was entering her back garden. But just as quickly, she wondered why. He should be going to her front door and waiting to be announced by her housekeeper if he wanted to see her. Did he think he could break every rule of Society?

Yes, he did.

For today, she didn't mind. Seeing him lifted her spirits and made her forget she was feeling as if no one needed her. She welcomed this unexpected *good* surprise.

# Chapter 13

Trying to tamp down the excitement filling her, Brina took off at a brisk pace and met up with the earl near the trellis. "My lord," she said, hoping she was breathless from her haste and not from the mere fact he'd stopped by. "I'm surprised to see you today and here in my garden."

"Your housekeeper told me you were at the school," he said, taking off his hat and running his hand through his shiny dark hair. "I decided to wait for you. Outside this time."

Brina couldn't stop staring at him. She was still amazed by how handsome he was, amazed how her heart beat faster every time she was near him, and amazed by how easily he evaded acceptable rules and manners.

"A gentleman doesn't wait for a lady to return," she answered, hoping she sounded at least a little annoyed when, really, she wasn't feeling irritation at all. But she should. "He leaves his card or a note as to when he might call again."

Seeming nonplussed by her explanation, he nodded as if he were understanding her but asked, "That's the proper way, is it?"

"Yes, and you must know it," she said with no scolding in her tone. "A gentleman doesn't wait because it might not be a convenient time for the lady to see him. It could turn into an awkward situation when she returns."

The earl kept his gaze on her and a smile curved the corners of his lips. "Do you feel awkward being with me right now?"

She hesitated for only a moment before answering honestly, "Well, no." Seeing him had made her feel better. Wonderful in fact. "I can't say I do."

Blacknight casually crossed his arms over his chest as his lids hooded his eyes enough to make her wonder what he was thinking and feeling.

"Neither do I," he said. "So that rule doesn't apply to us, right? Like kissing doesn't apply."

*Kissing?*

His comment sounded so sincere, it struck a nerve. There seemed to be several things that didn't apply to them. Brina wanted to be upset with him, but try as she might, she simply wasn't able to come up with any annoying feelings. She had been very close to feeling sorry for herself when she stepped out of the school and was glad he'd arrived and put a stop to that useless and weak emotion taking hold.

"Never mind kissing. What would the neighbors think if they saw you walking into my garden?" she asked, feigning irritation.

"That you have a visitor?"

Brina laughed at the truth of his statement and shook

her head as she looked into the depths of his brilliant blue eyes. "It so happens my neighbor across the street has a spyglass and a good friend who is a known gossip. No doubt it will be in tomorrow's edition of some scandal sheet that you were seen walking into my garden unaccompanied by me or anyone else. I'm supposed to be helping you remember your upbringing and how to behave so your family will be comfortable you have changed your rakish ways."

"And you are," he said softly, his gaze sweeping down her face. "You have already helped me with many things."

Her brows rose. "Doubtful."

He chuckled softly. "I want to take you for a ride. In a carriage this time. It seems the former earl recently had a well-sprung curricle built. I've taken it out a couple of times. The horses are well-matched and handle it with uncommon ease. It's warmed since our last outing and the afternoon is pleasant."

Brina hesitated. Not because she wouldn't adore a relaxing afternoon ride in one of the parks or about Town. She would. The day was beautiful. It was the idea of sitting next to him on a carriage seat, feeling the warmth of his body so close, and watching him smile at her that worried her. She hesitated, folded her arms together behind her back, and pretended to study on his invitation, trying hard not to look so eager to go with him.

But she was.

"My uncles, solicitor, and accountants have had me cooped up in my book room for three days. I needed to get out and you were the one I wanted to see. Come with me," he encouraged.

"We can sit in the garden if you don't want to go for a ride, or if you have other plans, we'll do it another time."

He was daring her to allow him to leave. And she should. But, just as when he'd brought horses for them to ride, she couldn't send him away. "No. Of course, I'll go, but a lady needs a proper invitation. I'm not dressed for an outing. I'll need to change my clothing and shoes, and get a—" He was shaking his head. The top of his hair fluttered attractively in the vagrant breeze and his smile was so charming she couldn't finish her sentence.

He stepped closer to her. "You are beautiful as you are. What you're wearing is perfectly acceptable for a ride with me."

His compliment made her feel as if she were glowing. She looked down at her simple day dress. The neckline of the bodice was a respectable height for a widow, but she wore no collar, no jewelry, and no frills of any kind.

Yet, he said she looked beautiful.

"Once you put on your cape," he added, "no one will know if you are wearing a morning dress, carriage dress, or evening dress, will they?"

"I suppose not," she conceded quickly. "I'll get my things and meet you out front." Brina turned and rushed inside.

Less than five minutes later, wearing a black cape, bonnet, and soft cotton gloves, she took the earl's hand so he could help her step into the curricle.

"I have a blanket if you think you need it," he offered, settling his body beside hers.

"Not right now." She knew from their last ride that being next to him would make her warm.

He nodded, and with a light tap of the ribbons on the horses' rumps, a slight jerk, and a familiar rattle of harness, the carriage started rolling down the street lined with cozy houses and perfectly kept lawns. There was something comforting about the familiar sounds of the wheels and harness, the smell of new and old leather, and horses lingering in the air, and there was something infinitely satisfying about sitting beside a man. No, she corrected her thought, sitting beside *this* man.

Mr. Inwood's attention had made her even more aware of how different she felt when she was with the earl. Like it or not, he was the one she was attracted to.

They rode in silence for a few moments before Blacknight looked over at her and asked, "What do you think?"

"Smooth as a hand gliding across silk," she said with a smile. "Your uncle had an excellent carriage built, my lord." Almost as soon as the words were out of her mouth, they hit a bump that startled her. She laughed and added, "If only the roads were as even as the wheels."

He laughed, too, as the horses clopped along. "I am getting used to being called *my lord*, but I'm not sure I'll ever like it."

"I would assume most peers appreciate the respect it shows."

"The problem is that I'm finding it hard to give up a name I've used for close to thirty years."

"Yes," she said. "I know exactly how you feel. Women do it when they marry and take their husband's last name."

He glanced at her and grinned. "I didn't think about it that way, but you're right. However, women don't change their first names and I don't want to change mine. It's difficult that it's not my choice, but I will comply. I will be *my lord* or Blacknight to family, peers, and to the ton, but I want you to call me Zane."

Brina blinked rapidly as she contemplated what that meant, and she felt as if a shield suddenly protected her. She would be giving up some of the distance Society had put between them if she agreed to his suggestion. She didn't need to be that close to him. It was an intimate endearment to call a man by his first name unless he was a family member or childhood friend.

"I couldn't possibly do that. It wouldn't be right."

"Not always," he said in casual tone. "Only when we're alone together." He glanced back to the road as they passed a carriage on the other side. "To others, you will continue to be Mrs. Feld. I'll call you Brina and you call me Zane."

The set of his strong jaw told her he was serious, but how could she possibly agree to something that simply wasn't done? Once a man gained a title, his first name was all but forgotten.

"You go too far, my lord. That would make us too familiar with each other."

"I'm all right with that." He turned toward her again, his expression serious, but not somber. "We can be ourselves with each other. Not a name someone else has given us. No Mrs. No lord. No title for either of us."

Her heart started racing at the thought. As horrific as it seemed, she liked that idea. She didn't want to be Mrs. Feld when she was with him. She wasn't married, yet she was a Mrs. She wanted to be Brina. But how could she agree to something so unacceptable to the elite of Society? Especially when she had promised to do all she could to see that Blacknight handled everything the proper way.

"Are you pondering?" he asked.

"Yes," she answered honestly.

"Fair enough. Think about it. In the meantime, I'll call you Brina."

Her name sounded nice coming from him. Proper or not. She settled more comfortably into the expensive leather-covered cushion and enjoyed the ride for a short time before saying, "You're suspiciously quiet. I hope you're not thinking about more rules you can break."

"I suppose I'll always break a rule once in a while, but I'll be careful which ones I do."

"Be sure that you do," she answered playfully, and then added with a mischievous grin, "I'm watching you."

"So is all of London, it seems," he mumbled under his breath, before turning to look over his shoulder again.

"You might like to know I saw your cousin Robert at a party a couple of nights ago."

"Was he behaving himself?"

"As far as I could tell. He was with Harper again. Both are quite accomplished young men and handle themselves well. They didn't stay very long, which surprised me. Apparently, they were eager to rush through the buffet and get to a card game."

The earl seemed to think on that for a few moments as he looked straight ahead, but for some reason it caused him to frown. "Did either of them happen to say where it was? The game they were joining?"

"No. But they seemed more interested in it than the bevy of young ladies who were there hoping one, if not both, would pay them some notice. Which neither did. They spoke, but I didn't see either one giving the ladies serious attention. It's the Season, and belles want to be courted by such handsome, sought-after gentlemen as they are. Perhaps when you stopped Mr. Browning from marrying in Paris, it put him off romance."

Blacknight shrugged. "It does appear the two friends are more interested in their games right now, but that's not so unusual. All men want to be good at the tables."

Their behavior hadn't seemed normal to Brina. Certainly not Harper's anyway. He'd always flattered the ladies with his cheerful smiles, and he'd never really been into cards and gambling—until he befriended Mr. Browning. For a moment, she thought she might tell the earl that but decided against it. She was sure he didn't want to hear his cousin was a bad influence on hers. Blacknight was probably as fond of his cousin as Brina was of Harper.

When they turned toward the business district of St. James's, the earl glanced at her and said, "Look behind us and tell me if you see a cabriolet in the distance."

She peered over her shoulder nearest Zane and caught the scents of his clean-shaven face and the fine wool coat, and it distracted her for a moment. "Yes. Why do you ask?"

"I saw it out of the corner of my eye when we made the turn. It's the same one that was parked on the street when we left your house."

She huffed a breath of doubt. "How can you know that?"

"A man knows carriages, Brina. Especially ones that aren't well-maintained."

She accepted the simple answer. "Is there something wrong with him falling in line behind us?"

"Not if that is all he's doing."

"Perhaps, like us, he's going nowhere specific and simply riding around to appreciate the lovely day."

"That's unlikely. If I slow down, he does. When I speed up, he does. I'm going to turn at the next street, which will put us going back in the direction we were coming from. Watch and tell me if he does the same."

That had her interest. After they made the turn, she strained her neck to keep looking and suddenly the cabriolet came into sight. "Yes," she said, growing more intrigued by what was happening. "It's still behind us."

Glancing her way, he frowned again and said, "I think we're being followed. I've had that feeling for the past couple of days. I've started watching my surroundings. In addition to spyglasses, as you mentioned, tailing people is one of the ways scandal sheets get the information they publish."

An uneasy feeling stole over Brina. Suddenly, she wanted to scoot closer to Zane and away from prying eyes. She wanted to reach over and lay her hand on his shoulder or his knee, anywhere as long as she felt his strength and comfort. But, if whoever was in that carriage actually followed them, it was best she not move.

"I've heard some people will go to extraordinary lengths to get gossip for their columns," she said, remembering some of the outlandish stories that had been written over the years, such as gentlemen having been seen jumping out of bedroom windows. "It's abhorrent really."

"Men have wagered a lot of money on whether or not you will accept my proposal by the end of the Season," Zane said. "Whether they win or lose depends on what I do or don't do."

"Because of the demands I put on you?"

"No," he said firmly. "You share no blame in this. It started by me making that first wager." He glanced over to her. "You have no need to worry that you are being watched when I'm not with you. It's not you they're worried about."

"You think someone is trying to catch you playing cards, having a sip of wine or—" It was odd and it really should mean nothing to her but she didn't want to think about him being with a woman.

"Yes. All of it. That's the way some men are. Unscrupulous men. It's no longer only the members of White's who have entered into the gaming of the original wager and the one between us. Others have taken them and made their own bets. Some men will either win or lose small fortunes depending on the outcome."

"I heard that too. It's appalling that so many people

are gaming on the outcome of our situation. You'll probably have someone watching you every day now. I didn't think about that."

He smiled. "I can handle the tailing, Brina. It matters not to me that I'm shadowed. But if anyone should start bothering you, I'll have to get involved."

Brina believed he would but really, what could he do?

They rode in silence for a few minutes. Long enough for her thoughts to expand on how outrageous people were being and for apprehensiveness to morph into outrage. She didn't like the idea of anyone invading her privacy. And for their own gain!

*Their privacy.*

She looked over at him and said, "It's true you started this wager, but now we are in it together. The nerve of some gossip-seeking scoundrel wanting to spy on us, no matter the reason, is beyond the pale."

"It could be someone who only wants to write about where we're going and what we're doing. It may not have anything to do with whether or not I take a drink or slip in a hand of cards."

"It's still wrong to spy on us. Speed up and we'll lose him."

Zane glanced at her and gave a questioning grin. "I can't believe you said that. Gentlemen are not supposed to drive fast when a lady is with them."

He was right, of course. She was being quite scandalous for a lady of the ton to suggest such a thing. "No. However, as you and I have established, some rules don't apply to us. Not today anyway. I'm not happy we are being followed."

"You aren't afraid to go fast?"

She thought about that. "No. I don't think so. I can't say I've ever been in a curricle that has been driven very fast. A coach once when Stewart and I were traveling to his brother's estate. We were running late, and he told the driver not to hold the leather. I don't remember it as being frightful."

"Speeding along in this lightweight carriage would be nothing like a fast jostling ride on a coach loaded with people and trunks."

She glanced over her shoulder again. The cabriolet was still behind them. Though he wasn't close, she could see there was only one man in the carriage. His hat and cloak were black, but she couldn't tell much else about him.

Brina gave him a defiant stare for a moment before stating firmly, "Let's lose him, Zane."

He angled his head toward her, his expression pensive. "I like your idea, but it would be too dangerous. Curricles can turn over easily."

"Are you not skillful with them and horses?"

"One of the best," he answered without sounding the least bit boastful.

"Then forget chivalry and let's do it. You are absolved of any responsibility for anything that may happen, Zane."

He seemed to study on that for a moment before sighing and then saying, "It won't be the first time I've done something dangerous. First, you must secure yourself. Feet flat to the floor. Take off your gloves and grab hold of the seat handle and—" He took his elbow and pushed his coat aside. "Grab hold of the waistband of my trousers." He stopped and smiled. "Don't worry. I'll be managing the reins so I'm not likely to accost you."

"That's not what I was thinking," she said, and then added, "I was wondering why I should take off my gloves."

"It's necessary. Your gloves aren't leather. The fabric might slip on the handle causing you to lose your grip. You need a firm, solid hold. Don't be shy. If we're going to do this, we have to do it right and with all caution for your safety."

She quickly took off her gloves, stuffed them into the pocket of her cape, and looked back to him for more instructions.

"One hand on the arm of the seat and with the other, slide your fingers about two inches past my waistband. Make a fist and don't let go for anything. We'll be taking some corners fast. I don't want you to get hurt."

Excitement built inside her. Instead of fleeing down underground tunnels in an old chateau with him, she would be speeding down the streets of London in a carriage with him.

Without further thought, she reached over and lifted the tail of his waistcoat and slid all four of her fingers between his shirt and trousers. His body was firm, lean, and warm as a winter fire. Closing her thumb around the outside of the fabric, she made a tight fist. She then steadied herself with her feet. She realized this was as intimate and as outrageous as calling an earl by his first name. It simply wasn't done. But for some reason, it felt freeing to make the decision to do it anyway.

Zane spread his legs. From the bottom of her hip to her knee, his thigh pressed tightly against hers. His warmth made her want to slip closer to him and snuggle deep into his strong, protective embrace.

His hands squeezed the reins. "Don't let go of me for any reason."

Brina gripped his trousers and the handle tighter and smiled at him. "I'll manage myself. You handle the horses."

"One. Two. Three."

The earl brought the reins down hard and yelled. The curricle lurched, and then jolted violently. She was thrown backward and then forward as the horses took off galloping. Wind whipped her face and tore at her bonnet. The road suddenly became bumpier, at times lifting Brina out of her seat. They came up quickly behind two riders. Zane didn't slow his pace but pulled on the reins and directed the horses around them.

"Slow down, you bloody jug-bitten hell-bounder!" one of the men shouted with his fist raised and pumping in the air.

Brina looked back at him and yelled, "Have some heart, you pickle-head! We're in a hurry!"

She heard Zane laughing and looked at him again. His concentration was on the horses, but he said, "Did you call him a pickle-head?"

Yes. She did. It surprised her too. It was so unlike her to be adventurous in her attitude. Being with Zane had her thinking and doing things she wouldn't have done or said before.

And it all felt natural.

"He deserved it." Brina braved another glance over her shoulder as the curricle raced along. Through the space between the angry riders, she could see the cabriolet. "Faster," she exclaimed excitedly. "He's still chasing us."

"Not for long."

Zane drew back hard on the reins, working them back and forth, pulling hard to the right, slowing the horses quickly. Brina's heart raced. She should have been scared out of her wits, but she was enjoying the bumpy, thrilling contest to escape the person trying to spy on them.

They turned the corner and the horses almost careened into a parked milk wagon. Brina's heart thundered. The action threw her against Zane's shoulder, but she held on as seconds later, she was thrown in the other direction.

She gasped.

Zane paid her no mind but kept his attention on the horses and maneuvered them out of harm's way and sped them up again. In no time, they were galloping fast again, flying past the buildings, more riders, a closed chaise, and a wagon loaded with baskets of vegetables.

"Did he make the turn?" Zane asked, the wind taking away some of his words.

She twisted around to look. "I don't see him—no wait!" Exhilaration bubbled in her chest. "Yes, it's him." The driver's arms were beating up and down as he let the reins slam against his horses. "He's still following. What are we going to do?"

"Don't worry and don't let go!"

Zane guided the horses to the far lane to bypass a mule and wagon and a very important-looking barouche with a fancy family crest on the door. Brina heard more shouts, but the earl paid no mind to them and kept his attention on manning the horses. She decided not to respond to the angry men and break Zane's concentration.

When Brina couldn't see the cabriolet, she started to relax but suddenly a landau pulled into traffic and headed directly toward them. Her heart felt as if it jumped to her throat and was strangling her. The horses' hooves pounded the earth like drums in her ears, the harness sounded as if it rattled deeply in her chest. She squeezed her eyes shut, certain the carriages were going to crash together and kill everyone.

But then Zane's warm leg pressed tighter against her. She felt his solid strength, heard his labored breathing, and sensed his focus and capabilities. A calm settled over her. She opened her eyes and sat upright in the seat again, watching as Zane pushed the horses to go faster and expertly pulled in front of the barouche a moment before they would have collided with the landau's horses.

Both drivers shouted obscenities.

Zane paid them no mind.

Caught up in the excitement, Brina was tempted to hurl insults right back at them, but once again refrained.

They were coming up fast behind a hackney. Zane slowed the horses and took another turn. At the very next street crossing, he took another, and then another. He seemed to know when to let the horses have their head and when to pull tight.

After taking several different roads, they came upon one with no traffic and much smaller buildings. Zane slowed the horses even more as another turn took them into a housing district. Brina loosened her grip on the seat handle and let go of his trousers and flexed her fingers. Her breathing calmed perceptibly, and she started relaxing again.

Zane smiled at her. She smiled too.

She realized that sometime during their wild ride, he'd lost his hat. His dark hair was tousled and wild. Her bonnet had fallen to the back of her shoulders. Her hair must look as windblown as his. She didn't care. She'd had the most stimulating experience of her life. And she didn't know how or why, but it was downright sensual too.

Twisting and turning around, she stared down the long empty street behind them. They had left the populated section of London. She had no idea where they were, but it wasn't near Mayfair or St. James's. The houses were small and farther apart, the lawns not as well-maintained. Rather than tall, crisply cut yew, there were small uneven hedges and fences that needed mending.

"Do you see him?" Zane asked.

"No. I think we lost him."

"I think so too, but best we find a place to park and get out of sight for a while."

He went a little farther and then turned the horses down a tall brush-covered trail and maneuvered them up and over a small slope, coming to a stop under a budding tree. He set the brake and immediately jumped down to check the horses. She watched him pat their necks and check their hooves before climbing back onto the seat beside her.

"Your cheeks are flushed and you're smiling," he offered. "I think you and the horses need a rest."

"How are they?"

He nodded and started taking off his gloves. "Winded, but all right. I'll see they have a good rubdown when I get them back to the stable. I thought you were going to be frightened, but I don't think you ever were."

"Frightened? No. Well, maybe for a few seconds," she answered truthfully, still feeling the intensity and madness of what had happened and very much protected by him too. "The ride was so exhilarating! You were so daring and masterful in the way you handled the horses with strength, yet care for their well-being. They followed your lead perfectly."

He placed his gloves on the seat between them and started untying his neckcloth.

"I've never seen or been a part of anything so unbelievably thrilling."

His gaze stayed on her face. "That's because it's dangerous and shouldn't be attempted often."

He unfastened his collar and loosened his neckcloth. Watching him heated Brina, and she pulled off her bonnet and placed it on top of his gloves.

"I understand now why young men like to race curricles," she said in an exuberant tone.

"It's something most men learn to get good at if they don't want to lose a lot of money or their self-esteem." He gave her a tweak of a grin. "Am I now forgiven for wanting to wait for you to return from the school so you could join me today?"

"Yes, you are," she maintained firmly. "Completely."

Brina continued to assess him. His windswept hair, the brightness of his eyes, and the look of strength in his face drew her. The longer she looked, the more her senses whirled. Tightness bound her chest. Zane's confidence and skill had been incredible.

He was incredible.

Without thinking about what she was doing or why she might be doing it, and despite every ounce of sanity she had, she threw herself into his arms and her lips came down on his with a demand she didn't know she was capable of issuing.

# Chapter 14

The force of her weight knocked Zane back into the corner of the carriage, lifting his feet off the floorboard, though he seemed not to notice. In one swift motion, his legs spread and he caught her between his thighs with a primitive groan. He accepted her hard, eager, and commanding kiss. With ease, his hands slid under her cape, circled her back, and pulled her close, pressing her breasts against the firmness of his powerful chest as if he were trying to bind her to him.

They clung together, his lips as hungry as hers. Neither seeming to get enough. His tongue probed deeply into her mouth over and over again. Their breaths came in ragged little gasps of infinite pleasure.

"Mmm," he whispered against her lips. "I needed to touch and kiss you like this."

Heart-throbbing impatience filled Brina with an eagerness she couldn't ever remember feeling before.

"Why did you make me wait so long?" she asked between deep, searching kisses.

The rumble of his chuckle thrilled her. "I was only waiting for you to let me know you were ready."

Brina leaned her weight onto him when he ran his hands down the sides of her body. Cupping her hips, he shifted his body to fit her softness against his hardness. Her womanhood clinched deliciously. Immense pleasure filled her, and she had no desire to stop what was happening between them.

She intended to relish every moment of it.

Her fingers curled into the fabric of his waistcoat before relaxing and brazenly skimming down the front of his trousers. A breathy, satisfying moan left his throat. Knowing her provocative caresses caused his body to tighten and tremble with need, she touched him again and again.

Their intense, ravenous kisses didn't slow. Neither did their searching caresses. Brina wasn't sure she understood the explosive spirals of sensation shooting through her at alarming speed. These were new to her but wondrous. She couldn't deny herself the exquisite vibrations that had taken control of her senses, her body, and her mind. The ecstasy of what she knew was about to happen between them was shaking her to the core.

It couldn't come fast enough.

Zane's lips left hers, and he kissed over her jaw and down the length of her neck. Gently he pulled on the neckline of her dress and it easily fell off on her shoulder. Her head fell back, and he kissed the small rise of her breast while his hand caressed and fondled it.

They shared every gasp, every moan, and every breath that passed from their lips as they kissed long, deep, and savoring. It pleased her to feel him tremble beneath her searching hands. She loved the way his arms tightened around her possessively as they teased, tasted, and enjoyed this time of being alone with each other to give into and explore the passion between them.

The thrills that swept through Brina were shattering all remembered thoughts of how kisses and caresses in the past had made her feel. Surely if she'd ever experienced this kind of earthly, raw, and heated desire, she would have remembered it.

The pressure of their kisses and touches became harder, deeper, and longer. She pressed her lower body against his, wanting more of him. Zane answered by reaching down and gathering her skirts, pulling them up to her thigh. Her knee came up, knocking her bonnet and his gloves off the seat. With natural ease, his hand slid beneath the soft cotton of her underclothes and his palm outlined the shape of her hips, buttocks, and thighs as they kissed and kissed and kissed again. When his hand moved over to her most womanly part, shivers and sensations of exquisite pleasure soared through her as his light touch pleased her swiftly all the way to a climax.

A whispered moan, a breathy "Yes" escaped past her lips as her body fell, weak and satisfied, against his. She buried her face into his hot, pulsating neck, unable to move.

Zane let go of her dress and caught the back of her head in his hand. His breaths came as deep and hard as hers, though she knew he had not finished what they had started, even though she had. She looked down into his eyes, her heart still beating frantically as she stared at him.

Breathless. Stunned. And more than a little confused that he had not carried through. Her whole being cried out for him to make their union complete. The tension of the moment was still holding him rigid.

"Don't ever think I don't want you," he whispered

huskily, and then winced as he shifted his weight beneath her, proving his words to be true.

Raising her head, Brina swallowed hard. She'd wanted him too. Completely. Not just this brief act of consolation.

"What happened?"

His eyes focused intimately on hers. "I intend to make you mine, but the first time I make love to you, it won't be in a carriage behind a tree."

She wanted him. Didn't he realize how distinct it made him? She hadn't even looked at a man with desire in over five years. He was the first she'd ever considered for a lover. Her skin tingled and she shivered slightly. All of a sudden, he was the one being sensible and she, the reckless one.

She stared down into his dark, fathomless blue eyes. He neither blinked nor retreated from the issue between them. "But there won't be many times we can be totally alone."

"I want you too much to do this now," he said earnestly, gripping her shoulders tightly to hold her against him.

Her heart continued to pound in her ears. Her pulse continued to beat in her chest. "It's not an ideal situation. A carriage, but we can manage."

Blacknight shook his head.

"Why?" she asked from a thick throat.

He reached up and brushed kisses across her bare shoulder, up her neck, to her lips for a deeper, longer kiss. Ripples of pleasure danced inside her and fed the hunger that hadn't been sated. She hadn't had enough of his touch, his kisses, and the thrill of his passion.

He pulled back from her but kept his gaze on her face. "If I am to make you mine for all time, I must not make you mine today. We have a bargain. Tempting though it is right now, I'm not going to break our pact."

Brina suddenly realized what he was saying.

*No women.*

But that didn't mean her. Did it? No, not her!

She struggled with what was between them as she continued to seek clarification from him. She supposed it did mean her. He was taking her at her word.

"Why do you all of a sudden have scruples?"

His brow and around his eyes wrinkled with concern. "I'm fighting for you," he answered earnestly. "I told you I always play to win."

But she didn't want him to win their wager. She wanted him for a lover. But as a husband? Her heart started beating faster. No, no. She couldn't go down that road again.

"I've never been so thoroughly seduced by anyone as I have by you," he whispered. "You are an inviting mix of a proper, innocent lady and a sinfully tantalizing woman." He gave her a faint smile. "And I want both. I was unbelievably tempted to disregard my promise to you. I was only one more kiss away from giving in to your desire for more and my yearning to make you mine. You must believe that."

Yes, she did. She didn't like it, and it shocked her. She averted her eyes and pushed at his chest. His hands tightened on her arms. He looked as if he wanted to say more but fell silent. Softening his grip, he slowly let go.

Pulling at her dress and cape, she straightened in the seat and moved away from him. She shouldn't be upset with him, but she was. It didn't matter that he was only following *her* dictates. Rules she never expected him to take to heart and actually follow. Demands she never expected to haunt her.

Yet, she had no one to blame but herself. Now she had to be levelheaded and get over it. He wanted marriage. She only wanted him for a time.

They were in each other's lives for the duration of the Season. For now, she had to leave it at that and hope he hurried to the nearest gaming house to have a drink and a game of cards. She certainly wasn't going to marry him.

She couldn't marry anyone.

Ever.

"I don't know what happened to me," she said, straightening her clothing. "I've never been so free before. I—I guess it was the thrill of the ride that caused me to forget myself to the point I lost all rational thought."

"It was your desire for me that had you mindless of all else," he said with a teasing grin as he picked up her bonnet from where it had fallen and handed it to her.

"What? No, no," she argued, half irritated and half amused by his assertion as he laid her hat in her lap. "You're a horrible person to insinuate that."

"I'm truthful. I fully admit you have seduced me like no other woman, but you won't admit I make you feel the same way."

He was right. It was hard enough admitting it to herself.

She placed the bonnet on her head and stuffed strands of hair underneath it.

"Are you upset with me?" he asked, tightening his collar and then his neckcloth.

"Of course I am," she said in a lighthearted tone. "You're a beast." But she was pleased that he had—well, by what he had done for her. "You ruined a perfectly good ending to an exceptional ride."

He chuckled, pulled the brake handle, and gave the

horses a gentle nudge to start moving. The harness rattled once more, and the curricle lurched as they moved out from under the tree's branches.

"What party are you attending tonight?" he asked.

"The Duke of Middlecastle's dinner," she answered, tying the ribbons under her chin. "He and Lyon are good friends. The duke is always at Lyon's card club—anyway, I know him fairly well, and I'm going with Adeline and Lyon."

"You know Lyon invited me to join his club," he said offhandedly, keeping his eyes straight ahead.

"Yes. I shouldn't have, but I jumped to conclusions and accused Adeline of asking him to do it so he could keep an eye on you."

Zane whipped his head around to look at her. "Did she?"

"No," Brina answered. "She assured me it was issued because of your reputation as a card player in London. I believe her and she forgave me. Apparently, many gentlemen are clamoring to play with you."

Seeming satisfied with her answer, he gave his attention back to the horses. "I told Lyon if he has an opening after the Season, I'd be happy to join."

"I am not opposed to you joining right now," she said with a hint of delivery in her tone.

Zane chuckled. "Your wishes will not persuade me to go back on my word to you. I wasn't going to attend Middlecastle's dinner, but if you're going, I will. Seated in a very small, uncomfortable chair, squeezed elbow to elbow at a table for a dinner that can last three hours is a form of torture."

"I just had an excellent idea," Brina said, before the plan had developed fully in her mind. "I think you should give a sit-down dinner party."

"No." He shook his head. "At my uncles' insistence, I had one for my family shortly after I returned. I want it to be a long time before I have another."

"Family dinners are easy."

"So my uncles said, but there is nothing easy about my family and the things they want. More allowance, trips to America, commissions in the military, and land. Their requests seem endless."

"You must decide about those things, but you say you want me to help you do things that are proper. A dinner party where you invite people such as the Duke of Middlecastle, the Earl of Lyonwood, and other peers who are in Town would be good for you. It will have to be toward the end of the Season as most evening dates are already filled for everyone, but I think we can fit one into everyone's schedules."

"No."

"Yes," she countered evenly. "I don't know why I didn't think of it before. It will please your family for you to have a grand dinner for such important guests and prove to other members of the peerage that you are serious about your place in Society. Mainly that you want to get to know them and are willing to work with them should they need you."

He grimaced. "They should know that anyway."

"Some people need to be told and shown things like that. It will strengthen all your relationships. This will be wonderful for you."

He flashed her a grin. "You sound as if you're already getting excited about this idea of a dinner party."

"Somewhat, I am. It would be refreshing to plan a party. I haven't had reason to in a very long time. Living with my parents in their home gave me very little to do. My mother is talented, efficient, and neither needs nor wants help. Besides, I promised to facilitate your transition into the world of London Society and the peerage, and help ease your family's concerns. I'll start planning it for you. With your permission, of course. Perhaps your sister will agree to act as your hostess."

"I'd rather you do it."

Brina frowned.

"No, wait," he quickly said. "Don't say anything. I already know. It wouldn't be the proper thing to do."

They laughed as he guided the horses back onto the trail that led to the main road.

# Chapter 15

He could have killed you!" were the first words out of Harper's mouth when Brina walked into the drawing room.

How did he find out and then get to her house so quickly? Brina had hardly been home half an hour. In fact, she was quite sure the blush from all Zane's kisses and caresses in the carriage hadn't yet left her cheeks.

Remaining calm, she said, "If you are talking about the carriage ride, I suppose you've never driven a curricle fast through Town."

"Of course I have," he insisted tightly. "But never when a lady was with me. From what I'm hearing, the earl was exceedingly reckless and showed no regard for you or your safety."

Her cousin's statement was pointed and damning. It wasn't easy to rile Harper. His nature was happy and easygoing. What happened had obviously perturbed him greatly.

"Oh, heavens, Harper," she said dismissively. "You are making way too much of this. The earl is six or seven years older than you and has had more practice. Who knows? By the time you are his age, perhaps you will have been reckless with a young lady as well."

"No," he answered firmly. "There are some things a gentleman doesn't do. But, lest I forget, the earl is no gentleman." He walked closer to her, his face contorted in anger. "I want you to stay away from him. In fact, I think I should pay a call to him and insist upon it. Your father would do it if he were here. I intend to do it for him."

Brina felt her hackles rise. "Now, wait a minute, Harper. I don't know what you heard but I don't want you speaking for me to Blacknight or anyone else. And, not that it's any of your business, but I will tell you, I am the one who encouraged the earl to go fast. He was quite reluctant to do so."

"You want to make excuses for him because you don't want me to do my family duty and protect you."

"I make excuses for no one, including you," she said, lifting onto her toes so she could look him eye to eye.

"I let it slide when he made the wager about marrying you. Men have a right to place their bets and wagers as they see fit, and what he did at White's will cause you no real harm. This was different."

She looked aghast at him. "Really?" How could he say that? Unless Zane started drinking, gambling, or carousing, she could very well end up married to him. And for the first time, she realized that idea thrilled her as well as terrified her. "If you really wanted to help me, you could be encouraging the earl to gamble."

Harper's eyes narrowed to serious-looking slits. "I don't think you are comprehending that he could have crashed the carriage and harmed or killed you. What I should do is call him out as a matter of honor."

"Stop talking such madness or I'll ask you to leave," Brina insisted hotly and turned away from him before sharply whirling back to face him again. "I won't hear such foolishness. What is wrong with you? Who is putting such nonsense in your head?"

He eyed her curiously. "No one. Why would you suggest that?"

"Because it's so unlike you to be this upset over anything. Besides, I need no one to defend me. I am perfectly capable of taking care of myself."

"Not with him, you aren't. You are fragile."

That brought Brina up short and she took in a long, deep breath. It wasn't easy hearing that. "Yes, I was for a time. Everyone in the family knows that. But I am fine now. Strong and confident. Living on my own and as you can see, happy and doing quite well."

"I want you to stay that way. Robert was with Blacknight in Paris and Vienna. I've heard stories about him. About the two of them that I'm not at liberty to talk about."

Brina felt a shiver shake her. She had experienced one of the earl's and Robert's stories. And it was as exciting as the ride they'd had today. She didn't need Harper to tell her anything about Zane. She knew firsthand exactly who he was.

"I agree," she said, knowing she was defending him and realizing she wanted to. "You shouldn't. He is a bachelor. What he has or hasn't done is of no concern of mine. Or yours, for that matter."

"I want him to leave you alone."

*No.*

For better or worse, she was bound to Zane right now. He was dangerous but she didn't want to give up the thrill of being with him. She couldn't tell Harper that, and he wasn't in a mood to listen anyway.

But she had to take control of this conversation and settle down her cousin. "Then let me be blunt and tell you the truth," Brina said, somehow remaining calm. "Someone was following us and spying upon us. I didn't appreciate it. I asked Blacknight to lose the carriage."

Harper's shoulders eased back, and he lifted his chin. "What do you mean?"

"Exactly what I'm saying. The earl is being followed—we assume that someone who has a large amount of money placed on one of the wagers at White's or one of the other clubs is pursuing him in hopes of seeing him take a drink, play cards, or—whatever. I felt violated by such an act as having my privacy invaded."

It was really anger she'd felt but wanted to use the stronger word of violation in hopes of quieting Harper even more. And his expression quickly changed to one of concern.

"You're serious about this?"

"Yes. The man was driving a poorly maintained cabriolet. Speeding up and slowing down when we did, and taking every turn we took. I insisted we must lose him so we could have the benefit of our afternoon without his watchful eyes. Blacknight finally acquiesced to my wishes. So if you are going to be mad with anyone, be that way with me."

Mrs. Lawton quietly walked into the room and put a tea tray on the small table between the two settees.

"Look," Brina said. "Mrs. Lawton brought the tea. And she has tarts." She turned to the housekeeper. "Apricot or figs?"

"Figs, Mrs. Feld."

"Good. Thank you." Brina looked at her cousin again. "Sit down, Harper, and I'll answer any more questions you have as long as you realize I am doing it because I want to and not because I have to."

"Very well."

Two cups of tea and half a dozen tarts later, Harper was calm and back to his usual cheerful self. She had no idea why, but she kept thinking that something else must have wound him tight and that what happened with the earl had set him off.

After telling him as much as she could about the afternoon with Blacknight, she'd changed the subject to one she knew he would like—cards. He was eager to talk about a new club he and Robert were trying to join. Thankfully, that had him parting on good terms, but she'd been unsettled about how his life seemed to be revolving around card games and clubs, and the parties of the Season all but forgotten. There should be more of a balance between the two.

Long after he left, she couldn't shake the feeling that something wasn't right with him. But what?

# Chapter 16

A light mist of rain dusted the top of Zane's hat and crest of his shoulders as he walked down the street toward the Brass Bull Gaming House in the early evening hour. Foot traffic was sparse because of a turn in the weather, but a steady stream of carriages rolled past him.

Zane chose to walk to his meeting with Harry. It gave him more time to think about Brina. It wasn't just having her in his arms, at her own volition, that had caused him to suffer unfulfilled passion that was still with him days later. It was that she'd wanted him as strongly and urgently as he had wanted her. She had been so tantalizing, he had to satisfy her.

But then he also had to deny her.

He had sensed the passion simmering beneath the prim exterior of her widow's clothing long before she had initiated the kiss in the carriage, but he hadn't expected her to act on it—being a proper lady. They were both hungry to fulfill their frantic need for each other and would have if she hadn't put those bloody damned and hellish restrictions on him. He shook his head in frustration as dampness sprinkled his neck.

Brina had been right. Inappropriate, vile curse words had become a habit for him—even in his thoughts.

Zane nodded to a gentleman he passed and then hunkered deeper into his cloak to keep the wet chill off the back of his collar. Whether or not he made the right decision to call a halt to what was about to happen between them in the carriage that afternoon still troubled him. His body would argue that he hadn't, but his mind disagreed.

Sometimes.

And sometimes he sensed that his heart was weighing in on the matter too. Which was troubling. Those thoughts and feelings he tried to stay away from. It was one thing to want her only for himself. As his bride and countess. Loving her, possibly being in love with her, was an entirely different matter and one he shied away from considering. A feeling such as love wasn't for gamblers like him.

Brina could never imagine the amount of willpower it had taken for him to set aside his desire for her. Every ounce he'd had, and then some.

The truth of it was that she'd left him no choice but to say no to what they both wanted. He didn't know if he could trust her not to use his being with a woman, even if it was her, against him at the last ball of the Season when he proposed to her.

Her vow to remain a widow was clear. He couldn't take her vow to herself lightly.

Her premise from the beginning was that she expected him to fail. And he'd come close a few days ago—which was why he was mostly staying away from her unless it was at a party—with other people watching them. That way, he was less likely to succumb to her desire to be with him.

Zane now knew, more than the day he'd made the wager for her hand, that he wanted her. All he had to do was stay firm on those promises and she would be his. He'd made it two weeks and would make it the rest of the time. His worry was, could he change *her* mind about him before he made it to the last ball of the Season?

There was still so much to know about her. Why had she been dressed in the pink satin gown in Paris? Did she harbor deep, lasting feelings for her husband as people claimed or was she, knowingly or not, using the perception as a protective guard against giving her heart to anyone? He wanted to know what had made her decide she never wanted to marry again. He needed to know more about her past to find answers.

Going without a glass of fine wine or a lively card game, difficult as it was, had been easy compared to staying away from her. He had relived the sensations of his lips against hers, the fullness of her soft breast beneath his hand, and her sweet, whispered feminine sounds of pleasure for endless hours. At times, he thought he might storm over to her house and insist she remove her demands from him so he could make her his.

But, after a fierce battle with himself, he'd come to his senses, pushed the treasured memories aside, and continued his studies to learn about the vast properties that were now under his command.

He also hoped the gossip about them would settle down now that he hadn't been seen with her for a couple of days. News traveled amazingly fast in the elite ton. By the time he'd made it to Middlecastle's house for dinner after their adventurous carriage ride, it was obvious everyone there had already heard he was seen driving the curricle recklessly through the city's streets with Brina on board. A hush had fallen over the drawing room when he entered, and everyone looked at him as if he'd suddenly grown two sharp thorny horns.

Some of the ladies quickly turned their heads away in protest that he had the gall to attend a dignified event after such ill-bred, dangerous, and careless behavior. Others gave him sly smiles of approval. Some merely looked surprised. None more so than his hostess, the Duchess of Middlecastle. It was only much later in the evening he discovered why Her Grace had gone running from the room at the sight of him. It had nothing to do with the race to dodge the spy.

Brina had been adequately protected all evening by her friends, Lady Lyonwood and Mrs. Stockton, and, so it seemed, the duke and duchess as well. Brina had been cordial when they spoke to each other, and meaningful glances had passed between them. There was no opportunity to have a private conversation about their event and the gossip surrounding it.

When dinner was served and they went into the dining room, he'd been seated on the opposite side from Brina and so far down the long, dimly lit table, he hadn't been able to get more than a glimpse of her for over three hours. Another reason not to appreciate dinners that took so long.

As he'd expected, the chairs were small, the seating tight, and the china, crystal, and silver abundant. So was the wine. The temptation to indulge was great. It had been difficult to deny himself but somehow he'd made it through the evening without sip.

Not one to grouse about anything for too long, Zane found a way to pass the evening by engaging in a lengthy conversation about Paris with the young widow,

Mrs. Pinewiffle, who was seated on his left, and a chatty young lady making her debut into Society to his right. After only two glasses of wine, she was spilling the reason why the duchess seemed so unhappy with him. Zane had failed to respond to her invitation that he would be attending. His lack of manners had caused her to delay dinner while the servants rushed to set a place for him at the table.

The fact that Brina was already planning such a lengthy evening for him to host was still an idea he was having to get used to. He'd much rather sit around a card table. Gentlemen were always given plenty of room when gaming. No elbows or knees ever touched. No one expected you to talk. You never had to wonder which glass was yours. However, if a long sit-down dinner would make Brina happy, he'd endure it. But she would damn well be sitting next to him and not at the other end of the table where he couldn't even see her face.

The mist had turned to a drizzle, Zane noticed, as he tipped his hat to a couple scurrying along as he passed them. He pulled his cloak tighter about his neck and kept walking. So did the man who'd been following him. When Zane decided to walk, he expected the man in the cabriolet to simply follow at a safe distance, but he'd jumped out of the carriage and was following on foot.

He wanted to court Brina the usual way a gentleman would pursue a widow. Candlelit dinners in her home. A friendly game of cards or chess. Smiles over a glass of wine, gentle touching of hands, and delicate kisses to start a night that would end in searing passion in her bedchamber.

Thoughts of that possibility kept him warm until he opened the door to the Brass Bull Gaming House and strode inside. The smell of liquor was strong. His stomach clinched. He had especially missed having a drink in the evenings. It was harder than he thought it would be not to pour himself a splash of brandy by habit when he was alone. By the third night without a drink, he'd considered having Fulton take every drop of port, claret, and brandy out of the house so he wouldn't accidently have a drink before he remembered promising Brina he would stay away from it.

Until she was his. And he would keep that promise.

Even if it killed him.

Brina Feld was a wicked woman to have trapped him into such a pact. But she was wonderfully wicked. Beautiful and enticing.

The hell of it was that he missed late-night and all-night card games too, but was getting used to going to bed earlier, waking earlier, and going for a ride in the park while the day was still quiet, and before Uncle Syl and Uncle Hector arrived for their daily hovering sessions with his solicitor.

After the brisk walk in the cool rain, he would have liked to settle around a table by the fire with a brandy to warm him before indulging in a game or two of cards. But he would do neither this night. He pushed the thoughts from his mind and hung his cloak on one of the pegs near the door.

Huffing a rueful breath, he popped his hat on top of his cloak. According to his uncles, none of the scandal sheets had been kind the past couple of days. Being called the Hellion Earl didn't matter to him, but it had Hector in an uproar and Sylvester desperate to calm his brother. Zane was close to telling his uncles he'd learned all he could about the earldom from them. It was time for them to get back to whatever normal lives they had before they decided to make themselves a daily fixture at his house.

What bothered Zane most was that one of the gossip sheets had slighted Brina by suggesting she'd been a willing participant in their wild ride. Which she was. An encourager, in fact, but he hadn't liked what was written about her in the column—*Mrs. Feld appeared to be enjoying the ride and draped herself over the earl's shoulders as the carriage sped wildly down the road.* Zane was fair game. Maligning her wasn't. It was no surprise at all that not one of the scandal sheets mentioned he and Brina were being chased by someone driving as fast.

The taproom was dim and noisy with chatter as he scanned it. Laughter and the solid clunk of tankards hitting wooden tables echoed around the room, but Zane heard a man from a nearby table whisper, "Can I buy you a drink, my lord?"

"In two weeks, three days, and seventeen hours," he quipped and kept on walking as the person chuckled. He didn't mind the remark or laughter that followed as he threaded his way around the tables. He had no idea how many weeks, days, or hours were left until midnight on the last ball of the Season and his bargain with Brina was at an end, but it couldn't come soon enough. Until then, only one thing mattered.

That she not win.

Very ungentlemanly of him, but necessary.

"I heard that was a mighty fine race you had a couple of days ago," a young bearded man said in a normal tone as Zane passed.

He gave the man a nod.

Another stranger from behind him called out, "Did you win the wager when you won the race?"

"No bet," he answered with good humor. "Just an pleasant afternoon ride."

Harry waved to him from a far corner table. Zane headed that way. He'd been enough of a scoundrel in his days not to let the ones in the taproom, nor the one who had followed him to the club, bother him.

It was close to ten years now that Harry Robins and Zane had been friends, having met at a gaming hell shortly after they were both old enough to enter. Their skills, looks, age, natures, and even allowances were equal, but not their social status. Zane's father was a gentleman. Harry's, a wealthy tradesman.

Ordinarily, the two such different lifestyles would never mix, but it hadn't kept them from becoming friends and often gaming partners—until an unfortunate event abruptly ended Harry's card playing.

While walking home late one night, Harry had come upon a man being robbed by thugs. Good fellow that he was, he stopped to help. One of the robbers had a long sharp blade and almost sliced Harry's palm in two. A surgeon stitched him up and saved the hand, but it was of little use to him. He couldn't shuffle a deck, make a fist, or even hold one card. He had his hand but no movement or feeling in his thumb and fingers.

Harry hadn't let that stop his gaming. He simply no longer played cards himself. He still haunted the gaming hells and found ways to wager with dice and other men's high stakes games, which was a common pastime for some.

"How are you, my lord?" he said, rising and offering a bow.

Zane nodded. "Managing." He pulled out a chair and sat. "How about you?"

"Managing quite well," Harry said, with a congenial smirk, before adding, "I was sorry to hear about what happened to your family."

"Thank you. Most everyone's recovered from the shock." A server walked over, and Zane pointed to his friend's glass of red wine. "Want another?" he asked. Harry shook his head, so Zane motioned the man away.

He was winning his battle over his desire to have a drink and play cards in the evenings, and he would win the battle for Brina's hand. It seemed as if everything in his life was changing. He knew it would be a struggle to adjust to being earl of the estate and head of his family. All he had to do was win one battle at a time.

"I was glad to hear you'd come by to see me. I had good intentions of getting in touch earlier."

Harry shrugged. "I knew you would eventually. You've had quite a lot happen recently—wagers and titles. Tell me, how does it feel being an earl?"

"Different, and the same. I still put on my clothing the same way every morning but learning to accept people I've known all my life or for years, like you, bowing and calling me 'my lord.'" He shook his head. "That, I'm still adjusting to."

Harry snorted a good-natured laugh. "I bet that has caused you some consternation. I'm surprised you still want to be seen with me. It was quite clear your uncles didn't want me hanging around when I went to your house."

"My uncles mean well—but live by old rules and traditions they aren't likely to give up."

"I would assume they didn't appreciate your terrorizing the Town with your out-of-control curricle a couple of days ago."

"Out of control? You bloody—" Zane caught himself and smiled. "Englishman."

Harry chuckled. "That's the nicest name you've ever called me."

"I promise not to make a habit of it. And you know, I am always in control of the horses. My uncles didn't mind the speeding carriage so much. They were livid I had Mrs. Feld with me."

His friend chuckled again, clearly embracing the fact he had riled Zane. "Was she frightened?"

"Not at all." Thoughts of Brina always distracted him. He took a moment to remember the exhilaration in her eyes and eagerness in her kiss. No matter what he was doing or who he was talking to, he always felt as if she were with him. "She loved every minute of it."

His friend eyed him skeptically. "That's surprising considering—"

Harry stopped midsentence but Zane knew what he was going to say. Her enjoying the fast ride was surprising because of Brina's reputation as the perfect widowed lady, the example every lady who had lost her husband should follow. He didn't mind people thinking of her that way. He had too. Now, he knew there was another side to her as well.

Deciding to ignore Harry's unspoken comment, Zane said, "I wanted to meet with you tonight because I need your help."

Harry leaned forward, and in a low voice asked, "Does it have anything to do with the man who walked in shortly after you did and hasn't taken his eyes off your back since you sat down?"

"No." Zane felt a twist between his shoulder blades and his gut tightened. He looked around the room. "Every time I leave the house, someone follows me. I assume hoping to catch me take a drink, gamble, or visit a mistress. I'm sure they are being paid by whomever has wagered the most money. If I stopped one spy, another would simply appear in his place, so I don't bother to confront them. Besides, I have nothing to hide."

"There are probably many men following you and watching the clubs. Every pair of eyes in here lit up when you entered the room. The amounts being entered in books all over Town is astounding everyone."

"Blast it—I never dreamed one little wager would turn into such madness."

"Maybe because it wasn't little."

"Seemed so at the time," he mumbled. "I only wanted to get *her* attention. Not notice from every gamester in England."

"But that has happened now, and you are being watched. What do you need me to do?"

"I was hoping you'd say that. I may have mentioned my cousin Robert to you before."

Harry shook his head and leaned farther back into his chair as he moved his wineglass closer. "You have too many cousins for me to remember the names of any of them."

It was true, so Zane nodded. "He's a young man thinking he wants to be skilled at cards, but still a greenhorn, impulsive and easily led. Apparently, now all the affection he used to have for women has turned to gaming."

Harry shrugged amiably and took a drink from his glass before saying, "He'll come back around to where he realizes he can handle both."

Zane blew out a derisive laugh. "The problem is, he doesn't want to take the time, as you and I did at his age, to study, learn, and get good at the games."

"Young men today have no patience or discipline for the finer details of card playing."

"Right," Zane agreed. "I have reason to suspect he may be getting into debt with someone or a card club. Maybe more than one."

"You think it's possible that some of the men are duping him and using him to plump their pockets?"

"Precisely," Zane said, and looked around the room again. "He's a good fellow but maybe with more swagger than he can back up. As you well know, there are a few men who make their living off a younger man's pockets. Until Robert learns to control his gaming limits, he's at risk. He's come to me twice for money since he's been home. That causes me worry."

"Is he giving you any details?"

"No, and I try to be careful. I appreciate his need for privacy. He wouldn't like it if he knew I was checking on him. I hope you can make some discreet inquiries for me."

"An easy enough request. Do you have names?"

"Not that I can confirm. Only suspicions right now."

"Your instincts are always good."

Zane hoped they didn't fail him this time. "Robert's spending a lot of time with a man his age who seems to have enough money to stay in the games, Harper Tabor. I haven't been around him often. He seems innocent enough, but I feel something isn't right. He doesn't have the attitude or style of an accomplished gamester."

"You think he might be a decoy to lure Robert into debt?"

For Brina's sake, he hoped that wasn't the case, but to Harry, he said, "Very possible."

"I've not heard Tabor's name mentioned in any of the clubs, nor a word about your cousin."

"Tabor could be one of the greenhorns being duped himself. He's young too. I don't want Robert getting in deeper than he should. I need to know if he's borrowing money to gamble from anyone else and who he might owe."

"The amount can't be huge. You know word like that gets around fast."

"That's why I'm asking now. If there are debts, I want to settle them before they get out of hand."

"Do you have any other details?"

"Robert mentioned a man named Remick who was having a series of games, and he didn't have the blunt to get in."

Harry shook his head. "Never heard his name, but games and clubs come and go so frequently."

Zane nodded. "I could be wrong, and both Tabor and Remick are square with Robert, and they are all having friendly games to improve his skills. I want to make sure before I leave him to stand on his own."

"I'll ask around and be in touch when there's something to report."

"The favor will be returned whenever you ask."

Harry straightened in his chair and picked up his glass and sipped. "You can grant me that favor right now."

"Tell me what you want."

"I want to hear about the widow who convinced you to give up wine, cards, and women."

# Chapter 17

$\mathcal{P}$assion was a peculiar thing, Brina decided, placing a large basket on the dining room table. She was certain she'd had as much of it for her husband as she now had for the earl. The problem was, she didn't remember it. The past couple of nights she'd lain awake in her bed trying to recall the memories of Stewart's touch.

She'd failed.

Once they were so vivid. Now, she couldn't bring them to mind.

Perhaps it wasn't so odd she couldn't summon them to comfort her anymore. It was so long ago. She was still practically a child when she married him. She'd been so eager to be his wife. At one time, recollections of her husband had overwhelmed her to the point she thought she'd never recover from the loss. The sad truth that she hated to admit even to herself was that feelings and memories of Stewart had started to fade before

Zane came into her life and disrupted it with his wager, his kisses, and his very presence.

Now it was Blacknight who took up too much space in her thoughts. If she wasn't thinking about him, she would see, hear, or touch something that would bring him to mind.

Especially when she was alone.

She hardly had room for other and more important things to ponder such as getting on with the preparations to give the girls painting lessons. The spring weather had been lovely so it was the perfect time to set up the easels outside. She believed it would be helpful to the girls in their sewing classes if they knew how to sketch a dress and then paint it in lovely colors.

Yet, time after time, she put those thoughts aside because she greatly enjoyed thinking about Zane and remembering his touch and kisses. How divinely delicious it was to feel desired again. For some reason, she'd always thought it would be a betrayal to Stewart to have wanton feelings of any kind for another man, but now that she actually had them for Zane, she didn't sense any disloyalty to Stewart's memory.

She only felt hard, fast, flowing *passion*.

And that was troublesome. She hadn't expected to be so enamored with Zane. He was supposed to be a rake. Why hadn't she heard that he was drinking and gambling—or, at the very least, swearing? That is what she needed the earl to do. And soon. Not give her kisses that made her feel as if she were melting into a pool of sensuous fantasy. Not proving he could change. That he could be a gentleman and refuse her invitation for more than kisses thrice.

*Thrice!*

She had no doubt he wanted her. The evidence had been clear, strong, and tempting. She desperately wanted

him—to be with him, but she hadn't changed her mind
about marriage. It was too hard. Too heartbreaking, and
she'd never live through that again for any man.

A knock on the front door made Brina jump. Her first
thought was that it was Zane. Anticipation gripped her.
And that aggravated her. Why did he have to be the first
person to come to mind?

"It could be anyone, you ninny," she whispered, and
shook her head at how easily she could get caught up
into thinking about the unforgettable earl. The man was
a constant drain on her thoughts.

Maybe Adeline had walked over with her rambunc-
tious little boy. Chatwyn loved to throw the ball to her
while she and Adeline chatted. Perhaps Julia had stopped
by for a visit or maybe even Mr. Inwood had sent more
flowers. The young bachelor had already sent two baskets. All of them pink. He was handsome, nice, and gentlemanly. A note asking if he might call on her always
accompanied the bouquets. Brina had absolutely no desire to have him court her. She had all she could handle
wrapped up in a man named Blacknight.

Heaven help her! The only time he should cross her
mind was when she was envisioning him going to his
club and drowning himself in brandy and gambling all
night long. That was the only thing that was going to save
her from a marriage she couldn't possibly accept.

Time was running out, and so far, he hadn't cooper-
ated.

"I'm only home for Adeline or Julia," Brina called
to Mrs. Lawton as she passed the dining room doorway
heading to the front of the house.

"I understand, Mrs. Feld," the housekeeper assured
her without breaking her stride.

Determined to rid herself of purely selfish thoughts,
Brina pulled a large, round tin out of her basket and

placed it on the table. Next, she grabbed the stack of thin cotton fabric she had cut into small squares, and then the lengths of string she'd carefully measured and snipped yesterday afternoon. She lined up everything perfectly on the table in the order she'd use them. This system made her project go faster.

After opening the tin, she shook most of the contents into the bowl and placed a teaspoon in the middle of it. That's when she heard a man's voice. A familiar voice. The earl's voice.

Anticipation filled her again. Followed by more annoyance with herself. It would be so much easier if she felt nothing but mere curiosity when he came to her door. Why did he refuse the usual manner of sending a note asking to call on her at an appointed time? Why did she want to see him? He'd been nothing but trouble since the first time she met him. She would have saved herself a lot of distress if she'd left him tied to the chair.

Mrs. Lawton quietly appeared. "I know you didn't want to be disturbed, Mrs. Feld, but it's Lord Blacknight. He says he's hoping you'll make an exception and see him. He has something important he needs to discuss with you."

"Important?" That got her interest. "Yes, thank you, Mrs. Lawton. Ask him to join me in here."

Any resolve she'd had not to be affected by him melted away the moment he appeared in the doorway of the dining room. Her heart and chest felt as if it expanded. His tall lean body looked exceptionally powerful. The color and texture of his thick black hair and the way he combed it away from his face gave a strong, handsomely fierce appearance that drew her. Now, she knew she would never grow tired of looking at him or being moved by the sight of him.

His dark blue eyes brushed softly over her face. She didn't know how, but she felt his deep desire for her.

"Good afternoon, Mrs. Feld."

Trying to tamp down all she was experiencing and her simple delight at seeing him, she said, "My lord, don't you think it would have been nice to let me know you wanted to come over this afternoon?"

"I thought you liked surprises."

His innocent comment made her smile. "Perhaps, but I'm not certain I always appreciate surprises from you."

"You seemed to have a good time when I brought horses for you to ride. And the fast curricle."

"Yes. I suppose I enjoyed both those things, but then there was the matter of the wager."

He winced and stepped farther into the dining room. "Not my finest hour."

"No, but we won't dwell on that. Mrs. Lawton said you had something important to discuss with me. Naturally that made me curious."

"I like it when you are curious."

So did she. "Never mind about that," she said with a quirk of her head.

He regarded her with barely concealed amusement. "I wanted to know if you've seen or heard from Harper in the past couple of days?"

"I've seen him recently. He came over and had tea with me. We had a lovely visit both times except for—"

He walked toward her slowly, determined, until he stood inches away. "For what?"

"He was very concerned about the curricle ride with you—as most everyone seemed to be."

Zane's features relaxed, and he nodded. "I received my share of lectures about how irresponsible I was to be so uncontrolled when you were in my care."

Brina huffed and folded her arms across her chest. "I really can't fathom the stir it has caused. I thought

Harper might really be on the verge of calling you out for endangering my life."

"Maybe he should have. I've heard several comments maligning my lack of restraint."

"Nonsense. Your handling of the horses saved us from crashing more than once."

He smiled and accepted her praise without comment.

"I had to tell him I'm the one who encouraged you because I didn't like being spied upon. The way everyone is acting, you'd think I was the first lady to ride in a carriage that was speeding along so fast."

He lifted one dark brow. "Maybe you were. We were almost flying." His voice lowered to almost a whisper as he continued, "More than that, I think everyone sees you as an angel, and I am the devil who is corrupt and leading you astray."

Brina tensed and turned away from him. She didn't like that characterization used for her. If people only knew what she'd done, they'd never call her that again. She wasn't an angel. Far from it.

She looked over to the table. Realizing she hadn't replaced the lid on the tin, she asked, "What was the particular reason you wanted to see me about Harper?"

He followed her over to the table and leaned a hip against it. "I wondered if he might have mentioned Robert during your visits. Uncle Hector said he hasn't been home in a couple of days, which is unusual, so he's worrying."

"Does Robert have a place of his own?"

"No. Since he and Harper have been spending time together in the evenings, I was hoping he might have mentioned Robert was staying with him."

"I suppose he could be, though it would be unlikely he'd stay with him for long. I've not actually been there, but my father has said that Harper's room is quite small.

If you're concerned, I could send a note and ask him to come see me about this."

The earl shook his head. "I'd rather you didn't. Young men don't usually want their fathers or uncles asking questions. Robert's impulsive. He could be staying at someone's house for a card party or other things."

She could imagine what the other things might be for a man of twenty-two years. "That's quite possible. Harper mentioned he'd gotten more involved in playing cards and hoped to be invited to join a club soon. He was quite excited about it."

Zane straightened. "Did he happen to give the name of the person who invited him?"

"Not that I recall."

"Can you think of anything else he might have said that was out of the ordinary conversation?"

"No but he was acting quite agitated. Harper is mild and usually hard to upset," Brina offered, but didn't want to say too much. She couldn't come out and accuse Zane's cousin of influencing Harper with his gambling. Not at this point anyway. Though there might come a time she'd have to say something. "It wouldn't have been proper for me to quiz him about it. Men love their gaming. As we've mentioned, Lyon certainly enjoys his private club."

"But it's very exclusive, Brina."

She returned the tin to the table after securing the lid, resisting the impulse to go further into this matter and say too much about what she really felt. "All men think their clubs are exclusive, do they not? Where or who Harper plays cards with is not any of my business. For now. Perhaps Robert's shouldn't be any of yours or his father's."

"I only want to satisfy Uncle Hector that all is well with his son. Apparently, if a problem arises within my family, I am the one duty bound to promptly take care of it. Besides, asking you about Robert gave me the opportunity to come see you." He gave her a twitch of a smile. "Robert wasn't my only reason for coming over."

Her lower abdomen tightened, and she hoped he couldn't sense how much that pleased her. "I guessed as much."

Nodding, he said, "I like being with you, looking at you, and desiring you as intensely as I am right now."

Brina's heart started beating faster. Glancing down at her dress, there was nothing suggestive about the loose-fitting pale brown gown she wore, but his words made her feel as if she were clothed in a luxurious silk gown with her hair beautifully adorned and her cheeks and lips as rosy as a babe's. He always made her feel that way.

"I—I don't know what to say to that. It's not the kind of thing a gentleman should say to a lady. 'Thank you' doesn't seem appropriate for such a comment concerning desire."

His gaze stayed softly on her face. "You don't have to say anything. I wanted you to know—in case you had any doubts. Let's go riding. I brought the horses."

She'd love to ride again. It was a beautiful afternoon. She glanced at the table and then down at her feet. The toes of her black satin slippers peeked from beneath the hem of her skirt. She didn't even have her riding boots. Much as she would like to ride again, she simply wasn't prepared. Why couldn't he give her notice so she could plan and be ready?

She sighed. "No. I can't possibly go this afternoon."

"You need to get on a horse and ride again so you won't forget how," he encouraged.

"I didn't forget in five years." Brina gave a soft chuckle. "I'm not likely to forget now."

"Let's make sure you don't. We'll be followed again. We can give the men who watch me a merry chase."

"That's such a beastly thing for them to do. I don't know how you put up with it."

He shrugged in a nonchalant manner and gave her a bit of a grin. "I am putting up with many things right now, Brina. Compared to some of them, these men don't bother me at all. I wave or tip my hat, so they know I see them."

She knew he was talking about the things she had forced him to give up. But he was kind enough not to spell that out, and she was grateful for that. There were still times she couldn't believe she'd issued all those demands. Or that, so far, he'd followed them all. That troubled her every time it crossed her mind. For that reason alone, it was best for her to send him on his merry way.

"No, I can't ride today. I must finish getting these ready for Pilwillow Crossings. I need to take them to the sisters tomorrow. Julia has already asked to go with me. I really can't change the day."

He glanced at her odd collection of items on the table. "What is it you're making?"

"Little bags of comfort is what I call them," she said softly. "I add a spoon of tea leaves to the center of the little squares and then tie up the ends with a string. These small sizes make enough for one cup of tea."

He studied on that for a moment before looking at her with a puzzled expression and asking, "Wouldn't it be far less trouble if you gave the entire tin?"

"You think it's for the sisters to drink?" She laughed. "No. These are for the sisters to hand out to people who aren't fortunate enough to have tea or even food every day. For some it will be the only tea they get. Three mornings a week, the sisters make soup and bread to give to the needy. They also provide poultices to those who may have an injury. I asked if I could help by making these little bags of tea to hand to everyone. Most of the people have few comforts in life. At times, something as simple as a warm cup of tea can make one feel better, no matter the circumstances."

He reached out and briefly caressed her cheek with his fingertips. His touch was warm and soothing. "They probably appreciate the tea as much as the soup."

"I don't know about that," she said honestly. "It's certainly not as nourishing. Yesterday, I rolled bandages for the sisters to give out." She looked down to the other end of the table at a large basket brimming with white rolls of cloth.

"You did all that?"

She nodded. "It's such an easy thing to do but means so much. Some have injuries that get very little care and most have nothing to cover the wounds to keep them clean. I take all I've made to the sisters once or sometimes twice a week."

"I'm understanding more now why my uncles kept telling me you were too good for me."

She turned away from his touch. "Please don't say things like that. It upsets me to be praised for doing something good for people in need."

His expression quizzed her. "Why? It's true."

She couldn't explain and didn't really want to try. Feeling a pang of sadness, she offered, "As you know, our Society frowns upon a lady doing anything that might be considered work, but I'm not bothered by that. It feels good to be needed, to help others have a better life. I wanted to help the sisters pass out the food. Unfortunately, Sister Francine wouldn't even consider it, but not because I am from Society."

"What then?"

"I'm not capable."

He looked at her as if she might have lost her mind. "No. I don't believe that."

"It's true. She was right to refuse my offer. I would be giving extra handfuls to the elderly or people with children and then others would be left without anything to take with them. The sisters do it as equitable as possible. They have learned how to be compassionate while being dispassionate. Very difficult to do. They are good at being kind and just to everyone who comes for help."

"What you're doing is kind too." His eyes softened. "Why does it trouble you so to be thought of that way?"

Because she knew how truly awful she'd once been.

Zane touched her cheek again, this time letting his fingers trail over her jaw, down her neck and arm, where he caught her hand in his. Squeezing her fingers, he brought her hand up to his lips and kissed the back of her palm. His touch was warm. The small gesture comforted her.

"How did you get started doing this?" he asked as he continued his hold on her hand and placed it on his chest over his heart. "Did the sisters ask for your help?"

Brina felt her defenses weakening. She didn't know why but suddenly wanted him to know. But how much did she want to tell him?

Understanding filled his eyes and expression. Brina was drawn even more to him. Beneath her hand, his chest was warm, solid. There was such strength in him and she wanted to rely on it.

He lightly squeezed her palm again. "Tell me."

"By chance I was riding by the abbey and saw a long line of poorly clothed men, women, and children. They passed by a table where a sister dipped into a large pot and filled their cups and bowls with soup. Another sister would hand them a piece of bread. Not far away, another table was set up where sisters handed out bandages and little bags, something like the ones I'm making here.

Later, I found out they were filled with herbs that had healing qualities. I went back several times to watch before I had the nerve to go inside and actually talk to one of the sisters."

His gaze was compelling. "Surely they were happy to have caught your interest."

All the inadequacies she felt after that first visit came crashing down on her and for an instant she didn't think she could continue but then she felt Zane's heartbeat beneath her hand. "Not at all, but surely you don't want to know about any of this," she said dismissively. It was another part of her past she kept hidden. She pulled her hand away from Zane's grasp and walked to the window to look over the small garden.

He followed and touched her shoulder affectionately. "Of course I do. I want to know everything about you."

Keeping her gaze set on the view from the windowpane, she whispered, "It's not easy to talk about one's shortcomings."

"Do you have any?"

His tone seemed sincere, not sarcastic, and without really knowing why, she turned to him and said, "I told Sister Francine I wanted to join the abbey to help them take care of unfortunate people."

He blinked and his brows rose.

"You look as shocked as Julia did the day I told her I wanted to leave my place in Society."

"I am," he admitted honestly. "Making it possible for unfortunate people to have a cup of tea is a long way from taking a vow of poverty, service, and celibacy."

"I know." She offered a bit of a sad smile. "The sisters do so much selfless work for others. They are strong, good-hearted women, and I have such admiration for them and all they do. I wanted to be a part of that. I felt if I could be good enough, help them, and help enough people, I could redeem—" She stopped and swallowed hard.

He gently took hold of her shoulders and squeezed only enough to let her know what she was saying was important to him. "Redeem what?"

She appreciated the shimmering light of concern that shone in his eyes and the earnest, honest appeal to have her tell him more, but she couldn't. She didn't want him or anyone to know all her past. As it was, she'd already said too much.

"Too many things," she finally said. "The sisters rise in the mornings thinking, *How many suffering people can I help today*? I rise and say, *What will I play on the piano-forte this morning? What dress will I wear to the park this afternoon or to a dinner party this evening?* My life was so empty, and helping people who truly need it was the only way I could think to help myself."

A sad laugh escaped past her lips and she shook her head. She didn't know if she could ever make up for her past. "Sister Francine took one look at me and knew I couldn't handle what would have been required of me physically or mentally. In my desperation at the time, I didn't believe her, but she was so right."

"I have my own reasons for being glad she recognized you shouldn't join the abbey." He pulled her close and wrapped his arms around her as he reached down and kissed her forehead, letting his lips trickle down to below her eyes before whispering, "But I refuse to believe you wouldn't have been strong enough to handle it. You certainly seem to grasp how to handle me, and that is no easy task."

Brina found herself amused by his last comment and snuggled deeper into his comforting embrace, laying her check against his warm chest. "I can't handle you at all. You frustrate me at almost every turn. And I found

I'm not suited for a complete life of servitude, no matter my protests to the opposite at the time. Unfortunately, it took me a while to realize that while my intentions were quite admirable, they were not practical for me."

"What happened to make you aware of it?"

"Actually, Julia helped me realize my inadequacies by proving to me that I didn't know how to care for myself, so I certainly couldn't take care of anyone else. I didn't realize how sheltered my life had been and how incapable I was until I tried to do something. After a disastrous afternoon in a kitchen, trying to cook a meal, I concluded it would be best to aid the sisters in other ways. As I do now."

Brina raised her head and glanced over at the tea, cloth, and string, before looking back to Zane.

"I don't know why I'm telling you all this. I've never told anyone I was thinking of joining the abbey. Adeline and Julia know, of course, and the sisters. But no one else. I've never wanted others to know I failed."

"Failed?" He grimaced. "What rubbish." His arms tightened around her and he kissed the top of her forehead again. "You didn't fail. You learned a lesson. An important lesson. Different people are suited for different lives."

"I do believe that now."

"You know, I feel the same way you felt. I'm not suited for the life of an earl. I would rather have the carefree life of a gamester than be deciding which of my family needs more allowance, which tenant needs the fees lowered, which party I'll support in Parliament. I don't want the responsibility for any of those things and many others. The only difference is that you had a choice. I don't. I am the earl whether or not I'm suited, so I must learn to be the best I can be. That's why I need you, Brina."

His words lifted her heart. She swallowed down the feelings of inadequacy that often rose inside her whenever she thought of the time she wanted to join the sisters. "I suppose you do understand. Your problem is that you don't like following accepted rules."

"Rules are enjoyable only if you are breaking them."

Brina heard laughter in his voice. It rumbled in his chest. She closed her eyes and took pleasure in the sound before turning her face to his again. "Now you have me curious. What rules have you been breaking since I last saw you?"

"None of yours, of course."

The mischievous light that touched his eyes made her realize how much she liked his sense of humor. "Are you sure? Not even a nip of brandy before you go to bed to settle your nerves?"

"What?" he asked, with a guileless smile. "You doubt me?"

"Spoken like a true rake."

He brushed his hand along the side of her face. "I've not broken any of the rules you set forth."

She stiffened at his words and pushed out of his arms. That was a problem. She needed him to.

He tried to pull her into his embrace again, but she resisted. "What kind of person neglects the needs of others to go for a ride in the park? We've talked far too long. I must get back to my work."

"All right," he said and walked over to the table and picked up a piece of the cloth. "Let me see if I can fig-ure this out. You hold it like this." He laid the white square in the palm of his hand and added a spoonful of the tea leaves to the center. After bringing all the ends together, he picked up a string and tied them in a bow. Holding it up to her, he smiled. "There. With me helping, it will take half the time to finish this, and we'll still have enough daylight for a short ride through the park."

Zane knew how to touch her heart to make her feel wonderful. He was an earl! It was almost unbelievable that he wanted to help her do something so menial, but she saw in his eyes he was sincere.

"That looks good," she praised him before adding in a lighthearted tone, "but you don't have it quite right." Taking the little sack from him, she untied the bow. "You must give the fabric a twist like this and then make a very tight reef knot." She quickly retied it and gave it to him to inspect. "That will secure it so it won't accidently come untied and the tea be lost to the wind before the person gets home."

"Understood," he said, then pulled out the chair in front of the items and sat down. He grabbed another square to make a sack as she had shown. "I'll keep doing this while you change into riding clothes. If I haven't filled all of them by the time you return, we will before we leave."

"What?" She eyed him with teasing annoyance. "You think you might complete these before I can change and return? There are one hundred squares here."

"Ninety-seven." He started on another one. "We'll see. I'm working and you are still standing there. I bet you I'll have more than half of them finished before you are down and ready to go."

Brina started for the stairs but stopped short of leaving the room and turned back to the earl. A breathy *oh* passed her lips as she gave him a knowing smile. She walked closer to him. "Did you just offer me a bet, my lord?"

His hands stilled on the string. His eyes narrowed enough to let her know that he knew immediately what she was referring to.

"No," he offered casually and finished tying the knot.

"You did," she insisted with mock seriousness, inching even closer to him. "You are caught. You said *I bet you.*"

Zane smiled up at her and placed the bag on the table with the others but she could see a tad of worry around his eyes. Good.

He rose from the chair, slid his hands around her waist, and pulled her close. His gaze locked solidly onto hers. "No," he insisted with an earnest expression. "I was not offering a wager. It was only a turn of phrase, a figure of speech, a slip of the tongue habit. Not a legitimate call for a bet."

His hold on her was friendly. She could have easily slipped out of his embrace, but she didn't want to. They were alone in her dining room and suddenly she wanted his heart-thudding kisses again.

"I'm not so sure about that, my lord," she answered in a lighthearted tone, their conversation delighting her. Her shoulders swayed lightly from side to side, her hips rocking against the firm hold of his hands. "Perhaps you should try to convince me what you claim is true."

His arms tightened on her and his face moved closer to hers. "I do believe you are tempting me to behave badly, Mrs. Feld."

She nodded her confession and asked, "What are you going to do about it?"

For a long moment he stared at her, taking stock of her teasing attitude to assess whether she was serious.

"I may have to kiss you," he said in a voice that was soft and enticingly husky.

Yes, that was exactly what she wanted. Their last time together was seared into her memory, and she ached to be that close, that intimate with him again.

He waited for a response from her. She remained

silent, but her gaze moved slowly over his face. It was impossible to deny the yearning he had caused inside her. She reached up and let her palm slowly drift down his cheek and across his closed lips, marking their shape with her fingertips. After she lowered her hand, he took the initiative, bowed his head, and tenderly kissed her briefly on the lips.

"Is that what you had in mind?" he whispered huskily.

"No," she answered on a gusty breath. "This is what I had in mind." Her arms slid underneath his coat and circled his slim waist. She lifted her lips to his and pressed ardently to show him she wanted to be kissed with passion. Her mouth clung to his while her hands slid up his wide, strong back.

Zane answered her kisses, and this time, held nothing back. His lips moved commandingly and hungrily over hers, his tongue probing and searching her mouth.

"Yes," she whispered.

This was what she'd wanted. To be held tightly, kissed thoroughly. Her head fell back, and his lips moved over her jawline, down her neck, and back to her lips. His hands caressed all around her shoulders, past her nape to where his fingers slid into the back of her hair. He held her head steady as he deepened the kiss.

Flames of passion flared between them. His mouth sought hers over and over again with ever-increasing pressure and pleasure. His hands molded over the contours of her back, her waist, and around to gently, but firmly caress her breasts.

Brina shivered slightly and murmured another soft, "Yes."

She clung to him as if some unknown force were trying to rip him away from her arms. This was the kind of devouring passion she wanted, and she gloried in the way it made her heart thunder in her chest and her head light. She took in the tension and urgency in his embrace and welcomed it, returned it.

Always, when she was in his arms, she came alive. Yet, all too soon his hands stilled, his kisses turned to short, parting pecks.

He lifted his head and stared at her with passion blazing in his eyes. "You have a decision to make," he whispered on a deep, aching gasp.

Her breaths were labored and as short as his. An ache filled her chest and squeezed her abdomen.

"Do we continue this upstairs or go for a ride?" she managed to ask past a thick throat.

Inhaling deeply, he shook his head. "Whether you will release me from the promise of no women."

*No women?*

Brina stiffened. She wasn't sure she believed what she heard him say. "You are still going to hold me to that knowing we both want to be together right now in the privacy of my home?"

He bent his head again and placed his cool lips to the base of her throat and trailed soft, moist kisses all the way up to her lips, where he gave her a few more sweet kisses before whispering, "You're the one I want. I'm trying to win your hand in marriage, Brina. Not just the afternoon in your bed. I must have the release from you."

There was no reason for it to, but his bluntness stung. She had invited him upstairs and he was declining. And making it her fault! Pushing out of his arms, she stepped away and huffed a breath of exasperation.

"That is a terrible thing to say to me," she said, tugging on the waistband of her dress as if somehow that would make her feel better.

"It was respectful and true," he argued with no anger in his expression.

"How dare you make no distinction between a paid woman—a mistress—and a lady."

He leaned in close to her. His gaze felt like a brush of velvet across her cheek. It was tantalizing. "I know the difference, Brina. It is you who must make the distinction. I will abide by your answer."

Her chest heaved. Drat the man. He was right. She hadn't made anything clear when she said *no women*. At the time, she didn't even know she was going to say it, much less try to qualify it.

"No bets are off between us, my lord," she issued firmly. "Our bargain stands as is. You best get busy if you are going to have more than half of those bags of tea finished by the time I am ready to ride."

Brina turned and headed for the stairs. She didn't mind the soft rumble of a masculine chuckle that drifted from behind her. The more she was around the earl, the more she liked him—no, no. It was more than mere like she felt for the earl. She liked several men, including Mr. Inwood.

She wanted Lord Blacknight in the most intimate way.

It made her vulnerable. It made deeper feelings for him grow and fill her with longing she didn't need but couldn't deny. She'd known she would have to endure his courtship when she made her bargain with him. What she hadn't expected was that she would find herself looking forward to it.

And why hadn't the rake taken a drink or picked up a deck? His willpower was far exceeding her expectations. She never anticipated him to last this long. Surely he would give in to temptation soon.

# Chapter 18

It had been a good day and a long time since Julia had accompanied Brina to Pilwillow Crossings. As was expected, the two didn't spend as much time together since Julia had married last year.

"We'll see you back here in an hour," Brina waved and called up to the driver as the two friends stepped out of the carriage and stood on the pavement in front of Brina's parents' house in Mayfair.

The landau rolled away at a jaunty clip, and she turned back to Julia and said, "A few days ago I was remembering when I first started going to the abbey. Before you knew. The ride home used to seem so long. I was always afraid someone would see me there and tell Mama where I'd been. Now, everyone knows I go once a week. Mama still doesn't want me to go, but like everyone else in the ton, she remains quiet."

Ladies of Society were encouraged to be benevolent to such organizations as abbeys, orphanages, and hospitals, but heaven forbid they ever be seen at one of the places. What others thought about her charity work no longer bothered Brina.

"I think it's because you go about it so quietly and you don't impose your will on anyone else," Julia said with a reminiscing smile. "Memories of the times I went with you last year will be with me forever. It was good to see the sisters today. There was a time I truly worried you would decide to give up your life with us and join their order."

"I came close, didn't I?"

Julia nodded.

"It's good they didn't want me. What I do now is more manageable than joining them would have been. Thank you for wanting to go with me today to deliver the tea and bandages."

"It was my pleasure to see Sister Francine again. Besides, I wanted to spend some time alone with you so I could see how you are really doing. We talk at parties, but we're often interrupted and there's always the worry someone will overhear us. How are things going with you and Blacknight?"

Hearing the earl's name swelled Brina's chest and made her abdomen tighten and tremble with a heavenly feeling. Brina looked up at the sky and breathed in deeply. Puffy white clouds dotted the azure blue. The air was cool but still. The neighborhood was quiet, and now that the landau was out of sight, there were no carriage wheels or voices to be heard along the street or in the distance.

"I kept thinking you would say something about him today," Julia continued when Brina remained silent. "Did I make you uncomfortable by mentioning him?"

"How could I feel uncomfortable on such a beautiful day? I haven't said anything because you haven't asked about him."

Julia pursed her lips and seemed to think on that before answering, "True. I kept hoping you would so you wouldn't think I was prying."

"Ha!" Brina said with a laugh. "When has that ever bothered you, my dear friend?"

"Always," Julia said with a knowing shrug. "I know you're a very private person, and I do respect that. At times. But not today," she added with a deliberate smile.

"You know I would never think you were prying. Only anxious for me."

"Good. I am. So tell me about him."

Brina looked up at the sky again as the turmoil of what was happening between her and the earl weighed on her. Her time with him was always exhilarating. *All of it.* "He continues to astound me," she admitted. "And probably everyone with his lack of appropriateness at times."

"Well, I'm not one to throw stones. As you know, Garrett forsook the role of a gentleman at one time."

"I remember. When Blacknight told me he disliked the tediousness of long, sit-down dinners such as the one at the Duke of Middlecastle's house, I said he must give one himself."

Julia's eyes widened with surprise. "You didn't."

Brina laughed. "I did. The date's been set and I'm working on the guest list. Hopefully, it will smooth over some of the feathers he ruffled for not responding to the duchess's dinner party and then attending."

"This was a clever idea, Brina. And it will be good for the earl to do this."

"I'm not sure how clever it was. Though his sister will be his hostess, I am doing all of the planning, which, of course, takes time."

"Are you seeing him often?"

Curls of pleasure tumbled in Brina's stomach. "I saw

him briefly last night at the Windhams' party, and a couple of days ago we went for a ride in the park."

"Hmm. Carriage or horse?"

"Horse," Brina said and started slowly walking up the stone path that led to her parents' front door. "I don't remember enjoying riding so much. I'm glad he reintroduced me to it. There's something peaceful and comforting about it. The animal is warm, gentle, and very easy to guide."

"And what about the earl? Is he all those things? Comforting, gentle, and easy to guide?"

Brina stopped. "Not in the least," she answered quickly, but frowned when she immediately remembered the gentle touch of his fingers against her cheek, the tenderness of soft kisses, and the caress of his hands on her breasts. Every time she had such thoughts, she wanted to be with him. "Well, he is gentle," she corrected. And eager and passionate too. "But no, he's not comforting because he disturbs me greatly. Continuously. In many ways. And he certainly isn't easy to guide—as everyone knows."

"Sometimes a man can disturb you in a good way. Does he do that?"

"Yes," Brina said casually and walked up to the door. She opened her reticule and took out the key. She squeezed it into her palm as they stood under the overhang of the small portico. It had been a long time since she'd talked so honestly with Julia, and it felt good. "His kisses make me tingle all the way down to my toes," she admitted freely.

"Oh," Julia whispered softly, clearly not expecting such a heartfelt answer from her. "I had wondered if the two of you were—kissing."

"How could we not. I admitted the attraction was there from the beginning. It's so hard for me to understand.

I've always been so adamant, no man would ever interest me again. I truly believed that, and for five years
no one has. Now, I'm interested. Not for marriage, of
course, but kisses and touches and all the rest of it. I can't
explain to you how good it feels to be that close to someone again. To be hugged so tightly, touched passionately,
and feel so wanted. No, more than that. He makes me
feel treasured. I could have kept kissing him forever."
She stopped and laughed at herself. "What am I saying?
I don't have to explain any of this. You know what I'm
talking about."

Julia nodded understandingly. "Have you done more
than kiss?"

"Not really." Brina struggled with her thoughts. "Not
because I'm not willing. He isn't."

Julia frowned in disbelief. "You can't mean that?"

"It's true." It had happened more than once, but no
need to tell that. "He reminded me that I had made him
promise there would be no women, and he included me
in that promise."

Julia twisted her lips around a couple of times, trying
not to smile. "He's making you suffer from your own
rule?"

"Yes," she exclaimed softly. "When I was in his arms,
I wasn't even thinking about our bargain. It was the far-
thest thing from my mind. Only loving how utterly wonderful he was making me feel. But, of course, that's not
the only reason he disturbs me. It's getting closer to the
end of the Season, and I haven't heard one slip of gossip from anyone accusing him of gambling, drinking, or
anything else. That night at the ball when I was making
all those demands, I truly didn't believe he could make
it through the night without a glass of wine or a card in
his hands."

"Garrett hasn't heard anything either. I've queried him

about what gossip is making the rounds in the clubs. He said Blacknight has been seen in the evenings, but he only talks with friends and watches others play their cards or billiards. If a man's not going to drink or gamble, there isn't much reason for him to spend a lot of time at the clubs. The problem is that you don't know what he might be doing in the privacy of his home. Who's to say he's not emptying the decanter every night?"

"You're right, of course," Brina said, with some ambivalence. He could be doing that, but it didn't feel right to Brina that he might be cheating in private. "I can't accuse him unless someone comes forward with proof they've seen or heard of him breaking our bargain. And believe me, I know men have tried to catch him in the act. Imagine someone watching your every step."

Brina inserted the key, the lock gave way, and she pushed open the door and stepped inside. The house was cold and quiet as a mouse creeping across a floor. For a moment, she missed her mother and wished she'd been there to greet them. She shook off the soft feeling of love and placed her reticule on the side table.

"My riding boots are in the wardrobe upstairs. I'll get those first. My mother's easel and painting supplies are in—"

Brina heard footsteps and, at the same time, saw the shadow of a man coming down the corridor. Startled, she spun to see Harper walking toward them with his lively step, happy and jovial as usual.

"Merciful heavens, Harper. I didn't know anyone was in the house. You frightened me."

"I didn't know I was in a frightful state, dear cousin. I'm sorry about that. Must be the wind." He brushed a hand through his hair and rearranged it. "Is that better? Such a lovely surprise to see you."

"What are you doing here?" Brina asked, trying to calm her racing heart.

He seemed momentarily at a loss but then spoke up to say, "I stopped by to check on the house and make sure everything was all right." He grabbed his cloak and swung it over his shoulders and fastened the hook at the neck before reaching down to give her the usual kisses on both cheeks. "Your father asked before he left."

Brina tried not to overreact, but it was difficult not to be more than a little surprised by his presence. "I do remember he asked you to check on me, but not that he'd asked you to check the house."

"Didn't I tell you?" he queried, putting his finger to his chin and striking a thoughtful pose. "You're sure? I thought I told you."

"No." And it seemed rather strange for her father to worry about the house. They lived in the safest section of Mayfair.

"I'm sorry." He guffawed. "I didn't make it clear he wanted me to look in on you and the house. Is there a problem? I don't have to come over, you know. If there—"

"No, there's no problem. I'm glad that I understand now. Please, yes, do whatever Papa asked you to do."

Harper nodded, then turning to Julia said, "How are you, Mrs. Stockton? Lovely to see you again."

"I'm good, Harper," Julia replied. "It's nice to see you too. Did you find anything amiss?"

"Missing? No, no. Or did you say amiss? I didn't look specifically." He turned back to Brina and gave her a nervous smile. "I checked all the windows and the doors. They were locked. Everything seemed to be in order. You don't have to bother to do that now if you don't want to."

Brina tried not to worry about Harper's strange behavior, but he had her wondering if all he said was true. She'd never seen him act nervous and on edge. Just as a few days ago she'd never seen him so angry over a ride in a fast curricle. What was happening to him? "I hadn't planned to check and make sure the windows were secure. I only came by to pick up my riding boots and some other things I need."

"Well, I'll not stay and hinder you. I'm sure you want to get right to it, so I'll be on my way."

"Wait. Before you go, there's something I'd like to ask you about, if you have time."

Harper looked at the front door and said, "Yes, of course. Anything."

"Why don't I go up to your room and look through your wardrobe for your boots while you two talk?"

"Thank you, Julia," Brina said, and waited until she was at the top of the stairs before turning back to Harper. Zane hadn't wanted her to say anything but things were at the point she felt she must and not worry about a young man's privacy.

"Since you are here and we have the time, I thought I'd ask you about Lord Blacknight's cousin, Mr. Browning."

Harper clasped his hands behind his back and kept silent. As if waiting for her to say more.

"I was wondering if perhaps you'd seen him in the past several days."

"Yes, of course."

That was easy. "The earl and his family have been concerned about him because they don't know his whereabouts. They hesitate to ask because they don't want him to think they are checking up on him. I thought perhaps you might know something."

"If that is all it is, I can put his lordship's and the family's minds at ease. He has been staying with me. I wasn't aware he hadn't sent a note around to let his family know he was with a friend."

Brina didn't know why, but she felt the need to add, "And he's fine? I mean, he hasn't been seen playing or drinking at any of the clubs, or that is, not as of last when I spoke to Blacknight at a party."

"Robert and I don't always go to the same parties or clubs as the earl," he said with an edge to his voice. "We're not in the same class with our skills or our money."

There was a bit of jealousy in that remark that startled her, but she let it pass. "All right. I'll tell him that Mr. Browning is well and staying with you."

Harper started shaking his head and his expression grew serious. She was beginning to wonder if this kind of behavior was the reason her father had asked her to keep up with him.

"I don't want you to tell Lord Blacknight you spoke with me about any of this, Brina. I'll see that Robert sends a note to his father or the earl that he is with a friend and all is fine. Let it stand. This isn't something that should involve you."

But it did because of Harper. "Why shouldn't they know he's with you?" she questioned, not appreciating his reticence on this subject. "You are quite acceptable."

"You've always been like an older sister to me, haven't you?" He smiled sweetly and suddenly seemed the Harper she knew. "And because you are, I will tell you the truth of it all. This mustn't go any further. Promise?"

Did she have a choice if she wanted to know? She nodded.

"After a late night of more than a few ales and a pint of wine, Robert took a fall and banged himself around quite badly. Bruised his ribs and gave himself a cut lip and black eye. But he's fine now."

That news sent a chill up her spine. Brina was suddenly reminded of when Harper's lip and mouth showed the same signs, and her worry grew. Had he fallen too? "That sounds serious and painful. Why didn't he go home?"

"Who am I to say?" he answered with a wave of his hands. "He came to me, and I took him in. And he is better. I don't think he wanted his family seeing him with his face swollen and in pain. Things like that can be embarrassing—for a young man to be so clumsy. They needn't be concerned for him. He's going to be all right. Best to get the worst past him before they see him, right? He'll go home in a few days." Harper took a step closer to her. "You keep this quiet, and I'll make sure his family knows, but I can't have them coming to my place to see him."

"All right," she said, as a shiver of unease affected her whole body. Something wasn't right about Harper's story. She didn't think a young man could fall and hurt himself so badly. "I'll stay quiet."

"I knew you would. I trust you." He gave her another genuine smile. "I'll be off now."

"One more thing before you go," she said, hoping she wouldn't sound as suspicious or interfering as she felt. "I wanted to know what happened about the card club you were thinking of joining. You seemed very excited about it. Did all that work out to your satisfaction?"

"Not yet. Mr. Remick is open to my joining and considering the possibility. He's quite skilled and is teaching me a few tricks about the games. I should be hearing from him soon."

"Good," she said, but really didn't feel it was. "And Mr. Browning?"

Harper smiled with confidence. "The same. We're finding it's better to have our own club where we can play with people we know are safe."

"Safe? That sounds disturbing, and I'm not sure what you mean."

"Nothing," he said with a quick smile and flippant tone. "It was an offhand remark that meant nothing. Listen, I don't want to keep you." He kissed her cheeks again. "Tell Mrs. Stockton how good it was to see her."

Not giving her time to question him more, he hurried out the door. He used the word "safe" and it troubled her.

Julia came walking down the stairs, holding a pair of dark-brown boots. "These must be the right ones. They are the only pair in your room."

"Yes, thank you."

Placing them beside the front door, she asked, "Did you find out why Harper was here?"

"You heard him," Brina said, more defensively than she intended, but Harper had her afraid to say anything about what she really felt. "To check on the house."

"No, no, there was more to it than that," Julia said, not letting Brina off the hook as easily as she'd hoped. "I think he was hiding something in his coat pocket."

"Hiding? What are you talking about?" She gave Julia a curious look.

"You probably didn't see it because you were so stunned to see him at all. I couldn't tell what it was. He put his cloak on before he even reached down to give you a kiss. Didn't you notice how strange that seemed?"

Brina hadn't noticed, but she knew he was clearly hiding things about Mr. Browning and the card club. That had her curious as well as worried, but she didn't want Julia to know that.

"What could he be hiding, and more to the point, why would he be hiding anything from us? I felt he was acting a little odd. Maybe even a little nervous, but so was I. Neither of us expected the other to be here, and it was quite unsettling at first."

"It was that and more," Julia insisted, refusing to give up her stance on the subject.

"You aren't suggesting he was taking anything from the house, are you?" Brina said, not willing to go that far with her suspicions, but agreeing there was cause for concern.

"I'm only commenting on my observation. I know Harper had something in his pocket, and it seemed to me he was trying to hide it with his cloak. I'm not saying he took anything from here. It could have been something he brought into the house with him that he didn't want you to see, but whichever, he didn't want you to ask about it."

Suddenly feeling warm, Brina unfastened her cape and laid it on the table with her reticule. She didn't know what to think. Yes, it was disturbing Harper was in her parents' home and that Mr. Browning had fallen and was convalescing at Harper's home.

"You may be right," Brina admitted with some reservation. She'd known Harper all her life. She couldn't start believing the worst of him. "But I'm not sure what I can do about a young man's secrets or habits. And I don't want to believe he was here for any bad reason."

Brina didn't like doubting Harper's story, but this was the second—no third—time Harper wasn't acting himself when he was with her. And it didn't help her feelings that Julia had been suspicious too. Something had turned Harper into a different person. No, someone. Mr. Robert Browning.

Julia folded her arms across her chest. "Then, we'll leave it at that."

"Yes," Brina said more confidently than she was feeling. "Let's do forget about this conversation with him and put our minds on something far more pleasant while we look through Mama's painting materials."

"You lead the way," Julia said. "I'll follow."

Brina started down the corridor. She wanted to talk with Zane about this. The earl might be a scoundrel and gambler at heart, but she had no doubt he cared for his cousin. He would want to know that Mr. Browning had been injured. Zane had proven he was quite fond of Mr. Browning, but how could she mention this to him when she'd promised Harper she'd keep quiet about where he was and the fall?

Besides, she couldn't start relying on the earl to help her. She had enough worries about what she was feeling about him, the approaching end to the Season, and what would be expected of her if the earl kept all her mandates.

Oh, what a troublesome man Zane was. If only he hadn't come into her life and upset it just as she was getting her balance again.

# Chapter 19

Zane placed his cup back into the saucer and set his empty plate to the side of the breakfast table. If not for Brina's unusual terms, he would still be in bed at this hour. Thanks to her, he'd already had a rousing early morning ride in the curricle, followed by over an hour of fencing at his club. Now, he'd eaten scrambled eggs, toast, and a thick slice of ham as if he'd been famished.

Since he was no longer staying up all night playing cards and sipping on a brandy, he found his energy level during the day had exceedingly improved. It was amazing how much one could get done in a day when he went to bed with the chickens—as he'd heard someone once say.

However, all the good things that were improving his life couldn't keep him from missing the stinging taste of a brandy, the satisfaction of winning a hand, or curb his desire to have Brina in his bed. His gaze strayed to the window overlooking the side garden. It didn't seem to matter what he was thinking. He found a way to bring his thoughts back to her.

Zane had never had to be proper about anything in order to win a wager. Skill had always accomplished it. He either won or lost on how tightly he stayed focused on the game before him and how well he read his opponent and the cards he'd laid down. It was difficult for most players not to show any emotion when they were in a well-matched game. Sometimes it was something as simple as squeezing the cards a little too tight with their fingers or breathing in a little too deep. The trick was to study enough men to know the small signs. Over the years, he had learned to discern when someone wasn't playing fair too.

And Brina Feld wasn't playing fair.

Whether or not she was doing so intentionally, he'd yet to completely settle in his mind. He didn't think so, but there was a little qualm of doubt that surfaced from time to time. Especially when she was so pliant and eager for his every touch, willing for him to thoroughly satisfy them both. Was she trying to get him to break his promise? She had said kisses were exempt but not anything else. He had no doubt her passion for him was real, but he had no doubt her desire to win their wager was real too.

One other thing he was sure of—he couldn't get her off his mind. Most especially when he imagined her lying in his arms, coming to life beneath him. Those images wouldn't leave him alone. Day or night. When he was with her, it was almost impossible to hold back his desire. When he held her, felt her shiver, and sensed the beat of her heart racing along in time with his, it thrilled him.

He had no doubt he was the first to awaken the sensual desires left dormant since her husband's death. That pleased him. Zane wanted her to experience every one of them to their fullest. He was sure she wanted that too. As desperately as he did. And they would have, except for the minor consequence of their bargain. He was caught in an unfortunate cat-and-mouse game with her when what he wanted to do was strip off her clothing, lay her on the bed, and kiss her softly curved body until he was rigid with pain. And then make love to her all night.

Grunting, he pushed away from the breakfast table and made himself more comfortable by placing the ankle of one leg on top of the knee of the other. Thinking about her so early in the day was not doing him any favors. Best he get her off his mind in a hurry. He picked up the *Times* and unfolded it.

A quick glance at the headlines told him amazing things were happening all over the world. The East Indian Company was going to establish a settlement in Singapore. Zane remembered talking with Garrett Stockton about that possibility at a party the first night they met. The adventurer had been to Singapore and agreed that it was a long way from England. Zane wouldn't mind going there some day. He wanted to get to know people whose cultures were different from his. But he would have to think on making the voyage. He wasn't sure he'd be happy with so many long days at sea before reaching land.

His eyes scanned down the rest of the front page. America was still trying to purchase Florida from Spain, and a steamship named *Savannah* had crossed the Atlantic in twenty-six days. The world was getting bigger and closer together every year. Reading those articles should keep his mind off Brina.

For a few minutes.

He shook out the newsprint and started on the article about the ship but had barely gotten two or three sentences into it when he sensed Fulton standing in the doorway.

"Excuse me, my lord."

Zane lowered the paper and looked at the butler. "Yes?"

"Your uncles and sister have arrived and are wondering if they might join you here or in your drawing room."

*Hells bells.* He hadn't heard them at the door. They usually came in chattering so energetically, they could be heard all over the house.

It seemed the earlier he rose in the mornings, the earlier his uncles arrived. And Patricia with them today too. That didn't bode well. She was usually reserved for only the most important issues. What in the hell had he done this time to upset his family?

"Have them come in here, Fulton, and see if they'd like tea or something to eat."

"No, we don't need anything, my lord," Hector said, coming from behind Fulton.

Zane had even missed the familiar tap of his uncle's cane on the wooden floor. He must have been deep in thought about Brina.

Sylvester and Patricia followed Hector into the breakfast room. They all stopped at the head of the table, greeted him properly, and then proceeded to stare down at him with disapproving expressions.

He refolded the paper, laid it aside, and rose. "Please, sit down and join me."

Sylvester remained staunch with his shoulders and back straight as a board, not moving a muscle. Patricia continued to stare at him but stiffly folded her arms on her chest and drummed the fingers of both hands on her forearms. Uncle Hector cleared his throat and bobbed his chin as he stared at Zane with great condemnation.

For a moment or two he had no idea what he might have done to warrant the rebuking stares, but then, by chance he noticed the sleeves of his shirt. Times like these were what reminded him of how much he disliked family gatherings.

"No," Zane said with a little more force than he intended. "I can bloody well sit alone at my own breakfast table, in my own house, without wearing my coat."

"Well, of course you *can* do it, my lord," Patricia said dryly, her tone almost as stiff as her frame. "The point is that you *shouldn't*."

"And why would you want to?" Sylvester asked, obviously feeling the need to straighten his own perfectly tailored clothing. "It's most undignified to present yourself that way."

"You need to remain respectfully clothed at all times for the benefit of your staff, if not for yourself," Hector added to make sure he wasn't left out of the criticism for what they considered such careless behavior for the mere satisfaction of being comfortable. "Besides, you are no longer alone. You have three guests."

"What?" Zane argued defiantly. "This is ridiculous. You aren't guests. You're family. And I doubt any of you or my staff would faint or go running to the gossipmongers for seeing me without my coat."

"Why take the chance?" Uncle Syl asked.

Zane fumed and continued with his steely expression. He hadn't asked to be the earl, but now that he was, he should be able to set his own standards in his own home. That should be the one place he could relax and be himself.

Yet, all three remained unyielding in their posture, along with Hector agitatedly tapping his cane. Frustrating as it was, Zane only had two viable options. He could extend and hold out and ignore their bluster about *his* rights in *his* house, or give into their demands, find out what they wanted, grant it to pacify them, and send them on their way as quickly as possible.

It was Sunday, for heaven's sake. Each one of them should have been in church, not pestering him.

"All right," he declared in a nonconciliatory tone, swinging his coat from the back of his chair.

This was why he didn't know if he had the fortitude to be a good earl. This was why his uncle, his uncle's son, and Zane's cousin should have never been riding in that carriage together, should have never died and left the unimaginable task of dealing with this family to him. He simply wasn't good at it.

He would never be patient enough. He had been quite happy with his life as it had been before the title fell to him.

Damnation, he wished it hadn't.

It wasn't in his nature to want to please people. He wanted to live *his* life *his* way and allow others to do as they wished. No doubt the previous earl and the previous two heirs would have loved sitting at the breakfast table buttoned up to the neck, wearing a coat that fit like a glove but was a hell of a lot less comfortable.

After shoving his arms through the sleeves and settling it properly over his shoulders, he walked over and held out a chair for Patricia. She smiled graciously, seeming perfectly happy now that he had donned his coat, and seated herself.

Zane and his uncles then joined her around the table.

"We wouldn't usually bother you on the Lord's day," Uncle Syl said. "Your aunt Beatrice is in a dither. Her daughter, Thelma, wants to marry Mr. Aldrich Clark," Uncle Syl said.

That didn't seem like earth-shattering news to Zane. "Patricia told me she unfortunately didn't make a match last year, so I would think that's good to hear she found someone to her liking," he answered, thinking this was easy enough to handle. "I give my permission."

Patricia's gasp, Hector's grunt, and Sylvester's harrumph left Zane no doubt that wasn't the answer they wanted.

"Do you know who he is?" Patricia asked in what could only be considered a scathing tone because he'd said something so incomprehensible.

Zane sluffed it off as he always had. If he got upset every time he displeased his sister or his uncles, he'd be in a perpetual state of agitation. "I don't personally know him, but if she wants to marry him, why should I have any objections?"

"His sister ran away from home over a year ago to become an actress," Uncle Syl replied, as if that was the most horrible thing to have happened in London in years. "And we have it on good authority she was actually seen on stage at one of the theatres."

Patricia sighed heavily. "It was devastating to all the Clarks. Not only his family, as you can imagine. You must go to Thelma and explain why he's not a suitable match and insist she needs to choose a different man to marry."

No. He wouldn't do that.

Zane looked at the three stern faces staring at him, remaining silent as he pondered.

He could easily tell them how unreasonable they were sounding, but he had set a precedent with Robert—though his sister and uncles didn't know about it. Was it unfair to allow Thelma to marry when he had prevented Robert from doing so?

But there was a difference. Robert was planning an elopement to a woman almost twice his age, and without an ounce of social standing.

Thelma's case was different. Even so, he knew he had to handle this delicately.

"We are all in agreement that Clark is a well-respected name in the ton, are we not?" Zane asked.

"Oh, yes," Patricia answered as if she adored every one of them. Quite so."

"Then what Mr. Clark's sister has or hasn't done is no reflection on what he might or might not do. Thelma shouldn't be punished for what someone else has done. Tell Aunt Beatrice that as long as he has adequate allowance to take care of her daughter in a style that's fitting, I see no reason to interfere."

"But what about the children?" Uncle Syl asked, looking at Zane as if he'd lost his mind.

Zane returned the expression. "What children?" Zane asked. "Does Mr. Clark have children by a previous marriage?"

"No," Uncle Hector said, jumping into the conversation with a strong tap of his cane to the floor.

Sylvester raised his hand to assuage and settle his brother's irritation. "The ones Thelma will have if she marries Mr. Clark. His daughters might have the same predisposition as his sister and think it's fine to defy one's family to run off and be an actress."

"What do you know about children?" Zane asked. "You've never had any. You don't know how they might behave."

"That's not to say I don't know about such things as bad blood in headstrong children, my lord. And how it can be passed down from family to family much like freckles."

*Freckles?*

What the hell was he talking about? Zane snorted. "I know nothing of the kind. And furthermore, neither do you."

"Well, I do." Patricia injected herself into the conversation. "I have children. And you know I take your side whenever possible, my lord, I always have, but there is such a thing as bad blood."

His sister had never taken his side in anything.

A long string of silent curses entered Zane's mind as Fulton quietly walked into the dining room and placed a small silver tray in front of him. A note. Probably an invitation to another party. He started to wave the butler away, but on second thought, he realized it didn't matter what the correspondence was. It gave him a much-needed reason to be diverted from his family.

"Excuse me," he said, rising from his chair. "This might be important."

He walked over to the window, broke the wax seal and opened the note. Glancing down at the signature, he felt a jump in his heart rate and smiled. It *was* important.

Dear Lord Blacknight,

    If you are not otherwise engaged this afternoon, I might be available at half past three for a ride in a carriage.

                      With regards,
                      Mrs. Feld

She was asking him to take her for a ride. A lady asking a gentleman? Surely that couldn't be proper, but blast it, if he didn't love it when she wasn't proper. Zane looked over at his uncles and sister. They continued to be in deep conversation over poor Thelma's love life and children she'd yet to have.

At least there would be a bright spot at the end of the day for him, and he'd do his best to see that Aunt Beatrice's daughter had a bright end to her afternoon as well. It they wanted him to be the head of the family, damnation, he would.

# Chapter 20

Sitting in the back of a well-polished landau on plush comfortable seats with the top down and being driven by a liveried driver was the proper way for a gentleman to take a lady on an afternoon ride through the park, Brina thought.

It would also be quite boring if not for the fact the dashing Earl of Blacknight was seated beside her. He made all the difference in how she felt.

The reason most everyone in the ton remained in their best clothing and took to the parks on a sunny Sunday afternoon during the Season was so they could see and be seen by others. The weather hadn't disappointed Londoners today. The sun was midway down the western sky with only a stray trace of white clouds breaking across the moderate shade of blue. Warm air didn't have a hint of breeze to stir it around, making the day pleasant. Cloaks, capes, and coats had come off in favor of lightweight clothing.

Brina held a pale gray parasol edged with a darker shade of braided ribbon to match her dress and pelisse. Zane wore a black hat and dark brown coat and trousers. The buttons on his dark-red quilted waistcoat were covered in the same fabric. Well-matched horses and expensive wheels allowed the carriage to move along the road at a smooth and gentle pace.

If not for Zane, Brina would have much rather been back at her house rolling bandages for the sisters, which was her usual Sunday afternoon project. However, she had agreed to such outings as this with the earl to show his family he had settled down, graciously accepted his place in Society, and was ready to be a respectable member of the ton.

Much to her surprise and dismay, he was doing a splendid job.

It also vexed her that time was passing quickly, and she still hadn't heard one hint of gossip that Zane might have slipped and taken a drink. No one had come forward to say he'd uttered so much as a swear—let alone an obscene one. He'd come close with her. But not close enough for him to surrender and agree she'd won. Some oft-used words of exclamation couldn't be considered obscene. Too many people said them or variations of them. She often said "merciful heavens" or "drat," which a few people would say are variations of "hellfire" and "damnation." Both words were in the Bible for goodness' sake! How could she insist they were obscene?

His strength troubled her, impressed her, and drew her. Drew her with such fearless abandonment, it would be so easy to give in to it and not even struggle. His sense of character was stronger than she'd suspected, than she was led to believe by all the gossips who said he cared nothing for his family or the responsibility of an earl that had fallen to him.

And she couldn't forget Paris.

But what was she to do? Go back on her word and not marry him? There might be no other choice but that seemed almost as dreadful as marrying him. There was the comment he said the other day in her house. *I bet you.* Though she was in a mind to let it slide at the time, she hadn't forgotten it. Slip of the tongue, well-used turn of phrase, or whatever he chose to call it, he couldn't deny he said those three little words and offered her a wager no matter his intention at the time. She must keep it as an arrow in her quiver if he didn't start drinking or gambling soon. She might have to use it.

Not only did she have to consider all that, she also had to reflect on the fact she enjoyed being with him. He made her laugh, but he'd never laughed at her. He desired her but hadn't taken advantage of her advances. How could she not appreciate a man who surprised her with a horse to ride and helped her make bags of tea for the poor? All these things had somehow helped her come to care for him. How deeply, she didn't know yet. Hadn't wanted to know. Which, of course, left her emotions in turmoil because she knew she could never trust herself to marry again.

So, what would she do if he somehow managed to refrain from all the gentlemen's vices she'd asked of him, and really expected her to marry him?

"You seem deep in thought, Mrs. Feld," the earl said as they crossed the busy street and headed onto the path that would put them in St. James's Park.

"Do I?" she asked, grateful he couldn't read her mind and hoping her cheeks weren't coloring as she answered.

He nodded. "You seem troubled. Are you not appreciating our proper afternoon ride?"

She looked over at him and smiled. "Very much."

"Really?" He gave her a half grin and moved more

into the corner of the landau and turned his body so he
could face her directly without having to continue turning his head. "Are you not missing the horses yet?"

"Yes, and I'm upset you know that I am," she teased.
While the thought of a neighborhood and park she'd seen
a thousand times might be boring, the man she was with
was not. She missed sitting atop a horse and guiding the
animal where she wanted it to go. It made her feel more
a part of her surroundings rather than someone who was
looking at them.

"Tell me," she said, "are we being followed by anyone today?"

"I'm followed every time I leave my house. I have
adapted much in the same way I am getting used to having a butler, a solicitor, and my uncles arriving every
day to go over yet more documents, account books, contracts, and requests for my help." A chuckle reverber-
ated softly in his throat. "Don't ask our driver to lose the
cabriolet shadowing us today. He's not capable and neither are the mares."

She gave Zane a confident smile. "I wouldn't. I trust
no one but you to handle a team of horses so expertly."

"I'm waiting for the day you will trust me with other,
more important matters."

His gaze swept over her face, making her feel she
could believe him, even though she didn't know specifically what he was referring to. It still made her want to
believe him. He was winning her over with his unpredict-
able, slightly ungentlemanly behavior. He'd never been
crass or rude to her or anyone else when he was with her.
Well, perhaps he was rude when he hadn't responded to
the duchess's dinner invitation to let the lady know he
would be attending. Now he was reluctantly, but graciously,
making amends for that with a party of his own.

"I do wish I could do something a little scandalous

today," he said. "Everyone we're passing seems stiff and in need of a reason to relax and take pleasure in the afternoon."

Brina laughed. There was something enchanting about him saying that. But everything about him seemed to be enticing. She tried to ignore the feeling by saying, "You have done enough for a lifetime."

He shook his head and his brow creased. "I was thinking how I'd like to reach over and kiss you right now."

Her breaths became rapid at the thought, but it would be madness. So instead of encouraging him, which she would have liked to do, she asked, "Is your book of poetry in your pocket? Reading it should curb your restless state."

He patted down the front of his coat and then looked around his booted feet. "How did I get away without it? It's been my constant companion since you gave it to me."

Brina laughed. "I don't believe you."

His eyes twinkled with mischief. "Nor should you."

"You probably don't even know where it is."

He leaned toward her once again, giving her a gentle smile. "Not true. I would never misplace something you gave me."

The way he looked at her meant he knew exactly where the book was, and that made her want to kiss him even more. But not now. Later. When they were alone. She would.

They fell silent as the driver maneuvered the horses and carriage to fall in line behind a queue of conveyances waiting to enter the congested traffic already in the park. While they were stopped, Brina listened to chatter from people in nearby carriages, the jingle and rattle of harnesses, and snorts from the horses as they hustled by pulling their load. Recent rains had turned buds into leaves on the trees and shrubs. Flowers had been planted at the entrance and many of the blooms had opened. Scattered patches of green grass flowed into brown patches of ground still dormant from the winter and made a patchwork of the area.

"Which reminds me," Brina said, changing the subject before either one of them acted on what they were both feeling. "Do you have any questions about your upcoming dinner?"

"None. I'll find a way to get through it. Patricia and my uncles are excited. They were all over to my house this morning and they think your idea for me to host the evening was superb. They keep asking Fulton questions, and he continues to assure them his staff has everything in order and under control. It should be a perfect dinner party for us."

"Us?" she questioned. "Why do you say that? I sent over the menu, guest list, and seating arrangements for Fulton, but the evening is for you alone."

"No," he said huskily, reaching over to let his hand rub down her arm. "It's for us. For our future. Together."

Thoughts of the future made her heart race again. As a lover, yes. Yes, she'd be willing to find a way to make that happen. She looked away from him, and on a grassy area not far away she saw people standing and waving. "Isn't that your uncle Hector and his wife waving to you?"

"Yes, and Uncle Syl with them." Zane paid them no mind. "It seems I can't go anywhere without seeing them these days."

She turned back to him and smiled. "We should go over and speak to them."

"No," he said unequivocally.

His short answer and clipped tone irritated her. "It's the polite thing to do."

"It's torture. I told you I spent part of the morning with them. That was more than enough for today."

"You can't just ignore them," she insisted. "They are motioning for us to drive over and say hello. Look, they have refreshments and will probably ask us to join them for a while. This is something you need to do. Something you wanted to do. Learn how to make your family feel you care about them and that what is important to them is important to you. Furthermore, I can't help you be polite and proper if you don't take my recommendations."

Zane rose up in the seat, looked their way, and gave them a long, hearty wave. He then turned back to Brina, smiled engagingly, settled back into the cushion in a much too casual manner for being in public, and said, "That is all they are getting this afternoon. Besides," he continued as they started up a small rise, "I told the driver to take us down to the abbey after our ride through the park. We'll stop there and take a stroll to look at the buildings you wanted to see in that area. I've wanted to do it before now, but decided I'd rather take a closer look at the area with you."

"Oh," she said, touched by his words. Just when he was ignoring his family and she was thinking him irredeemable, he surprised her with his kindness. "You remembered I wanted to do that?"

His eyes swept over her face. He leaned in toward her again. "I recall everything about you, Brina. I remember how you taste, how you feel in my arms. At night in my dreams, I hear your sighs. When I wake, your scent surrounds me like a garden of sweet-smelling flowers. I am never without thoughts of you and that makes you always with me."

His voice was husky, persuasive, and delighted every one of her senses. His gaze was so penetrating, it was as if Brina were living every word he said. She remembered all those things about him too. As surely as he was sitting beside her, she wanted to kiss him and show him her pleasure.

It didn't matter there were other people walking near their carriage, riding on horseback, and wagons and carts passing by, moving along in front, or trailing behind them. That very real, stimulating attraction was always between them. She moved to reach over and slip her hand into his, press her lips on his, but thankfully the carriage wheel hit a bump in the ground and they were jostled. The moment to touch and kiss was lost.

"You are being bad, my lord," she said in a voice that was only half teasing. Sometimes he made her feel so good, she wondered if she might wake up to find him a dream.

"If you only knew how desperately I wanted to take you in my arms right now, you would know that I am actually being very good."

She believed him, and that was why she changed the subject to one that she'd been debating even mentioning. "Have you seen Robert or had word from him?"

"No one has seen him," Zane responded. "Uncle Hector had a terse note saying he was with a friend and there was no need to worry about him. He'd return in a few days."

"Hmm," she said thoughtfully. It was good to know that Harper had kept his word about having Robert alert his family, but it did little to ease her suspicions all was not as Harper had told it.

Zane looked at her as if he were giving himself time to digest her words. "Why did you say that?" he asked. "And do that?"

"Do what?" she asked in all seriousness.

"Frown."

"I didn't," she rebutted.

His bright, delicious blue eyes locked on hers. "You know you did and what does 'hmm' mean?"

Meeting his unwavering stare, she quirked her head a little and asked, "What does it mean when you say it?"

"That I'm unsure of the meaning of what the person has either asked me or answered me. And *that* usually concerns me, Brina. So what do you know about Robert that I don't know?"

"Well, of course, I have no idea. Why don't you tell me everything you know about him?"

He smiled, and as if without thinking, he reached over and ran his gloved hand down her cheek before drawing it away. "Gentlemen allow ladies to go first."

She watched him as closely as he watched her. Their cat-and-mouse game had returned. "I defer to you."

"All right. Because of Robert's recent behavior, I've asked a friend to check around to see if he has accumulated gambling debts."

Anxiety she'd had about Harper being friends with Mr. Browning returned full force. Suddenly she was worrying that Harper might have debts. "I'm glad you are checking into that."

"I'm also checking on the man named Remick. Robert has mentioned him. I don't know but he may be hustling both our cousins to join a club so he can get them into debt with him."

Brina was really treading on unfamiliar ground here. She didn't know much about men's gambling habits but she hoped no one was deliberately deceiving Harper to get money from him. His allowance was generous, but it wasn't bottomless.

"That doesn't make sense. Why would he want them in a club only to get them into debt to him?"

"So they will eventually harass their families for more money to pay what they owe."

"Oh, that's an absolutely wretched thing for a man to do."

"But it happens more often than you might think. Now, what do you know?"

Unsure of how much to say for fear of betraying Harper, she offered, "I saw Harper two or three days ago and asked about Robert."

The corners around his eyes tightened. "I need to know everything he said."

She stared at Zane. She appreciated his honesty. It let her know things were more serious than she suspected. Perhaps she needed to tell him what she knew, even though it would mean betraying Harper and ruining her relationship with him should he ever find out. It wasn't an easy decision to make.

"Brina." He huffed her name impatiently. "Do you know something that will help me help Robert?"

After another brief hesitation, she bit back her resistance and said, "I might. Robert is staying with Harper."

He gave her a disbelieving look and grunted. "You knew this days ago and you are just now seeing fit to tell me?"

"Harper said he would see to it Robert let his family know he was fine now and with a friend. He obviously did that."

"Wait." Zane kept his tone level, but leaned in close to her. "What did you mean by he is fine *now*?"

She swallowed hard, fearing she was jeopardizing her relationship with Harper for Zane and his cousin. Lifting her shoulder a little, she turned and stared into the distance, listening to the sounds of the carriage and the horses clopping along.

"You are giving me cause to worry, Brina. I suddenly have the feeling you are not telling me truth."

"I am," she said, taking umbrage at his words and facing him again.

"Then perhaps it's just you aren't telling me all of it. Why is it so hard for you to trust me?" he asked sharply.

"I don't appreciate your tone, my lord. Even if I don't tell you everything I know, it doesn't make what I do say less true."

He averted his gaze and muttered something so low she couldn't hear it, but was certain it was a curse word. Whether or not it was obscene she didn't know.

When he looked back at her, anger dominated his face. "I need to know everything if I'm trying to help my cousin."

"And I am trying to help mine," she said just as hotly, folding her hands tightly across her chest. "If you want to know all the truth, it's that I don't think Robert is a very good influence on Harper. He had no problems enjoying young ladies and staying away from excessive gambling until he started gaming with Robert, and I wish they weren't friends."

"Is that so?" He gave a short derisive laugh. "It just so happens I think the exact thing about Harper. He could very well be the one who has been leading Robert astray."

"What?" she exclaimed more loudly than she should and leaned in close to him. They stared at each other, equal in passion about their cousins. "I'll have you know that Harper is a gentleman and has never done anything wrong in his life. He's only recently started gambling, sir—since spending all his time with Robert, who was obviously taught everything he knows by you in Paris and Vienna."

Zane's grimace hardened. "Fine. Don't tell me," he retorted and leaned back in the seat with bounce. "I'll talk to Harper."

"Heavens, no!" She reached over and placed her hand on his upper arm as if worried he might try to immediately leave the carriage. "You mustn't do that. Ever. Harper would never trust me with anything again. Promise me you won't mention this conversation to Harper or Robert, and I'll tell you."

His expression softened. "All right, but tell me everything you know."

Zane listened attentively as Brina relayed her last conversation with Harper. "So it seemed suspicious a young man would fall and injure himself so badly—but it could be true. Except Harper recently showed signs of bruising."

Nodding, Zane offered, "It sounds like they both might be gaming at a house or club where ruffians play."

Brina closed her eyes for a moment and shook her head. That is not what she wanted to hear him say. "What can we do about it?"

He shook his head decisively. "There is no 'we' in this, Brina. I am already looking into this."

"Zane, you must promise me again that you won't go to Harper's to talk to Robert."

He gave her a conciliatory smile. "I might get angry with you from time to time, but I won't go back on my word to you. You should know that by now."

Yes, to her detriment, she was learning just how seriously he took giving his word.

"Besides, if Robert is staying out of sight while his bruises heal, for now he is safe. That gives me time to find out what's going on."

"If Harper is mixed up in any trouble, will you tell me?"

His eyes swept down her face and lingered on her lips. "Of course, I will."

"Thank you. I'd want to—"

"My lord, Mrs. Feld, how are you on this lovely afternoon?"

Brina looked over to the carriage that had driven up beside them to see Zane's uncle, Mr. Sylvester Browning, and his brother and his wife smiling at them.

She heard Zane mutter another oath under his breath, and she smiled. When he didn't go to family, they came to him.

After a short chat with the Brownings and a lengthy ride through the park with more than a few nods, waves, and calls of greeting to people they knew, the earl's carriage rolled to a stop in front of the abbey. The large stone building with its plain wooden door stood out like a stalwart beacon among all the smaller buildings surrounding it. There was nothing notable about it other than its size. A small sign out front read THE SISTERS OF PILWILLOW CROSSINGS. The good work that went on inside for the poor made it a formidable and a majestic place to Brina.

Zane hopped out and reached to help her down onto the pavement. "This isn't a part of London I'm familiar with," he offered as he looked around the street.

"I wonder why. No gaming hells nearby?" she offered with a smile, knowing it wasn't a busy section of London for shoppers or many businesses.

"If you keep teasing me in such an attractive manner, Brina, I'm going to have to go against my better judgment, that of my uncles, and the entirety of my family and most of the ton, and kiss you right here on the street."

"You wouldn't."

He took a step forward and reached for her. She whirled away and laughed. "You must behave, my lord, or you'll have it where neither of us are welcomed in Society again."

His gaze swept seductively up and down her face.

"There will be no promises about that from me on this afternoon."

Deciding it was best to leave that subject alone, Brina cleared her throat, pointed, and said, "The sisters set up tables and give out the food there in front of the main entrance."

"The building is bigger than I thought it was. How many women live there?"

"I don't know for sure. I never asked. Probably thirty."

"Are all of them nuns?"

"No. Maybe half. In this abbey, you don't have to take the vows of the church and join the order to unite with them. But everyone is to follow all their rules. Remaining chaste, participating in prayers, and performing whatever duties you're assigned without grumblings or rancor. Otherwise, they would be dismissed from the sisterhood."

"Sounds reasonable," he commented.

When she showed Zane where the tea and bandages she'd prepared were handed out, Brina noticed the now-familiar cabriolet had stopped in front of a building not far behind them. The driver looked the same, standard black top hat and hunkered down in a black cloak. Though he'd never been close enough she could see his face. It angered her the man continued to follow Zane. He had no right to watch the earl's every move. She supposed it was a testament to Zane's willpower that he hadn't flattened the man.

For a few moments she thought about grabbing Zane's hand and racing down the street, ducking between buildings with him, much in the way she had imagined racing through underground tunnels when they were in the chateau in Paris. But she then remembered how upset everyone was about the curricle ride, and she pushed the exciting thought of escaping with the earl aside.

There were only a few other people on the street, so Brina started walking and Zane fell in beside her. Three men walked ahead of them and a couple strolled leisurely on the opposite side of the street. The road was free of traffic, except when the cabriolet rolled slowly behind them.

"This building behind the abbey that we're going to look at, have you checked to see if it is for sale?"

"Yes," she said confidently as they continued to walk. "It's not currently available."

"Perhaps I could put in a good word—"

"No, thank you, my lord," she said, looking over at him pointedly. "This is my project for the sisters, and I will handle it myself in due time. I'm in no hurry. Besides, Sister Francine *is* the type of person who will need to be gently coaxed into seeing that the sisters could make use of a separate chapel for the abbey. Their wants and needs are few and simple, but their service and hearts are pure. I only want to—"

From the corner of her eye, a splash of color caught Brina's attention. She glanced at the window she was passing. There, displayed in the seamstress shop, was a gown almost the exact shade of the pink costume she wore to the masquerade ball.

Her heart skipped a beat.

# Chapter 21

 he gown was gorgeous.

Brina stopped to stare at it. The round neckline was low but wouldn't be considered shockingly racy. The high waist and short capped sleeves were banded with beaded velvet ribbon of the same bright shade. The skirt flowed in wispy waves of short, curled flounces trimmed with the same exquisite ribbon. The late afternoon sun was at the right angle to shine on the beading. It sparkled, twinkled, and called to her hidden desire to permanently shed her widow's weeds and wear something soft and beautifully feminine again.

And then, of all things, she imagined herself dressed in it, walking into a glittering ballroom in London, the skirt swishing from side to side and around her legs with every step.

Toward Zane.

An intense swelling of something she didn't quite understand filled her chest. Right then, all she wanted him to do was sweep her up into his arms and never let her go.

He smiled reflectively. "That looks like—"

"Yes, I know," she interrupted him and answered simply. Beautiful as it was, the gown wasn't something a widow should wear. And it didn't matter how many fantasies she had about Zane and love and all the rest of it. She would remain a widow.

Brina turned and started walking again. Faster this time, feeling as if she needed to get away from that gown, that color, and Zane. He was making her want things she shouldn't want, feel things she shouldn't feel. The all too sudden and real fear that she had already lost her heart to him hit her with such force, she was finding it difficult to manage.

There was nothing she could do. She couldn't marry again.

Zane easily kept up with her hurried stride. They walked in silence for a few moments before he asked, "Why don't you want to look at the gown?"

"It's not for me," she answered in a clipped tone.

"Why? You looked glorious when you rushed into the room wearing that color in Paris. I remember thinking that fate had an evil sense of humor. Sending in the most beautiful lady I had ever seen, and I was bound to a chair."

His words took the edge off her tense feelings and her footsteps slowed. She laughed softly. It was wonderful the way he could change her outlook with just a few words. "You were so angry that night, I'm surprised you remember what I was wearing."

"I told you. I can't forget one thing about you. That night will be with me always."

"Me too," she said, returning to her more somber state.

"I'll never forget the shock of hearing you say, 'Come untie me.'"

The hint of a chuckle in his chest was soothing.

"I was desperate," he admitted without reservation.

"So was I."

"You never told me why you were at the ball," he said, intentionally bumping her arm softly with his elbow.

"We decided the reason for the mask was so people didn't have to talk about what happened or why they were there."

"But you know the reason for my presence. I want to know everything about you. Being there, dressed as you were, and now knowing who you are, puzzles me."

Her steps slowed and she stared at the backs of three men walking in front of them. She supposed there was no harm in telling him since he already knew about her connection to the abbey. "I foolishly thought that since I had looked into a life of celibacy and servitude that I should look into a life of entertainment and debauchery." She continued to amble along the street without looking at him. "Does that surprise you?"

"No. It sounds like a human reaction."

She sighed. He was being kind. "The minute my aunt left me on my own, I knew I wasn't made for that kind of life any more than I would take to life at the abbey. When I entered the room you were in that night, I only wanted a safe place to hide until it was time to meet my aunt and leave."

"Did something happen after I left you in the room?"

"No, I locked myself inside and thought about you."

That caused him to glance at her. "Me? Why?"

She stopped again and so did he. "I was wondering if you were doing more than kissing her. The woman who tied you."

"Brina," he said her name on a husky breath as he looked deeply into her eyes and shook his head. "Don't ask about my past."

"Why can't I be as curious as you? It's not like I don't know you've been with countless women. You are known as a scoundrel and rake as well as a gambler."

"Who has mended his ways," Zane emphasized. His eyes stayed steady on hers. "For you. I've not thought about kissing anyone but you since I saw you walking down the street the day after I arrived in London."

She looked into his eyes and felt a horrible, over-whelming sense of loss because she knew she couldn't have him. "I'm not available. I've tried to tell you I am committed to being—"

"No," he said earnestly. "I don't want you to be a widow, Brina. I don't want you to be Mrs. Feld. I want you to be my wife, my countess, Lady Blacknight. I am committed to keeping my word and you must be—"

The sudden squeal of youthful laughter startled Brina and Zane. They looked down the street. Not far from them, a boy the age of nine or ten and thin as a sapling was jumping up and down in a jubilant way and in a singsong voice saying, "I won again. I won again." His friend, younger by more than a couple of years, with full cheeks and a chunky build, stayed huddled against the side of a building, holding cards in his hands.

Thankful for the children's interruption, Brina said, "It looks as if they are having a good time with their game. I like to see children who are happy and playing."

"I'm not sure what's happening," Zane said, seeming to study the boys intently.

"What do you mean?" she asked.

"Only one of them appears to be happy. Wait here." He started walking directly toward the boys.

Brina wasn't about to stay behind. She was as inquisitive as he was. Catching up to him, she asked, "What are you going to do?"

"I'm going to talk to them." He looked over at her and smiled. "Don't worry, I'm not going to join their game."

She returned his smile with a rueful chuckle. "I think you should."

The two boys weren't wearing the best of clothing, but it didn't appear they were street urchins who'd been left to their own care by unfortunate circumstances. They were clean and too well-fed not to have someone looking after them. Brina scanned the area but didn't see anyone else paying attention to the boys.

As she and Zane neared the pair, Brina drew closer to Zane. He immediately knelt down to be on the smallest boy's level. Startled, the youngster shrank away from him.

"Don't be frightened," he said in a calm voice and tone. "I only came over to talk to you because I heard you playing. Who's winning?"

"I am," the tallest boy said, looking at Zane. "He's not a very good player."

Zane eyed the cards the younger child held and then picked up some of the ones that lay on the pavement and looked at them.

"What do you think you're doing, Mister?" the oldest boy asked, staring at Zane with a menacing expression. "We aren't causing anyone trouble. Those are my cards you have in your hands, and I'll thank you not to take them."

Zane shrugged. "I'm not going to take them from you. I'm going to give your friend a lesson in card playing." He looked up at Brina and repeated, "A lesson. So his next game will be a fair one. Don't you agree every game should be fair?"

The youth rolled his small brown eyes from side to side and wiped his forearm under his nose before declaring, "Of course I do."

Zane nodded and gave his attention back to the youngest. "What's your name?"

"William," he answered shyly.

"What's his name?" Zane asked with a quirk of his head toward the taller boy.

"Claude."

"We don't need you in our game," Claude piped up in a high-pitched tone. "We aren't doing anything wrong. You have no cause to bother us."

Zane ignored him and kept his attention on William. Big green eyes stared back at him. "Do you mind if I see your cards?"

"It's all right," Brina said, stepping closer to William. "You can trust him. He only wants to help you."

Timidly, the little one handed the cards to Zane. "Do you see this smudge on the card right here?" He pointed to the top left corner.

William nodded.

"It's the ten of hearts. So, if you saw this card in his hands"—he motioned with his head to the taller kid—"what would you think?"

"He's holding the ten of hearts."

"That's right," Zane said with a nod. "It would help you win if you knew what cards he was holding, right?"

"I didn't know that smudge was on the card," Claude defended. "I swear I didn't."

Zane continued to ignore him. "This card has a little dot of red right there." He pointed. "And this one has the edge frayed. See them?"

The youngster nodded again.

"The next time someone asks you to play a game, check all the cards over carefully for markings, and if there are any, don't play. It won't be a fair game. Do you understand?"

"I had no idea the cards had markings," Claude interjected dramatically. "Found them in the rubbish. Thanks for letting me know, Mister. That was right kind of you."

William scrambled to his feet, one chubby hand made a fist and the other he held out, palm up, as he glared at his friend. "You cheated. Give me back my money."

"I didn't cheat," Claude declared in an angry tone, putting both fists up in a threatening manner. "You want to fight?"

Brina was about to speak up when Zane calmly said, "There will be no fighting over this. Give him back the money you won off him." He rose to tower over the older boy. "Go on, do it. All of it."

Claude scowled at Zane.

"We can do this your way or my way. Makes no difference to me."

The youngster slowly relaxed his hands and lowered his arms. He shook his shoulders a time or two, shoved his hand into his pocket, produced two pence, and returned it. William's round cheeks filled out more with his wide smile before he turned and ran away.

Zane gave the cards back to Claude. "Take your marked cards and peddle them on boys your own age."

"Hey, mister," Claude said as he slipped the cards into his pocket, "do you and the lady want to see some kittens? I'll show you where they are for three pence." He held out his hand.

Brina stepped closer to him. "A kitten?"

"Two of them." He held up two fingers. "Soft as the hair on a baby's face, my mum always says. And the momma cat is friendly." He continued to hold out his hand.

Zane looked over at Brina. "You want to see them?"

She felt a leap of delight. "I'd love to if you think it

will be all right. I haven't seen a kitten in—well, a very
long time."

"How do I know you won't take my coins and run?"
Zane asked the lad.

"I give you my word," Claude said, lifting his chin
proudly.

Zane reached into his pocket and pulled out a small
coin. "I'm going to give you one. If you really have a kitten you can show the lady, I'll give you the rest."

Brina slipped her hand around Zane's arm and smiled.
It felt good to touch him. He laid his hand over hers and
gently squeezed. They followed Claude a short distance
down a side street before entering an alleyway. At the
end of it was a small, rundown shed. The door was missing, and the roof had caved in. Claude scrambled underneath the two steps and out of sight.

All was quiet for a few moments, and then she heard
several soft meows and his hand shot out from under the
step holding a small gray kitten with the biggest, most
beautiful gray eyes Brina had ever seen. Its belly, neck,
and paws were white as snow.

Zane reached down and plucked the kitten from the
boy's hand and gave it to Brina.

She took the squirming ball of fur and immediately
put it up to her neck so she could feel its softness and
warmth. The kitty pawed at her chin and wiggled. Its
meow was so faint, she almost hadn't heard it. She felt
such joy just holding the thin, soft-as-a-tuff-of-cotton
body close to her.

"Do you want me to bring the other one out?" Claude
called from underneath the dilapidated porch.

"Yes, of course," she answered the lad.

Zane looked at her, and for a moment she could have
sworn he saw the love she was feeling for him shining
in her eyes.

# Chapter 22

Zane shut the ledger and pushed back his chair. "I think that settles it, Uncles."

"Settles what?" Hector asked from his seat across the massive oak desk.

"Your tutelage. I have now been through every account book, looked over every contract, and been briefed on every tenant. I know where every piece of property is located, the size of it and approximate value, and the type of land it is: grazing, waste, fertile, or inhabited. I will continue to seek your guidance in the future when needed, but for now, I see no reason for you two to make daily visits."

Uncle Syl shifted in his chair and sniffed. Uncle Hector tapped his cane once on the floor as they looked at each other for a considerable amount of time. Surely they had known this time was coming, but clearly not that it would be today.

Finally, Hector's chin bobbed. "What about the

family?" he asked. "Many requests have been made of you that you haven't addressed."

"That's true. I've delayed that until my review of everything was finished." There were so many different family members asking for favors of different magnitudes, he didn't remember them all. "I admit this is a way the two of you can continue to help me."

Hector glanced over at Sylvester, and they both smiled, thinking that would signal a reason to maintain their routine.

"Put together a list for me of all the people and requests that have been made so far. In fact, make me a list of all my relatives and what relation they are to me. Are they second or third cousin—niece, aunt, or uncle. You know what I mean. All of them. My mother's family as well. Once that is done, I'll set aside a time to meet with you and go over everyone's requests."

That wasn't what they wanted to hear.

Hector's brows grew closer together by the second. "I'm not sure I know the names of all of them."

"Neither do I," Uncle Syl said, looking puzzled by the thought of what Zane suggested. "You know how it is. Cousins, nieces, and nephews get married and have children, which makes you have more cousins, nieces, and nephews. How far down the family tree do you want us to go?"

"As far as you think is necessary. I'll leave that decision to the two of you. I would also like a recommendation from you as to the merits of their requests."

Sylvester was the first to give in. He bowed from his lower back toward Zane. "We'll get it done. Your great-aunt Imogene will probably know everyone in the family. If not, she'll know who does."

"Yes. Leave it to us." Hector moved his cane around and placed it between his knees, resting both his palms on the handle, and leaned forward. "But we were hoping we might continue in our assistance of you until after you are settled."

"I am," Zane said. He hadn't indulged in a vice in three weeks. How more settled could he get?

"But you're not wed yet," Sylvester argued, as if Zane didn't know that.

His uncle was unbelievable. "Neither are you. I appreciate the two of you wanting to keep helping, but for the reasons I indicated, it's unnecessary. Besides, I don't know when I will wed."

Or if he would wed.

He and Brina had seen each other several times since their visit to the abbey. She always seemed happy to him. They enjoyed each other, but he still wasn't certain he could trust Brina to fulfill her part of their agreement, even though he'd followed to the letter the rules she laid down—well, except for a swear or two. And then there was that troubling mistake he'd made in her dining room when he'd mentioned making a bet with her. That caused him some worry. She could choose to hold that against him. He had actually said the words to her, innocent though they were.

"But you have Mrs. Feld's assurance she will wed you after the last ball," Uncle Hector said. "Unless you have done something to keep her from accepting your proposal? Something we don't know about?"

"No," he said firmly. And he didn't intend to. "I have kept my word to her. I'll propose to her per our agreement. That is all I have to say about it. You have taught me well, Uncles. It's time I take over on my own going forward."

Zane saw Fulton step into the doorway. "Yes, Fulton."

"Mr. Robins is here to see you, my lord. He says it's about your previous discussion with him."

"Show him to the drawing room and tell him I'll be right there." Zane rose. "Uncles, I have more things to take care of. I'll see you back here tomorrow *night* for dinner."

"Yes," Hector said, relying on his cane to help him rise. "And with Parliament ending its session a week early, the last ball of the Season was moved up to the night after."

"What?" Zane froze. "I thought it was still a week away."

"It was until late yesterday. The committee moved it up. You know how it is, once Parliament's finished everyone's ready to escape Town and head to their summer homes and begin their house parties."

That didn't give Zane much time. He needed the extra days to win Brina's love.

*Love?*

That was such a big little word!

But yes, he not only wanted to win her hand, he wanted her love. She was loyal and tenderhearted. There was no doubt she loved her family, her friends, the sisters, and the girls at the school. He'd wanted her to love him too. He didn't want her holding back any part of herself from him. She was attracted to him. She took pleasure in the way he made her feel. What he didn't know was why she still continued to proclaim she wanted to be a widow.

That remained a mystery and kept her from being ready to commit to him. If she had loved her husband so much that she'd pined after him for years, why wouldn't she want to find that kind of love and happiness again?

He looked at his uncles. "I don't intend to miss the ball. I'll let Fulton get your coats and see you out."

Zane strode into the drawing room and joined Harry, who stood near the far wall looking up at a large tapestry depicting a battle scene. "I didn't mean to keep you waiting, Harry."

Harry looked at Zane; a quizzical expression narrowed his eyes and pursed his lips. "So, when you became the earl, this house and everything in it became yours? Is that right?"

Nodding, Zane stopped beside him. "It all becomes part of the entailed property of whoever is the earl. It can't be sold. It can only be passed down to the next man to inherit the title."

Harry chuckled. "That's a good way to keep it all in the family. Just declare it can't be sold."

"There are a lot of rules to follow. Most of them go back hundreds of years. I hope you have some news."

"Some," he said. "Not as much as I'd like. I don't know if it will help you much."

Zane heard his uncles coming down the corridor. He pointed to chairs by the far window. "Let's sit over there. Can I get you something to drink? A port or brandy?"

"No," he said, settling himself into one of the wide-striped blue-and-beige-covered chairs. "I've asked around on Remick. He's from America and it appears he's been in London about three months. He purports to have various business ventures there—but no one seems to know exactly what they are. But, he always has plenty of money to play, so no one really cares."

"Understandable. As long as he pays he plays."

"The odd thing about what I've heard is that he does most of his playing at the smaller gambling houses—Hillspot, York and Petly's, Buck and Doe's. Places like that. His bets are in line with most everyone's there, and he seldom loses. He goes to gaming houses such as the Brass Bull, and when he's there, his bets are large, and he usually wins there too."

"Cheating?"

"Not that anyone has ever accused him," Harry said. "Just damn good, like you are. But it's like he's two different men. One night he's at the Brass Bull betting hundreds of pounds and the next he's at the Hillspot, where bets are limited to five pounds. The same places where your cousin and Mr. Harper Tabor do most of their playing."

"So, he makes money off the small bets where players aren't as good and then plays with the skilled players?"

"That's what I'm thinking. And the rumor is he's starting his own club to teach younger players how to become skilled."

"And they have to pay in order to get in these clubs?"

Harry nodded. "There's one other interesting bit of information you might find useful. I heard Remick asked if he might be a guest at Lord Lyonwood's card club and he was refused. Now that you are an earl too, you might want to ask Lord Lyonwood what he knows about the man."

"I'll do that."

Harry shook his head. "Imagine an American wanting a seat at the earl's gaming table."

Zane nodded as he looked over at the clock. It was almost four. Rather late in the afternoon to call on someone. Brina wouldn't approve, but he didn't want to wait until tomorrow to talk to Lyon. Besides, Lyon lived right beside Brina. Why pass up an opportunity to see her?

By the time Zane saw Harry out and had his landau brought around, half an hour had passed. His carriage stopped in front of Lyon's house alongside four other carriages, including those of the Duke of Middlecastle and the Duke of Marksworth, Lyon's father. That's when Zane remembered it was Lyon's card club day. He wasn't one to interrupt a man's game. He didn't know how long they played but he'd wait.

With Brina.

He stepped out onto the pavement and sent his driver away, not knowing how long he might have to wait. As he started toward Brina's house, he heard talking coming from the back of her house. After he passed the tall hedge that separated her house from Lyon's, he saw the top of Brina's head. He walked about halfway down the side of her house and looked over the garden wall. She wasn't alone. There looked to be a dozen girls with her.

Zane huffed a silent laugh at them. They wore what looked to be men's long-sleeved shirts over the top of their dresses. Easels were in front of them, paint brushes were in their hands. Brina stood in front of them talking. Crouching low enough not to be seen, he quietly moved in closer so he could hear.

"A good painting of a flower begins with a well-drawn flower. You will see, I've already drawn the flower for you to make your first lesson easy. You are going to start with the stem. I want all of you to dip your paint brush into the green paint. Don't look at your partner or her work. You are only interested in your drawing. Pretend you have the entire easel to yourself and not just half of it. What the other girls are doing or how they are doing it should not affect what you do. After you have paint on your brush, make slow, easy strokes like this."

Zane continued to watch her. The way her hands moved and her shoulders rolled as she colored in the stem of her flower. Her voice remained calm as she continued to instruct. She would make a few strokes and turn back to her students and explain something else before placing her brush on the canvas again. The girls were quiet and attentive as they watched her and made the same strokes.

After her stem was finished, Brina walked over and looked at their paintings. The girls asked questions. Pointing to their work with her brush, she answered by making suggestions. He was mesmerized watching how unruffled she was with them and how much they seemed to adore her, sometimes all of them talking at the same time and vying for her attention by gathering around her. Without much effort, she'd quiet them and send them back to their easels.

Zane relaxed and folded his arms comfortably over his chest. He could watch her all day. She was a patient teacher. She would be a good and patient mother. To his children. Their children. He didn't just want to marry her; he didn't want to live without her. He loved everything about her.

And that was a damn good feeling.

He didn't know how long he continued to watch her, but he finally heard talking from Lyon's house and the sound of carriages leaving. He would wait and see her after his visit with the earl next door.

When the last carriage rolled out of sight, Zane rapped the knocker.

"Lord Blacknight to see Lord Lyonwood if he's available," he said to the staunch-looking butler.

"Wait here, my lord," the butler said, and moments later Lyon came walking down the corridor and motioned for Zane to come.

"Blacknight," Lyon called. "Come join us. Garrett's with me. We're having a drink."

Zane's stomach twisted and one of his hands made a tight fist of frustration. He would enjoy a drink right now. "Nothing for me," he mumbled to himself and headed toward Lyon. The men shook hands, and once inside the book room, Zane greeted Garrett as well.

"Sit down," Lyon offered, pointing to a chair.

"Thank you. I won't stay long. How did the games go this afternoon?"

"My father and Garrett won most of the money. The rest of us didn't fare as well."

"That happens." Zane gave Garrett a nod of approval before giving his attention back to Lyon. "I dropped by because I wanted to ask you about a man named Remick. I heard he wanted to play with your club and was wondering if you could tell me anything about the man."

Lyon scoffed and then sipped his drink. "The American? No, I can't tell you much. He asked to see me, so out of courtesy, I met with him. Apparently, he's a skilled player and wanted an opportunity to play with my group."

"But you didn't agree."

"Of course not. It's not that men like him aren't good. They usually are an interesting challenge. But if I allowed one man to play with us, it would get around and others would want to test our skills too. Best not to start. I'm sure you know that."

Zane nodded. He was hoping for more information.

"Some men travel from town to town to test their skills and see how many men they can beat. The same way a man wants to test his thoroughbred against others. Once they're satisfied they move on."

"That's an observation I hadn't thought about. I guess he felt he had nothing to lose by asking to play."

"I didn't mind him asking once," Lyon said. "I didn't like it when he waited for me outside White's and asked the second time."

"That didn't set well with you. Did you find out anything about him?"

"No. Does he want to play you?"

Zane shook his head. "I think everyone in London knows I'm not playing right now. I'm asking about him because of my cousin. Remick appears to have started a private club. I have reason to believe my cousin might be involved with him, and I wanted to make sure the man plays fair and is not out to line his pockets with a young man's wealthy family."

"I had no reason to ask him any questions. I wasn't interested. If I'd known, I would have been happy to." He looked at Garrett. "You've met him, Garrett. What do you think of him?"

"I agree with all you said. He's obviously skilled and knows it."

Zane turned to Garrett and asked, "You've gambled all over the world. Do you think he's a master gamester and out to get an impulsive young man's blunt?"

Garrett weighed his words before saying, "Something about him doesn't add up. Most skilled players are trustworthy. They probably wouldn't stay alive very long if they weren't. Usually the important thing for them is the bragging rights. Money is secondary and only to feed their habit. However, I wouldn't trust an American who's come to London to set up a card club."

"Nor do I," Zane said.

After a few more minutes of discussing Remick's possible motives, Zane left Lyonwood's house and walked over to Brina's. It was early evening and dusk had settled. Lights were showing in houses up and down the street. It was a highly inappropriate time to pay a call on a lady. Proper gentlemen would wait until tomorrow, send over a note, and wait for a reply.

Zane had always known the rules for a gentleman.

But he had always preferred just being a man.

He rapped the doorknocker once and took off his hat while he waited. When the housekeeper opened the door, he said, "Good evening, Mrs. Lawton."

"My lord," she said with a proper greeting.

"If Mrs. Feld is home, I'd like to see her. I have some important news for her."

The housekeeper looked behind him as if to make sure no one else was with him before saying, "She's just finished her evening meal. I'll have to ask her. Come inside to wait while I ask."

Zane walked in behind the woman and placed his hat on the side table. When she turned and started down the corridor, so did he.

Quietly.

As he neared the double doors leading into the dining room, he saw Brina pushed back from the table. In one hand, she held a glass of red wine and in the other, a book. She was so beautiful, a longing quiver started in his loins. She'd been reading while eating. A silver branch with five lit candles flickered near the book. Her lush blond hair fell long and enticingly around her shoulders.

He was sure she had no idea how lovely she was sitting there, nor what it did to him to see her so beautiful and serene. His breaths quickened and he swallowed slowly. Suddenly he wanted her more than he'd ever wanted anything. He wanted to take her in his arms and feel the shape of her body, feel it pressed next to his, and beneath his.

"Mrs. Feld, the—"

"Earl is here," he said, stepping from behind the housekeeper.

Startled, Brina looked up. "My lord, what are you doing here at this hour?" She placed the book and glass on the table.

"Obviously the wrong thing. Interrupting your dinner. Behaving badly."

She gave him an unusually shy smile before giving the housekeeper the nod to leave. "No," she answered him, almost whispering as she rose from her chair. "It's all right. I'm finished. Why are you here?"

"I wanted to see you." No, it was more than that. He wanted to kiss her until she was breathless and sighing with pleasure, and then he wanted to possess her and show her how deeply his feelings were for her.

"We'll go into the drawing room so Mrs. Lawton can finish in here."

"Please bring your wine with you." He gave her a teasing smile. "Just because I can't drink doesn't mean you can't."

Brina gave him a lopsided grin. "I'm finished with that too."

He walked beside her down the dimly lit corridor, all the while thinking what he wanted to do was take her in his arms, shove her against the wall, and well . . . That was not the reason he came over. He had every intention of telling her what he'd discovered about Remick and what he thought Robert and Harper had gotten themselves involved in. Right now, he had no desire to visit that subject. Their cousins' problems were fading from his mind. He wanted only to think about her. What he felt when he looked at her. How he felt when he touched her. Tonight, he wanted her to know just how much he desired her, and he wasn't going to give a damn about anything else.

Zane knew how dangerous it was to bet everything he had on one game. He would caution anyone about being so foolish. You always left something to play again. But time wasn't on his side. The last ball was only a couple of nights away. Tonight he was going to bet it all.

They walked into the drawing room. The draperies

were still open and the room was shadowed in early evening twilight.

"I'll light the lamps," she said. "Sometimes, I go straight upstairs after dinner and never come into—"

"Wait," he said, taking hold of her hand when she reached to turn up the wick. In the darkness, she turned toward him and stepped into his arms.

Their lips met softly, brushing lightly back and forth in delicate, feathery motions that were meant to stir and entice. The kisses stayed that way until Brina's arms wound around his neck and she pressed her body against his.

Zane was lost to the hunger he had for her and he couldn't keep his passion at bay.

Soft, reverent kisses turned fervent and deep. With eager hands he felt the shape of her slender, womanly body. Desire for her soared. He tasted the warmth of her mouth, teasing her with his tongue. His hands pressed firmly into her buttocks to hold her tighter against him. Breathless gasps fell from her lips and he groaned as they both fed on the spiraling sensations that swept through them.

Brina matched his yearning and dug her fingers into the fabric of his coat as she tried to hold him tighter. His lips left hers and he kissed his way down her neck and quickly back up to cover her cheeks, her lips with more kisses.

He lifted his head and looked into her eyes. The only light in the room came from the corridor, but Zane saw she was as passionate for him as he was for her. He'd seen and felt her love for him as she held the kitten. Now, with the last ball moved up, he had run out of time and he had to show he loved her.

It was dangerous. She could use this night against him,

but he had faith it was time for him to *trust* her with his love, time to *trust* himself and put all his cards on the table.

"I love you, Brina. I don't want any wagers or bargains between us. Just me and you tonight. Nothing else," he whispered huskily.

# Chapter 23

Brina didn't know how they got up to her room. Did they walk? Run? Did he carry her? It didn't matter. It was bathed in moonlight, and they were completely alone for the first time.

She had been attracted to Zane and wanted him to make love to her almost since he'd come to London, but he had rightly denied her. Somehow, he'd known tonight was the right time. All through their brief courtship he'd surprised her, teased her, and made her laugh. He knew how to listen to her innermost feelings without passing judgment, and she had fallen in love with him.

After she had locked them inside her room, it seemed their lips never parted. At times their kisses were short and fierce, and sometimes they were long and passion-ate. Still, at other times his lips caressed their way over her cheek, down her chin, and along the column of her neck, causing shivers of delight to cover her before sear-ing her lips with his once more. She felt and accepted the pent-up desire he had for her and gave it back to him with full measure.

They tumbled onto the bed without removing the bed-covers or pillows. No care was taken for their clothing or shoes. Those things were easily disposed of as they kissed and touched and explored each other's body. Their passion was fierce, driving, and desperate, but always loving. His hands tangled in her hair and her hands raked over his shoulders, back and down his slim hips. She gloried in the feel of his warm flesh beneath her hands. He whispered her name over and over again.

Each touch and kiss was frantic but loving when without reservations, she opened her heart and body to him and he took her for his own. There were moans of sweet, satisfying pleasure from both of them until they were breathless, happy, and sated.

Even though Brina already had some knowledge of loving from her brief marriage, she'd never felt the all-consuming sensual world Zane had introduced her to. Every kiss, every touch, every breath he drew showed her he wanted her. No one else. And that made her love him all the more.

Moments later Zane lifted his weight from her and rolled over. When he pulled her into the circle of his arms, Brina realized it was over and she suddenly felt like crying. Their coming together had been so passionate, so complete that she knew the depth of her love for Stewart had been only a young girl's flight of fancy with her first beau.

Tears flooded her eyes. Stewart had loved her but never with such fierce passion, never making her feel as if she were the only woman he had ever wanted. As if she were the only one who could make him feel complete.

Memories tore through her mind at rapid speed. She

knew what had just happened meant that after all these years, she'd given up her undying love for Stewart and replaced it with unyielding, undying love for Zane.

The pain was intense. Guilt crushed down on her. She rose up in the bed and whispered, "I hated him. I hated—" Her voice broke on a sob before she managed to say, "Stewart."

Zane was beside her instantly, placing his arm lightly around her shoulder. "What are you saying? Brina, no. You couldn't have hated him."

"It's true," she whispered as tears spilled from her eyes and rolled down her cheeks.

He softly raked his thumb across her cheek and gave her an incredulous stare. "You loved him."

"Yes, I loved him, but I hated him for saving all those people." She clutched at the sheet covering her chest as the familiar rush of intense shame filled her. "I hated him for that."

Zane tried to pull her close, but she brushed away his arm, revulsion for having to admit that ripping at her soul. "I've told you I'm not good. I'm not a good person like everyone thinks. I hated my husband for putting all those people above me and saving them."

"Don't say that," Zane whispered softly.

"It's true and you might as well know what kind of person I am." Another sob fell past her lips. "I couldn't understand why he didn't save himself and come home to me? They were strangers to him. So yes, I hated every one of them for taking him away from me. They were all alive and going on with their lives, and my husband was dead. I was so selfish. I hated him when Stewart was anything but selfish. He was a hero. That's what makes me a horrible person."

She choked back a sob but the next one she couldn't hold inside. Nor the next. Suddenly she was wrapped in Zane's strong arms, her face pressed into his naked chest as she poured her heart out.

He held her close, rubbed her back, kissed the top of her head, and all she could do was weep.

When her tears and sniffling subsided, Zane took hold of her shoulders and forced her to face him. "You're not a bad person for feeling that way. I'd bloody well be furious too."

"You would?"

"Anyone would be," he said in a tender voice. "There's no greater sorrow than the bone-shuddering loss of a loved one. All your feelings are understandable." He reached and pulled the sheet around her shoulders. "You're not selfish, Brina. At nineteen, your soul had been shattered. You were sad and hurting."

"But I hated him for a time. I hated all of them, and I live every day with such scorching regret that I ever thought such things as wishing they'd never been saved."

"I know," he whispered softly, drying her face with his hand. "You were human. That's all."

"I've tried so hard every day to make up for those terrible feelings. I want to help everyone, hoping I can in some way make atonement for all those revolting things I thought and felt for a time."

"First," he said and lifted her chin with his fingertips. He gave her a smile. "You don't have to work off feelings you had while mourning. No one expects that of anyone. But even if you did, believe me—with all that you have done for the sisters, the girls, and everyone else in Town—you have more than made up for any bad feelings you had. Brina, you can't carry guilt for emotions that are natural, a part of life, and even expected when a loved one dies."

"Mine were excessively so," she added, blinking away more tears. "I know that. I felt so much anguish, I thought I might be losing my mind. So did my parents. They were so worried they wouldn't allow me to be alone for fear I might harm myself."

He looked directly in her eyes. "But you didn't."

She shook her head and swallowed hard.

"What happened to help you get over the hurt?"

"Meeting Julia and Adeline, and their idea for the school to help girls whose family members died with ours. Suddenly there was someone who needed something from me in the same way as Stewart had helped those who needed him. Stewart was gone, but I was alive and could continue his example by helping others. The school gave me the opportunity to not think about myself or my loss, but to think about what I could do for others."

Zane reached over and tenderly kissed her forehead again. "You are a person who feels emotions deeply. That's why you were so extremely wounded. It takes time for hurts like that to mend."

"It's why I never want to marry again."

"No, Brina," he whispered.

"It's true. I never want the possibility of feeling that intense anger at someone I love. I never want to bear the guilt again for hating someone I never met. Loving is too hard and brings out the worst in me. I don't want to ever be that way again. That's why I didn't want to love you. And that's why I can't marry you."

"Wait." He brushed her hair again and softly kissed her lips. "You don't want to love me, but you do?"

She nodded. "I do love you, but I can't marry you because I couldn't bear going through what happened after Stewart died again."

Zane held her close and breathed in long and deep. "Let's start with you loving me as I love you. Just love me, Brina. That's all I'm asking for. We'll get to marriage tomorrow or the next day, or next month. All I want to hear you say right now is that you love me. All the rest will come later."

"I love you, and—" He placed his fingertips over her lips.

"No. Don't say any more. Not tonight. Let's have this time together with just the two of us. Loving each other. No past for either of us. No guilt, no bargains. Not even tomorrow. Only us tonight."

Brina reached over and claimed his lips.

# Chapter 24

Zane looked in the mirror as he tied his neckcloth. A simple but elegant knot and a small amount of lace around the cuff of his sleeve would please Brina. He'd shaved that morning but had wanted to shave again before dressing for the dinner in his home. It hadn't taken long, and he wanted to do everything within his power to make sure she was happy for this event she had planned.

Perhaps hosting all the peers in Town was a good idea. There would be matters they'd have to work on together from time to time. He wanted to get to know Lord Lyonwood better and, once his bargain with Brina was at an end, he hoped to join the man's club. But for tonight, he wanted to make sure every duke, earl, and viscount knew they could count on him for whatever they might need if the occasion arose.

He slipped on his light beige waistcoat and started fastening the tiny pearl buttons. For some reason his tailor had seen fit to make the damn things smaller on his evening waistcoat. He supposed that had something to do with the elegance of the evening too.

Zane's hand stilled when from below he heard the door knocker clanking hard and fast—as if someone were frantically banging. He glanced over at the clock on his dressing table. Guests weren't due to start arriving for another half hour. Obviously Fulton hadn't heard the first knock, and whoever it was wanted to make sure he heard the second time. Zane kept buttoning his waistcoat.

The thought that it might be Brina hurried him along. But then he heard loud masculine shouts.

He tensed. One of the voices was Harry's.

Zane grabbed his dinner coat and started out the door, shoving his arms into the sleeves as he went. From the top of the stairs he could see that Fulton and Harry held on to each other's lapels.

"What's going on?" he called and started down.

They released each other and both started to speak at once.

*Damnation.* Zane couldn't make sense of either one of them. "Fulton, enough," he said.

"He was barging in, my lord."

"I understand. Thank you, but I'll handle this now."

"Yes, my lord."

Before Fulton turned to walk away, Harry said, "You must come with me now. There's no time to waste. I'll tell you about it on the way. My carriage is outside."

Zane's blood ran cold. Harry wasn't one to be excitable or to exaggerate. Still, Zane said, "I can't leave. I'm expecting more than twenty people for dinner in a little over an hour."

"Then be prepared to never see your cousin Robert again."

"What do you mean?"

"Believe me when I tell you there is no time to waste. It might be too late even as we speak."

"All right, let's go." Zane then raced out the door behind Harry, who yelled to the driver, "Brass Bull and don't slow for anyone."

The carriage lurched before the door closed. Zane had to reach out to grab it and slam it shut before being jolted back into the seat.

"Hellfire, Harry, what the devil is going on?"

"Remick isn't just another skilled player out to dupe your cousin out of his money. He's a crimp."

Zane tensed again. "A crimp?" he said disbelievingly.

"Yes. Apparently Remick lures young men into a gambling club, gets them heavily in debt to him, and when they fail to pay, he sells their indebtedness to either the military or a boarding master. Robert is already his captive."

"Damnation! How did you find out about this? And do you know for sure Robert's debts have already been sold?"

"Remick apparently discovered I've been asking about him. I received a note to meet him this evening so I did. That's when he told me he has Robert, and unless I could get you to the gaming house in twenty minutes, he would leave and Robert would be on a ship far out of your reach."

Zane's stomach tightened like a fist. "I knew the blade was in debt. I refused to help him again. I thought it best he learn to stand on his own. I never dreamed his ineptness would be to a crimp."

Zane seldom had dealings with the unsavory, yet still somehow lawful, act of crimping—forcing men into the military or service on a ship. Both occupations were always in need of young, strong, able-bodied men. Neither was an easy life.

"Did he name the ship?"

"Of course not. He didn't even say if he was still in a crimping house. Only for me to get you. Even if we follow him after he leaves the gaming house, we have no way of knowing whether or not he'll go to where he's holding Robert."

"I will pay whatever he asks to free him."

Zane looked out of the small window on the coach door. Lights from buildings flashed by quickly as they jostled along, reminding him of how Brina's eyes sparkled at him. Hellfire, he would be late for his own dinner party. This would be a tough one to explain but he believed she would understand.

Zane reached up and struck his fist against the roof of the carriage. "Faster," he yelled.

Minutes later Zane and Harry rushed into the taproom of the Brass Bull. It was dimly lit, noisy, and smelled of dried ale. "Do you see him?"

"The bearded man sitting alone at the corner table."

Zane's hand curled into a fist as he strode toward the man. He wanted to jerk him up by his neck and pound his face, but he had to think about Robert. This needed to be handled with a well-tempered head.

It would be difficult. He would manage.

He pulled on the lace cuff of his sleeve and calmly strode toward Remick. The tall, robust man slipped a watch back into the small pocket of his waistcoat and rose. In his mind, Zane had imagined Remick an older, shorter, and more rotund man with small eyes. To the contrary of all Zane thought, the man's clothing and air of superiority might suggest to some he was a gentleman.

"I'm impressed, my lord," he said and bowed. "Your man did his job well."

The man's pleasantness only angered Zane more.

"You made it here in seventeen minutes," Remick continued. "I was of a mind to give you more than the twenty indicated."

Zane didn't want to be reminded of the time. Brina, his uncles, and sister were probably arriving at his house right now and would be wondering where in the hell he was.

"How much do I owe you?" Zane asked in a clipped voice.

The man chuckled, showing white even teeth. "Now that you are here, there's no hurry."

Oh, but there was.

"I'll pay whatever Robert owes and your fee for holding his debt." He glanced over to Harry. "Find the gaming controller and ask him to come over with quill and paper." Turning his attention back to Remick, he said, "I'll write a promissory note that you can have exchanged for pounds tomorrow. How much do I owe you?"

The man chuckled again and eased himself back into his chair. "Sit down, Lord Blacknight. It's going to be a long night. Do you really think I'm going to just accept payment for Mr. Browning's debt? Don't tell me you thought it would be that simple?"

"Paying another man's gambling debts is never a simple matter. If you were a true gamester, you would know that."

Remick's shoulders twitched. "I think you and I are about to find out. Ever since I've been in London, I've heard you're skilled at cards. One of the best, but I've never seen you play. I was looking forward to matching my skills against yours. Then I heard about a certain wager you had with a lady."

This man wasn't making it easy for Zane to remain calm. Mentioning Brina was the wrong thing for him to do. He'd never challenged a man to a duel, but now it looked as if he might have met his first. But for Brina and his love for her, he was going to give the man another chance. "None of that concerns the matter at hand. Robert has a debt and I'll pay it. We can settle it with money or we can settle it at dawn with pistols."

The man chuckled again and Zane wanted to yank him out of the chair and rip his head off.

"That's not how we settle things in America. I've heard enough about you to know I'd be a fool to go against you in a duel of any kind—except cards. You're going to play games with me. If you want to pay Mr. Browning's debt, you're going to have to win it one hand at a time."

Zane took a step toward him, his gaze dead on Remick's. So he was a card marksman who dealt in the underworld of crimping too.

"I'm not."

"Then I guess your cousin will end up on a ship heading to Singapore after all. A promissory note won't change that." He picked up his glass of port and took a sip, but he never let his gaze leave Zane's.

"Singapore?" Zane's hand made a fist again. "That's halfway around the world."

"That's why it's difficult for boarding masters to find young healthy seamen to make the voyage. It's long and arduous. So many don't make it there. Or back." He put his glass down on the table with a clunk. "I want to match my skill against yours. I don't want your money. I already have enough wagered that you will gamble before midnight tomorrow night."

"You bloody thief. I'll see you in hell first. You deliberately allowed him to fall into debt to you."

"It's a dirty business but a lawful one. He could have paid me what they owed and walked away at any time. He doesn't know anything about hard work but he'll learn. And, should I go to hell, I'll be sure to say hello to Mr. Harper Tabor while I'm there. He'll be on the same ship with Mr. Browning."

Zane's heart slammed against his chest. "You bloody fool, I'll choke their whereabouts out of your—" Zane lunged for Remick but was grabbed by the shoulders. He struggled against Harry and another man, trying to shake them off, but they pinned his arms behind his back.

"No, Zane," Harry said. "Calm down. Think!"

He couldn't think. The man held Robert and Harper captive. What was he going to do? He'd promised Brina he wouldn't play. He was little more than twenty-fours from keeping his bargain with her.

"I'm not playing," he said again.

"You have no choice. You have no idea where the young men are. When is the last time you saw either of them? Are they in a crimping house here in London? Bound for Southampton? Or already on ship ready to sail out of Liverpool? They'd be gone before you could beat their whereabouts out of me."

"Let me try," he ground out as he tried to free himself again.

Remick chuckled. "I know you aren't afraid to test your skills against mine. But if you care so little for your cousin and Mrs. Feld's cousin, I'll take my leave. They'll return one day. If they survive the voyage. But remember, it takes years to work off a gambling debt on a ship."

Zane was at a crossroads like no other. He was damned if he did and damned if he didn't. The man was right. Crimping wasn't against the law. Robert and Harper legally owed their gambling debts. The man was using that to force him to play. The man had no vendetta to settle, he just wanted to add one more gambler to his list.

"The clock is ticking. If no one hears from me by dawn, it will be too late."

"You bloody rotten guttersnipe."

"That's where you're wrong. I live for playing cards and matching my skill against others'. I've been planning this for several days. Once I realized Mr. Browning was your cousin and his friend the widow's, the idea came to me. Both men were so eager to learn all my secrets. It was easy to get them into debt and it didn't take long. Being American, I don't have the title of earl, but I know how to be a gentleman. We'll play each game for one hundred pounds. If you've won enough hands to pay off their debt by midnight, I'll tell you where they are. There's no time to waste. You need to sit down now."

"How do I know I can trust you?"

Remick grinned and sniffed. "I'm a gambling man. I always pay my debts. But if it will make you feel better, I'll let your friend put it in writing. Keep everything legal. I'm not really after sending the young men to Singapore. It's you I want to defeat."

Zane had no choice. He had no damn choice. He thought to send Harry to tell Brina what had happened, but no, he couldn't. This was something he'd need to explain to her himself and make her understand why he had to break his promise to her. He couldn't leave that to another man.

"Reserve the private room upstairs."

"No, no," Remick said. "Right here in the gaming room. So everyone can see that every game is fair."

Zane turned to Harry. "See that there's a table for us in the gaming room and bring over a fresh deck of playing cards."

# Chapter 25

Brina stepped down from her carriage in front of Zane's home. Thankfully, Adeline hadn't questioned her when she said she wanted to take her own carriage to the earl's house. It was scandalous. A widow arriving alone to a bachelor's dinner party.

But tonight, Brina didn't care.

It would be a late evening. She would be one of the last to leave and she didn't want Lyon and Adeline to wait around for her. She wanted time to be alone with Zane as they were last night.

She'd done a lot of thinking since he'd left her bed in the early hours of morning. And because of his gentle concern and insights, she had come to terms with her fears of marrying again. Just as she had put away the hurt of losing Stewart and all the debilitating emotions that had followed. Sharing her burden of guilt for her past feelings seemed to lift it from her. Zane was right. She was young and devastated. It was time to forgive herself.

And she had.

She was ready to begin a new life of feeling free from her past, and she was going to start by telling Zane tonight she would accept his proposal at the ball.

That had her smiling and humming all day.

Her dark rose-colored gown had been made especially for this evening. A simple high-waisted gown with long, sheer sleeves. At the last fitting she'd had the seamstress add an overlay of white sheer silk so the color wouldn't look so stark. She'd also had the neckline lowered more than usual, but not so low eyebrows would be raised at the party. Her only jewelry consisted of an ivory-circled amethyst on a white ribbon at her throat.

"Good evening, Fulton," she said when he opened the door. After handing off her cape and reticule, she followed him to the drawing room to find it empty. She was a little early, but not much. She thought for sure Zane would be down, ready to greet his first guest. No matter. She would take a peek at the table to make sure her written instructions had been followed.

The dining room looked warm and inviting. It wasn't large, but the staff had managed to seat twenty-four chairs around the table. A wide gilt-framed mirror bracketed by crystal candle sconces hung over the fireplace. On one wall hung a large tapestry of a classical garden with a waterfall scene. The other had a life-size wall painting of a man who looked as if he could have been Zane's father or the first Earl of Blacknight. His hair was as black as Zane's, though longer. He had the same classically handsome features with dark blue eyes that held a hint of devil-may-care humor and a twitch of mischief showing around the corners of his mouth.

The long rectangular table was almost the length of the room and covered with white linen. A single silver candlestick had been placed in front of every other chair down the center of the cloth. Woven throughout the candlesticks were bits of greenery and small English tea roses.

The china and crystal gleamed even though the candles hadn't yet been lit. That would come closer to serving the first course. Zane would be at the head; she would be seated to his left as he'd instructed. As his hostess for the evening, Patricia would sit at the other end.

Brina smiled. It was going to be a good evening for Zane. And tomorrow evening would be even better. When he asked for her hand, she was going to give it to him in front of his family and everyone. He had proven he could be a gentleman, but she was going to marry him because she loved him more than she could have ever thought possible.

Only a few weeks ago, she swore she could never love or marry again. Zane's gentle but constant pursuit had changed her heart. He had challenged her, made her laugh, made her happy. He helped her understand she no longer needed to feel such heavy guilt for the anger and selfishness that had festered in her for so long after Stewart's death. Grief caused terrible feelings. They shouldn't be compounded by continuing to relive them. She could never be good enough or ever do enough beneficial things to make up for what she'd felt at those terrible times in her life. All she could do was forgive herself.

And she had.

"Fulton and his staff have done an amazing presentation."

At the sound of the voice behind her, Brina turned and saw Zane's sister, Mrs. Cranston, standing in the doorway. "Yes. It's as beautiful as I imagined."

"Indeed. Very sweet and reserved, Mrs. Feld. Much like you. It was clever not to try and top the extravagance of the Duchess of Middlecastle's table. She'll be pleased it's so simple."

Brina wasn't sure what to say about that, so she merely smiled and answered, "I'm sure Zane didn't mean to—"

Mrs. Cranston's eyebrows rose almost to her hairline. Brina immediately recognized her mistake. *Zane.* She had used his first name. She should have known it was bound to happen sooner or later. For most, it was an unforgivable error to refer to an earl in such a manner.

"I'm sorry, Mrs. Cranston. I shouldn't have referred to him in a familiar manner."

"You don't have to worry about slip-ups with me, Mrs. Feld," she responded in a matter-of-fact tone. "I am all for you helping my brother any way you can. I do believe you've been good for him, and I wouldn't mind having you in the family. I would have never believed anyone could help him settle down, but you seem to have. For a month, at least. Only time will tell if it will last any longer. It won't be the first time we've thought he had changed only to find that he hadn't. But, we're always willing to hold out hope. Ah—I hear voices. Let's go see who's arrived. Perhaps by now even our host."

Brina had been almost to the point of tapping her foot in frustration before Mrs. Cranston left the room. It was no wonder Zane felt his family was such a challenge.

They were! How could his own sister be so unbelieving in him?

As she entered the drawing room, Brina looked for Zane. His uncles had arrived. So had Viscount Mountgate, Julia, Adeline, and their husbands, but she didn't see Zane. Thinking he must be greeting someone in the vestibule, she headed over to speak to her friends.

Other guests continued to arrive, but Zane was noticeably absent. Unable to stop herself, she'd glanced at Mrs. Cranston, who was in turn, glancing at her. The last to arrive were the Duke and Duchess of Middlecastle. After they entered, Brina went in search of Fulton and found him standing by the door.

"Fulton, is the earl still in his chambers?"

"No, Mrs. Feld. I've already told Mrs. Cranston, he hasn't returned home yet."

Brina felt as if something had slammed into her body and it almost drove her to her knees. "What do you mean? He's not home?" It was a foolish question, but nothing else would come to mind.

"That's correct."

"Do you know where he is?"

"The earl didn't inform me of where he was going or when he expected to return."

"Can you tell me how long he's been gone?" Her breaths were so short, she could hardly speak. "All day? The afternoon? When did he leave?"

"More than an hour ago."

Her heartbeat raced. "Then he's coming back. He's been delayed."

"He said he would be back for the dinner."

"Good. Thank you."

Brina walked back into the drawing room on shaky legs. Chatter was lively, and if anyone was missing the host, it wasn't showing to anyone but her and Mrs. Cranston.

Yet.

But the minutes passed. She began to think maybe he'd had a carriage accident. She knew how dangerously he could drive. He was excellent managing the horses, but what if— No. Then minutes later she was thinking perhaps he'd been attacked by footpads. What if he were lying hurt in an alley? Maybe she should ask someone to go look for him, but where would they start? Where would they go?

So, no. She wouldn't ask anyone to look for him. He wasn't an errant schoolboy. Anger was beginning to creep inside her. He knew where he should be.

"Have you seen Blacknight this evening?"

Brina turned to see both Zane's uncles standing beside her. In the distance she saw Mrs. Cranston heading toward them. Brina's heart pounded and her throat went dry. They were going to be looking to her for answers she didn't have.

"Not yet," she said calmly when she couldn't have felt more tense as Mrs. Cranston stopped beside her.

Zane's Uncle Hector stared at her and started tapping his cane on the floor. "I assumed he was in his chambers getting dressed, waiting late to make a grand entrance."

"No," Brina defended Zane. "I don't believe the earl would do anything that pretentious."

"Then where is he? If he's not here, where?"

"I don't know," she answered truthfully, sadly, and bewildered that he wasn't on time for his own party when he knew how important it was to do everything right this night. Why was his uncle giving her a difficult time about it? Didn't they know how badly she wanted Zane to be with them right now?

"What do you mean you don't know? You are the one who planned this evening for him. Did you forget to ask if he'd be attending his own dinner party?"

"Now, Hector, there's no call for that kind of talk. If we weren't able to tame him, why should we think Mrs. Feld could do it?"

"Enough of this," Mrs. Cranston offered in a tone that let them know she was tired of the exchange. "I do believe my uncles are stressing you, Mrs. Feld. Don't let them. Put a smile on your face." She looked from one uncle to the other. "As we all shall and enjoy this evening. What you don't realize, Mrs. Feld, is that this isn't the first time my brother has snubbed his nose at Society or the family. He says he will attend an event, and then he doesn't. But don't worry, we'll see him Christmas Day. We always do."

No, Brina couldn't believe he simply didn't care enough about them or about her to attend. He had told her he loved her last night. She believed him. She felt it in his touch, his words. She had to believe he would come.

"He will be here," she said confidently, and denying the shiver of apprehension that washed over her. "There's no need to worry. We'll hold dinner. He will come."

But half an hour later, the crowd was restless. Glasses were empty again, murmurings of discontent had settled in. Like his sister, Brina kept a smile on her face. Adeline and Julia were worried for her and had tried to cheer her, but nothing could take away the ache in her chest.

Twenty-three people were waiting for a dinner that should have been served an hour ago. Brina had to tell Mrs. Cranston they couldn't delay dinner any longer. She was afraid people would start leaving.

Something was wrong.

But what?

Within ten minutes everyone was seated, but Zane's chair was empty. With great effort Brina smiled and chatted with the Duke of Middlecastle, who was seated across from her, and Viscount Mountgate, who was beside her. Thankfully, he didn't seem to even notice that the host wasn't occupying his seat as he kept a steady stream of conversation going, but the duke was not as forgiving. He kept turning his head and staring at the empty chair.

Brina couldn't bring herself to give up on Zane. She was constantly glancing at the doorway. In her heart, she knew he was going to rush in at any moment and

explain the terrible event that had delayed him. However, she was inclined to now agree with Zane that sit-
down dinners with five courses were excruciatingly long.
They started with steaming onion broth, followed by the
beautifully prepared sole caught fresh from the coast of
Dover. The breast of pheasant had been drizzled with
butter and the lamb chops covered in a honey and fig
sauce. The delicate fluff of sugary confection that was
now being served should have been the crowning end to
the meal and successful dinner, but the chatter and clink
of silver and glasses that could be heard all around the
table made it clear no one was in a joyful mood. There
were no raised voices or bouts of laughter that usually
graced the ending of such an elite slate of dinners.

While dessert was being consumed, a man Brina
didn't recognize came into the room and whispered
something to the duke. She couldn't hear what was said,
but the duke's eyes widened and swept over to Brina. He
then cleared his throat and dug into his dessert. Brina's
heart beat so loud and fast, she felt sure everyone in the
room could hear it. Moments later, the duke leaned over
and whispered to his wife. She looked aghast and whispered to the gentleman beside her.

That's when Brina heard. *"He's gambling at the Brass
Bull."*

Brina's stomach twisted and she stopped breathing. For
how long, she didn't know. Other whispers reached her.

*"And he has a woman hanging on each shoulder."*

No. That wasn't true. It couldn't be true.

*"No one is surprised."*

*"Perhaps Mrs. Feld is. Look at her."*

Brina felt light-headed and took in several deep
breaths. That was when she knew Zane wasn't coming. She froze and watched in unspeakable horror as the
hushed words being passed down the table. After what

seemed like an eternity, Mrs. Cranston laid down her spoon and rose.

So did everyone else, including Brina.

"Because of unfortunate circumstances," Zane's sister said. "We won't be serving the gentlemen brandy or tea for the ladies. We've been pleased to have you join us this evening."

Chairs scraped against the floor and murmurings continued as everyone made their way out of the dining room and into the vestibule, where they collected their wraps. Julia and Adeline flanked Brina and tried to shield her from others making their way to the entrance.

"Brina," Julia said, "let's stand over here and let everyone else say good night to Blacknight's family first. It will be easier if you are the last to leave."

"Yes," Brina agreed, leaning against a wall in the corridor, watching Zane's sister and two uncles hurry everyone out the door.

"I know it's not the time to talk," Julia said.

"No, it isn't," Brina agreed, feeling numb with disbelief.

"We never expected the earl wouldn't show. What can we do to help?" Julia asked earnestly.

Brina gave herself a mental shake and straightened. "Nothing. I am fine. This is what I wanted. Remember?"

"We'll come over to see you tomorrow," Julia offered.

"I'm not waiting that long," Adeline said firmly. "Lyon and I are going to take you home, and I'll stay with you as long as you want me to."

"What?" Brina, said, confident she was doing a good job of holding herself together and showing no signs of the unbearable ache inside her. "No. Go."

"We are not leaving you to handle this hurt by yourself," Julia insisted. "Adeline and I might be married, but the three of us stick together."

"Yes. We do," Brina said, not knowing where she found the willpower to sound so strong but grateful she had it. "But sometimes we must stand on our own. I planned this evening, and I will see it through to the end. I need no help from the two of you tonight." She smiled. "My carriage is outside. I'll see myself home and see both of you at the ball tomorrow night when I accept my apology from the earl. Now, time for you two to get your husbands and go. I'm going to visit the retiring room before saying good night to Mrs. Cranston. I've not been there all evening, and I simply must go before the ride home."

Brina reached over and kissed both of Adeline's and then Julia's cheeks. "Go on, both of you. I want to be alone but promise we'll talk later. I must speak to Mrs. Cranston and Lord Blacknight's uncles before I leave."

In the retiring room, Brina almost broke down and sobbed. How could he have done this after last night? After how he'd made her feel? After he'd told her he loved her? Wanted only her? It had been a lie. All of it.

Alone as she was, it would have been so easy to let the hurt show. But instead, she replaced it with anger to keep her eyes dry until she could get home.

Zane had not only done this to her but to his peers? To his family? Now, she finally understood why his family had no faith in him. All they believed about him was true. He wasn't capable of giving up his carefree life to handle his responsibilities. She had only thought she had made a difference in his behavior.

But no. He was still the man she'd seen tied to a chair in Paris. And that was crushing.

Perhaps he'd simply wanted to bed her—the widow no one else had touched. And gambling and drinking tonight was his way of getting out of his wager with her and winning his own. But it really didn't matter what his reasons were. The outcome was the same. Why couldn't she have seen that? Why did she fall for his charming ways and his load of poppycock?

And why should she blame him? He was only doing what came natural to him. She was the one who had changed. Not him. She had fallen in love with a rake of the highest order.

When Brina walked back into the vestibule, Mrs. Cranston was the only one left standing by the front door.

"Sylvester and Hector have already left," Zane's sister said. "I am leaving as well. I suggest you do so too. The earl probably won't be coming home before midmorning. And just think, my dear, you won your wager. The earl has violated the terms of your agreement with him. You'll be getting that apology you wanted tomorrow night. That must make you feel good."

If what she was feeling was good, she never wanted to feel bad.

"Serves him right," Mrs. Cranston continued. "Maybe that will take him down a peg or two. Do take some comfort in that. Most men hate to admit they are wrong."

She hadn't lost him to a woman. There might have been women hanging on him while he was gambling and drinking, but she lost him to himself.

"I'm sorry for you, dear." She gave Brina a sympathetic smile and placed her hand on top of Brina's shoulder, giving it a quick, tight squeeze. "I know you hoped for better from him. I really thought he was changing too. He'd just settled a lot of things in the family that needed his attention, and everyone had seemed quite happy with his generous increase in allowances."

"That's good," Brina answered with the tiniest of smiles. "So, there was some improvement. You know what they say. We must be thankful for small blessings."

"I can't help but notice Lord and Lady Lyonwood didn't stay to see you home."

There was no use hiding anything at this point. "Yes. I came in my own carriage. Dreadfully scandalous of me, I know. If you feel you must tell someone, I will understand."

Mrs. Cranston gave her a swaggering smile. "I like you, Mrs. Feld."

"Thank you," Brina whispered. "Now, I hope you don't mind, but I asked Fulton if I might leave the earl a note. He's laying out paper and quill for me in the drawing room. I'll write that, collect my wrap, and be on my way."

"To the Brass Bull, I hope, to drag the earl out by his ear."

Brina gave a soft laugh. "Well, if I thought I was strong enough, I might try it."

"I'm rather sorry it didn't turn out better for you two. I know I don't show it, but I really do love my brother. I'll say good night and be on my way. Fulton will close up after you leave, Mrs. Feld."

She turned, not giving Brina time to respond. Which was probably best. Her last words had stung. Brina had thought that after last night, after tonight, after tomorrow night, she would no longer be Mrs. Feld.

Brina walked back into the drawing room and sat down at the secretary.

Dear Lord Blacknight,
    I will see you tomorrow evening at mid—

No, that wasn't right. It was already after midnight. Tomorrow was already here.

Dear Lord Blacknight,
    I will see you this evening for the apology you owe me.
                                                        Mrs. Feld

As Brina replaced the quill to its stand, she heard a door open and slam shut, and masculine footsteps ran down the corridor. She looked up as Zane rounded the doorway. His neckcloth was hanging limp and untied. His hair was rumpled as if he'd just risen from sleep. He looked handsome, vibrant. Happy to see her.

How dare he!

And how could he be so inconsiderate as to still make her heartbeat race at the sight of him?

"Thank God, you're still here," he whispered.

Was that a smile of relief she saw on his face? Relief that she was still there? Anguish festered inside her. "That's obvious," she managed to say and rose.

"I was sure you'd be gone."

She should have been. It was clear he'd been carousing. She supposed she did look like the dutiful, faithful lady waiting at home for him to return. "I'm sorry I failed to leave before you arrived," she said tightly.

"I know you're angry but—"

"You do, do you?" She cut him off and walked toward him. "Angry? Really? No, I'm hurt."

"Brina, I'm sorry I—"

"You're about five hours too late for such words, my lord."

She went to rush past him, but he caught her arm. "Look at me," he said earnestly.

"No," she whispered, keeping her head down. She bit back tears that collected in her throat but was unable to keep them from pooling in her eyes as she remembered how he had held and loved her. She choked down a sob. "I don't want to look at you. I don't want you to touch me."

"Listen to me, Brina." His hand tightened on her arm.

She lifted her head, and then her lashes and what she saw made her want to forget who she was, what she had vowed. She was deeply, madly in love with him, but she was overcome with such grief.

Zane's eyes were gleaming too. A breathy sigh of despair pushed forth from her aching lungs. Only with the will of an inner strength she'd developed since being alone did she manage to give him a steely gaze and say, "Let go of me and don't say anything."

His face was etched hard with indecision, but finally, he dropped his hand.

"I don't want your explanation," she said past a thick throat.

He struck his thumb to his chest. "I deserve to be heard."

"You don't deserve any consideration from me!" she lashed out at him. "Gambling, drinking, with women hanging all over you!"

His eyes widened with outrage. "No!" he said bitterly. "No. Listen to me. Gambling yes, but there were no women and no drinking, I swear!"

"As if that matters! What you did tonight was wrong. It shows you don't care for me or anyone. I made a fool of myself to ever think you cared for me or that I could trust you. I did my best, but I was misled to think you had or could change."

"That's not true," he demanded angrily. "I'm not going to let you say things that aren't true and get by with it."

"I don't have to say anything. Your actions prove it." Brina bit back the tears again. "You have made choices like this throughout your life."

"Let me explain, damn—" He bit off the last of the word but swore under his breath as he raked his hands through his tousled hair.

"I thought nothing could ever hurt me as deeply as when my husband didn't come back to me. But he didn't mean to hurt me. He didn't do it by choice. You did. He hurt me by doing something good for other people. But you? You knew exactly what you were doing. So, I am going to walk out of here with my head held high and no tears on my face."

"Brina." He whispered her name almost desperately.

"Not one more word. I can't wait for you to apologize tomor—tonight at midnight, at the ball. I came on my own because I wanted to be the last one to leave tonight. So you see, you aren't the only one who can break the rules."

She kept her chin up, her shoulders straight, and looked straight ahead as she walked past him. Somehow, she managed to make it to the carriage and climb inside before a heaving sob of heartache left her mouth. A second and third came rushing out before she was able to stop the flow and hold the rest of her anguish inside her aching throat.

There was nothing to compare to the hurt of realizing he had chosen his wayward life over her.

How could she ever get over that?

# Chapter 26

Brina always felt better after visiting with the sisters at Pilwillow Crossings. She had deliberately stayed away from her house until darkness covered the sky. Not only did it nourish her spirit to be at the abbey, but today it kept her from having to talk with Adeline and Julia. They meant well, but she wasn't up to bearing their concern for her. She hadn't actually told them how deeply she felt for Zane, but she was sure they knew. Probably from the first time they saw her with him, they knew she felt differently about him than any other man. She'd never hidden that from them.

Having been too numb to sleep for very long, she'd sent them both a note early in the morning saying she'd be out all day and would see them at the ball. She wanted no one going with her, acting as a companion, and certainly not as the dedicated friends they were. They would respect her need for privacy. Part of her healing would be handling this on her own. She couldn't let losing Zane affect her the way losing Stewart had. From that, her recovery had been long. Now she was older and wiser, but she knew she would miss Zane all the days of her life.

A tired laugh passed her throat as she walked up to her front door. It appeared Zane had changed her more than she had changed him. Imagine her—a widow showing up at a ball without a companion. It simply wasn't done, but she would. If the old guard of Society were so inclined, they could shun her. Right now, she'd welcome it. She was feeling very much alone anyway.

She wouldn't be spending the rest of her life any different than she'd expected for the past five years. She had always said she'd never marry again and believed it— until Zane had her dreaming of happily-ever-afters. For a short time, he had given her hope she could have the incomparable feeling of true love.

Oh, why had she fallen in love with London's most notorious rake?

What hurt the worst was that he never truly loved her. Why else would he have gone to the club and spent the night gambling and—and? Her thoughts paused. He'd said there were no women.

She swallowed hard. Even now, she wanted to believe that was true. Only the need to play cards.

But again, it didn't change the outcome. Any or all, it was the one sure way he wouldn't have to marry her.

Staying at the abbey also kept her from the possibility of seeing Zane should he even want to see her and try once again to explain his unforgivable actions last night.

After they made love, she had lay bare her deepest soul to him, telling him things she'd never told anyone. How could he have been so callous with her love?

Brina opened the door and started taking off her gloves.

"Is that you, Mrs. Feld?" Mrs. Lawton called from above the stairs.

"Yes," she answered.

"Lord Blacknight has called on you three times today and waited more than an hour each time."

"Thank you for letting me know, Mrs. Lawton," she answered, untying her bonnet.

"You best hurry on up. You're already late getting ready for the ball."

Brina placed her bonnet, gloves, and reticule on the side table. There, lined in a neat row, were three notes. Her name written in the bold lettering of a man. She wanted to swipe them all off the table and fling them as far as she could. How dare he start trying to follow accepted rules now!

She turned away and headed up the stairs. After all the times he came over without asking, how dare he leave her notes today? She walked into her room and gasped. Hanging on her wardrobe was the gorgeous bright pink gown that had been in the shop window near the abbey.

"It arrived this afternoon," Mrs. Lawton said with a beaming smile. "I figured you wanted to wear it tonight, so I pressed it for you and laid out your stockings, shoes, and jewelry for you to choose from."

Brina's heartache over the earl had been so great, she'd forgotten she'd gone to the shop yesterday and had been fitted for the gown.

To wear tonight.

When she thought she'd be accepting Zane's proposal and could put away her widow's clothing.

Not an apology.

Anger jumped on her so fast, she was suddenly reeling. She couldn't believe she was such an idiot. To want Zane to see her in that color again. No! No! She would remain a widow, wearing dark, drab widow's weeds.

Why would she want to ever wear that dress? She didn't even want to go to the ball. An apology from Lord Blacknight meant nothing to her. His word meant nothing to her or anyone else. She'd hung so much hope on him. On that gown. Now she hated it. She never wanted to see the color pink again.

Brina ripped the dress off the wardrobe, wadded and squeezed it into a tight ball. She rushed over to the window, and with amazing strength, threw it open and hurled the gown out.

"Mrs. Feld, what are you doing?" Mrs. Lawton exclaimed.

In the bright moonlight, Brina watched as the wind caught under the thin gossamer fabric and lifted it higher for a moment before slowly allowing the gown to flutter down and fall in a heap on top of the purple rhododendron bush. She stared down at discarded silk and should have felt better.

But she didn't.

Zane's apology wouldn't make her feel better either. He wouldn't mean it anyway. If *he* even showed up publicly to give it. Fine. She didn't want it. It no longer mattered. All she felt was loss.

Another terrible, terrible loss.

"Mrs. Feld?"

Brina heard the housekeeper's worried voice behind her. She straightened from the window and faced Mrs. Lawton, doing her best to act as if the woman hadn't witnessed her display of anger.

"Yes?"

"Should I mix you a tonic of brandy and honey?"

"No." She softly closed the widow. "But I think I will have a brandy. I didn't sleep well last night, and I'm told it will help settle the nerves." She turned and saw her bed, where Mrs. Lawton had laid out her shoes, stockings, and lace-trimmed stays. "I've decided I'm not going to the ball tonight. You can put away my jewelry and other things and lay out my robe. I'll be back up shortly."

She walked downstairs and was headed down the corridor for the drawing room to pour a nip of brandy when she heard a light tap on the front door. Her heart felt as if it jumped to her throat as her first thought was of Zane. Her first thought was always Zane. But then the sound came again, and she realized it sounded like Harper's knock. She started to call up to Mrs. Lawton to answer the door but stopped. Even if it was the earl, she couldn't be afraid to face him. What was done, was done.

Cautiously opening the door, she saw it was Harper and fell into his arms. She was so happy it wasn't Zane. If it had been him, she might have wanted to listen to his excuses, to hear an apology.

"Brina, dearest," he said, holding her tight. "I'm all right. Everything is fine now. Don't be upset."

"I'm just glad it's you."

"Who else would it be? Everyone else is at the ball. Where you should be dancing and having a wonderful time." He held her for a moment longer and then set her away from him. "Why aren't you?"

She breathed in heavily and suddenly noticed his face. His lip was swollen and there was a cut above his eye.

"I'm not going—but, Harper, by the heavens! What happened to you? Who did this? Don't tell me you fell as Robert did. I won't believe you."

"No, no. I didn't want you to see me like this. I didn't think you would be here. I only came to return this." He reached into his coat pocket and pulled out a note and one of her mother's fine porcelain figurines and placed them on the side table by her bonnet.

What had happened at her parents' house came back

to Brina, and she said, "I don't understand. What were you doing with it?"

"I stole it from their house. That's why I was there the afternoon you saw me. I was going to sell it to help pay my debts to Mr. Remick."

She gasped. "Gambling debts?" She knew Zane's cousin had been a bad influence on him. This was proof.

"In the end, I didn't have the nerve to sell it. At first, I thought to just slip back into their house and replace it, but Lord Blacknight told us last night that when you've done something wrong, you should make it right."

She tensed even more. "You saw the earl last night?"

"Not at first."

"Did he do this to your face?" She could hardly breathe. "He will hear from me about this." She started toward the door. "Tonight!"

"What? Brina, wait. What are you thinking? He didn't do this. As heaven is my witness, Blacknight saved us last night. I'll always be grateful to him."

Brina blinked. Her mind seemed to be going faster than her ears could hear. "Us? You and Robert? Saved you from what? It looks to me as if he's taught the two of you how to be brawling gamesters just like he is."

"No." Harper's eyes narrowed in disbelief, and he shook his head. "Didn't the earl tell you what happened? He was in such a hurry to get back to you. I've never seen a man so on edge about the time."

Brina felt as if her body were going limp as Harper's words sunk in. "No, and I don't want to hear anything he has to say. He's not a gentleman. He's not a man of his word, and I hope I never see him again."

"You really don't know what he did last night, do you?"

"I know he gambled." Thinking about that renewed her strength. "That's enough."

"But it appears you don't know why he played cards. You need to." He took both her hands in his. "You'll listen to me about this," he said firmly, making sure her gaze stayed on his. "Robert and I were duped into a high stakes games with Mr. Remick, and when we couldn't pay our debts, he forcibly took us to a crimping house. He wouldn't accept money from the earl because Remick considers himself a master of cards. He insisted Lord Blacknight had to play him one game at a time to win our freedom. If he hadn't done it, Robert and I would be on a ship heading to Singapore right now as payment for our debt."

"Singapore!"

"Yes. We were crimped. It's what Mr. Remick does. Lord Blacknight had no choice. With his skill, he finally won enough games to save us from months or years at sea."

Brina couldn't think straight. The only thing she could manage was to shake her head and hug Harper again. "I'm so glad he saved you from that."

"I can't stay any longer. Lord Blacknight thought it would be best if I stayed out of London for a while. He's hired a coach to take me to Northumberland. It's waiting for me. He's sending Robert away too. I didn't ask where. We're both happy to still be in England, not to have been sold to a boarding master."

Zane played to save Harper and Robert.

"Don't be angry with the earl for gambling. He was so furious, he railed at us because he had to break his promise to you. It truly upset him greatly."

"He saved you?" she whispered.

Harper nodded again. "I hope one day he'll forgive me, and that you will too. And I hope you'll forgive him for breaking his promise to you. He's in love with you. That was clear to me and Robert. So, it's our fault he—"

"Excuse me, Harper. I must hurry." She turned and started rushing up the stairs. "Mrs. Lawton," she called. "I've changed my mind. I'm going to the ball. Heat your iron. But first, run outside and get the pink gown off the rhododendron."

# Chapter 27

Zane stood near the entryway and watched for Brina. Everyone else in the ballroom watched him.

He'd purposefully arrived late. Very late. Midnight wasn't far away. He'd scanned the crowd twice. Brina wasn't in the room. He wondered if she just hadn't arrived or if she were waiting out of sight in one of the alcoves. If she had arrived with her friends, Lady Lyonwood and Mrs. Garrett were no longer with her. He spotted them across the room with their husbands. They, like several others, were trying their best not to stare at him. Perhaps Brina was feeling the same way he was. That tonight wasn't something she wanted to be a part of.

He could understand that. He sure as hell didn't want to be there.

Yet, he was the one who started this with his wager, she expanded it, and he would finish it this evening.

As promised.

The hell of it was that he was a different person now.

Because of Brina, he no longer saw the mischievous humor of trying to get a lady's attention by making a wager. Brina had helped him see a lot of things differently. And he liked to think he had helped her see some things differently too.

Not that it mattered to her now.

Usually, the last ball of the Season wasn't well attended. For various reasons. By the time it rolled around, all but an ardent few in the ton were tired of the endless parties. The young ladies and gentlemen who had already made a match were more interested in making plans for their own wedding parties. The last ball also signaled Parliament had ended its session. Once the House of Lords and House of Commons finished with their business, they were eager to forgo the last party and travel to their summer estates to escape the approaching heat in London and begin their summer house parties.

But this year's ball was different.

It was a crush.

The orchestra played, but few danced. Most stood in little groups chatting with whomever happened to be by their side. Zane had no doubt that everyone far and wide knew he had gambled last night, and tonight at midnight, he had to give an apology to Brina.

And he would.

Whether or not she attended to receive it.

He huffed out a rueful chuckle when he saw his uncles and sister had spotted him and were heading his way. The day before he thought he'd settled into his new role in life. Earl, provider and protector of his family. Lover and soon-to-be husband of Brina. But somehow, one good deed changed all that.

He couldn't argue with Brina that he'd had a choice whether or not to hurt her, where Stewart had not. Damn, but that pierced his heart as surely as the blade of a rapier. When she'd told Zane he had hurt her more than her husband, it had torn his heart to shreds. He knew how deeply she felt emotions. He knew he couldn't, *wouldn't* hurt her anymore. That was why he had waited at her house on and off throughout the day. He had wanted to demand she see him, force her to listen, and make her understand he'd done the right thing. Not for her, but for Robert and Harper. But in the end, he didn't want to cause her more pain.

He'd give the apology. It was all she wanted from him.

Sins of his gambling past had finally caught up with him. He now realized what a mistake it had been to try to teach Robert to be a well-seasoned gamester when they were in Vienna. Few people ever became really good at it, but Robert was a Browning, so there was a chance. At the time, Zane needed something to take Robert's mind off the French woman. And it had, but it gave him a far bigger problem.

The American crimp who'd held Robert and Harper in his makeshift prison had been one good card player. For a time, it looked as if Zane weren't going to win enough money to pay their debts before time was up. He simply wasn't winning enough games. Brina and the dinner party kept coming to his mind, causing him to lose focus in the beginning. He was doing all the things he knew not to do. Sweat, hold the cards tight, blink too rapidly, and so many little telling hints of what he held in his hand.

But those same thoughts of Brina and getting back to her eventually calmed him. His skill and intuitive nature took over, and just before the hour Remick had given him was up, Zane had won more than enough to pay for Robert and Harper's freedom.

Remick reluctantly conceded and assured Zane the young men would be released. Zane wasn't about to let the crimp out of his sight until he had the young men in his hands and they were safe from being thrown onto a ship bound for the East. That was when Zane pulled the knife Harry had slipped into his pocket and forced Remick to take him to Robert and Harper.

Only after he had the young fools with him and seen they were not too badly hurt did he let Remick go—with the warning he never peddle his skills or his crimping in London again. Zane was certain word that he'd been seen gambling at the Brass Bull had made it to his house.

News like that traveled fast.

He had been equally confident everyone would be gone by the time he made it back home. However, Brina was still there.

For one very good reason. To let him know she had won.

"It's about time you got here," Uncle Hector said. "Not that it's pertinent to this evening, but I had a note from Robert this morning saying he was going to visit one of his aunt Lorraine's son's in Dorset. I thought it was sudden. Did you know about that?"

"Not any particulars," Zane said. "I'm sure he'll write once he gets there. Young men like to travel."

"Now that we have that out of the way," Uncle Syl said, "what happened to you last night?"

"We know what happened, Uncle," Patricia informed him dryly and rolled her eyes toward Zane to ask her own question. "What I want to know, dear brother, is if you have spoken to Mrs. Feld today?"

"No."

"No?" Hector said, stomping his cane. "Why not? You have some explaining to do and today was the time to do it."

"Not to mention an apology," Patricia added.

"Well, you can't do it now," Sylvester said calmly.

"She's not here. Who can blame her? She probably wouldn't listen anyway. You didn't make it to your own dinner last night. She obviously isn't going to make it to your apology."

"Well, she should," Uncle Hector insisted. "They were almost engaged. There's still hope this can be settled for a good outcome. She was doing such a fine job helping you be more of a gentleman. Until you strayed."

"What I want to know is what happens between Zane and the widow," Patricia said, keeping her eyes on his face.

The *widow*. Zane grimaced and gave a silent growl. How he'd come to detest that description of her.

"Maybe all is not lost," Uncle Syl said in a placating tone. "Perhaps if you tried writing her a poem? Ladies love poetry. You know, something about flowers, moonglow, and how beautiful she is might go a long way to soothing her and help her overlook your lesser points."

"A poem?" Patricia asked in an unbelievably indignant voice. "At this point, a poem is not going to win her hand."

"If romantic words won't ease her disposition," Syl countered, "tell her in no uncertain terms that she will sit down and listen to you because you are an earl. Though we don't know exactly what they were, I'm sure you had good reasons for your behavior with that gentleman last night, and she needs to accept them without further ado."

"And thinking like that," Patricia remarked sharply, "is why you never married."

Hector stomped his cane again. "Everyone is growing restless. It's time for you to speak. While you are apologizing, you might as well extend your regrets to your peers as well for missing your own dinner party. Most of them are here."

When hell freezes over, Zane thought.

"I think it best he never mention it again, but go forward from here," Patricia said, offering her bit of advice. "No matter how you decide to handle what you are about to say, we will stand with you." She gave him a sincere smile. "We are family."

Zane gave his sister a nod of appreciation. "My actions are my responsibility."

There was no clock to chime the midnight hour, but Zane agreed with Hector. Every gentleman in the room was ready to go to White's and other places they may have placed a bet to either collect their winnings or pay their debts.

It was time to end this, even though Brina wasn't present.

He started walking toward the center of the room. The place quieted. Everyone stepped aside, giving him plenty of space, and once he stopped, they formed a wide circle around him.

Zane had recollection of telling Brina he'd give a grand speech, but he wouldn't. It would be two short words. He started to speak but saw her rush into the entryway. It felt as if his heart stopped beating for a few seconds and then suddenly thundered like the sound of a hundred galloping horses in his chest. She was wearing the bright pink gown they'd seen in the shop near the abbey. She looked glorious dressed in it. It shimmered with every step and so did she.

Watching her made losing her all the harder.

Some in the ballroom must have noticed her too. The quietness just moments before turned to murmurings. The whispers got louder. Her chin was demurely high, her shoulders softly confident. She was breathtaking as she walked down the three steps into the room and started toward him. His admiration for her grew. She wasn't ducking out. She wasn't going to stand on the other side of the room from him or cower near the door. No, damnation. Not her. She was going to come right up to him and make him look her in the eyes when he apologized.

Good.

He was glad she decided to make him pay for hurting her. The crowd parted as they had for him, and she stopped in front of him. All he could think for a moment was that she was the most beautiful person in the world, and he loved her with all his heart. If there was anything he could say or do to win back her love, he would do it.

With the same poise she always had, she curtsied before looking at him with serenity settled in her lovely features. "Permit me to go first, my lord."

He bowed. "A gentleman always allows a lady to go first."

How was he going to live without her?

"Thank you," she answered softly. She turned away from him and addressed the room. "I know that all of you gentlemen here tonight are far too proper and kind to wager on anything concerning a lady. Especially something as delicate as a lady—a *widow's* hand in marriage. I appreciate your restraint in that matter and your resolve not to resort to gossip about it either. You have set the standard for all gentlemen."

Zane kept his eyes riveted on Brina. Her statement was odd. What was she doing? She knew almost every man in the place had wagered on his proposal to her.

There were more than a few clearings of throats, and men looking down at their toes in hopes of hiding their guilt.

"But," she continued, "if you have friends or acquaintances who wagered that I would reject Lord Blacknight's offer of marriage tonight, please tell them they lost."

Zane felt a jolt of hope slam his chest. Had she said what he thought she had? He took a small step toward her as a roar of cheers mingled with some jeers resounded around the crowd.

"However, however," she hastened to quiet the crowd with a loud voice and movement of her hands, "if you happen to have friends or acquaintances who wagered that I would accept Lord Blacknight's proposal, you can tell them they also lost."

Zane's heartbeat suddenly thundered in his chest again. The cheers and jeers turned to rumblings of discontent and confusion. Zane had no idea what she was talking about, and judging from the mutterings, neither did anyone else.

*"How can she accept his proposal if she rejects it?"* someone asked.

*"What does she mean?"* asked another.

*"What about his apology?"* another commented.

Brina seemed to hear the last question, as she glanced in the direction from which it came before saying, "You see," she continued, still addressing the crowd, "I do not wish to hear an apology or proposal tonight from Lord Blacknight, but I would like to ask him to answer one question."

The room fell silent as she turned to him. She looked up at him with her big bright eyes and held out her hand to him, and said, "Lord Blacknight, will you marry me and be my husband?"

Zane felt as if his heart might beat out of his chest as his fingers closed around her hand. He took it to his lips and kissed it. He smiled and said, "I accept with pleasure."

He then did a very ungentlemanly thing and swooped her up into his arms and kissed her quickly but soundly in front of everyone before setting her back onto her feet.

Brina looked up at him and smiled as gasps and sounds of horror echoed, and mumblings and rumbles of confusion continued to circulate around the room. Her eyes squinted a little in mock concern. "Must you always do the wrong thing, my lord?"

His gaze swept down her face as his hands tightened on her back. Zane swelled with love. "I do believe I still need training from you."

"Gladly."

"You are amazing, Brina Feld."

Love for him shone in her eyes and she laughed softly. "Thank you. So are you, Lord Blacknight."

He nodded. "You realize you just conquered every man in this room and canceled all their bets by asking me to marry you, don't you?"

The gathering scattered and the orchestra started playing. She looked around the room and smiled triumphantly at the grumbling crowd before settling her attention back on him again. "Of course I do. It's what they deserved, but I only wanted to conquer you."

Brina knew how to go straight for his heart. He nodded. "I surrender to you," he whispered softly before saying in a teasing tone, "You also realize that I won. I got you."

"Yes, you did. I think I like it when you win. Dance with me, Lord Blacknight. We just got engaged."

# Epilogue

The September sky was bluer than Brina could ever remember seeing it. A faint hint of autumn stirred in the late afternoon air as she and Zane rode their horses. The grass, leaves on the trees, bushes, and under-growth were just beginning to show signs of cooler days ahead.

For Brina, everything looked brighter, fresher, and newer since she and Zane had married. After their nuptials they'd made the long trek up to Northumberland to visit with her parents. They couldn't have been happier that she'd married an earl, though she knew it would take her mother a bit of time to get used to the fact the earl was the once-notorious black sheep of the Blacknight family. Her mother would adjust.

Harper was doing well, and Zane suggested he not be in any hurry to return to London. Surprisingly Harper agreed. After a visit there, they had journeyed down to

Dorset to see Robert. He was doing well too, and had changed his affections once again to a lady, having decided ladies were safer than cards.

Both young men had sworn off gambling. Whether or not it would last forever, only time would tell. They seemed to have put their scare with the crimp behind them, and neither were in a hurry to return to their previous lives.

After their wedding journey, Zane had joined Lyon's card club and seemed perfectly happy playing only once a week, except for a friendly game at the occasional summer garden party Londoners relished in the late afternoons. Brina had assured him she wouldn't mind if he wanted to go to White's for a game or two during the week. He insisted he'd much rather have his brandy sitting with her in front of the fire in the evenings than furthering skills he no longer needed to use.

His life was full with her, his duties as the earl, and his family. His uncles persisted with their offers of help, and Zane was always kind when he declined. Brina continued her work for the sisters and the girls' school. The painting lessons weren't going as smoothly as she'd hoped, but she was determined not to give up. If just one girl showed a natural talent for the art, it would be worth the trouble.

"What are you thinking about?" Zane asked as he halted his horse and folded his hands over the pummel.

Brina reined in her mount too, and looked at Zane with all the love she was feeling. She thought about asking him to remove his hat. She loved to see his wind-blown hair and the sun's rays shining on it. But, of course, it was proper he keep it on until they were seated to have their refreshments. She was so blessed to have him love her.

"I was thinking about you."

He chuckled. "Good. I was thinking about you too."

"Were you?" she asked teasingly. "Thinking about me doing what?"

"Racing."

She quirked her head and narrowed her eyes. She liked that idea. "If you wanted to race the curricles again, why are we on horseback?"

He shook his head. "Not curricles this time. Horses. You are seasoned now. Your horse against mine."

She rather liked that idea. "Do you mean it?"

"Of course. You are doing so well, I was thinking it's time we had a short race. Longer when you are more comfortable. But for today, if I win—I get to take you to our bed as soon as we get home."

Her breaths increased at the thought he was suggesting. The racing and the prize. "And what do I get if I win?"

"You get to take me to our bed as soon as we get home."

She gave him a completely unserious frown. "You are impossible."

He laughed, but said, "I'm serious. You've been riding again for several months now. I think you can handle yourself."

"Hmm," she said. "A lady and a gentleman are not supposed to race horses in the park."

He grinned affectionately. "I know, but are you game?"

"Ha!" she said in good humor. "I think I can handle myself, the horse, and you, my lord."

"Prove it. To the tree?" He pointed. "I'll let you have a generous—"

Brina didn't wait to hear the rest of his sentence. She'd already snapped her heels against the horse's flank and the mare took off faster than she'd expected. It took her a moment to settle into the saddle at the faster pace, but she felt safe, comfortable. Wind quickly brushed her cheeks, swept her lightly tied bonnet to the back of her shoulders, and grabbed at strands of her hair. She laughed, so pleased with herself that she had gotten a head start until she heard Zane's horse coming up fast behind her.

She saw the head of his horse edging up beside her. She urged her mount to go faster. Zane actually wanted to win. She was so close to the tree. So close, but no, he passed by her the length of his horse's nose.

"No fair," she complained in jest as they stopped the horses under the tree. "You are a beast."

"I told you. I always win."

"You are no gentleman, and you never will be, Zane Browning."

He jumped down and rushed over to help her dismount. "I love it when you are upset with me."

"I shouldn't call you by your first name, you know." She put her hands on his shoulders as his hands circled her waist and lifted her to the ground. "I called you by your first name in front of your sister once."

He looked into her eyes. "It doesn't bother her. She forgets and calls me Zane sometimes too. And I forget where we are sometimes and do this." He bent his head and kissed her lips softly, wonderfully.

She stepped away. "And I never mind when you do."

Brina reached back and grabbed the blanket roll from her horse while Zane untied the basket from the saddle. After they'd settled themselves, she started to open the hamper, but Zane put his hand over hers, squeezed lightly, and said, "I have something I want to share with you before we have refreshment."

He looked serious. Too serious. "All right. I like surprises. That is as long as they are good ones."

"You will have to decide that, but I thought it was something you needed to know."

She pulled her hand out from under his. "Now you

are making me quite uncomfortable. I do hope you don't have bad news."

He pulled a sheet of foolscap from the pocket inside his coat and unfolded it. "I hope you don't feel that way by the time I finish. I think of it as good news. May I read it?"

Her heart was pounding. "Yes, of course."

"Mrs. Caroline Hawkins had her second child last week. Mother and child are doing fine."

Brina didn't know that name and had no idea why he was reading it to her, but she remained quiet and let him continue.

"Mr. Arnold Pendergrass just entered his first year at Oxford. Mr. and Mrs. Richard Graves celebrated twenty years marriage this month."

"What are you doing?" she asked. "I don't understand. You have my interest. I'm quite happy to hear about these people, but I'm also quite befuddled. Why are you telling me things about people I don't know?"

"Because I thought you needed to know their names and stories. The first person I mentioned was Miss Caroline Smithers when Stewart saved her. She's now married with two children."

Tears came to Brina's eyes so quickly, so fully, she didn't have time to stop them from overflowing or blink them away. She quickly wiped her cheeks.

"Arnold was only eleven when he was saved," Zane continued in a somber tone, after glancing at her. "Mrs. Graves was pregnant when Stewart helped her onto a piece of wreckage. She lost the child she was carrying, but because of your husband, she's alive and taking care of her other three children. There's more, but you can read them when we get home. I see this has upset you."

"Yes." Brina choked down a sob and wiped more tears from her cheeks. "Of course it has. You know how

I once felt. How do you know all this? Why are you doing this?"

"I thought it was important for you to know. After we made love the first time, you shared your feelings about Stewart with me. I could see that you were still sad, and I just kept thinking you should be happy. Look what your husband did so unselfishly so others might live. Just as you do good things for the sisters at Pilwillow Crossings. You are happy when you roll bandages and make tea for them to hand out. Look, you, Adeline, and Julia—you've saved nine girls by starting that school. All these are reasons to be happy, not sad. And Stewart should be remembered in your heart as he is in their hearts with happiness. You said Stewart had saved five people, but it really was more than that because of how life goes on and touches others."

Brina sniffed again and looked into the eyes of the husband she loved so dearly. "Thank you for doing this for me. I should have looked into finding them myself."

He shook his head. "I wanted to do it for you. I want to make you happy about your past, your present, and your future with me. You are my life."

"I am the happiest person in the world because of you," she whispered. "I love you, Zane. I'm so glad I found you in that room in Paris."

Zane grinned. "You are never going to let me forget that, are you?"

She laughed and reached over and hugged him tightly. "Not in a million years."

His strong arms circled her waist and he kissed the top of her head. "That's the amount of time I want to have to love you."

"I want that too."

Zane reached over and kissed her. Brina thrilled to her husband's touch.

# Author's Note

My Dear Readers,

I hope you have enjoyed the last book in my First Comes Love series, and that Brina and Zane's story has touched your heart as it did mine. It's always a challenge not to keep telling the same story when you have an event that holds three characters together as was the case in this series with the sinking of the passenger ship *Salty Dove*.

During the Regency, crimping was lawful. Crimps thrived in port cities and were paid to coerce men into military service or as a seaman onboard a ship using a variety of methods including indebtedness, trickery, intimidation, and sometimes drugging and violence. For ships in particular, the boarding master relied on crimps to bring him young, able-bodied men strong enough to withstand the harsh life.

Particularly when it was difficult to find seamen who wanted to sail to places as far away as
India and Singapore.

I always look forward to hearing from readers. If you haven't read book one and two in
this series, I hope you'll order *The Earl Next Door*
and *Gone with the Rogue* from your favorite local
bookstore or e-retailer.

You can email me at ameliagreyauthor@gmail
.com, follow me on Facebook at FaceBook.com
/AmeliaGreyBooks, or visit my website at ame-
liagrey.com

Happy reading to all!
Amelia